Grieve More, Bodymore
Bodymore Book Three

Ian Kirkpatrick

**STEAK HOUSE
BOOKS**

First publication in the USA
Steak House edition published in 2023
Copyright © 2023 by Ian Kirkpatrick

All rights reserved.
Paperback ISBN: 978-1-7368870-9-7
ebook ISBN: 978-1-7368870-7-3
LCCN: 2023917311

Our books may be purchased in bulk for promotional, educational, or business use. Please contact your local bookseller to order.

Cover by Samuel Johnson
www.SpoopySamuel.com

Printed in the United States of America.

31   10   23   1

CONTENTS

ONE.

"Right. I'll be there soon, D. I gotta talk to her first, ya know? Some shit happened yesterday. No, nothing to do with the badges this time. *Personal* stuff. Gimme thirty, yeah? Thanks." Jag's voice is soft, muffled by the wall. It comes into the bedroom through the door left open. The air smells like fresh coffee, paint, cigarettes, and him. My fingers curl into the sheets nicer than the ones I have back at my house. His side of the bed, left empty, is so big and even though I hear him shifting in the other room, he feels far away. The bed's so soft; the blankets are warm, wrapped around me; it doesn't feel real to be here.

Last night, I was so dumb...

I gave Jag my heart—The necklace Ralph gave me. I don't even know what it all means. Just that hungry ravens were watching me on the way here and the moment Jag had it in his hands, I felt a peace I've never known. I spent the night for the first time without worrying about how I'd sneak away and back into my house without my dad noticing so he wouldn't get mad because my dad's gone.

This is my home now.

The brick walls, the big windows, the fresh air, and the sounds of morning traffic outside… None of it seems right or where I should be. None of it's normal. None of this is mine.

I'm waiting for a loud crash of something falling over, a broken bottle, the TV ringing with Drew Carey telling someone they were right about the cost of that Jeep, next year's model, because there was also a huge jug of detergent inside and somehow, they knew that and so the price was right—Or my dad'll be yelling and hungry and sobbing and going, "Josephine, are you still here? Am I finally alone? Is this all I have? I can't believe you actually left, you ungrateful bitch!" and that'll be my call to get the hell out of bed and assure him I'm still there. Then, he won't believe I never left. "You just climb in the window?"

It'd be a gamble whether he'd reach to smother me cause he's desperate, but it was always a risk I didn't mind taking.

For the longest time, waking up hasn't felt this normal. The air in the apartment's still. Jag's gone quiet.

His movements are a soft echo only because of how heavy his boots are and the apartment's eerie now that he's not talking. He puts his mug down on the counter. More shuffling. The coffee maker's bubbling makes it through the open door like tiptoeing feet.

I roll onto my back. The ceiling's bright from the fresh coat of paint the landlord put over all the graffiti yesterday or the day before that or the day before that. Whenever it was they fixed the messages Wayland left all over Jag's apartment. I'm not sure when it was anymore. Everything from the last few weeks has blurred together, one thing running into another that shouldn't exist or shouldn't have been happening and never going to bed so it's all one, long day, but somehow I'm lying on my back and not feeling angry or anxious like I've gotten so used to.

My eyes burn, feel puffy and swollen and my cheeks are crispy from crying last night. I hope that didn't happen when Jag and I were having sex; I hope he didn't see it when he got up.

I wipe my eyes. My fingers come away, wet still. "Fuck," I exhale. My chest is so tight, my breathing goes shallow and my heart's starting to race. Tears leak from the corners of my eyes. I wipe them again and say, "Stop it, Jo." Again, my muttered words come out more like a sigh.

I roll onto my side. A glance at the bedside table, my phone's plugged into the charger, screen still cracked from when I threw it out the window at the badge station in Font Hill. My hard chuckle feels more like a groan. That moment feels so far away now, when the ravens were chasing me, watching, counting the seconds until I found my death three blocks away.

It was so stupid.

I was so stupid.

I feel the Big Guy's hands around my neck, the brick wall against my back. His face flashes through my mind, his eyes angry, dark, and possessed by red shadows and tendrils driving hatred to his hands. It wasn't like the way my dad looked at me. Yeah, he had his really bad days, but he never looked at me with that kind of poison. Then, dad always stopped; the Big Guy was so desperate, he couldn't. I don't know what I was to him, but something he had to get rid of.

My skin prickles. My breaths are shallower until I can't breathe at all.

I sit up, reach for my phone. My lungs release. I brush the screen with my thumb, teasing the cracks in the glass as my skin catches. I tap the blank screen away. I don't know why I'm expecting messages from Jag when he's in the other room. Something asking me to come over or how I am or what my dad's doing or what my schedule's like tomorrow, even though I know he knows it since it's posted at work right next to his.

Always just an excuse to make conversation.

I knew he was checking up on me, to see if Dad had killed me yet or something, even if he never said it. I pretended I didn't know better and told myself he was just being annoying and needy because I couldn't believe the alternative.

My inbox this morning shows nothing from him. Makes sense, even if it feels weird. Still, the drop-down shows there's 1 unread message. At the name, my skin goes cold, but sweaty. My chest hurts.

The banner reads WAYLAND CROSS.

I open the dialer and call his phone. I press the speaker to my ear. The ringing goes on and on and on and on until his voicemail opens with a soft, "Hey, sorry I missed you—"

I toss my phone onto the bed. It slides off the edge and makes a sound as it clatters to the hard floor.

"You awake, Joey?" Jag's voice startles me, coming in from the other room.

"Yeah—" I say quickly. "Just… waking up. Almost fell out of bed."

"You need help?"

"No. I'm good. Just gimme a sec." Tears blur my vision. I take a deep breath, wipe my eyes with the back of my hand. Eyeliner smudges my skin darker and I'm wondering how the hell there's anything left around my eyes after everything that's happened. "I'm just putting something on."

"We need to talk," he says.

"I know. I'll be right there." I search the floor for the jeans I was wearing last night, but they aren't there. In the hamper, they're hanging over the edge. I pull them out. They're still wet and they smell so bad. Sulfur, blood, the rot of Leakin… I search through the pocket, muttering to myself that the ring's still in there, it didn't fall out, Jag didn't find it and take it and get rid of it. He wouldn't do that, right?

The ring's wedged into the bottom of the pocket.

I pull it out, exhale, and breathe, trying to feel relief, but the air's so heavy and again, my skin prickles as heat builds behind my eyes. I'm standing in the bar in Mortem; the ring's the last thing Wayland gave to me while he backed away to forget everything about his life with Sol's help.

"Goodbye, Jo," was the last thing he said to me.

I remember him, but he didn't want any more of this.

Did he hate me? After everything I did to him, I wouldn't blame him.

I slip the ring onto my finger and throw the jeans back into the hamper. The belt catches on the edge. The sound startles me. I yank the pants off the edge of the basket and shove them all the way in. The room spins. I grab onto the nearby dresser for balance, lean over, and twist the ring around the base of my finger, again and again and again like it'll make the spinning stop or it'll attach to my thoughts that are just wishing my phone would buzz with a message from him telling me he was never gone; he's around; did I need a ride to work today?

I know he's not calling.

I watched Sol take him from me, but rationality has

never really been a strength of mine.

I open a drawer and put on a pair of black boyshorts, then grab a hoodie from the laundry basket. I pull the hoodie over my hips. The bottom of it reaches mid-thigh, covering my underwear. It's Jag's. Smells like his cologne and oil and cigarettes and somehow that makes it feel warmer when it's on me. I don't know what my face looks like. The bathroom's right there. I'm kind of scared to look. I pull the hood up instead. It's hard to open my eyes, tears keep slipping out, and the trails left behind from the night have left my skin feeling dehydrated and tight.

I *really* hope I wasn't crying last night when I was with Jag.

How pathetic is that shit?

I used to laugh about the people who would cry while fucking. Didn't matter if it was because the sex was too good or too bad or she was just getting over a breakup, and everything just reminded her of the guy she didn't have any more or the guy's dick was too big or she thought he was too good for her. All of it was pathetic but look at me. I've joined the ranks.

I don't want to be crying; I don't want to be needy. I don't want to look like I'm so much work to take care of that Jag starts thinking about when and how to get rid of me. He accepted my heart, but it's not too late for him to change his mind, you know?

I still can't believe he took it. He didn't even ask me what it meant.

"You okay in there?" Jag says.

"Yeah, sorry," I say. "Just moving a little slow, I guess."

"Take your time."

"Didn't you tell Donny *thirty*?"

Jag chuckles. "How long've you been awake?"

"Long enough to hear you jacking it to *Aerosmith*—"

"I would never jack it to *Aerosmith*."

"You say that, but I heard it."

"Don't start any rumors, Joey."

I'm watching the door for Jag to come in. I don't know why I'm still expecting to see some of Wayland's words left behind. I don't want to believe that he's gone. ESCAPE had been written on the wall by the door the other day. I can't help but feel like it was his cry to himself of what he should've been doing with me, the same way Jag had told me to escape from my dad three years ago.

I really am the worst, you know?

I'm wiping my face with the hoodie sleeve as I come out of the bedroom. Jag's standing in the kitchen, leaning against the counter with a coffee cup beside his arm and a cigarette pinched between his fingers. The kitchen window's open, a living room window's open, and he's got a bottle of Febreze on the counter. He pulls the glass ashtray on the kitchen island toward him.

I suck in a breath that catches in my nose like it's clogged. "Allergies," I say.

Jag sucks on his cigarette. His exhale tells me he doesn't believe me, but he says, "That time of year."

"Yeah." I wipe my eyes again, my cheeks next, pretending it's to get at the smudges of eyeliner or dirt from the river or sleep that I haven't gotten off of me yet. I hold the cuff to my nose a little longer, letting the scent give me a bit of passing comfort. The cigarettes on the kitchen counter are tempting, but my legs won't move me closer. "Why didn't anyone tell me I looked like shit?" I laugh weakly.

"You've had a shit week. Figured you could use a break on *gussying up*." Jag smiles. He nods toward the coffee pot. "You want anything?"

"I don't know." I'm standing outside the kitchen, just beside the edge of the island now. My legs tremble. I tell myself it's the cold air, even though I don't believe it. My body resists going closer. I shake my head slowly. Light catches on something around Jag's neck. It's the pendant Ralph gave me to give him. Shaped like a heart, the metal's not gold, but something darker, black, looking tainted, stained, aged, and decayed. The stone's black along the edges, but thick, wiry streams of red wrap over the center like organs or blood splatter, turning brighter red the closer it gets to the center until there's almost a soft glow of red in the middle. The morning sun lights it up, but the black around the edges devours any attempt at brightness.

"So… That really happened." I nod toward Jag. My eyes are still on the necklace.

He looks down, then back at me. "Yeah. *That* really happened." He smiles. "Embarrassed?"

"Why would I be embarrassed?"

"I've never seen you so sentimental before."

"Chh… It was a weird kind of night."

"Yeah, it was."

My chest tightens, heart racing so fast I can't breathe. I cross my arms and look at the floor. It's not the kind of panic I'm used to feeling in the morning; it's not a worry of leaving, but a worry of being left behind. Irrational—I know. I hated my dad so many times for making me feel like shit for leaving and I'm over here now wanting to beg Jag not to leave when he's already late for work.

I move into the kitchen and go to Jag. My hand slides along his arm. He sets his cigarette in the ashtray and turns away from the counter, making it easier for me to access his body. I grab a handful of his shirt. My fingers slide up his chest and around the back of his neck while I stand on my toes to meet his lips. He leans down, neck craning, closing the gap between his lips and mine. He turns us so my hips are against the counter and he's pressing into me. My back arches. His hands are under my thighs, gently lifting me onto the counter while his lips move from mine to my jaw, then my neck. I brace myself; my hands land on the counter behind me.

The ring on my finger clicks against the hard surface.

Jag pulls back, his eyes dropping to my hand. He sees the ring. He picks up his coffee cup and takes another step back, no longer standing between my knees. I shove my hands into my hoodie's pouch pocket. Jag looks back at my face. "Alright." He sets his coffee cup on the counter beside the coffee maker. His cigarette's back out of the ashtray and in his mouth. He takes a puff. "Is that Cross's ring?"

"Yeah." My head drops; my face burns with shame.

"What's it mean that you're wearing it?"

"That I'm not fucking over it." I grab the box of cigarettes and the lighter beside me on the counter. It's seconds before I'm lit up.

Jag leans against the counter. His cigarette's pinched between his lips. Arms crossed; his head drops to the side. He plucks the cigarette from his mouth. "Was there something going on between you two?"

My body suddenly feels cold, making me tingle. Tears pool in my eyes, obscuring Jag's face, and dread pulls at my insides. I slowly shake my head. "No, Jag. I told you—We never... He was just my best friend, but we never... *I never...*" The heat's building up from every stupid implication I missed, every bit of pain that I felt in the way that Wayland kissed me yesterday. I couldn't do anything to help him. My eyes close.

"You help him hide a body, Joey?"

"Isn't that what best friends do?"

I look at Jag. He's watching me. Arms uncrossed,

cigarette in his hand. I don't want to see his face; I don't want to risk seeing what he's thinking about me in his expression. "Did you help him kill anyone?"

"No… I haven't killed anyone, J. I'm not like that—"

"And before this ghost shit, neither was he, right?"

"Yeah." My skin prickles, making my ass feel numb. The chill of the air is against my bare skin. I'm panting a little. My hand touches the counter. The ring clicks again. "Shit." I slide off the counter and go through the kitchen until I'm at the fridge. In the back of it are a couple of beers. I take one out. Shutting the fridge door, I turn away from Jag to pop the cap off in a way he won't see. The hiss of the carbonation gives me away before I'm ready.

"Shut up," I mutter.

"It's a little early, isn't it?"

"No."

"You need to be careful you don't pick up a habit."

"I'm not picking up a habit. I'm not my dad." I go into the living room and drop onto the couch when I get there. "*Three* times is a habit."

"Shit happens, Joey."

"I'm not my fucking dad!" I turn back to the kitchen, but I can't stand looking at him, over there with his coffee and his combed hair and pity he's ready to go to work with. But facing forward, I'm just looking at the TV reflecting him at me instead, making it feel more like there's a window between us where I can barely see him, but he can still watch me with the clarity to determine how big the mistake is that he just made. "You said it yourself. It's been a shit week." I mutter into the bottle, then take a drink. I hate how much it makes me feel like Dad's habits are mine. His sitting in that chair is now me with Jag looking at me like I looked at my dad before I went to work. I set the bottle on the coffee table and bury my face in my hands. "I'm not doing anything…"

Jag rubs his eyes. He exhales hard. I hear him turn back to the coffee maker, take it off the plate, and pour himself another cup. He sighs again, sets his cup down. "I'm not saying you're like your dad or that you're gonna be like your dad, just that… I've seen people spiral, okay? I know what it looks like. It starts out as something small and you don't see it coming. A little bit of comfort turns into a routine and that turns into a habit and that turns into something you can't live without." His foot's tapping. I glance over the back of the couch at him. His hand's resting on the counter again, his thumb's hitting the surface there too. He doesn't normally fidget like that. Actually, he's never fidgeted like that. When he's full of it, he's pacing or something, not making little movements like that.

His small ticks are getting to me, making me nervous and my leg's bouncing a little more now. I grab the beer off the coffee table. The drink goes down with the hope of giving me enough of a morning buzz to take the edge off. "It's one beer, J."

"I know, just…" He takes a breath. Shaky. Nervous.

What the hell is wrong with him?

"You need to be careful. It's really easy to fall into something bad when shit happens. Relapsing. Whatever. I've seen it."

"You have to have a problem in the first place to relapse."

"Yeah, and I don't want to see anything happen to you *again*."

"I get it."

"So…" He licks his lower lip. His jaw's tight. "Tell me what happened with Cross. Do I gotta worry about him stalking my place again?"

I'm chewing on my lip. My drink's between my

crossed legs and my empty hand's now twisting the ring. The stone keeps catching on the neighboring fingers, but I keep twisting it loose. "Cross is gone." I run my fingers under the hoodie sleeves to smooth down the goosebumps on my arms. "After what happened at the house, he and I talked and… he said he didn't want to be a burden. I tried to stop him, but he thought it was better to move on. So, I took him to Mortem and Mortem took him." Tears build in my eyes. I wipe my face with my sleeve. The bottle's at my lips again. "I think I just… I didn't want to believe he was gone or that things were different or that he wasn't… himself, you know? Like if you could hide it all and wash what was left down the drain, then it wasn't real, and Wayland wasn't really dead and I didn't have to think about what came after that."

"You know how bad that shit is for you?"

I look up at Jag; he's waiting for me with that look on his face that I always hated. The one that says he feels sorry for me and I'm kind of pathetic, but I know that's not actually what he means. I drop my head again, blink a couple of times, bring the cigarette to my lips and just breathe to push the heat and tears and everything back. The pressure builds into a laugh that's too tight to sound natural. "Sorry, Jag. I've said that so many times in the last couple of days. I know it's gotta seem like I don't mean it or something, but that's not it… I'm just like… I'm really bad at this shit, you know?" Another strangled laugh works its way out while I'm wiping my face again. "It's Bodymore, right? People die around here… a lot and it just keeps happening to me too, like…" I look at Jag and the scene at my house from yesterday plays in my head. I can't count how many times I thought something might happen to him. Maybe it would've been one of the nights Jag dropped me off and my dad would've had just enough willpower to come out the door and meet Jag in the grass and they'd throw hands and my dad would surprise me with how agile he was compared to Jag.

Unrealistic, yeah, but I'd seen it play out a couple different ways where Jag ended up on the ground. I knew how determined my dad was to not be alone; I knew what his hands and rage and dejection felt like; I knew how far determination could go.

I knew he always had that gun in the chair with him.

Jag's cigarette is in the ashtray on the counter. He's at the couch, pulling the coffee table up so there's no space between us. He takes the bottle from my hand and places it on the table. He grabs hold of me. I'm falling into him. My arms go around his body; my fingers desperately grip his shirt. "I'm sorry," he mutters against my head.

"I know you didn't like him—"

"That's not it, Joey."

The heat's building too fast. My vision's blurring and it's mashing Jag's apartment into something that doesn't make sense. Ghosts and anger and shadows that aren't there, judging me like the bodies hanging around Mortem, telling me I should be there too, not here, haunting Jag with a life that expired way before I actually died. Shoving my face into his shoulder, I close my eyes. My nose is too stuffy, and I choke on a sob.

"He couldn't be here anymore," Jag says.

The week with him flashes through my head, from finding his abandoned car at Leakin in the middle of the night to the body in the trunk and the bodies at Fort Armistead and him standing in the trees at Leakin in my dad's clothes and the way he bashed that guy's head in back at his house when it was on fire. He didn't look like himself and all I can think of is every time he was in his body, watching the ghost that inspires Bodymore to destroy life, again and again, using his hands and he was powerless to stop it. Wayland wasn't that person. "I know." My fingers twist in his shirt. "What if it happens to me next?"

"What?"

"The anger and resentment and destruction and I just... I kill everything that moves. J—What if I hurt you?"

"It's not going to happen—"

"How do you know that?"

"Because I know *you*, Joey." Jag pulls back. He forces space between us. I don't look at him, even though he's waiting. His fingers gently slide along my jaw. I'm waiting for him to hook my chin and make me see him, but instead, all he does is stroke my skin with his thumb. "You're not going to become like *him*."

My chest aches with so much pain, I can't process it and all that's happening in my head is my voice saying *I can't, I can't, I can't* with flashes of Wayland's name being on the banner of my phone. It hurts so much and the ring's burning my skin every time I twist it around. I keep hoping if I go back to the bedroom, there'll be three more messages from Wayland.

Jag runs his hand through his hair with a sigh and says, "Fuck," while looking at his phone. "I need to go." He slips his phone into his pocket. The mug's off the counter and in the sink. It hits the dishes, crashing. He swears again. I'm pretty sure something just broke and he says, "Leave it alone. I'll take care of it when I get back. I need *you* to relax, you got it?" His voice is sterner, louder, closer to a growl through his teeth. The anger isn't like him. No matter how many times we've gotten into it— Even in the last couple of days with me being a complete idiot, he's never sounded or looked like this. His eyes reflect differently. Glossy, hurt. His hand curls harder into my shoulder and it's not like I'm not used to him touching me or pinning me down or stopping me from burning the hell out, but his hand feels like poison right then and I'm getting off the couch, stepping back with the bottle in my hand and a wet spot on my leg. My heart's throbbing so hard, my fingers are trembling.

He grabs his cigarettes off the counter. I throw the bottle I'm holding—Not at him, near him. It hits the floor and crashes to pieces. "Shit—"

Jag smashes his fist into the nearby wall. "What the hell, Joey!" His knuckles are raw. He hisses and there's a little bit of a hole in the wall and he's saying, "Shit," and "Fuck," and "Are you alright?" and "I don't know why I did that."

My face is burning still. Tears roll down my cheeks as panic sets in. "It's fine, J. It's fine. Are you okay?" I wipe my face. Force a laugh. My voice quivers. My legs want to drop me. "I've been dealing with this kinda shit for a while now. Fuck. I can't believe I brought it to your house. It really is me, isn't it? I did this to my dad and now I'm doing it to you."

"Stop it, Joey. It's fine." Jag growls. "Fuck. No, it's not fine. But it's not whatever you think it is." He steps over the glass. At the sink, he's pulling a small first aid kit out from the cabinet. A bit of blood goes down his knuckles as he sets the supplies on the counter. The wall he punched is caved in with jagged wooden edges the landlord's going to need to know about. Jag wraps his knuckles while cursing under his breath and every time he hisses, I feel it under my skin, echoing in the back of my head like his words are my thoughts and I'm saying, "I didn't mean to do this," and he's like, "What are you talking about, Joey?" in a growl.

"Nothing, J. Nothing—I just... I don't know." I go to the bathroom so I can get away for a second. I turn on the sink. My hands are under the cold water. I lean over and bring it to my face, like maybe this'll cool me down a little bit. I hate the way I look in the mirror. Puffy eyes, trails of black running down my face and eyeliner I can't get off leaving black trails where my tears and fingers have been. My red cheeks further highlight just how bad I look and the blue of my eyes makes me look so much more pathetic. Dark strangulation marks still color my neck, reminding me of both the last minutes I spent with my dad and the last moment I was alive.

I don't know what the hell Jag sees in me or why he wants to talk to me anymore. I look like shit, I act worse. The only thing I've done for him in the last few weeks is destroy his life and give him a little sex. How many times has he almost died?

"Stop saying that shit about yourself, Joey!" Jag says from the other room.

"I didn't say anything!"

"Then what the fuck am I hearing?"

"I don't know, J! Your own thoughts?" A tear rolls down my cheek.

"I've never thought that shit about you!!" A cabinet drawer bangs. He's tossing something away in the other room.

My head's tight. I lean onto the counter cause I can't stand on my own anymore. A sob shakes my body. He knows. He's finally getting who I really am and he's going to step out. You know you can feel a disaster when it's on the way. That's why it's so dumb when people who see it coming keep standing where they're gonna get hit.

I use one more splash of water to try and clean up my face. Most of the black is gone, but without the mess of leftover makeup, there's only the violence left behind on my body by the places I've been. When I go back to the living room, the first aid kit isn't on the counter anymore. Jag's hand is wrapped in a fresh white bandage.

"After all this, you still want anything to do with me?"

Jag's in front of me, his arms go around me and he pulls me in. I hold him, tighter than he's holding me. "If we're going to get through this, we have to be a team. You can't hide shit from me anymore, got it?"

"There's so much, J—"

"So, we'll find a place to start and go through it, one thing at a time." Jag leans back. He reaches for the necklace hanging over his chest. "Last night, you said this was your heart. What did that mean?"

"I don't know."

"Bullshit."

My hands are fists. How does he always know exactly what I don't want to tell him? Just the things that make me feel weak or stupid, that'll give him power, that'll make it so he can break me whenever he wants? "Ralph… said it was my heart."

"Literally or figuratively?"

"Literally." I look at the necklace. He didn't even have to put it on this morning, but he did, without explanation or anything beyond the fact I gave it to him last night. "I was something bad when I was dead. Angry voices in my head and pictures of death and everything was making me crazy. I couldn't stop wanting to mess shit up. Ralph said this thing is my second chance, but I can't do it alone." I meet Jag's eyes. "He said when you die, a raven comes from somewhere, I don't know where—but it rips your chest open and eats your heart. Then the reaper comes and takes your soul and your body stays here and rots. These three things make a person a person, and once they're separated, you're not supposed to get them back, but Ralph's different. He can talk to *that* side. When he had us get that stuff, it was so he could talk to whatever's on the other side of forever to get my heart back and *that's* it." I nod toward the necklace. "If anything happens to that necklace or if you don't have it, then I go back to the way I was because we're sharing your body since mine died. I don't know the logistics of it all. I don't even know if that makes sense. I was kind of in a rush to get the hell away from everything last night, but he said whoever holds my heart will feel what I feel."

Jag releases me. He reaches for the necklace and lifts it to examine it. The morning light catches on the clear, red parts of the gem, illuminating the hole in the center that looks more like a bullet hole through the dark swathes of black and red ligaments. "Maybe that's what happened with the cup and the wall." He nods toward the sink. "You were freaking out and I was freaking out and… I don't remember ever feeling like that. I mean, yeah, I've been angry before, but not anything like that, not with you."

"You believe me?"

Jag meets my eyes. He chuckles, drops the necklace. His glance goes toward the bedroom as he rubs the back of his neck. "Right now, I don't think I have too many options. With what I've seen, I'd be crazy if I don't believe it… or I could be someone holding onto something too hard because I don't want to let *her* go. I don't want to believe that though." He leans down and catches my chin with his fingers. His lips press to mine and it's so much warmer and more comfortable than anything else I've ever had. I don't even feel like myself when he's touching me. All the bad shit melts away and I can't remember what the trailer smells like or what my dad looks like or how bad the last couple of days have been. My lips part and I'm curling a hand in his shirt, pulling it up while I step back toward the bedroom, tugging him with me. He's following, hand on my hip, saying, "You feel real to me though."

"I am real," I say. "I just died once."

Something buzzes.

His phone on the counter.

"Shit," Jag mutters. His hands are off me and he's back in the kitchen. He picks up his phone. The screen lights up. "Shit." He grabs his keys from the counter, checks his pocket for his lighter, cigarettes, and wallet. "Sorry, Joey. I gotta go. I told Donny I'd be there like fifteen minutes ago. We can talk about this more later, yeah?" He's at the door, keys jingling in his hand.

I'm following him across the house and I can't stop the nerves and fear and panic from building with every repetition of *he's leaving, he's leaving, he's leaving* and the belief that he's never coming back.

"I'm off at five, maybe six," Jag says. You hang out here today, huh? Relax. There's pizza in the fridge." He nods toward it. "Let me know if anything happens."

"Like what?"

"I dunno." His hand releases the door to comb through the hair on the back of his head. "I never know what's next with you. Crazy shit always seems to find its way around though."

"Yeah…"

Jag laughs one more time, then the door's shut. He's loud when he walks and this building doesn't do much to quiet movement. You can hear the neighbors come in no matter what time it is, the elevators down the hall ring from one end to the other, and every opening door on the floor echoes like it's slamming.

The closing stairwell door behind Jag is loud, echoing into the apartment and then I'm actually alone.

A raven laughs from outside the window.

So, I'm alone, but not *that* alone.

TWO.

I stare at the apartment. My insides are twisting, heart racing, I feel like I'm going to vomit. Is it too pathetic to pull the door open and see if maybe he's still on the other side even though I heard the elevator down the hall?

It's a weird feeling—Seeing someone walk out the door like that, like he took a part of me with him. Usually, I'm not around when he goes to work or heads out because I've never spent the night like this. I've always left while he was sleeping or I'd go home in the middle of the day when we both had something else to do anyway because walking out the door on someone has always felt wrong to me. Like, you might not think they're never coming back, but what if something happens? What if they get distracted or run off or find something better to do and never come back?

I can't blame Dad anymore for being so weird when I

left. I pace the apartment, fueled by panic. I know he's coming back; I know where he's going; I still don't want him to leave. What the hell's wrong with me?

I check myself for cigarettes. I'm not wearing pants, so there's nothing there. There's nothing on the counter, either. I go to the closet where Jag keeps his cartons and pull out a box and a spare lighter. The cigarette's lit and pinched between my lips while I say to myself, "He's coming back," again and again and again. "You're being dumb, Jo. Nothing's gonna happen. He's always fine. He's been fine for twenty-seven years and he's going to come back, okay? So, don't be like Dad."

My eyes catch on the mug in the sink, the wet mess on the floor from where my bottle burst, the pieces of broken glass Jag cleaned up while I was in the bathroom. "Don't be like Dad."

The fridge is right there.

I open it.

There are three more bottles in the back. I lick my lips, reach, grab the box of pizza, and shut the door without taking a bottle. "Don't be like Dad, Jo." I toss the pizza box onto the counter. One bite's all I can take without feeling sick. I toss the pizza back into the box, exchanging the taste of cheese for cigarette. The nicotine soothes my anxiety and coaxes me into taking another bite.

I stare at the coffee pot on the counter for a while. The smell's filling the apartment, overtaking most of Jag's scent. It can't get rid of the cigarette smoke though. My hands curl at my sides. Adrenaline courses through me restlessly and my foot's tapping again whenever I stand still. I pace the room again. Everything's blotting red and black and red again and I'm reaching for the counter. Is this what a actual panic feels like or am I just going crazy?

Jag's voice echoes in my ear from last night. I feel his hand on my hip while he's saying, *"Breathe."* I do it like he's telling me now.

I open my eyes again and the house is clear. No spots, no dizziness, no darkness. My heart's slowing down. I hold my breath, waiting for the sound of the ravens who haven't been able to leave Jag or me alone for the last couple of weeks.

Moments go by.

There's only the throbbing sound of someone's car radio blasting as they pass in the street below.

A car horn from the city getting the better of someone.

A responding horn and echo of, "Fuck you!"

The throbbing base subsides.

The cackle of a raven.

It doesn't feel like laughing, but a threat. *Get to the job you promised you'd do or I will take something you care about.* I don't think that's how Charon and Val work, but I can't help thinking it anyway.

I look toward the window. Take a step, stop. Look at the fridge. My lips flick at the cigarette before taking it out of my mouth. "Don't be like Dad," I mutter.

I put the cigarette into the ash tray on the kitchen counter and go to the bedroom.

My reflection catches me in the mirror on the other side of Jag's bed. The bruising that I saw just a little bit ago is lighter now. The discoloration on my legs, arms, and neck are more yellow or almost the color of my skin. The cut Ralph had made in my arm for our deal isn't glowing and puckered anymore, but has softened into a light-colored scar, mixing in with every other piece of history my body has recorded.

I run my finger along the new line on my arm. My skin tingles under the touch. A chill goes through me.

Another caw penetrates the bedroom.

I need to move.

I grab a pair of jeans out of the drawer Jag's set aside for me. My throat's feeling dry, and I'm thinking about the beer in the fridge again. My tongue flicks over my bottom lip. The skin feels busted beside my lip ring and the taste of crusty blood comes away. I take the laundry basket to the other room and the closet where the laundry machines are. The jeans I'd been wearing yesterday sit on top of everything. They're still damp with the water from Styx and Dead Run and reek like sulfur. I reach into the pockets to check for anything else left behind. The ring catches on the fabric.

Jag's face comes back to me. The moment he heard it when it tapped on the counter, then the way he looked at me like I betrayed him. He says he gets it, but I know I'm just hurting him again with this shit. I slip the ring off my finger and take it to the kitchen island. My hands shake as I put it down on the counter.

I'm not forgetting him; I promised I wouldn't. Putting the ring on the counter just means I don't want it to get caught on the clothing and thrown in the washer by accident or something.

I return to the basket. There's already clothing in the washing machine, but it doesn't belong to Jag or me. It's my dad's sweater—the one I gave Wayland to wear back at my house. I look toward the bedroom, then the laundry closet. The dryer's on top of the washing machine. I open it. There's nothing inside of it. The sweater smells wet, moldy, and sulfuric too.

I'm so sick of that smell.

I guess I never finished the wash the other day. So much of the shirt and pants are discolored with mistakes that won't come out because Wayland and I weren't fast enough to wash out the failure.

My shirt's sticking to my back.

I need to check on Wayland.

I throw the shirt into the washing machine and run to the bedroom. My phone's laying where Jag and I used to be, pressing the blanket down with the only weight still there. My fingers tingle at my sides as I approach. My knees press into the mattress. A lump grows in my throat and a chill goes through my skin. The room's spinning. I blink that away. The phone buzzes against the sheets.

Short, sharp, a text.

I reach for it thinking it's *him*. The screen reads three unread messages. One from Wayland, two others from Jag with a received time telling me he was the one who just messaged me.

I'm dumb.

I know better.

I still hoped.

I carefully open my messages to get to Jag's without accidentally opening Wayland's. He's said, "You ok?" and "Got a bad feeling."

I take a picture of the apartment, but delete it because it'd be more insulting than anything to pretend he doesn't trust me at this point, right? Instead, I respond:

JOEY	I'm fine.
	Cleaning the room.
	Doing laundry.
	Domestic shit.
	Got light-headed for a sec.
	That's all.
JAG	Take it easy.
JOEY	I am.
JAG	Yesterday was
JOEY	I know
JAG	something

	Watch some TV.
JOEY	My cut's gone tho.
JAG	Which one?
JOEY	Mostly.
	The one Ralph gave me for the thing.
JAG	How much did he tell you about this stuff?
	Or being dead?
JOEY	Not a lot.
	tbh, I didn't ask.
JAG	Maybe that's something we should do later.
JOEY	Probably.
	I guess.
JAG	This thing seems kind of important, Joey.
JOEY	And I could use a drink.
JAG	Right.
JOEY	That was a joke.
	He runs a bar.
	….
	I'm not an alcoholic J.
JAG	I know.
	but relax.
JOEY	I'm doing laundry.
	What's more relaxing than that?

I put my phone into my pocket and go back to the laundry machine. Next piece of clothing is one of Jag's black work shirts. The smell of grease and sweat is almost totally overpowered by the scent of sulfur left behind by my clothing having been on top of his.

I dump everything from the basket into the washing machine as quickly as I can. This doesn't need to be sorted; it should probably all be burned though. Death versus not death is the only split now and everything in the laundry basket's infected by my trip to Mortem.

I grab the detergent and don't worry about measuring. The laundry's started, the basket's in the closet, and I close the door. My back presses against it to keep me up. I cover my eyes. The sound of the quiet apartment is somehow overwhelming. No screaming TV, no tension thick in the air keeping all the doors closed, no hesitation to move because Dad's waiting for me to make a sound and flip his lid.

It's like an alternate dimension. As shit as stuff was before, I don't think I can do this. I need my dad to be angry. I need the TV roaring because that'll tell me Wayland's also waiting. I go to Jag's TV and turn it on. I flip to Dad's favorite channel and crank the sound up.

The ringing of a contestant's correct answer fills the apartment.

A caw cuts through the sound. A fat raven sits on the window sill. "Fuck you, Val!" I yell. I run across the room. The raven sees me coming and flees. I slam the window shut and lock it.

My phone vibrates against my thigh. I cover my lips like it was my voice that got the attention. My phone's in my hand. The blind says it's Jag. The text reads, "Still ok?"

I laugh into my hand, shaking my head. My eyes water, blurring the screen and Jag's words and I'm thinking if I can't read it, then I can't understand it and I can't answer it, right? But that's a lie since I've already read it and I can't lie to Jag anymore. He knows. He always knows. I don't want him to see me like this, but I don't have a choice anymore, do I?

Have I always been this bad?

I wipe my eyes clear and respond.

JOEY   Still ok.

	Thanks.
	u should get to work tho
	Don't worry about me. :p
JAG	Nah.
JOEY	legit, I'm fine.
JAG	Always been a problem.
JOEY	Thanks.
	But I'm fine, J.
JAG	That's what you always say.
	Can't remember the last time it was true.
JOEY	This time I mean it.
JAG	I've heard that one before too.
JOEY	u always been this clingy?
JAG	don't call me out like that.
	My cred'll be shot.

I give it a couple of moments, staring at the message, waiting for more to come in. Jag doesn't say anything else. My heart's slowing down now. The smell of laundry detergent's hitting the room. The soft roll of the machine forces normalcy back while the soap gets rid of the paint smell. I tap out of the messages from him. Sitting in my inbox, there's only one unread message left. Wayland's name is bold. It says it came in some time last night. Between everything that happened, I don't know if that was before or after I dropped him off in Mortem. Everything's kind of a blur from the bar to the house to the blackout and river and open sky and the pain eating at my body from the way regret consumes you. I think it hurt worse than the time I did it when Jag was with me and both of those hurt worse than the first time.

My thumb hangs over Wayland's message. My chest's tight. The laundry room door's the only think keeping me standing. I will myself to touch the message.

I can't.

The phone goes black.

Fresh tears obscure my vision. I wipe my cheek, though I don't know if there's anything there yet. It feels like the camera on my phone is staring at me with the way my face reflects in the screen. I look so goddamn pathetic and everyone on the other side of the phone can see it too.

"Touch the screen," I mutter.

My thumb gets closer, and pulls away.

"Touch the goddamn screen, Jo." My thumb sinks and the screen fills with the chain of messages from Wayland. Our last conversation still show at the top:

JOEY	You still at my place?
WAYLAND	YEAH.
JOEY	Stay there, ok?
WAYLAND	OK.

Despite his assurance, he's not there anymore and I'm the reason for it. Underneath Wayland's OK is one more message from him. An address in West Baltimore, not far from the Poe Museum and just south of Leakin Park. Along with the address is the word BUSHES. There's nothing else. I know I shouldn't go. It's a shitty part of town for a couple of reasons and the daylight offers only a little bit of disinfectant, but it's Wayland's last message and the apartment's feeling cramped, I can't stop the feeling that Val's watching me and Charon's gonna bust down my door any second because I'm not doing what he thinks I'm supposed to be doing.

I thought I got out of this shit when I dropped out of school; I thought checking out of society meant making my own decisions. Somehow, I went from one pressure to another and I don't know how to get out from under the expectations of yet another creature pretending to be an authority figure.

My eyes slowly run over the word BUSHES again.

I keep reading it like he's saying it to me again and again and again. The wet smell of Leakin Park creeps in around me. My jeans, the blood, the sulfur, the inside of Wayland's car. The weight hits me, and I slide down the laundry closet door to the floor. Tears roll down my cheeks. A sob shakes my body, forcing air into my lungs, but I can't breathe. That was it. That was the last message Wayland will ever send to me. His name will never show at the top of my messages again; his name will never appear on my phone unless I go looking for it; he'll never call or text or send me anything saying he's waiting for me outside or he saw this stupid thing at the store and thought of me or "Are you busy?" in the middle of the night because he's anxious and needs someone to talk to and that's the least I can do after everything he's done for me. I'll never get, "I just finished my exam. You wanna celebrate?" or "Hey! My residency's over! I'm going to be a doctor, Jo!"

I stare at the message. Jag's name pops down at the top of the screen beside my assurance to Wayland that everything's going to be okay. I wait to see if another message is gonna come through, but nothing does.

It's stupid.

I know Wayland doesn't have his phone on the other side, right?

They take that shit away from you when they process you like it's prison, right?

Cause of all the stupid shit I've discovered by going to the other side, the idea that you can make calls without service any time you want from Heaven or Hell or wherever would be the dumbest thing I've ever heard in my life.

For a second, I hold my breath. The shaking and

crying subsides while I type a message to Wayland. I doubt it'll get to him, but it doesn't matter. I didn't tell him enough when he was alive. I didn't give him enough of my time when he needed it. I wasn't a good enough friend and this hardly makes up for it, but I'm desperate for anything that might tell me he's still here and I didn't mess up *that* bad.

JOEY   I love you, Way.
            Don't forget.

The moment I press send, electricity goes through my fingers. My phone smacks into the floor. "What the fuck," I say through my teeth. I pick the phone back up. Turn on the screen. Wayland's messages are gone. All of them. His entire thread, our history, past, friendship. At the top of the inbox is a new chain from a scramble of symbols that don't make sense. The only message in the thread reads YOU CHOSE THE DARK.

I type YOU STOLE HIM FROM ME and FUCK YOU. Again, hitting send zaps me. I drop my phone again. Pick it up. The messages are gone. "For real," I growl. I use the wall to pull myself to my feet. "I know it's you."

Another caw comes from the kitchen this time.

The fat raven's sitting in the open kitchen window hanging over the sink.

"Fuck you too, Val!" I shove my phone in my pocket. My approach makes the bird fly away. I close the window. A glance around the apartment betrays no other open windows.

Good.

I check my pocket for my wallet, keys, and pat my phone again like I'm not expecting it to be there. I grab my skateboard from the living room where it's leaned against an end table by the couch. I close the door louder than I mean to. My key's in the socket. Someone comes out of the room down the hall with a garbage bag in his hand. It looks heavy, weighed down with inhuman liquid and it's too much like the bags I tossed in the woods with Wayland a couple days ago. The guy's wearing a short sleeve shirt and black shorts that don't hide the thick black tendrils crawling from his eyes and moving down his skin. His fingertips are slightly blackened by the coils that go down his arms, gather at his wrists, and disperse into his hands. Light catches on his eyes. They're too red, almost black. It's not drugs; he's dead red.

He turns down the other end of the hall in the direction of the trash shoot.

"Is every goddamn building in this city haunted?" I yank my key from the door. They're traded for the phone and I immediately punch Charon's number into the caller.

I'm at the elevator. It starts with a soft rattle of chains. Then ravens being to fill the window frames in the elevator lobby. The light's flicker overhead. The elevator on the left arrives, dings, the doors open. A group of ravens flies out in what feels like a never-ending swarm as they fill the lobby, the halls, and line the floor creating a walk way. The second elevator hits the floor. The doors part. Inside, the elevator lights aren't on and more ravens pack against the walls in such an unnatural way, the thing looks like it's made of feathers and obsidian eyes. In the middle of it all is the reaper, his white suit appears glowing against the sheen of black feathers. Cyan eyes illuminate his pale cheeks. He steps out of the elevator toward me. The biggest of the ravens sits on his shoulder, its head cocked to the side in momentary observation of me. Then, it turns away to stare down the hall.

"I was wondering when you would approach even a modicum of responsibility," Charon says.

My eyes burn, the tears wanting to start up again. My jaw tightens so I don't cry. "There's a ghost over there. Room 314 probably."

Charon glances down the hall. At the end of it, the guy I saw with the bag a second ago is on his way back, empty-handed. He pauses when he sees Charon. He turns to run. Charon marches down the hallway with the rattling chains that follow him getting louder, coming out of his peacoat like tentacles that throw themselves at the ghost so it can't get away.

The panic's building in me and I get into the empty elevator as quickly as I can so Charon can't turn his sights on me next. I push the lobby button over and over and over again until the doors close. The guy down the hall's screaming. I cover my ears and lean hard against the wall, closing my eyes and pretending I don't hear it. This shit didn't bother me before, but it feels like there's no escape now.

I reach the ground floor where everything's normal. No birds, no streaks of darkness, no messy handprints. The receptionist at the package counter's not dead. I loosen the grip on my phone and look down at Jag's messages, still flagged on the screen.

I have to write him something.

JOEY   Have a good day, J.
JAG   U 2.

I run out the front door of the apartment complex like giving me space from the house and Charon is all it'll take to assure me everything's fine. The birds that should be on the window aren't there or they're not visible from here.

I put in the coordinates for the park Wayland had sent me and stuff my phone in my pocket. I'm not at the house, but I'm just going for a walk, getting some air, getting the hell away from the house only because the reaper's here and I'm supposed to be doing shit. Even though Jag told me to stay put, I can't, this is better than sitting around an empty house panicking and throwing shit and pissing the grim reaper off. I'll be back before he notices I'm gone anyway, so, it's not a big deal.

With that thought, I set off in the direction of Wayland's last wish: Mt. Olivet Park.

THREE.

The air's cold; fall's here and with my hoodie sleeves pulled up, the chill's pecking at my exposed arms. I kick the ground to propel forward a little faster, hoping to warm up after a little while. Brick townhouses pressed shoulder to shoulder are going from gray to tan. The wrought iron fencing around some of them make the neighborhood look better until you get to the neighboring building where the paint's chipped, the fence is rusted, or there's a busted up sign hanging on the gate in front of an overgrown yard saying STAY OUT and BEWARE OF DOG. Most of the houses I pass are a mix of blasted out windows, some with ashes splashed toward the roof or rotting boards on the lower entry because at some point, someone had thought there was something worth protecting inside. Now, they're all broken and dilapidated or torn out and hanging on the stoops, forgotten, discarded, devalued, or too dangerous for anyone to bother with anymore.

There's more trash on the right side of the street than the left. A red brick townhouse has a window covered in white, peeling paint on the first floor. The window beside that one is busted out, but it's so dark inside, you can't see anything. The mail slot's rusted shut on the next three houses. Paint on the sidewalk reads:

DROP OUT
    FUCK OFF
        FUCK MEE   E
NO
PLZ BABE I SAID IM S ORRY.
    IM DED.
                    SHIT

It's all written in different handwriting, different people having different conversations with each other whether they like it or not.

There are too many condom wrappers in the gutter and I've seen at least one actual plumpy, used condom. I wouldn't even be looking down if I didn't have to watch for cracks and protruding edges in the busted sidewalk. I swerve around a can and candy wrapper so they don't jam my wheels. At the end of the block are a couple more red townhouses, all brick, the last one's boarded up on the first floor with the windows open on the second. A torn, black curtain blows gently in the breeze. Something moves behind it. A small shadow, a kid or a ghost. I don't know. I should call Charon if it's a ghost. If it's a dead kid, are they really as bad as dead assholes? At least their coming back could put a parent at ease, right?

If that's not some kid in the window, it's someone who gave up on the city a long time ago, but stuck around, just like the rest of us.

When you're born here, this city carves itself into you.

No matter how good that place in Virginia or Pennsylvania might look, it'll never be home.

I don't know why I care so much about this damn city. Maybe I identify with it too much. Bruised and rebellious and tired. Everyone shits on it, just like everyone's always shit on me, but they don't know Baltimore's heart. They see what she looks like on the outside and cast judgment, just like very few ever bothered to get to know me. I don't think every ghost here is bent on destruction. I mean, *I'm* not and KC seems fine. We can't be the only ones, right? There's gotta be something else here.

I feel like I'm being watched. Each building I pass, someone's peeking out the window, looking for hope or a message telling them things'll get better. Instead, they see DON'T JUMP on the sidewalk below or LOOK BACK across the street or YOU STILL HERE? LOLOLOL is on the pavement in the street because the city's just as surprised as any of us that we're still here.

A raven's sitting on the empty sill of a second story townhouse window. Its reflective eyes follow me as I pass.

My phone's tight in my hand with the map taking me to Olivet Park. Leakin's entrance is just a bit north from here. It's so close that Gwynn's Falls runs through Olivet too. If I stop rolling and stand still enough, I can even hear the rushing waters of the falls. Though Olivet's near, it's not as sketchy as Leakin. It's not as big and people don't go jogging there the same way and there's a playground kids actually use.

The houses are getting more aggressive, multiplying the chains or boards on the door and the continual yelling of KEEP OUT and MAKE ME's written against everything in chalk and the paint they use for lines in the street. The busted-out windows and broken bottles spilling onto the cement are a menagerie of bodies and bullet casings and a knife catches in the sunlight; violence is a broken river that runs down the sidewalk for kids to play in. I don't know who has the time to write this shit all over the city, but the voices never seem to stop. The graffiti's been a fixture ever since I was old enough to notice, like a population of its own and everyone in Baltimore's always got something to say. Even when the voices aren't in your head, it feels like the city's trying to talk to you through the buildings.

The discount food market on the corner lets me know the park's just a few more blocks down. White graffiti on red brick says RUN BITCH RUN!

The Big Guy's in my head, holding my neck. The voice snarls. My fingers curl. I'm seeing the guy from the bar about to smash my head in while standing over me saying, "Goodbye, bitch!" as Wayland lays on the ground beside me, his dark eyes wide with fear and pain and sorrow.

I press my foot into the ground and kick off faster without looking back.

Closer to Mt. Olivet, the town houses turn to brick duplexes with rusted chain-link fences. A popped ball sits in uncut grass mixed with weeds. Not abandoned. Summer's over. The driveway before one brick house reads CLOSER in black and feels like it's talking to me.

Come to the house, come deeper into the trees, find the darkness.

Like every time I've stumbled through the woods, it's a promise I'll find another one of the secrets this city's been hiding. Maybe that's the real reason why no one asks questions around here. We live on top of Baltimore's history. To see the worst of it, you just gotta open your eyes. We know that, so we keep our heads down and don't get involved. It's not a big deal if you don't talk about it.

Mt. Olivet's surrounded by trees, lush and green in the summer, but now the branches are anemic and the red in the leaves looks brown in the light so you can tell yourself it's just natural rot instead of mistakes and disagreement between people who just couldn't live together anymore.

A man on a billboard at the side of the road has a loopy mustache and a bottle of pills in his hands. He's winking beside a headline that reads CALL YOUR DOCTOR. Graffiti overwrites the brand name with RULE #2: FIGHT OR FUCK OR DO DRUGS. Tires look out of place in the gravel and weeds, mixed with the rocks and an abandoned off-white trailer reading DON'T LEAVE on the side. Much smaller bubbly, light blue letters read I DIDN'T, U DID underneath. A bottle of opened pills lay spilled in the grass. The name's something the TV tried to sell my dad in the case he had a floppy dick. All across the label it reads DEATH, DEATH, DEATH in a formal typeface.

A raven sits on top of the billboard; it doesn't notice me.

I keep going.

The trees have taken over entirely now where the houses used to be and cars are parked along the sidewalk. At the end of the street's another billboard with a guy in a gray suit, smiling wide and the caption GOT A LAWYER? GET A LIAR is written in graffiti. Someone's also drawn a mustache and an eye patch on him.

A couple of croaks slip out of the trees. Branches ruffle. A car slows down as it passes me. The driver's staring as he goes by. His face is making a determination about his future; am I worth the risk? He speeds off. I turn back around to the billboard and now there's an eye crudely drawn at the edge beside me.

The sidewalk turns into grass, so I skate in the street. The road turns into an underpass. Against the concrete wall are signs of a life gone by. A used needle, a dirty sneaker with the sole ripped out, a spilled bottle of what could've been Mountain Dew. Modest scratch marks like JK&DJ and RIP. Blue and black and gray and white turn the bottom of the bridge into a wave of bubbly letters saying KILL, ANGEL, RESIST, and ILU. Black lettering that's harder to read wraps beneath a shadow-like figure with talons and the words CAN'T RUN FROM HIM.

LOL

CHOSE THE CHURCH

    ORIANDA IS CURSED

        ITS CALLED HAUNTED

WHO TF CARES?

Beside the creature is blue handwriting that looks too familiar saying KEEP GOING. PARK. YOU CAN'T SEE.

The paint on the E drags away like someone lost control at the hand. The writing got looser, but the more I stare at it, the more it looks like it belongs to Wayland.

Just out the other side of the underpass is an entrance to a grassy walkway that leads away from the road, into the trees, and toward a little brook that's an appendage of Gwynns Falls.

I'm on the dirt path. A gust presses into my back like a hand leading me through the bushes. I turn around, step back, keep going while I look from the bare trees to the bushes for someone standing behind me. It feels too familiar and too real to be in my head. I press my hand to my neck. A caw comes from the trees behind me. I turn around again. Another caw echoes from a different direction. I survey the branches.

A raven sits on the ledge of the top of the bridge by

the road. A hand's on my back again, pushing me forward. "Stop that!" I say.

No one's behind me.

Train tracks run under one of the bridges at Olivet and they're all made up of arches and pale stone with white paint tossed against them that speckles like bird shit.

Dead grass crackles under my sneakers. My shoe sinks into the grass where it shouldn't. Mushy mud climbs my pant leg. Going faster and deeper into the park, the mud holds onto my foot in a way that feels too much like a hand trying to keep me still. I drop my board. Stepping back, something catches my leg. A scream catches in my teeth while I pinch my lip so I don't open my mouth. A couple of thin sticks with too much power wrap around my ankle. I continue forward, pulling myself free. I'm hearing things; it's the city's dead that's always around; I'm losing it.

Something's not feeling right about Olivet. It's not like I haven't been here before. I've boarded around here at least half as many times as I've gone through Leakin, but something about this place is different. The air's colder and it smells so bad. Rotten eggs, mold, decay. I reach for my back pocket to grab my cigarettes. My teeth pull at my lip ring to give them something to do while I light the cigarette. The time it takes me to get it into my mouth is enough to make me taste the nasty air. The nicotine's tainted from the way Olivet's flavor sticks to my tongue.

I pick my board back up. In the morning light, the arches of the bridge almost look like they're glimmering with a bit of gold. It's the secret beauty Baltimore hides from visitors who only see the point in visiting the abandoned wreckage here like we live in a deserted theme park. A feeling of familiarity and dread seeps from the cutouts closer to the top of the bridge. In the arch nearest to me, the stone reads SRY, SRY, SRY, SRY, starting out with big letters and going down until they're at my height. Blue. Shaking.

Familiar again.

"Cross?" I say, breathy, too loud it echoes back.

The dirt and gross or whatever underneath me has a slight indent, a shadow like the outline of someone who jumped off the bridge at some point and left their mark. It blends in enough you wouldn't notice it unless you're looking.

The trill of a raven echoes off the stone.

There's a breath in the back of my ear.

A warm hand touches my shoulder.

I gasp, turn around swinging and screaming, aiming for whoever's standing behind me. I hit air. A wave of dizziness grabs me, and I fall against the bridge wall. My cigarette falls out of my mouth and I'm sweating.

The tastes in the air's worse.

I don't know what a body tastes like, but with the sulfur and the water of Styx and the rotting corpse from the back of Wayland's car—This is what I'd imagine. I cover my face with my hoodie sleeve in an attempt to filter the air while picking my cigarette back up. It's not a great idea to put it in my mouth, but it's still lit, and I need something to calm me down.

I need to get a hold of myself.

I take a deep breath; a chuckle comes out.

Not mine. A bird, maybe? There's nothing in the trees. The raven I saw earlier isn't there.

My hand's on the bridge pillar, giving me balance again. I hold still, hold my breath, wait to see if my feet will sink again.

They don't and the silence betrays nothing but the cars going over the bridge above me. A chain link fence bounces nearby.

"Jo," he mutters.

The back of my neck prickles. My head dips to the side. His fingers draw down my arm. I turn around, looking for him. "Way? You there?" I stumble forward. Fingers caress my arm again, leading me to the pillar across the way. Neat, but frantic blue lettering appears where it wasn't before, reading: UNDER THE BUSH, OFF THE PATH. Next to it is

BITCH'S NUMBER and

BITCH LIED and

BITCH GOT CHLAMYDIA

DON'T TRUST DOLORES!

YA'LL B FOOLS.

The feeling of someone touching my arm tugs me forward gently. The sound of the falls is louder, like it's trying to cover the voice I just heard in my ear. It's trying to hide Wayland from me. It might sound crazy, but I know the falls is doing it because the cars on the bridge have gotten quiet too and that shouldn't have happened. A raven makes a couple clicking sounds that are less like a bird and more mechanical. Another one makes a sound like a human, unnatural, distorted, going, "Hey, hey, hey, hey. What are you doing?"

"This way, Jo," the familiar voice says.

I know it's him. A hand pulling mine, fingers feeling interlaced even though there's nothing there. I'm walking faster. My hand loosens and I almost drop my skateboard. "You there?"

It's dumb to ask; I know the answer. I saw him off and ghosts aren't the invisible creatures the stories and folklore would have you believe. They're much more destructive than that.

My jaw tightens and I pull my phone out of my pocket to look at the map. I'm in the right place. I just have to find the bushes he means. I glance back from where I came. Look over the arches, the bridge. There's a shadow standing under there and something that looks like a hand reaches out of the mud. I move away faster, pushing through the bushes and away from the normal side of the park where families actually go to play with their kids.

A chain link fence cuts off where I am from more bushes and trees. There's no path over there, but one created by consistent foot traffic. A KWIK N GO foam cup sits in the dirt, half covered. A cut in the fence makes it easier for me to get to the other side. I pull some of the chain back, crouch, and go through. A sharp edge catches my sleeve; I pull it loose. A soft string burns along my arm, but looking at the fabric, my hoodie's fine. A little irritation's coming through from a scratch maybe, but it doesn't matter.

The smell of it comes first. Rot and ammonia and… I know it too well cause it smells a lot like my dad; it's the smell that was in the back of Wayland's car. The decay of a corpse.

He's never coming back.

Red paint in the grass reads SORRY.

It *has* to be paint.

Then, the tree in front of me says DIDN'T MEAN IT and SRY, JO and ONLY U with an arrow pointing deeper into the trees. The bushes are still full of brown and gold leaves though the branches above are skeletons decorating the park.

I know what's behind the branches before looking.

The air's thick with decomposition. My skin puckers with goosebumps and there's just as much a feeling pressing into my back, urging me closer as there is repelling me. I advance carefully, gently tugging back bush branches. His foot comes into view first. The stained leg of his jeans I've seen him wearing so many times before. He's not wearing a jacket, though he should've been. If he left at night, they took his jacket or maybe if he was lucky, he took his jacket off when he left himself here. His chest's open, animals have taken bites out of his exposed body and dragged some of his innards into the grass to continue eating. A soft buzz is accompanied by flies and a couple of maggots crawling around the open wounds. His skin's discolored, red where blood's pressing into the side of his body he's leaning on. The other side of his face is pale, his hand's white and stiff and lifeless. His eyelids are closed, cheeks hollow. Does he even have eyes anymore?

A burn builds in the back of my throat while my vision blurs. Everything's spinning around me while the sound of the park disappears. The breakfast I dared to eat goes into the bushes. A little bit of leftover pizza and beer I didn't need anyway. I should've just had the cigarette.

Legs shaking, I fall to my knees. My arms tremble with barely enough strength to keep me on all four while my stomach tries to toss anything left inside of me into the grass.

Everything until now wasn't real.

He wasn't really gone and there was still that chance to wake up, even if I said goodbye to him. This all could've been a sick joke or a drunken stupor of my worst nightmare. He still could've returned since there hadn't been a body.

Now? There's nothing left of him to hope for.

I catch the stained shirt in my periphery, going from blue to purple to brown, with the loss of life spilled from selfishness born of someone who valued car keys and a wallet more than Wayland's life.

"What the fuck is wrong with people?" I spit out a bit

of bile mixed with stringy saliva.

My phone buzzes against my thigh, again and again and again like someone's calling. I fall onto my ass. My hands are still shaking as they get my phone out of my pocket. Jag's name's on the screen, accompanying the sign of an incoming call.

I wait for the call to subside. He immediately sends a text.

JAG	Answer the phone, Joey.
JOEY	Sry.
	Was in the shower.
	I'm fine.
	u don't have to worry so much.
JAG	Yeah I do.
JOEY	lol
	When'd you get so clingy?
JAG	kinda happened when u died.

My chest constricts. I look up. Get dizzy. Focus on the phone again. I don't have a good response, so I just write, "that's fair," and shove my phone in my pocket again. It buzzes again. I can't ignore it.

JAG	Do I need 2 come home?
JOEY	No.
	Work.
	I'm fine.
	I mean it.
	Shit's just
	Hard
	But I'm ok.
JAG	ok.
	I'm trusting you.

My phone's in my pocket again so I'm not tempted to lie more and feel worse. The more I talk, the more lies I'm telling him and I can't help the feeling he's catching it every time, even when there's nothing to read into with stupid text messages that on any other day wouldn't be a big deal.

My hands rub down my thighs, pretending to pat my pockets while I actually slap myself to make me feel like I'm back in my body again. The sound of the forest comes back. The cars in the distance roar on the bridge. Some kids laugh at the playground wherever it is.

God.

It's so like Baltimore to be staring at a body and hearing kids laughing, totally ignorant of what he's just a little bit away from. Someday he'll see it and the laughing won't be the same. It happens to all of us at some point.

I roll onto one cheek so I can get my wallet out of my ass pocket. I flip through it until I find the recycled cardboard business card with gold lettering reading DETECTIVE STONE GRANT in a font that pretends it's so strong, the guy it belongs to has real power. I turn the card over and put his number into my phone. It only rings twice before his deep voice picks up on the other end saying, "This is Stone."

I don't know why it's so startling to hear him. It takes me a minute to collect myself. I'd been hoping to catch his voice mail, not have to do this live. Maybe I should hang up and try again in five minutes. Out of the corner of my eye, Wayland convinces me not to do that. My voice shakes as I suck in a breath. "You taking tips?"

"Whatcha got?" he says.

I've seen him too many times—I know what his thinking face looks like when paired with that voice. The skepticism, the "your name's not Barbara, is it? Why would you lie to me?" He's asking if I made the body before I even tell him there is one.

"You take bodies?" I say.

"You make one?"

I snort; my nose burns. The pain pulls at the back of my eyes, making my head hurt. I turn further away from Wayland's body. Not fast enough because I catch a glimpse of him again and gag. A tear rolls down my cheek. I wipe it with the back of my hand. "How'd I know you were gonna ask that?"

He chuckles, sounding way less sick than me and I kinda hate him for it. "Do I know you?"

"Why would you say that?"

"You talk like we have a history."

"Do you want the body or not?"

The line's quiet. He's probably waiting for the badge tracker to pick me up because that's how they do it in all the shows, right? Keep the criminal on the line, find their GPS, tag them. Maybe that was the old way and new phones have a different way the badges can get you. Rocky'd only be too happy to get into my phone. Read my contacts, the text messages, affirm I had some part in the murdering spree he'd always thought I was guilty of while connecting dots that aren't really there. Would he be able to see the messages I sent to Wayland since he died if he's been laying here the whole time? What if my phone zaps him?

"Running out of time, R—" I bite my tongue.

"Where are you?" Rocky says.

"Stay focused." I shake my head. The dizziness comes in fast. I close my eyes again. My palm presses to my face. I didn't realize my hand had gotten so cold; the air had gotten so cold; I had gotten so cold. "You have to pick up the body. I need you to find it." I breathe in, shaking. "He needs to be put to rest."

"Who is it?"

"*Wayland Cross*," I whisper.

"Where?" Rocky's voice is stiffer than before. Suddenly, the laughter and jokes and playing with me are gone. I can even hear his chairs squeak as he stands up.

"Mt. Olivet. Past the bridges. In the bushes behind the fence. Follow the signs."

"What signs?"

"You'll see them."

"You make those too?"

"I didn't do any of this shit, Rocky." I snort. "I can't help I keep finding bodies."

"What'd you just call me?"

"Shit. At this point, I'm just doing your job for you. Pick him up. Tell his family. They deserve it." I hang up before anything worse comes out.

Tears roll down my cheeks more freely now. I rub them away with the back of my hand and get to my feet. My phone's in my pocket. I don't have time to stick around. If Rocky thought he could get here and catch a killer, he was already in his car before I gave him a direction to drive in. The badge lights and sirens will be echoing off the bridge within minutes—if I even have *that* long. Font Hill's literally across the street.

My body's suddenly heavy and I have to fight to get through the bushes. I use my skateboard to knock away branches. Three swings though, and I can barely lift it anymore. I keep going North toward Leakin and the Northwest entrance until I come out on the other side of the road. I've barely touched the pavement when the whirring of a badge car warning echoes off the trees from the other side of Mt. Olivet. I set my board down and ride Hilton Avenue past the highway until it turns into Leakin.

Then, the familiar roads of the park become the cover for   my   escape.

FOUR.

My legs have a mind of their own and that's fine, because I think if I stopped moving, I'd collapse, and I wouldn't be able to get up again. For a while, there's nothing in my head but a need to keep going and it's the same heat and pressure and pain I felt every time I ran to Wayland's place after I got into it with my dad or the same thing I felt when I ran to Jag so he could get me the hell off this plane of existence for a little while.

Now, I can't go to either of them.

I recognize the light poles first.

The trees on the corner three blocks from Deadwood with the tire swing hanging from a rope to snap when met with just a little too much weight. I've been waiting for the neighbor next door to trip into it during a drunken stupor for months now, but every time he's made it outside, he's avoided falling into it. The trailer across from mine was blinking Christmas lights in the window. They're strobing too fast; something doesn't seem right about it. The flamingos in the yard next to mine are kicked over with broken legs. My lawn's grass is overgrown and crowded with weeds, dandelions that've given up, the pile of dead grass I pulled at while sitting there with Wayland not even 24 hours ago.

A sob rattles my lungs. My body's finally slowing down, getting heavier again, wanting to sink into the ground and give up and not exist anymore the closer I get to my house. My fingers tingle with the urge to smack someone, the wall, myself if nothing else is there. I don't know. I want pain because I just want a distraction from this fucking disaster that is my entire life. I want the sting or burn or screaming to pull me out of my head. The wooden stairs outside my house creek as I climb them. My shoulder slams into the front door while I'm reaching for the knob.

It's still unlocked.

"Dad?" I go inside and shut the door behind me all in the same movement. "You here?"

My dad's chair's empty. Everything's so damn quiet. My back presses against the door. My board falls to the floor with a loud *slap*. I gasp, freeze, press harder to the door. I close my eyes and wait for the sting and the yelling to start. The bottle falling out of his lap, his standing in front of me, his voice in my ear.

There's nothing.

I breathe in the smell of the house. Rot and shit and piss and yesterday's beer that stayed too long erase the overcooked mac and cheese and pizza and dirty laundry that needs to be done. I don't remember it being this bad. Has it always been like this?

I look over the room.

The kitchen I've grown up with next to the living

room my dad never left and the chair he couldn't get out of; the chair he pressed me into; the chair I shot him in a couple of days ago. A week ago? I don't know anymore.

His TV's off.

The house should never be this quiet; it's never been this quiet and it's making me nervous. I go to the TV and press the button on the screen.

It doesn't turn on.

I pull it away from the wall. Blindly, I search the TV table until I find the cable, hanging unplugged. I put it into the wall. Hit the button. The TV turns on. My dad's favorite channel's playing a loud commercial that says GO TO THE STORE, YOU LIKE MEAT, DON'T YA GET THE MEAT TO FEEL GOOD? PICK UP YOUR LOTTO AND BEER AND BENEDRYL TOO. CAN'T BEAT THE MEAT ANY OTHER WAY.

I'm not sure I'm hearing the TV right. Things have been off for a while now. Like that commercial that told my dad to kill himself. That shit couldn't be real, right? Sirens come on next from some show about badges, I think. Or maybe they're coming into the neighborhood cause my neighbors are getting into it again or maybe Rocky saw me leaving the park and followed me here and I'm about to go down, finally, for real.

I grab the remote from dad's chair, cranking the TV up as loud as it'll go. My skateboard's under my arm. I'm going down the hall to my room saying, "Let me know if you need anything," under my breath. I slam the door shut. The TV's screaming through the walls. I toss my board onto my bed. My bedside lamp's still on the floor, broken from when I knocked it over a couple days ago to prove to Wayland we were still alive.

I was so fucking stupid then.

I'm so fucking stupid right now.

I turn back around to the door. Bloody handprints mar the chipped, white paint. I place my hand over one of them. It's too small to be my dad's. I think it's Wayland's from when he was in here with me the other day. When Jag was here. When I told myself that everything was going to be fine. A fuzzy feeling of electricity goes through my body. I sob, pull my hand back, and stumble away until I'm tripping over some shit on my floor. A spare wheel? A sock. I put my hand to my mouth to catch the sounds I'm making while I retreat.

I don't know what else I can do, so I climb into the closet. Clothing lays piled on the floor in one corner, a mix of clean and *probably* clean. My toolbox is underneath that, stuck open with the spare rails and wax and risers and grip tape hanging out. A blue-green hoodie sits on top the pile. Lightning bolts stream across the back.

Something Wayland loaned me forever ago.

I throw myself onto the floor and pull the door shut behind me the best I can. I grab the hoodie and sit back. A loose sneaker pushes into my ass. The hoodie's against my face. I breathe in. His smell's still here, mixed with mine and the cigarettes and a little bit of alcohol.

Tears spill down my cheeks. My breath's short and I can't stop it from hitching and moaning and turning into whiny hiccups I hate myself for. My hands are trembling.

I take off the hoodie I'm wearing and put Wayland's on. The next time I breathe in, I smell him less. A scream comes out. He's disappearing before my eyes in every single way and he's not coming back, and I can't do this—I can't exist without him—and now Dad's going to hear me and come in here to make me shut up. I lean over, hitting my head as hard as I can against the wall. My teeth chatter; my lip busts; I taste blood. My hand covers my mouth to shield another sob as I pull my legs to my chest. I bite my lip ring to hold my mouth shut. My arms go around my legs to pull them in closer, make me smaller so he won't see me hiding in the closet. I close my eyes, hold my beath, *don't find me.*

The TV rings with another siren, someone yells at someone else to stop. A couple of pops. Every time I think I've got it, another sob breaks through me and I can't stop the cascade it starts. I don't have control of anything; everything's being taken away from me again and again and again. I squeeze my eyes shut tighter and keep telling myself everything's fine, like I'm that naive. Dad's in his chair, Wayland's at home, and I'm screwed, but not for the reasons I think. I don't know when I started rocking. I don't know when I fell onto my side. My face feels tight and wet and getting to sleep in the closet is the closest I come to getting control of myself.

The sounds of the house fade. I'm floating in my dark room with nothing around me until it's replaced by someone saying, "Joey?"

My bedroom door slaps hard against the wall. I press my hand to the floor to sit up. My swollen eyes make it hard to see.

"Joey? You here?" he says again, closer this time.

"Jag?" I whisper.

I use my sleeve to wipe my face. Get all the red and shame and evidence of anything off before he sees me. I dig my phone out of my pocket. My screen says there are nine messages and seven calls. It's after six. The closet door opens. He's standing on the other side; back lit by the bedroom light he must've turned on whenever he came in.

"Joey." My name is a sigh of relief he doesn't try to hide. "What are you doing here?"

"I… don't know." I try to keep my voice even, but at the end, tears fight me. One goes down my cheek. I wipe it away quickly as if moving fast enough will make it so Jag didn't see it. "How did you know I was here?"

"I had a feeling—"

"I want to go back, J—I just want it all to go back! I don't care that he beat me or made me feel like shit sometimes or that I didn't want to be here. I just want his stupid ass in that chair! Cause—You know, if he's over there, it means the last couple of weeks never happened and I don't know that he's dead and rotting and Wayland's just home with his family and his house isn't burnt up, trying to take his memory with him. J—" My voice breaks.

Jag's on the floor with me. He holds me and pulls me into him in the way that I've always liked, making me feel safer than I've ever had any right to feel.

My arms go around him, hands grabbing at his shirt in desperation to hold onto him, so he doesn't disappear too as I bury my face into his chest. He smells like sweat and grease and cigarettes and him. I close my eyes and fall into him harder. His arms tighten more. "All I ever wanted was a dad just like everyone else got. He didn't have to be nice all the time, but maybe he could've said I love you sometimes—or like, made dinner or pretended to be happy to see me for more than five seconds—even if he didn't mean it." A sob breaks through my words. "Pretending's better than nothing—but he couldn't even do that!" My nails dig into his back; he doesn't let go. "J—He chose being dead over being my dad. What the hell's that? Like what the hell's so wrong with me? I don't know what I did—I don't know what I could've done to make him care more about me. Maybe if he talked to me—If he asked—All I ever wanted was for him to want me and I hate myself for how much I still want him."

Tears stream down my face. Jag's shirt absorbs them.

My body weakens. My hands keep loosening, but then I panic and grab him again because I don't want him to go. Even seeing me like this, I don't fucking care, I need him. Jag's hold gets tighter. He sits on the floor with me, pulling my body into his lap.

"Why is everything taken from me?" My voice cracks with a whine. I'm embarrassed at myself, but I can't stop. Jag's heard every stupid, pathetic thought I've had about myself for God knows how many years because I'm goddamn pathetic enough to think them in the first place. He can take that as the final sign he'd been waiting for to leave. "What did I do to deserve this? My mom, my dad, my best friend, my life? Everything's just gone. I don't deserve anything. I never did. When are you gonna go too?"

His hand's sliding along my back. My body shakes. Everything's too weak, I can't hold onto him anymore, but I don't want distance between us.

His lips press into the top of my head. "I'm not going anywhere," he mutters.

"What makes you so sure? I'm annoying as fuck, J. Everyone thinks so."

"I made the decision, Joey. I'm not going anywhere."

My hand slides around Jag's body to wipe my running nose again. My arms are too weak. Jag loosens his grip just enough to give me space to move and I hate it. It means he can look me in the face if he tries. I keep my head down so he can't.

"You said you were fine earlier… Why do you keep lying to me," he says.

"Don't feel so special." Snot tries to choke me. "I was lying to me too."

"What were you doing?"

My throat goes tight. It shouldn't be so hard to speak. The words are running laps in my head like each time they pass, they should get further away. Instead, the stomping gets louder. *You should've stopped. He's gone and it's your fault. If he hadn't known you. The way you found him? That was you. Every time they say you haven't killed anyone, maybe, but you're just like your dad, aren't you? How long until you do to Jag what you did to Wayland? How long are you gonna hang around someone who is worse off for it?*

"Joey," Jag says. "Stop saying shit about yourself and tell me what happened."

"I put Wayland to rest." My fingers curl into Jag's shirt. I bury my face in him. I don't deserve the comfort his body gives to me. His hand doesn't leave my neck, but he tilts my head back until his lips gently press against mine. His fingers stroke my cheek. I lean into him.

We stay in my bedroom's dark closet for a while and I can't remember anything else.

FIVE.

Soft buzzing wakes me up first. Then, it's the shower. I'm going in and out of sleep. I reach across the mattress, searching for companionship. He's not lying next to me anymore. My face is swollen; I can't open my eyes. I grab the blankets and wrap them tightly around me like it'll make the emptiness of the bed less obvious.

The shower shuts off. The bathroom door opens. The smell of shampoo comes into the room with leftover mist from the shower. Then, there's Jag's body. Bare hips go for the dresser. My eyes flutter mostly shut, only so maybe he won't see that I'm awake yet. He opens the drawer and slips on a pair of underwear. Next are the jeans and black shirt. Same thing, different day, every day.

I like the routine. Predictable. It lets me know what to expect so I can pretend there will never be any surprises.

Jag turns toward the bed, toward me. His arms cross.

"You're awake," he says.

I roll onto my back so I'm not facing him anymore. A small smile tugs onto my lips. My fingers gently work the blanket between them. "Couldn't miss this."

"I can't believe you're not asleep."

"When did we get here?"

"I dunno. Late. Sometime after you passed out at your trailer last night."

I push myself up. Everything's heavy; my muscles ache. I groan before realizing that's my voice and make it stop. I'm leaning forward because my back's not strong enough to hold me. I wipe my face, hoping that maybe it'll take some of the tightness away because I know every bit of tightness is sadness waiting for Jag to see it, ask me about it and bash me up again with the things I don't want to think about. I pull the blanket over my lap while trying not to bite the inside of my lip ring.

It doesn't work.

I need a cigarette, but those aren't allowed in the bedroom.

I'm still wearing Wayland's light blue hoodie, though my skinnies are gone. My phone's sitting on the nightstand, plugged in. I grab it and look at the clock. It's almost eight. I track Jag. He's still at the dresser, moving shit around, but it's more like busywork than he's actually doing anything. "Shouldn't you be on your way to work?" My thumb hits the button on the side of my phone. The screen goes off.

Shutting the drawer, Jag turns back to me. "I needed to check on you first. Yesterday… wasn't good." He leans against the dresser, arms crossed. "Lately, it's like every time I go out the door, you're getting into something."

"I didn't have much of a choice on this one." My eyes drop. I pull the blanket further over me.

"You could've told me where you were going—"

"And you would've said, '*yeah, sure, honey. Good luck with that?*'"

"No, but you said you wouldn't hide shit from me anymore."

"I didn't hide shit from you—"

"'*I'm fine*' sound familiar?"

The coffee pot hisses from the kitchen. There's a soft throb from a radio passing outside, the open window in the other room lets the sound in. Jag's place is kind of central, so it's always at least a little noisy. A couple stories up and made of brick, the noise isn't the worst when the windows are closed and they're better than anything you hear at Deadwood.

"How the hell'd you end up at your place?"

"You wouldn't believe me—"

"Try it."

I pull at my lip ring while my mind races to come up with an excuse that Jag will actually believe—or something he at least won't mock. It's all lies. There's nothing that I can say that doesn't suck. "I was looking for Wayland—"

"You're doing that again?" Jag pushes off the dresser with a grunt.

"Gimme a second to explain, would you?"

Jag uncrosses his arms in a gesture meant to invite me to talk, but it feels mocking.

My knee bounces softly. I pick harder at the loose strings on the comforter. "After I dropped Wayland off downstairs, I got a text from him—Or his number—I don't know—but it was a location. He never told me where his body was. The text didn't even say I'd find his body there, but he sent me an address and I followed it—"

"Joey—Are you stupid? That could've been so many

other people—"

"It just went to Mt. Olivet." My throat's dry. Bile and the taste of leftover pizza burn the inside of my nose again. I swallow. "I found his body in the bushes… Whatever was left of it, anyway."

"What happened to him?" Jag's voice is softer than it was a second ago.

"Baltimore." My fingers curl into the blanket. "He wasn't even doing anything shady, J. Some jackass killed him for a wallet and his keys!"

Jag's lips are tight. His fists ball hard enough, his knuckles are white. That's the first time I notice his skin's puckered up the arm. A long, red scratch runs along his forearm. A slight prickle resonates from my arm, remembering the sting I felt yesterday when I went through the fence. I pull my hoodie sleeve up to see the same line going down my arm in the same place.

"Where did you get that cut?" I point to the line on my arm. He eyes my cut then surveys his arm, starting with the wrong side. A look of genuine surprise crosses his face, like he didn't know the cut was there before. "I dunno. I guess I rubbed against something yesterday at work." He shrugs.

"In the same spot I got cut?"

"How'd you get that?'

"I think I got it when I was ducking under a fence at Olivet."

Jag sighs hard. He rubs his eyes as he turns away. His hand goes to his neck as he drops his head back. "You know how shit West Baltimore is.

"It was during the day and the badges were right there." The excuse doesn't make me feel any better. The breath I take is shaky and doesn't stop my heart from racing. "Nothing's gonna happen to me that isn't my own doing."

"Most of the shit that happens to you is your own doing, Joey." Jag's laugh is bitter. "Not the shit with your dad and not that you ask for it, you just like to get into situations that make it easy for you to get hurt. You don't ever know when to slow down, it's *borderline* suicidal." Jag pushes off the dresser and leaves the bedroom. "And that's being nice."

"Sorry."

"For what?" He stops in the doorway.

I pull my sleeve back down my arm. "Because… everything that happens to you has happened because of me."

"No, Joey. That's not what you should be sorry for."

"How can you say that? I don't even know what the hell I'm doing most of the time." A wave of sadness hits with a feeling like I'm losing him. Not because he's going, but because I can't stop pushing him away. I don't want anything bad to happen to him and the truth is outside of Wayland and Jag and Donny, it's only bad shit that happens to me. "The cut? The body thing? The necklace? I don't think I really understood it yesterday when I asked you to carry that for me."

Jag sighs again, rubbing the back of his neck. "I made a decision to work with your shit a couple years ago when I got involved with you, Joey. Whatever you think you're apologizing for, you don't need to. I'll take an apology for the lying though."

"Sorry," I say.

"See? Was that so hard?"

I lower my head, grabbing at my phone and hitting the button on the side so the screen lights up. Another expectation there'll be something there.

I'm not disappointed, I know better.

I feel tears coming back. I'm so sick of crying and you'd think I'd run out of tears at some point, but every time I think it's over, it comes back. I wipe my eyes with my fingers like I'm getting crust out of them.

"You call the badges?" Jag's still standing in the door.

"About Cross?" I exhale the words. Using his last name doesn't make it any easier to speak. I can't distance him from the way I saw him yesterday and that's overwhelming the last time I saw him in Mortem. "Yeah."

"Good."

"He deserved so much better than what he got."

"I know."

My fingers curl around my phone. The screen goes black. Weight presses into the side of the mattress. The bed creaks. I look up. Jag's on his knees, leaning beside me. His arms are on either side of my lap and he's towering over me. I lay back, giving him more room to come on top.

He leans in so our faces are close; I wait for his lips. "You did everything you could," he says.

"Only after it was too late."

"You can't hold onto that, Jo."

The name sets my skin on fire. Everything's tingling, even my ears are hot. I meet Jag's eyes. He's so close. His fingers cup my jaw. He leans in a little, I go in the rest of the way, so our lips meet. My hand curls into his shirt to pull him down on top of me. It slides down his body, pressing into his strong chest, his stomach, reaching for his belt. Damn—He got that on fast. Doesn't matter. My fingers work it open while my head lands back on the bed. His nose urges my chin up and he assaults my neck with comfort while he works my hoodie off.

"Don't you have somewhere to be?" I mutter.

"Donny can wait." The gentle baritone of his voice, his hot breath, and the strong touch to put me at ease. This is what Jag's been doing for me since the day we first hooked up. Every time I came to him with something on my mind or a fresh bruise on my skin and the overwhelming desire to get the hell out of here, he could bring me back, calm me down, and make me feel like someone gave a shit.

It happened so fast after that first time.

Anything that went wrong, he was there to give me comfort and I didn't think much about it because he never complained. I guess that's how we sort of became serious. Instead of turning to Wayland for a distraction when I was upset, I came to Jag, who was always willing to argue against my thoughts with his affection. Everything in moments like this have been an exchange of emotion and fears and vulnerability kept between the two of us. The fears and panic and guilt that had told me to check my phone or hide or look out the window or run are gone in the way only Jag could stop them. There's something different about the way his body feels against mine. It sounds so cliche to say he fills in the parts of me that are missing, but like, what the hell else can you say?

I was either born broken or busted up from everything I've been through, and it's being with him that makes me feel like maybe I'm not so far away from being functional.

I didn't have any experience before Jag; I never wanted hands on me, knowing what they could do at their worst. Not to mention, taking anything off meant showing someone else my dad's anger and giving them something to laugh at or ignore or pretend to care about just to look the other way at the first chance they got.

Jag never did that though, even when I expected it to be a one-time thing; even when I figured he'd make a joke the next day or he wouldn't go for it again or he'd bounce out of Donny's because what happened made working with me awkward. He never overlooked me or thought less of me, even when I pretended I wished he would.

My body's tingling with the feeling left behind by his lips. As he slides off the bed, I still feel his hands on my arms and hips and the way he holds me when we're together. My racing heart's slowing down, coming to a contented place it wasn't at earlier. He slides his pants back up his hips. I watch the fabric cover his body again. His shirt drops over his belt once it's secured. He catches me watching him and smiles. "Donny can only wait so long, Joey."

"I know."

"I've got Sunday off. We can do something then."

"Okay." I sit up. My hand blindly searches the bed, not for my shirt or bra or anything, but my phone. It's buried in the comforter by the edge of the mattress. I pick it up. On impulse, I hit the button on the side. The screen illuminates. No messages. The panics coming back. I throw my phone to the other side of the bed. "Jag?"

"Yeah?" He's patting down his pockets, doing his usual check.

"You think Donny would kick me out if I came to work with you?"

"He might." Jag looks at me. "You're supposed to be taking a break."

"I think I might get a *habit* if I stay here."

Jag sighs. His lips are pursed. He crosses his arms as his hips drop to the side. "Take a quick shower. Clean up. I'll let D know we're on our way."

"He think I'm gonna be like Veronica when I come back?

Jag laughs. "From what I hear, you could never be like Veronica."

"That's a relief." I'm out of bed, grabbing the jeans I wore yesterday from the floor by the hamper, a shirt from Jag's partially open drawer, and a pair of clean underwear. I go into the bathroom and shut the door a little too fast. It claps. "Sorry!" My voice echoes off the tiled walls.

"Did you want coffee?"

"I don't know." I bite my lip.

"I'll make some more." Jag's voice is getting farther away.

"Thanks." I toss my stuff onto the counter and climb into the shower as fast as I can. The water's hot enough I burn my skin a little. The puckered, red skin helps me keep my mind off the footprints still in the tile where Wayland stood a couple days ago, showering when I made the stupid decision to bring him here. Most of him's been washed away already, but the grout between the tile's clung onto some of the grime he brought into the house. The brownish-red color says it's not just mud.

The oil of life is what Ralph called it.

Does it mean something else when splattered everywhere? When it feeds the Baltimore, does it really have an effect? Seeing the rage and loss in one person can't be where it ends. The city has too much of an identity of its own. Everyone who lives here sees it. Everyone on the outside sees something else. Maybe it's the same reason Jag and Donny keep giving me chances. It's not charity, but something else.

I turn the water up hotter to try and wash the shame of the last couple of weeks off me. My mind's racing, coming up with what I'll say to Donny when I show up again. I need to calm down, figure it out, and don't be fucking crazy or Jag won't take me anywhere anymore. I know it's why I never liked staying at his house for long. If I'm at work, then he doesn't have to look at me for who I am or how I am or when I'm breaking apart. You know how many people don't have time for that shit?

I've never wanted to expose myself too much because I know what happens when you let yourself be honest. The more someone realizes who you are, the more personal it is when they leave.

I turn the water off. I don't remember washing anything, but there's soap in the bottom of the shower around my toes, my hair smells nice, and the prints left behind by Wayland are less. The fog in the mirror obscures my face into a blurry knot of color. I apply my normal eyeliner.

When I'm done with that, at least I look a little more normal than before.

In the kitchen, Jag's leaning against the counter with coffee in front of him and a cigarette pinched between his lips. He straightens when I open the bedroom door and come out. "We can stop by Ralph's after work, yeah? Ask him about some things."

"Okay."

The coffee maker hisses. If it wasn't there and hot and if Jag hadn't put the effort into making it, I would've left without it just to get to a cigarette faster. But I know I'll regret it by the time we get to Donny's if I skip it. I make a cup and turn the pot off, rinsing the filter and kettle before we leave. I've got a cigarette by the time we reach Jag's car. He's playing the radio low this time around.

I hope he doesn't want to talk more.

My hand's sitting on the center console, waiting for his when he's not shifting gears. I close my eyes and the image of my living room comes back to me and the repeating thoughts I need to check on my dad, it's been a while since I saw him, something might've happened. It doesn't matter how many times I tell myself he's not there and he doesn't need me. There's still a nagging voice telling me I'm wrong and I should check just to prove it to myself.

What's the worst that could happen if he's not there?

My foot's bouncing against the floor. I open my eyes.

Graffiti on the passing stop sign reads TAKE A BREATH in white.

I do what it says and the cigarette tastes pretty good.

At the body shop, Jag and I go through the backdoor by employee parking. I'm at the lockers before Jag. I open mine. There's someone else's jacket inside.

"Felix has been using that." Jag stuff's his jacket into his locker. "You can put your stuff in mine."

"Party." I grunt, hanging my hoodie in the locker along with Jag's coat. We step out of the break room and Jag takes a look around the garage.

Donny's not anywhere visible, though his voice is carrying. "No, we can't fit you in. Look, I've got a callback sheet the size of a divorcee's wish list. Yeah, if something opens up, I can add you, but I doubt we're doing anything for ya today." Donny's standing behind the front counter with the phone pressed to his ear. He sighs. His fingers tap the counter rapidly. "Yeah, yeah. I'll put you on the list, alright—No, there's nothing I can do about the placement. No… That ain't gonna work either. Been there, done that, mistake every time. You're written down, but that's the best I can do for you. Yeah, yeah. Good one to you too." His voice carries into the shop through the open garage door.

Mustache guy waves from what's been my spot since I was seventeen.

"Hey, Felix," Jag enters the lobby without stopping.

Donny's hanging the phone up as he groans. His hand presses into his face as he looks over the computer screen and sighs again. "You're late, Jag," He grunts.

"I know."

"How's Joey?"

"Didn't you get my text?"

"What do you think? I've been on the phone since I got here. What happened?"

I come through the garage door. The large window overlooking the shop gives Donny a chance to see me before I come in. He only spares a glance at first. Then, it takes him a second to realize it's me or he's confused because he's gotta look again. When I enter the lobby, he says, "Joey, you're here."

"Morning to you too, Donny." I fight the tightness in my throat with a smile that's just as tight. With all the time I've spent here, I've never felt so nervous. "Don't sound so excited to see me or anything. I might get the wrong impression."

"That's not it. I just wasn't expecting ya for at least a little while," Donny says. "You're supposed to be taking a break."

"Yeah." Jag steps around the back of the counter. He flicks through the bin holding the files pulled for the jobs expected today. The three of them in front already have keys at the bottom of the bags along with the paperwork. "We decided it might be good for her to get out of the house. Too much trash on TV to be a distraction. If life's not making you drink, that shit sure will." Jag pulls one of the files out, seemingly finding what he was looking for. "Hope you understand."

"Sure," Donny says slowly, looking from Jag to me. "Either way, glad to have you back, Joey, cause goddamn do I hate the phone." He laughs more boisterously than before. There's no one sitting in the waiting room and the TV's not on yet, which makes his voice carry more than usual. "Not that I can't do it, but I hate arguing with customers. Men think they can fight me, women think they can seduce me, and nah. I'm not about any of that. Blowjobs don't pay the alimony, you know?"

"What if I want to work on cars?" I say.

"Mmm, yeah… I think it's only fair you manage the phones today since that was your thing anyway. Also, consider it payment for all the chaos you've knocked into the current schedule, eh?"

I glance at Jag. I really didn't want to be stationary today. I'd been hoping to get back to something that kept me busy. Listening to music, moving, maybe zapping myself a little by going too fast and getting doused in grease and grime and crumbs from someone else's car while I drive it to the lift. Instead, I sigh and move behind the counter. There's no argument, especially if Donny's not sending me home.

A stack of notes lays beside the phone. The lights on it blink with who knows how many missed calls and messages. I look at the computer screen that shows a list of numbers next to the appointment planning program. You have to scroll to see them all. "Fine. I'm on counter. Thanks Donny…"

"Great." He pats me on the shoulder. I stiffen and he laughs again. This one's a little more awkward than the last.

"If I'm gonna be dealing with the phone, I think I'm gonna need more coffee though." I follow Donny back into the shop.

"You're in luck. We got some actual flavored creamer now. It helps cover the nasty taste of the coffee. Doesn't do much for the aftertaste though," Donny says.

"You know, it'd probably help if you changed the filter every once in a while."

"Look, Joey, I'm a mechanic, not a woman." Donny elbows me, laughs again, notices I'm not laughing. "It's a joke, kid."

"I know." I enter the break room. The sink's running. Mustache has a foam cup in his hand and the coffee pot's sitting on the sink. The air's stale and smells like watered down brew. "S'cuse me," I mutter, taking the space in front of the sink. I glance in the cup on the counter. The color's a little too light. I'm anticipating what the filter looks like as I fill the coffee pot.

"Felix, have you met Joey yet?" Jag says, standing in the break room door.

"No," Mustache says. His voice is higher pitch and nicer than I was expecting.

"Well," Jag says slowly. "Joey, Felix, Felix, Joey."

"Hey—"

"Thanks, J. I never would've figured that one out." I toss the filter into the trash. It doesn't look as bad as I thought it would, but maybe that's because I just cleaned the filter out a day or two ago. I don't know anymore. We still have the Artisan Cherrywood stuff in the cabinet which is surprising. I thought he would've run out of it by now. Once the pot's set to drip, I turn from the counter. Felix is still standing there and Jag and him are standing still like they just stopped talking to stare at me. Were they talking or did they ask me something and somehow I missed it? "Sorry," I say. "I'm kind of distracted. I got a lot of work to do today."

"I get that," Felix says. "But thanks for cleaning the break room the other day."

I still can't believe the way he sounds or his big, brown eyes or the smile that feels too genuine to be in a place like this, talking to me. "For the record, you're probably being too nice to me." I step out of the break room, sliding between Jag and Felix since they're standing in front of the door.

As I return to the lobby, I hear Felix say, "Did I do something wrong?" and Jag says, "Nah. Give her a couple of days to warm up to you. Thing's've been a little rough lately."

"So, I heard," Felix says.

I close the lobby door, so I don't have to hear them anymore. I don't want to hear Jag say, "She's not so bad once you get to know her," or worse, "Don't worry about the lockers; she's probably not coming back to the garage side." With the door shut, I can't hear the music from the radio that Jag's always in control of. My foot's bouncing. I already want another cigarette. The silence is getting to me, so I turn the TV on. I'm kind of pissed there aren't any regular cable channels that play music anymore.

I open the schedule and emails and message log to start going through them. At least there's not a lack of things to focus on, even if I'm not in the garage. My cellphone's on the counter now too. I hit the button on the side to make the screen light up.

No messages.

Cursing under my breath, I rock against the counter. The phone rings. I answer with, "Hello," while spinning my cellphone around against the glass. "Yeah, let me check the schedule," I say. My hand's on the work computer mouse. I scroll through a couple of days. "We don't have anything until Saturday." I tap the counter just beneath my cell phone. "Yeah, yeah, I can get you in. Three work? Party. See you then." Just as soon as I hang up, I'm holding my cellphone again. My inbox is open. Wayland's not there.

"I know. I'm a fucking idiot," I say to myself. I shake my head to fight the impulse to grab my phone again and start going through the backlog of messages and callbacks as a way to not wonder if he'll ever message me again.

SIX.

The day at the auto shop goes by and I don't check my phone as often as I expect, though I still look at it too often to feel proud of myself. The schedule's caught up with everyone in the call queue given a time slot. Most of the customers didn't yell when I told them we couldn't see them precisely when they thought we would. Besides getting my coffee, I avoided going into the garage because I still don't want to see Mustache's shit in my place at the lift. At some point, I propped the shop door open because I missed the sound of the radio and Jag muttering to it while he worked. That came with laughter from jokes I wasn't a part of and I'd look up to see Jag and Donny and Mustache saying something too quiet that it got lost on its way to the lobby. Is this what it was like without me? They all got along, probably better than whenever I've been here because none of them carry around the attitude I can't seem to get rid of. Mustache probably knows more about cars than me too and is like Jag, so he's stronger than me, making everything just so much easier when I'm not at the lift.

Maybe Wayland had it right and there's nothing left for me here either. Nothing but Jag, but what do I even give him that makes me worth the trouble?

It's closing time and they've already started putting away their tools. The phone on the counter rings. I pick up saying, "Bodymore, Body Shop. How can I help?"

"I need a tow," an urgent voice says.

"We close in like, ten minutes. I don't know if we can help you," I say.

Donny comes into the lobby holding a couple folders for the cars still being worked on in the shop. "What's up?" He slides the folders into the file cabinet behind the counter.

"Someone's asking for a tow," I say.

"Where they at?" Donny says.

I ask the caller and he tells me, "Leakin Park."

"Shit. Really?" Donny leans against the wall behind me. "I don't like leaving people hanging out there after dark. Jag, can you take it?" His voice carries through the open door.

"Yeah." Jag comes into the lobby from the garage while working grease stains from his fingers with a rag. Large globs of black darken his skin. The casual rubbing he's been doing isn't helping much to remove the color. "I can go." He tosses the rag onto the counter. He stops in front of me. Leaning against the surface with his elbows, he watches me as I take down the caller's details.

Once I've confirmed everything with them, I hang up. Jag takes the notepad and flips it around to read what I got. He mutters everything as he reads it. My chest gets tight with returning panic. He glances up, seeming to notice at just the right time. His hand reaches across the counter to mine. I pull it away before he touches me, crossing my arms casually in an attempt to look like I don't care. "Can't Mustache go?"

"Who?" Donny says.

"*Felix*," I say.

"Aw... You've already got a nickname for him? That's cute," Donny says.

"Right..." My jaw tightens. "So, can he go or not?"

"He left two hours ago," Donny says.

"What?" I say. "I swear I just saw him in there—"

"He's been the opener, Joey. Unlike you guys, he's getting up at the asscrack to start before we open the gate."

"It's fine." Jag pushes off the counter. "I can go, no problem. You wait here and it'll be like thirty minutes, forty-five, tops." He winks.

"I want to go with you." I turn back to him.

Jag's lips purse. I'm not sure if he's pursing them at me or to hold back a smile. What's the judgment in his eyes? He's thinking something, but I'm not daring enough to look at him directly in case he'll get a better look inside my head while I try to see inside of his. "You sure?"

"Yeah. Why wouldn't I want to go?" I snort. "Leakin's pretty much my second home at this point."

"Is it?"

"For how many times I've gotten laid out in Dead Run? Feels like I can't get away from Baltimore's burial ground." I'm tapping my foot. I glance down as Jag rips the details from the notepad by the phone.

Donny levels with the front counter. He glances between Jag and I and back to Jag. "If you're fine with it," he says to Jag. "She can go. Just be back before nine, yeah? I'd like to get *some* sleep tonight."

"Don't worry, D. With two of us, the job should go

twice as fast, right?" Jag shoves the paper into his pocket. He grabs the tow truck key from the lock box.

"I'm not so sure about that." Donny laughs. He waves us off while dipping into the garage.

"Just don't blame us if we come back with a body," I say. "You know what it means to send us to Leakin after dark!"

"Don't even say that!" Donny says without stopping. As he disappears into his office, he swears under his breath. A couple moments later, the sound of his squeaky door closing echoes softly against the empty work room. Jag's leaving the lobby, making his way to the break room. I follow.

At the lockers, he slips his jacket on and waits for me to grab my hoodie. He leans against the locker beside his, still got the same dumb expression on his face from the other room. Lips pursed. Head downcast, his goofy smile is freed once my hoodie's over my head. "You sure you wanna come?" he says.

"It's just Leakin."

"Yeah."

"Yeah. Is there supposed to be something more to it?"

Jag looks me in the eye, then down, and there's an assessment in his expression. "Nah." He shakes his head while pushing off the locker.

I check my pockets to make sure I have everything. My phone's not there. "Shit."

"What?"

I go back to the lobby; Jag's in tow. My phone's still in the drawer underneath the computer. I pull it out and slide it into my pocket. When Jag sees what I'm grabbing, he just says, "Oh. Expecting a call from me?" He spins the key around his finger.

"Maybe." As I walk by, I take the keys from him and

run. I'm out the back door; he's chasing me. I'm not even off the sidewalk when his arm goes around my waist. His free hand closes around the one I'm holding the keys in. He pulls me to him and his grip tightens around me. I stubbornly hold the keys against my palm. It's only as I loosen my grip that he loosens his.

"I just wanted to carry those for you," I say. "Least I could do after everything you carry for me."

"Appreciate it, but I got it." He's got the keys now. He climbs into the driver's side and I'm in the passenger. The city's passing by quickly. Messages on homes read MAYDAY and UR MOM and have pictures of bombs and gang tags I try not to think about. Every other message feels like something left behind by the dead, too morose to be something left by the living here.

Sometimes it doesn't feel like it was even ever human.

While everybody's got something to say, some of the warnings read like charity instead of a threat, but it's hard to imagine anyone sharing charity on the walls after they've suffered the worst Baltimore has to offer. I close my eyes until I feel the bump in the road I've gotten used to telling me we've reached the west side. Jag says, "Where'd you say the car would be?"

"Dead Run."

"Is it just me or is this side of the park cursed?"

I snort. "The whole park's cursed, J."

"Yeah, but like, that spot specifically feels extra."

"It's not called *Dead Run* for no reason. Kinda where Mortem jailbreaks happen if you think about it." My skin puckers and stings with the memory of jumping into Styx too many times. My pocket's itching for a buzz. I squeeze my hands between my thighs, telling myself I'm not allowed. Jag will notice if I get out my phone and maybe he'll ask who I'm waiting for. I won't want to say Wayland so that'll turn into another lie, and I can't keep doing that to him. "You think the people who named it know about that?"

"Maybe," Jag says. "All things considered, doesn't sound that wild." He pulls into the East entrance at Leakin. The windows are cracked a little and a little cold air blows in. A soft caw reverberates from the other side. I'm sure it was a caw. Maybe a cackle. It was one of those damn birds. A breeze catches in the trees where there wasn't one before. The sun's not fully down yet, but it's dark enough that the streetlamps that are working are on, buzzing and flickering and giving just enough light to give some visibility, but busted enough to flicker and make you think you're seeing something move when the darkness gives it a chance.

Another criminal, another neighbor, another friend, another bag of trash. It's incredible how many lives can be thrown into the woods and forgotten about.

I shouldn't judge.

I was part of that a couple days ago.

I didn't feel bad.

I still don't feel bad.

Because none of it seems real yet.

Even being in Leakin again doesn't feel real. As much as I know about this park and the city it's housed in, this doesn't feel like the same place I've been pulled to over the last couple of weeks. The trees are familiar, but it's more like I know them in a way that you know when you're in a dream. A vague kinship or memories that leave feelings inside of you that you know not to trust, but somehow, they still feel like they've got substance. The trees have a purple tinge to them; the sky carries that color too while half of the stars darken to glowing, black spots.

Another caw, a couple of clicks like wood and false laughter.

"You hear that, J?"

"The ravens."

"Nothing's going to happen to us, Joey." Jag turns the radio down. The silence says he's holding his breath. He drives slower so the car doesn't bounce to minimize its sound. "I'm not feeling like dying today. Are you?"

"You don't always have a choice in that shit."

"Right." Jag goes back to normal speed. "You never did tell me how you died."

"Some giant asshole stalked me from Mortem to the badge station and strangled me when I jumped out the window."

There's a pause. The breaks squeak as Jag comes to a stop. He leans on the steering wheel as he turns to me. "You jumped out the window at the station?"

"I didn't mean to say that—"

"Yeah, but you did. What the hell were you in custody for?"

"Don't worry about it, J. It's over."

"Nuh-uh." He shakes his head. "Not good enough. No more secrets, Joey." His stare burns into my side, even when I'm not looking at him. My foot's bouncing more rapidly and his starts to bounce at a slower pace while his thumb beats the steering wheel. It's not like him. "Joey…"

"It's because of the email I sent from Way's laptop, okay? Rocky showed up at my house with a warrant. That's it."

"I told you that would happen." Jag takes his foot off the break and continues forward. "You should listen to me sometimes. It might keep you out of trouble."

"I know. Shut up." I groan. I turn back to the window, watching the trees. Maybe not so much that as looking at the trail, looking for movement between the anemic branches. They aren't bare, but they're getting there with the threat of winter looming.

It was only a couple days ago that I crossed the bridge over Dead Run looking for Wayland in the forest. Like many others that visit the park at this time, he was hiding secrets in the mud, hiding himself by a log no one could see while just going for a walk. I wonder how many of the garbage bags we dropped are still here, hidden in the brush, innocuous with the trash and clothing dumps and bully bags. The deeper, off-trail parts of the woods have always been a decent cover for anything Baltimorons worried about getting rid of. People are too lazy to look though sometimes, it feels like if you wander too deep into Leakin, you go somewhere else and maybe you won't come back. So it's better to leave the dead where they lie.

I'm not excluded from that. I know better. I've passed so many bags and never asked questions about the smell. I didn't want to get involved. Now, there's so much more to lose.

Up ahead, a silver Honda Corolla sits off the side of the road. "That should be it," I say.

"And they didn't want to stick around?"

"Nope."

Jag groans a string of "ughs" under his breath. I get it. I hate when drivers aren't around to figure out what they want either, but they've got our number and we've got theirs. They knew they weren't recovering their car tonight. If we want to get out of here quicker, it's probably better like this anyway because you never know if a random customer call is gonna turn into a socially deprived person who goes on for three hours about the last five years of his life he hasn't been able to share with anyone. If we don't get back by nine, Donny might kill us anyway. So, whatever. Reasonable. The guy's just gonna be frustrated tomorrow when he doesn't get what he'd been expecting even though he didn't tell us anything.

"He said the engine was making noise and smoking. Overheat signal was coming on, there was a smell, and something under the hood popped, then it shit the bed," I say.

"He describe the smell?"

"No. Just that it might stick around the car."

Jag curses again. He pulls the truck in front of the Honda and backs it up for mounting. I take off my seatbelt before he's cut the engine.

"You don't need to get out," Jag says.

"Why would I stay here?"

"We said we'd be quick."

"I am quick."

Jag shrugs.

"I'm not afraid of this park if that's what you're thinking."

"Not what I was thinking."

"Then why wouldn't I get out?"

Jag shrugs again. His door's open before mine. The sun's a little lower now. Give it twenty minutes and it'll be gone. My feet touch the pavement, goosebumps form along my skin. The stink of the park's coming out, thick and stagnant. Mud, iron, sulfur, rot.

My skin's on fire with a feeling of familiarity. The waters of Dead Run bounce off the trees from just a little way down. Thudding in my ears is accompanied by soft purrs that sound like imitations of something less dangerous and they're coming from three different directions. A bit of flickering light catches on something shiny on a branch. A black body. A raven with an eye, glowing like a ruby when it catches light. The branch moves, whispers pass between trees. Sticks crack in the bushes just a little further down. The rotten smell's getting worse. Something splashes in Dead Run. Big. Not a fish.

How many ravens are there?

I step off the road into the brush, careful where I'm putting my feet. I don't want to sink into the ground again. I don't even know what turned that one spot into a puddle of Styx before, which means it can happen anywhere. I scan the darkness. A silhouette of shadows moves with another gust. I squint and lean forward. I'm sure that's a person moving between the trees. It has to be.

"Joey?" Jag calls.

My hands curl into fists. "We need to hurry." I go back to the road.

"Planned on it." He's already at the car.

"I think there's someone out there."

"They say where the keys would be?"

"Glove compartment." I reach the passenger side door. It's unlocked. The inside of the car's dark, catching none of the light from the streetlamp a little ways down the road. Nothing's visible in the back seat. The car smells of stale fast food. Old burger wrappers litter the floor. An empty cup from Burger King sits in the foot space under the seat and another foam cup from a gas station's in the cup holder. Sand or dirt or something is spilled on the light-colored fabric. Stains go up the cushion and the glass on the sedan's windshield is bubbled. "Someone's really taking care of their ride."

"Thing looks like it's at the end of its life."

"Then it came to the right place to die." I chuckle.

There's a resistance in my body to not sit down inside the car. I force myself through it. The seat's not just stained, but wet. The feeling of water going through my jeans runs a chill through me. The glove compartment's open. There's no registration paperwork or insurance inside, but the key falls to the floor between my feet. I hold them out the door for Jag to see. He gives me a nod. Leaning back, the seat's hard, lumpy, doesn't feel right. The inside of the car smells rancid.

I snap the glove compartment shut. The key's go into the ignition. I climb over the center console to get to the driver's seat. I don't know if it's because my jeans are already wet or what, but this seat feels wetter than the other one. My foot's on the break. I move the car into neutral. The windows are manual. The locks are also manual. Key in my pocket, I get out of the car. I shut the door a little harder than I mean to. Jag snaps around going, "Something happen?"

I shake my head. "We're good to go."

"Okay." Jag's already pulling the straps off the back of the tow. He wraps the first tan cord around the front of the tire on the driver's side.

"Jay?" I say.

"Yeah?"

"Does my ass look wet to you?" I turn around so my back's to him. There's not much light, so I don't know if he'll see anything. I'm looking over my shoulder at him but surveying the trees behind him.

He glances up from the wheel well of the passenger tire. He's sporting a grin. His tongue wipes across his lip. "You know, if you want me to look at your ass, you just gotta ask."

"What about the birds? Have you heard any of them yet?"

Jag secures the band around the second tire and straightens again. "Yeah. I've heard the birds and I still don't feel like dying." He speaks so casually like all the things I've warned him about aren't going to come true. He laughs like I'm not dead. He laughs like shit's not as dark as the park makes it. My heart flutters lighter because of his influence.

I wish I could see things more like him.

"I'm not saying *you're* the one that's dying, but there might be someone out here who's going to." I turn back around to face Jag.

"You might be thinking too hard about this," Jag says.

"You might not be thinking hard enough about it. I was here last time. I know what the park felt like around Way's car and this… I don't like it."

"You can wait in the truck."

"I'm not waiting in the truck, J." Scanning the trees, I watch every branch, every soft crunch, every bit of movement the shadows let me see against the purple sky of dusk. "I think there might be someone out there."

Another raven's scream goes through the trees. A soft bell whispers or those are the chains or ringing I keep hearing when Charon shows up. I shake my head and they all disappear. My heart's pulsing in my fingers, and my hands are shaking now. I should look in the trunk, but I don't want to. Jag's gonna think I'm crazy if I say anything. *It's just me overthinking this*, he'll say and then next time there's an evening pickup, he won't let me come.

Jag's at the tow, using the lift to elevate the front of the car. When he sees me going back to the car, he says, "What are you doing?"

"Just looking the car over. Gimme a second." I pull my keyring from my pocket and open the driver's side door to reach the backseat lock.

All of it's manual.

I open the backseat. The light on my keyring's weak, but the illumination's enough to see if there's anything there. There's a little discoloration on the cushions. Wrappers, old cups, a shirt, and some newspaper on the floor, but nothing really stands out. I close the door.

"The park really is different after dark, huh?" Jag's voice startles and he laughs.

I don't know if he's laughing at me or the circumstances, but I laugh back. "Yeah… And cold as hell." I shove my hands into my pocket to grab the sedan key again. The tag on it clicks with my hand shaking as I make my way to the back side of the car. "Fuck, J." I laugh again. "We need to stop accepting jobs like this."

"I'll talk to D about it."

"If it helps, you can even tell him it scares the shit out of me."

"That bad, huh?"

"Little bit." I chuckle. It goes fast, tight with anxiety. The key goes into place in the trunk. Sticks crackle behind me and something grabs the back of my shirt, yanking me back. "Gotcha, bitch!" someone growls as Jag runs from the tow yelling, "Joey!" Whoever's there flips me around. A hand goes around my throat while he mashes me over the trunk lid. The guy's got a jean shirt, sleeves rolled down, a chain bracelet and thick, square rings on his fingers. He presses me harder into the car by the hold on my throat. My feet are off the ground, my back's screaming. Jag growls in pain.

"Always the throat, huh?" I choke out. I reach for the guy, but his arms are longer than mine and I can't do anything but grab and tear at his arms with my nails. My fingers do nothing against his thick jacket. I gasp for air. I'm kicking, looking for his stomach. They find nothing or when they hit him, he feels like a tree, and he doesn't let go. His fingers are cold. Black and blue veins throb against his skin, curling around his black, inhuman eyes. What the hell happened to him? He's not just a dead guy. The pools of malice in his face. He's so much worse than my dad, but what the hell happened?

Jag's fist slams into the guy's face. The guy staggers

back, forced to let me go. I fall off the trunk and hit the ground. Jag's panting with me with a desperation for air that's almost as bad as mine.

"You alright, Joey?" he says without turning from the attacker.

"Yeah." I suck in a hard, choppy, shallow breath. "Thanks." I use the car to get back to my feet.

The guy throws a returning blow, fist aimed at Jag's head. He misses as Jag ducks to the side with more agility than I've ever seen him use, but a second fist lands a cross against Jag's stomach. Jag and I gasp at the same time. I dig my phone out of my pocket and tap at the screen for the dialer. Enter Charon's number, I hit call.

Jag's got his arms up in a defensive posture as the dead guy charges him, fist in air. One punch, then another, then another. He jabs in quick succession. A blow hits Jag in the chest and I gasp as pressure rocks my ribs. Jag grabs the dead guy's arm and slams his fist into the guy's face. He groans and staggers back as Jag releases him. He repositions himself to go at Jag again.

Ghost recovery in a fight's too good, like shit doesn't affect them and the only way to stop the fight is for the dead to want it to stop. The dead guy's hand goes behind his back, digging something out of his waist. Light catches on metal.

"Jag—Knife!" I say.

"I see it—"

I run at the dead guy, shoulder ramming into him with all the strength I can get. He's got a lot of weight on me and the push barely makes him stumble. His grip tightens around the knife's handle. He draws it back and swings at me. The sharp edge catches on my shirt. I feel the blade touch my skin, but there's no burn of a fresh cut.

Jag comes from behind me, slamming into the dead

guy. Both of them hit the ground. The weapon flies out of his hand and I run to pick it up; the knife's weighty. My fingers tingle against its cold hilt. I suck in a breath through my teeth, taking a couple of steps back.

Jag's pinning the dead guy down with his weight while the guy's on his belly, his arms pulled behind his back. He rolls, struggles, grunts, doing anything he can to reach for an escape. The dead guy presses his knee into the pavement, lifting his hips for a moment just to be pushed back down again as Jag struggles to stay on top. Unlike when he dealt with Wayland, Jag has to fight to keep control. The guy's relentless, thrusting, fighting, screaming, "Cocksucker!" again and again as saliva dribbles down from his mouth.

My hand's trembling. Nausea curls my stomach, but the adrenaline's making me restless to the point of pacing. I should shove the knife through that bastard's skull and put him out of his misery until Charon arrives.

The dead guy thrusts up again, almost bucking Jag off. Jag slams him back into the ground. He pulls his hand away from pinning the guy's arm for just a second. The hand flails, racing to the ground for more leverage. Jag grabs it again and pulls it harder behind the guy's back.

"I'm gonna fuckin' kill you, bastard bitch-ass fuck!" the dead guy screams.

I cross the pavement, holding the knife at ready. I squat beside the flailing. I can't stop looking at him. I feel all the pressure and anger and hatred coming back to my face. This is the kind of bastard that took Wayland away from me and he wants to do the same thing to Jag. This is the kind of bastard that doesn't deserve to live and if he jumped into the river, he should be miserable every second he's walking this goddamn planet a second time. I draw the blade back.

"Joey!" Jag snaps. "Calm down! I got him—You need to call the badges."

"I've already called for help, J. All we gotta do now is waste time until it gets here, and I got a couple of ideas," I say.

"Snap out of it, Joey!"

The trees around us rustle with a gust that wasn't there before. Chains rattle within the leaves. A long, low whistle hides among them. A couple of ravens fly overhead and land beside us, on the sedan, on the tow truck. More and more, they gather around us on the street and in the trees like they're paving an entry for something bigger. The dark sky turns more purple. The visible stars, once white, quickly flicker into black spots as black and purple mist infiltrates the park. The rattling sound of chains gets louder. The dead guy on the ground is screaming now, turning from anger to fear and begging as he thrashes for a new reason. It doesn't work. Jag gets into the rhythm and looks more like he's riding the guy, even as his muscles tense and he grunts and he flies back just a little with a surprising push, he's still not losing his grip.

Down the street, Charon materializes through the mist. His glowing blue eyes appear first, then, his all-white peacoat and suit crystallize as he steps forward. Behind him is a shadow of a figure, taller than him by at least a foot. The shadow in black clothing comes without detail until the two of them are just a couple feet from Jag and me. Black pants, black jacket, black hair and nails. Val appears as a sulking figure following death with raised shoulders, a hanging head, and the grin of a troublemaker.

"Leggo of me!" the dead man growls.

Val's smile fades into pursed lips. He looks at Jag with disinterest, then away toward the bushes like he can't focus or see the fight in front of him. Bits of red discolor his fingers as he brings them to his mouth and licks them slowly.

He must've been eating before he got here.

Charon produces the crystal on a chain from his jacket. He steps up to the body without looking at me. His presence makes me step back as the rattling gets louder. The approach startles Jag, but more than that, he appears repelled. His grip loosens on the dead man enough that it gives him room to push. Jag's knocked back. The dead guy's on his feet and running, yelling obscenities as he makes for his escape.

It's too late. The chains, lit by a soft glow not too different from whatever magic Charon carries, shoot toward the fleeing soul. As the chains wrap around the dead guy, his screaming turns from fear and panic to pain. The guy on the ground can't do anything against the chains that've hooked into his skin now and squeeze harder and harder forcing bits of him loose. My skin's on fire. I hold onto the sedan to keep from hitting the ground, but I can't breathe. I'm rocking and bouncing and Jag must've noticed because he comes over and tries to put his arms around me but I tell him no. I can't. I don't know what's wrong with me. I keep backing away. Maybe it's the closeness to *him*. It's not the first time I've seen Charon collect, and I'm not even a ghost anymore, technically. Heat's building in my eyes as this asshole's scream starts to sound like my dad's and then I'm remembering what the chains felt like when they were on me and Wayland and I had to escape by any means necessary.

I run into something backing up. I gasp. The smell of blood's strong. Blood and dirt and breath. Val's standing behind me. He cranes his head to the side, a finger still pressed against his lips as he licks it to the end of his long, black nail. "What's wrong with you?" He laughs. "You look like you're gonna be sick."

"Something like that," is all I manage with a pant.

I'm dizzy, my head's throbbing, the forest is spinning, and I think I'm going to pass out. Against every instinct my body's screaming at me, I sit on the ground. Just breathe. I need to just not think of anything.

The dead guy screams as his soul's torn apart. There's noise and violent pressure in the air, building in a way that makes me feel like it'll never stop. I shove my palms into my ears, hoping to dampen the sounds and the panic that come with them. Then suddenly, it's over and the feeling of absolute horror is gone. My body relaxes totally and the emotions of a moment ago are a forgotten feeling I just know I had.

The screaming echoes in the empty park only a couple seconds past his disappearance, like thunder after a strike of lightning. Then, there's nothing left of whoever that guy used to be.

I'm still panting, my heart's still racing, and everything around me's still spinning. I lean back to rock but hit something again. Val's standing over me. "Did you follow me?" I snap.

Val laughs. "No. Why would I do that?"

"Liar." My jaw tightens. I don't understand what all that feeling was. I've turned a couple of ghosts in before and have never felt like that. None of them were running. I didn't stick around to watch Charon collect the one at the apartment, though I felt some kind of something while I got in the elevator. I couldn't stick around. My dad's collection didn't make me feel like this though. Why? Everything I just went through, it had to be from the dead guy, right?

"You okay?" Jag squats down beside me. I don't know when he got there.

I rub my face to wipe away anything that feels wet or might've been running eyeliner. I look away from him like it'll hide what I'm doing, but I nod. "Yeah."

"What the hell was that?" he says.

"Collections," Charon says.

"What?" Jag stands up again. "Who the hell are you again?"

"He's here for work," I say. "Uh, Jag—meet Death." I wipe my face again. My skin's moist with sweat. I'm still panting. Jag's not. Once I'm pretty sure I'm okay, I get back up. "Charon, this is Jag."

"My name is not Death," Charon says.

"I said Charon," I say. "I was just giving him extra context."

"Joey?" Jag says.

"Sorry, J." My ability to think's coming back, but now I have to figure out how to explain everything I've figured out in the last few weeks in the fewest number of words without looking crazy. I mean, what Jag just saw is crazy enough, but did it mean anything without an explanation? "You know the grim reaper?"

"Yeah…"

"That's him." I point to Charon. "The guy in black's like his pet raven or something. He helps find bodies by their heart. I can't explain how it all works 'cause I don't even know, just… Charon collects the souls of the dead, but if they're ghosts, the bird can't find them. There's nothing the badges could have done about this."

"Pet?" Val's nose scrunches. His laugh is partially a growl. "I'm better than that."

Jag looks from Charon to Val to me. His eyes are narrow. He's skeptical when he knows he can't be. He rubs the bridge of his nose before crossing his arms. "How did they get here?"

"You remember when you saw the guy in white haul

my dad off at my house?" I say. "Same person, same thing. You just thought I was insane."

"The *grim reaper* has a *cell phone*?" Jag says.

"I don't... really know how it works." I turn to Charon, hoping he'll come up with some kind of explanation that I can't give. Instead, he doesn't say anything, choosing to stare at me flatly. It's not like he's overlooking me, but seeing through me. It's not as invasive as what it felt like to have Ralph's glowing eyes look at me. Does that mean he can't see as deep as Ralph or he just doesn't care or did I care more because Ralph's a person and Charon's not. I shake the thought from my head. "All I know is that I was told to put this number down somewhere if I ran into a dead guy. Anywhere, doesn't matter. Wayland used blood once."

"Cross... was writing numbers in blood?" Jag sighs.

"It's not what you think, okay?" I say. "The guy burned his house down and was already dead. It didn't matter."

"Joey..."

Val moves past me. Long strides take him back to being Charon's shadow. His arms slide around Charon's shoulders and he leans against him, acting like a bird sitting on Death's shoulder, though instead, he's a tall man hanging off a smaller one. His dark, empty eyes still focus on me in a way they didn't seem able to before. Charon doesn't respond to the way Val leans against him.

"I don't know how I'm supposed to take any of this." Jag sighs.

"I don't either, okay?" I say. "I'm just... I'm trying to figure it out and that's all I can do. Unfortunately, in a moment of desperation, I made a deal to work with this guy and so that's where I am. Acting like a narc for Hell."

"I don't work for Hell," Charon says.

"Whatever," I say. "Mortem's close enough."

"If he collects the dead, then why's he helping you?" Jag turns from me to them. His muscles are stiff, suspicion overtakes his posture. Though he doesn't lift a hand like he's ready to fight so much as he's waiting for them to make a move. He takes a step-in front of me, acting like a wall.

"We have a deal," I say.

"Oh, great. *A deal with the devil?*" Jag turns back to me. "Again?" He growls.

"Circumstances have somewhat changed," Charon says. "You've performed a ritual with a medium. Now that Jagger Ashley Locke is carrying your heart, you are not a rogue spirit, but breaking the contract you've made with me will result in punishment beyond my control."

"What do you mean?" I say.

"Violation of our agreement will strike your *soul* and your *body*." Charon's eyes flicker behind me.

I glance toward Jag. The park lights illuminate his outline. His expression's vague. My necklace isn't visible against his chest. "J—Where's the necklace?"

Jag touches his chest. He looks down. His hand slides up his shoulder to the base of his neck. His thumb dips under the collar of his shirt and pulls at the small, dark chain. The heart-shaped stone comes out from underneath his clothing.

"You couldn't feel that was near?" Charon says.

"Gimme a break. I'm new to this stuff, okay?" I'm tapping my foot again to expel the excess anxiety I'm feeling, hoping he doesn't notice, but now Jag's thumb's tapping against his thigh, so he knows.

"If your heart is severed from the body, you will know," Charon says. "The calls from the Darkness will return to you again and so will your desire for destruction. Your ritual was not a perfect return. It is reliant on duty, responsibility, and partnership. Something that you would do well to learn."

"What are you talking about?" I say.

"Mistakes you've made while alive continue to grow the longer you ignore them. You must see your choices through and follow-up on your promises," Charon says.

"Are you mad at me for not catching more ghosts?" I say. "I've had other things I've been dealing with, but I've also sent you a lot of them. You didn't tell me there was a quota—"

"I'm not asking for a quota," Charon says. "I'm telling you that *ignoring* your mistakes as an attempt to *consider them dealt* with will only results in tragedy. If you want to find peace, then you must deal with your past before it returns to settle your growing debt." Charon's attention shifts from me to Jag. Val's dark eyes follow and it makes me feel like he's getting ready to eat. There's a little bit of red still on the bird's jaw. His tongue laps his lower lip. His knuckles wipe at a spot on his chin, which he then licks and spreads the blood from his tongue onto the back of his hand.

"What do you know that I don't?" I say.

"Very little that I am permitted to tell you," Charon says.

"You don't smell like you're dying anymore," Val says with eyes locked on Jag. A little bit of light catches on his abyss-like eyes. A sheen of red illuminates, then disappears back to black as his head cocks. He leans up, pulling himself away from Charon. He's wearing a contented grin as his head tips to the side. "Your hearts actually smell alike now."

"What do you mean?" I say.

"Did you learn nothing about the contract you signed?"

"I didn't sign a contract—I just brought Ralph some

stuff he asked for," I say.

"Ah." Charon mutters. "So, you have done as little to understand your current condition as you have to understand your duty to me."

"Shut up," I say. "I'm doing fine with both."

The glow of Charon's eyes gets brighter. The almost white glow reflects a soft blue on his cheeks in the night shade. "It is not a requirement of mine to provide warnings to the living, but understand this, Josephine: Your heart is no longer your own. While the darkness could corrupt you *alone* before, if you allow it in, it will poison the body that keeps your humanity. What you do will now affect Jagger Locke more deeply than you know. Do you understand that?"

"My pain is his pain," I say.

"Your enemies are his enemies," Charon says. "Your anger is his anger. Your corruption is his corruption. Your death is his death. Tracking the listless is not a simple, passive, or easy task. Your body is now separate from you. Be prepared for your past mistakes to understand your weaknesses. They will seek you out, ravenously, for there is something much bigger here that feeds on disaster."

My skin puckers as a chill goes through me. I can't help but look at Jag who's just as focused on Charon as I am. His fists are tight and he's fishing out his box of cigarettes from his pocket. His tongue flicks with dismissal. "Appreciate the warning, but we're gonna be fine, guy. Don't worry about it."

"Moronic," Charon says.

"Thanks," Jag says through the cigarette pinched in his lips.

"You would do that before knowing anything about what you have chosen?" Charon says.

"I made my choice long before Joey gave me a

necklace," Jag says.

Charon stares for a long, quiet moment. "There's a hunger in this city that you do not understand. Regret. Resentment. Revenge. Rage. Rapture. The *Grief Eater* has more influence than you can imagine. You need not see him to see his power. Your name is moving in the air for business you did not complete." Charon's eyes flicker to me. "The longer you allow it to fester, the worse it will become. As it builds, so too does the damage to bystanders in the quest for perceived equity."

"You mean someone's hunting me?" I say.

"It is not a coincidence that there was a dead man waiting for you in this park," Charon says.

"I knew the dead talked," I say.

"They do, and they trade anger. As you've experienced, the destruction of another becomes your own. Guard your heart before you are the next creature Val feeds upon." Charon comes toward me. Val follows behind, hands shoved in his pockets now. His movements are a slacker's slow swagger while Charon steps with deliberate authority that makes my legs quiver. I need to step back or run or something. The feeling of the end is coming back, just like when that guy was taken away. Jag stiffens, moving further in front of me to block Charon from coming too close. Charon continues forward without a pause to even give Jag acknowledgment. He's not coming toward me though, but moving past me. Val trails behind. His dark eyes lock with mine. He grins. A bit of blood still clings to his teeth, and he looks like a kid who forgot to brush. A couple long strides, and Val's form is gone, turning into a bird that flies the length of space between him and Charon in order to land on Charon's shoulder.

"Wait—" I turn around to face Charon. The mist in the park's already consumed parts of Charon's body. He stands half eaten by darkness; his face disturbed to the point his human mask is gone. One eye glows while the other is a blur behind purple and black and the forest. The streetlights have caught on Val, making his black eyes glow red with almost as much luminescence as Charon's. He's so inhuman, he's more like a feeling of dread and fear and finality within a shape I can see. "If the heart is supposed to be my second chance and mean that I'm alive again, why do I still feel like you're coming for me?"

"Even with a second chance, the dead cannot escape the fear of finality," Charon says. "All creatures of the universe live within the structure, even when you believe you have cheated it. Resistance to influence is not immediate or permanent. The experiences you have at your core will be transferred to your partner. You would be wise to remember that upon forfeiting your control to another."

Charon turns away and continues forward. The darkness devours him quickly. What remains is the street, the night, and Leakin Park. Still, in the quiet is the whisper of ravens sharing secrets among the rustling leaves. Something that sounds like a person's voice says, "Dead bitch!" I don't know if it's another guy waiting his turn or a bird.

I grab the car key from the ground and run to Jag. Passing him, I hook my arm around him to pull him toward the tow. I'm not stronger than him, but he lets me lead him.

"This is hella weird, Joey," Jag says.

"I know." I turn to face him while I keep walking backwards, still pulling, maybe with more urgency now. My eyes water. His face is threatened with obscurity. I blink a couple of times and smile, but every time I close my eyes, I'm thinking he's not gonna be there when I open them. He is though. "I'm sorry."

"Stop sayings sorry for shit you didn't do." He plants his feet. We're at the driver's side of the tow. He touches the back of his neck, then the back of his head, then his face. His eyes drop. He hits the cigarette. Blows out. Rubs his eyes again. "I'm just gonna need a minute to process this. It's kind of a lot, you know?"

"Yeah… I know… It is."

His chuckle comes out with a sigh. His eyes meet mine. I nod to him, then I'm going around the truck to the passenger's side because I want to get the hell out of here and everything in Jag's face is saying the same thing. We don't need to find out if that voice is another guy waiting his turn or a delusion born out of my new paranoia.

I barely get my door closed before Jag's pulling forward. His cigarettes are in the center console cup holders. I grab them and light one up.

It's quiet until we get out of the park. Then, another laugh and Jag says, "There's a Grim Reaper…"

"Yeah, there is." I chuckle back.

I sink into my seat, trying to focus on the cigarette and what Charon said. The radio's on low and Jag's muttering along with every song because he knows the channel so well and it makes it, so he doesn't have to think. My fingers tap on the door as I watch the neighborhood pass by. A door says GET OUT WHILE UR ALIVE in white.

Does that mean the house? The neighborhood? Baltimore?

I know I wasn't the most pleasant person while alive. I've pissed off a lot of people in twenty-three years, but to get someone so bad, they'd chase me in death? With my dad gone, the only person I can think of is the Big Guy from the bar. I don't even understand his obsession though. I didn't do anything to him, but see he exists and watch him make a run for it. That's all, but that was enough for him to lock in on me as the person who destroyed his life? Is he really going to keep coming at me in every way until I either die or he destroys everything around me? What about the guy at the bar that burnt Wayland's place down? Was that one of his guys too? Is Charon right that everyone around me is doomed to be a casualty of this guy's anger because I… What? Looked at him just once and didn't stop him from getting away?

What the hell is it about me that makes me worth destroying so much? Or is it really so simple that the pain blinds the dead so much that he thinks his freedom and happiness will really come when he's finally gotten rid of me? What happens if I go and he still hasn't found the peace he's looking for? Would he go after Jag thinking he's the next block holding him back?

I lean forward. My seatbelt keeps me from going as far as I'd like. I pinch my cigarette between my lips to run my fingers through my hair. "Jag, I'm s—"

"You better not be apologizing again."

"Don't worry, I'm not. Jeez."

"So, what were you gonna say?"

"Just that I'm glad you're here and I'm glad I came, okay?"

"Yeah…" His lips purse into a tight smile. "Me too." He looks down at the console, maybe to see if my hand's there. That feels too narcissistic to think. As good as the sex might be sometimes and as much as I can say I'd go to Hell for him, I don't understand why he'd put up with so much for me. My mom was the first to see there was nothing worth sticking around for when she looked at me, and my dad didn't take long to follow suit. Jag's better than both of them which means he's too good for me. I've heard people say it at the shop, at Jag's house, when we're at the grocery store. I know I've heard random people who don't even know me say it because they can look at us and just tell.

It's hard to miss how much of a mess I am.

I put out my cigarette. Sigh. My empty hand rests on the center console. Seconds pass, but then his warm hand's on top of mine. "Whatever's gonna happen, we're gonna deal with it together, alright?" He glances sidelong at me. "We'll stop by the bar after we drop the car off and we can ask your guy some questions about all this stuff. He should have answers, yeah?"

"Yeah." I sigh. I can't think of what else there might be at BAIT's. This necklace was the help he had, but at least Jag's better than me at coming up with questions. He's always been good at stuff like that… He's got a lot more patience than me.

I squeeze Jag's hand. He squeezes mine back.

"Thanks, J," I say.

"Any time."

I let my eyes close and stop paying attention. The sounds of Jag's favorite oldies fill the car. The same Nirvana song that plays a million times a day followed by the Bee Gees followed by Madonna and someone else and he knows all the words. It's so stupid, but the familiar routine of it makes me feel better until the fight inside of me dies out.

SEVEN.

Back at the shop, Donny must've seen us pulling into the parking lot, because he's already opening the garage door to let us bring the car in. Jag cuts the engine and climbs out of the cab to Donny saying, "Any trouble?"

"Nah," Jag says, already at the lift on the back of the truck, lowering the car down.

The shop lights are harsher than anything at the park. Maybe I was just in the dark for too long, because they feel like a lot. Jag's got a bruise forming on the left side of his face. I dip into the bathroom off to the side of the garage, flick the light on without closing the door. A brief glance in the mirror and I've got discoloration on my face too. A cut on my right cheek. A little bit of blue around my neck. "Shit," I say.

"You're looking a little rough," Donny says.

I come out of the bathroom.

"Kinda just wanna go home, D," Jag says.

"You give the car a look over?" Donny says.

"It was too dark at the park for much of anything," I say. "And the driver bounced, so we booked it."

"Suppose I can't blame you," Donny says. "The shit that happens in the dark…"

"Yup." Jag's taking the second strap off the sedan's tires. When he's done, he climbs back into the cab. The tow's parked in the side lot again. I close the shop door. I don't like the smell that's immediately apparent. My skin prickles at the familiarity. My nose is burning and the taste of bile builds in the back of my throat.

We brought Leakin Park back with us.

We should've checked the trunk.

Jag comes into the garage from the lobby. "What's up, Joey?" he says.

"You smell that?" For once, I'm hoping he says no and thinks I'm crazy and paranoid and need to take a break for real this time. I'm taking the keys out of my pocket. The overhead lights of the shop flood the inside of the car, showing nothing I didn't already see at the park. A wadded-up shirt from Burger King sits on the floor in the back. It's stained in a way I didn't notice at Leakin. Not grease. The pair of black slacks beside it are a little discolored with a random splash of mud, though it doesn't look entirely like mud.

I go around the car to the trunk. My heart's throbbing so hard, I only catch Jag when he's standing next to me and he says, "You hear what I just said?"

"Sorry, what?"

"I smell something, but it's not garbage." He's grimacing.

"No, it's not." I slide the key into the hook. Close my eyes. I know what's going to be inside before opening it, but I really don't want to be right. I don't believe in any kind of god, but I've still thrown wishes into the universe

110

like it'll make some kind of difference more times than I care to admit. With my fingers hooked at the bottom edge of the trunk, I do it again, begging, *please, let me be wrong.*

I pull the trunk open. Sickness runs through me not unlike the first time with Wayland's car or his corpse at the park. I pull away with vomit burning the inside of my nose and chunks making it into my mouth before I'm at the sink. I'm heaving over the drain when I hear Jag saying, "Shit."

A hand touches my back and I startle, straighten up with a fist. I'm pulling away, turning, red faced and swinging before I realize it's just Jag. Another heave bends me over the sink. Once I can breathe again, I say, "Sorry. I don't know when I got so sensitive," and he says, "It's okay." I suck in a breath, holding onto the side of the sink to keep myself balanced. My legs are shaking. There's still a bit of wetness dribbling down my lip. I turn the sink water on to give the room some white noise and wash down my mess. I lean in for a drink. Still lukewarm; pipes still unfixed.

I grab the rag hanging over the edge of the sink to wipe my face with. I turn to Jag; he's watching me. "We don't really have to call the badges, do we?" I say.

"Yeah… We kinda do."

"Fuck."

Donny comes out of his office, lights off now and keys in his hand. "Ready to close up?" He looks between the two of us, the sink, then Jag, then me again. The slight smile he had on his face fades into a scowl. His nose crinkles at the bridge with recognition he doesn't want. "Please tell me your pregnant, Joey." The way he says it, he already knows what I'm going to say. He's just hoping I'm punking him, that things aren't as bad as they really are, but that's just how things go in Bodymore.

Never admit what you're looking at. Never see the carnage. Step over the bodies and bullet casings in the street. Ignore the guy getting mugged between the houses. If you're lucky enough to live in a good part of town, you can close your eyes when you drive through. Pretend every gang tag is the signature of an artist you'd like to hire when you hit the next income bracket rather than it being a threat to everything you have, including your life.

Slowly, I shake my head. "Check the trunk."

Donny turns around. There's hesitation in his step before he's approaching the car. He's not even halfway there when he mutters, "Not again," and goes to the office instead.

I meet Jag's stare. The body's not as bad now as it was when Wayland mangled that banger. This one was stabbed a couple of times and the mess is pooling in the carpet beneath him. That's probably the worst of it. And he's fresh. Like, still bleeding, fresh. Jag picks up a cloth rag and closes the trunk with it over his hand. I lean against the sink a little while longer. Drink a little more. Shut the water off. I wipe my mouth with the back of my sleeve.

The office light's on again and Donny's voice comes out the door. "I told you last time," he sighs. "We're not *that* kind of *body shop*. Yeah, yeah. I know, but we're not doing any kind of under the table work, alright? Just a clean place with some bad luck. Fine. Come back with a warrant and you can even do a cavity search for all I care. Short of that, you're not getting more than I gotta give. Yeah, yeah. Whatever. At this rate, we're not gonna run anymore pickups at Leakin." He laughs. "You're welcome to the body if you want it. Again, ring the bell when you get here. No one's leaving. You can ask your questions then." He hangs up.

Coming out of the office, Donny leaves the light on. A heavy sigh drops as he looks between us. "You know, Joey… For the week and a half you were gone, not a single body was brought in here."

"It's not like I'm trying," I say.

"You got a knack kid." Donny sighs.

"I don't wanna talk to the badges…" My voice is whinier than I want it to be.

"Shoulda thought about that before bringing in another corpse." Donny wipes the frustration from his eyes.

"Then stop sending us to that stupid park when the sun goes down!" I shove my hands into my pockets.

"That's the plan going forward, okay?" Donny crosses his arms, his button-up shirt pulls tight over his chest. "The last time this happened, it wasn't great for business. Regardless of what they say on TV, people ain't racing to drop their cars off at a gore factory. All ya get's the weirdos hoping to see something nasty they can post online, blocking the parking lot. Ask for a review? Good luck with that. They give you the finger and tell ya to fuck off while trying to sneak in. We're not doing this shit again."

Jag glances between Donny, me, and the car. He paces toward the sedan, stops halfway, stares at it, and comes back while running a hand through his hair. Rubbing the back of his neck. His jaw's tight, working slowly to hold back whatever's going on in his head. "Donny," Jag says. "We got attacked at the park."

"What?" Donny says.

"Some rando came out of the woods and jumped Joey."

"Jag!" I say.

"What kind of trouble are you in, Joey?" Donny says.

"I'm not *in* anything," I say.

"I don't wanna say I don't believe ya, but c'mon kid!" Donny's saying.

"She had a run-in with some thug at a bar a couple weeks back." Jag glances at me. I'm shaking my head, mouthing for him to shut up. He knows better than to share anything going on with me, especially with Donny and I'm getting the feeling that they say so much more about me when I'm not here, then pretend they don't. My skin's hot. Sweat's matting my shirt to me again. I turn back to the sink and thrust my hands under the water. I'm splashing it on my face to cool down before I say something I'm gonna regret. The chill isn't good enough. Water turned off again, I cross to Jag and swipe his box of cigarettes from his ass pocket. One cig's in my hand before the box is in the back of my jeans. I check myself for a lighter.

I don't have one.

Though, I can't light up in here anyway. I stick the cigarette in my mouth to chew on the filter.

"But she didn't do anything," Jag says. "Guy mistook her for someone else, started something, and got chased out of the bar. We think the guy at the park was one of his buddies. It's hard to know since we didn't get to talk to him."

Donny's expression drops. The bags under his eyes look darker as he blinks a couple of times. "And what the hell happened to him?"

"Ran into the trees when I knocked him on his ass," Jag says.

I'm pacing the garage. I feel like I'm suffocating and light-headed. The air's too thin and it's filled with the putrid smell of death that was bad before, but much worse now. I can't stand it. The thickness in the air reminds me too much of running through the trees in Mortem when the mist was strangling me with memories. Sharply, quickly, I'm making my way for the garage's back entrance.

"Where are you going?" Donny says.

"I need a smoke." I hold my cigarette up between my fingers.

"I could use one too." Suddenly, Jag's behind me. His closeness isn't good enough to stop the chaotic energy bouncing around inside of me, telling me to get out of here. Maybe I dealt with the badges just fine last time, but another body? Another explanation? They're suspicious enough, even when they don't remember me. How the hell am I supposed to explain how this keeps happening to me when they'll never remember the people who keep doing it? To the living, there is no believable explanation but my guilt.

"Don't wander too far." Donny turns back to his office.

I'm not sure if he's just filling the space or if he really doesn't trust us.

"We're just going for a smoke, D," Jag says. "Relax."

"Yeah, right." Donny waves. "Say it again as my business deteriorates into a funeral home." Donny chuckles bitterly. He pauses in the doorway of his office. "You guys need something to eat?"

"Joey?" Jag says.

"No. I don't think I could stomach anything if I tried. But thanks for looking out for me, Donny." With that, I'm out the back door and to the dumpster where Donny and Jag both park. The air's fresher than the garbage, but it's still thicker than I remember the city ever being. Maybe my body's finally busted in a way I can't come back from. The vomit, the strangling, something inside of me's broken where I can't get away from the stench of this damn city and the death tailing me through it.

Standing next to me, Jag holds out his hand. I trade

him the box of cigarettes for his lighter. A bit of nicotine helps cover the smell sticking to the inside of my nose. I sit on the curb by Jag's car, legs kicked out. The moisture in my pants presses into my ass; the night air's making everything chillier.

This is why the smell's following me.

My legs itch with the soft burn of Styx against them. I'm half tempted to take my pants off. Another hit. I drop my head into my hands. My foot taps against the cracked cement. Jag sits down next to me saying, "You gonna be alright?"

I snort, turning my head away while sucking my cigarette. "I've gotta be, you know?"

"Right."

"I don't know what Baltimore's got against me. Maybe it's mad I didn't die when I was supposed to."

"What'd you mean?"

"Death's been following me for a while, J. My dad, Wayland, me, you… I can't help but think it's gotten so much worse cause it's not hiding how much it wants me dead anymore. Maybe that's because I shouldn't be alive." My skin prickles in anticipation of what I'm going to say. "I was supposed to follow my dad's example. I was supposed to kill myself seven years ago. Ravens were following me, waiting for my heart to drop, but… Wayland got to me first. He made me feel like there was a reason to keep living for a little while longer, so I didn't *step out*."

"I'm glad you had a friend like him, Joey."

I look up to see Jag watching me. The parking lot lights reflect in his brown eyes. They're soft, concerned. He's got something else to say, but instead, he brings his cigarette to his lips and turns away. Across the small parking area, a fat raven lands on the grass. It doesn't look our way, but slowly, it moves across the lawn. The sound of a screaming raven comes from above the garage or the other side of the dumpster, but it's too dark to see anything.

"Don't you got something better to do than follow me all the time, Val?" I stand up. "There's nothing for you to eat here! Go away!" My voice echoes off the empty parking lot, the couple of cars still here, and the dumpster. The raven either doesn't notice me or is pretending I'm as invisible as I've ever been. The only people to ever really take notice of me were the badges and that's because they could flex their power.

Apparently, creatures that work on the side of supernatural aren't that different. Put your hand around my throat, drag me into a lake or whatever, fine. I'm just another person's punching bag. Just like Wayland. That's all any of us have ever been to our so-called *neighbors*. Who really gives a shit about anyone else but for what they can take? Someone else's hard work is your glory if you know when to stick your hands in it.

Timing is everything.

After death might be the best time to take everything you ever wanted without consequence since no one can really stop you.

Red and blue lights flash down the street with the howling call of the badge cars on the way. I put my cigarette out on the cement and stand up. "I'm not ready for this," I say.

Jag stands with me. A couple more puffs and he puts his cigarette out on the garbage can by the back door. "You think you can get away from them if you have a head start?" His stub goes into the cigarette bin beside mine.

I turn around to face him while stepping back. "Nah. Just putting off the inevitable for a couple of seconds. If I ran, they'd they just come back with a warrant and a feeling they can stick their hand up my ass." I give him a couple of finger guns. My lips pull into a weak smile; he smiles back.

Jag grabs the garage door ahead of me. He waits for me to go first, then locks it behind us. The place smells like freshly brewed coffee, but it doesn't do enough to hide the rot. All I can think is, "We're gonna be here all night, aren't we?" I'm going to the break room more so to put space between the front of the shop and me than anything else. I might not be running, but that doesn't mean I won't take every second I can to stall. "Donny! Badges are here!" I call out. I don't like how loud my voice is. In the break room, I look at the coffee pot running on the counter. It's dark. At least Donny started with a fresh filter. That also means Mustache is the lazy ass who can't be bothered to change it.

I go to the lockers, open Jag's, and close it without doing anything. I grab a couple of paper towels from the wall, wet them, and start wiping down the counter. I don't know. I just need to do something. My body's unbelievably heavy, I want to close my eyes, lay down, and forget the world exists for a couple of hours, but I can't. The small, tinny radio in the other room's playing again. Mixing with the drip of the coffee machine, it almost makes everything feel better.

"Yeah, nice seeing you again too, officers," Donny's voice makes it into the break room from the lobby. He sounds worse than me. I toss the paper towels into the trash and go to the break room door. In the garage, Jag's looking this way. I rub my eyes as I walk to him.

"You ready?" Jag says.

"Not really." I glance toward the car we picked up. It still doesn't seem real to be doing this again. "But what can we do at this point?" I laugh a little.

Jag laughs back.

"Jagger Locke?" Rocky's too familiar, too friendly, too deep voice comes from the lobby door. "You here?"

"Yeah?" Jag says.

Rocky's looking like he always does. Night or day, pressed slacks, blazer, loose tie, itching to get something in his hand. He'd say notes, I'd say addiction. He makes a beeline for Jag. "You're under arrest. Your choice if we do this the easy way."

"What do you need?" Jag says.

"Turn around." He twirls his finger in the air as if demonstrating. His other hand has cuffs waiting, probably a pair one of his buddies gave him because he's got another set on his hips. Jag turns around in compliance. The cuffs go on his wrists, and one of Rocky's buddies approaches to detain him.

"Arrested for *what* exactly? I say, stepping forward. "Just like the other one, we *found* it."

Rocky's eyes fall to me next. His lips turn into a flat smile I don't believe. I don't think it's meant to be believed either because he says, "Josephine Bourgeois…" Trailing off like he's almost remembering something or he's thinking in the same way that made me slow down when my dad put together more than a few sentences and none of them were angry.

"What's with the face, Rocky?" I say. "Almost looks like you've seen a ghost."

"Almost feels like it." His usual friendliness comes back into his voice.

"I've heard the rumors. Apparently, around here, the dead don't stay that way."

"You know? I've been hearing rumors like that for a while." His smile reminds me too much of Sol. Too big, too forced, too sweet. It's not in his eyes either. He closes the space between us and lunges, putting a hand on my wrist and flipping me around with force he's never used on me before. "Anyway, long time no see." Cuffs are digging into my wrists before I even realize his grip's been replaced.

"Yeah? When was the last time, anyway?" I say.

"I believe I left you in an interrogation room and you disappeared on me," Rocky says.

"I wasn't told I was being detained," I say.

"We had a warrant."

"Mm… Sorry, high school drop out here. I don't know what that means."

"You weren't free to go."

"I guess I had to use the bathroom pretty bad and your place just wasn't cutting it."

"I hope it works out for you this time," Rocky says.

"Okay, fine. I get what your problem is with me, but what did *he* do?" I nod toward Jag.

Rocky stares down at me for a while. A glance across the way to Jag, and he keeps his eye on him while his hand remains tight on my shoulder. "We found the blood of a missing person on the washing machine at his apartment. And in this line of work, there is no such thing as a coincidence."

"Excuse me?" Jag says.

"Shit," I mutter.

"Joey?" Jag growls.

"It's not what you think," I say. There's nothing in my head that says Jag ever did anything wrong. He's always been the laidback guy, probably too laid back if I'm honest. The worst thing he's ever done is get a little too worked up in traffic or angry over stupid shit when there was something else bothering him. When that happens, he can sometimes go a little over the top, but so can everyone in Baltimore.

I'm going back to when I brought Wayland to his place after finding him in Leakin, covered in blood, surrounded by garbage bags filled with someone the city has already forgotten; Wayland's messy clothes I put in the wash while Wayland showered; the staining in the grout where he'd stood; whatever Way might've touched on his way to the bathroom and what I didn't clean up after him because I was too busy trying to figure out how to stop him from making Baltimore's next ghost. "Shit," I say again.

"I don't know what you're talking about," Jag says.

"We can talk details at the station," Rocky says.

"Jag didn't do anything," I say.

"We'll talk about it at the station," Rocky repeats. With a hand on my shoulder and another on my arm, he leads me out while one of his buddies has his hands on Jag, though that guy is way less controlling of Jag than Rocky is of me. I'm sure Rocky wouldn't admit it, but he definitely has something against me now. You jump a fence once or twice and everyone who has any bit of power suddenly thinks they need to be *extra*. I get it. I'm slippery, but you would be too if you'd been playing the same games I have with badges all this time.

On the way out of the shop, Donny's saying, "Damn it, damn it, shit, fuck, goddamn it, Joey," again and again while looking Jag and I over. "What the hell did you do?" Donny follows as the badges lead us out the front.

"Nothing," Jag says. "Don't worry about it."

"Easy for you to say," Donny groans as he walks away.

Jag and I are in the back of the same cruiser. We're on our way to the Font Hill station before they've even bothered to look at the car we brought back. My feet are bouncing. Wired again. Jag's leg pulses at a slower pace. He mutters, "Calm down, Joey," and I say, "I fucking can't." A wall outside next to a convenience store says DUN GOOFED. I turn away from the window and press my back into the corner between the seat and the door. My knee bumps into Jag's. I look up to meet his stare. My face is burning. Feels like I've been in the back of a badge car more than my dad ever was and something about this is stupid and funny and embarrassing.

How did I get so bad that the city thinks I'm worse than my dad? Like how the hell does that happen when you live the way my dad did? I can't make it make sense without admitting that I'm just the worst person in this stupid town. Jag's seen me in all kinds of positions. Bruised and bloody and crying and naked, but I've never wanted him to see me like this. I've never wanted to drag him down to the gutter with me.

I shouldn't have waited for him to leave me to bounce out.

"I'm sorry, Jag," I mutter. "This wasn't supposed to happen. I… You still sure about your decision?" My voice shakes with the feelings I can't suppress.

"Yeah." He looks me in the eye. He's seeing through me. I'm filled with so much shame; I can't hold his stare. "But you gotta stop hiding shit from me, Joey. For real."

"I'm not hiding shit. I just forgot a couple of things—"

"How'd you forget about running from the badges? You called *yourself* a fugitive."

"I thought it was cute at the time."

"Joey," my name is a growl. He leans back, closes his eyes, and takes a deep breath. "This isn't a joke. If we're gonna be a team, then you need to let me know when shit happens. I don't care how stupid you think it is or if you think I'll be mad. You have to clue me in. Like how the hell did blood get into my apartment?" He glances at the screen separating the backseat from the front. He lowers his voice. "You told me you didn't kill anybody."

I can't say anything in this place. Everything would be taken out of context by the badge and while Jag's seen enough to believe me about the ghosts and the hauntings and everything, I doubt Rocky would take it with as much sincerity.

It shouldn't be this scary to think about telling him what I know, but I guess I've never been that honest with anyone. Thinking of the stupid shit I kept to myself because who wanted to hear about my life or worries or what I was freaked about? Thinking Wayland and Jag and Donny would laugh at me in the wrong way if they knew I was serious or worried, it was better to never put it out there so I didn't feel dismissed when I cared. Or every time you open up to someone about the mess you really are, it gives them a chance to see how deep all the trash goes and it won't be a pretty girl walking into the shop that makes him call it. She'll just be the one to scoop him up when he's moved on.

No one thinks I'm worth the time already, but being honest and having someone say, *"Wow, you're right. You are garbage,"* is something I've never been prepared to handle.

I bite my lip ring. The cigarette I had thirty minutes ago wasn't enough to help me now. "I'll explain everything later, okay? I promise. Start to finish, any question you have, everything I can remember, it's yours."

"Alright." Jag nods. "See you in twenty-five to life." He winks chuckles, and smiles, tired. Then he leans back.

I don't get it; I don't get how he's always been able to smile when shit seems so bad. Here I am, panicking, again, trying to figure out what the hell I'll tell Rocky or Garnet or whatever piece of trash they leave me with next, but Jag looks so content and sure and when I look at him, when he smiles, I want to calm down too.

Rocky turns the radio on. The Beatles are playing. Jag glances through the screen separating the front and back seats. "I love this station," Jag says.

"Me too," Rocky says.

The two of them mutter with the radio, off-key, relaxed, and like they're in their own bubbles. Considering the circumstances, it's probably one of the most ridiculous things I've ever seen, but I don't mind it.

The seat in the badge car's hard, but not hard enough to be uncomfortable when pitted against everything else. I scoot so I'm not leaning against the door anymore, and I drop my head on Jag's shoulder. He lays his head on mine. It's nice. I just wish I could hold his hand.

Instead, I'm going to have to settle for this and it's no one's fault but my own.

EIGHT.

I hate everything about this.

They put me in an interrogation room about an hour ago. I think it's been an hour, but I can't see the clock. All I can do is hear it ticking, like it's laughing at me forever because I can't see it. There aren't any windows in here and I'm pretty sure it's colder than the last time. The lights are so bright, my head's starting to hurt again, and I need to pee. Though, something tells me that if I ask, they wouldn't believe me. My wrists are handcuffed to the room's table. I've tried asking for someone a couple of times, but if there's anyone behind the one-way mirror I'm facing, they aren't listening. Maybe they think I'll crack easier if they make me wait long enough while freezing my ass off. I lean back in my seat. The cuffs tug on my skin. Hard, sharp edges burrow into my wrists just a little bit. I sit upright again and lean forward so my head falls into my arms. Not a great pillow. The position hurts my shoulders. My back's screaming.

"Rocky!" I try to groan; it comes out a pathetic whine.

I lift my head, look at the mirror glass, drop my head again, groan. My foot won't stop bouncing and I'm worried about Jag. Bringing me in, they took all my shit from me, did they take the necklace from him. What happens to my heart if it's not in his possession? Didn't Charon say something about going back to the dead? I don't know if it's just because I don't want to be here or if it's because they took my heart away, but I'm jittering so bad. My foot's almost pounding, I'm kinda rocking in my seat. The cuffs keep digging deeper into my wrist every time I pull.

I probably look insane.

I don't blame the badges for ignoring me, but I still hate them for it.

I lean back in the seat again. My elbows hang out. My ass is slipping down the chair and I'm staring at my face in the reflective window housing the badges again. My hair's messy as hell and the darkness around my eyes is more than eyeliner. I'm sure it's part shadow of the dead. At least they let me grab my hoodie on the way out or I'd be freezing. Even with it on, I'm cold.

I drop my head over the back of my chair. Counting to ten in my head's not stopping the impatience. Something moves out of the corner of my eye. I sit up. There's something moving in the glass, a shadow against the wall that shouldn't be there. I squint. That can't be a body on the other side of the mirror, right? I turn. The cuffs at the table dig harder into my skin and stop me.

I hiss. I got this feeling on my back like someone's there. A weight touches my shoulder. I startle. There's no one there, but that shadow like a splotch of thin, misty paint in the mirror. I pant softly; a voice mutters in my ear. There's something familiar about it, but I don't know what it's saying. Too quiet, the words don't make sense, I don't know, but it's making my heart race and stoking the desire to pull at the cuffs until my hands pop off. "C'mon!" My voice bounces off the walls. "At least torture me or something! Like, insult me, pluck out my fingernails—Do your evil badge shit! You want answers, don't you? Then don't leave me in here like this!" My voice gets louder and rougher until the last word's a scream that doesn't even sound like me. I never even went that high-pitched with my dad before.

The thing in the mirror moves again.

My elbows jerk back. I'm not in control of them. I lean forward, hard, pressing my chest into the table to try and fight against the impulse to tug away. Yeah, I hate the badges, but I need one of them in here now, at least to make me feel like I'm not in a new kind of purgatory.

I pull hard at the cuffs. They dig further into my wrists. My angry growl turns into a squeal of pain and frustration as I slump into the seat with another groan. My fingers curl and I'm panting against the table, making me hyperventilate or something. I need to stop the impulses.

A moment later, there are voices in the room. More of those goddamn voices. I don't want to look up in case there are shadows in the glass again, and I can see them for real now. It takes me a second to register the voices aren't a mutter in my ear, but a conversation on the other side of the interrogation room door.

At least two of them, and one of them is definitely Rocky's. The door's lock clicks. It opens. Rocky's not wearing his blazer anymore. His hair's kind of messy in a 'it's been a long day' kind of way. Probably just part of the act—look less put together, more of a wreck like me. I'll talk if we've got shit in common, right?

He's not wearing a tie either when I'm sure he had been back at the shop. He flashes me a smile and nods.

"Rough night?" he says with a gesture to my hands.

"Like Hell." My cheek's still against my arm. "What time is it?"

"About a quarter after eleven."

"Great. Thanks."

"You're welcome, Joey."

"You actually remember me now?" I lift my head.

"Of course." Rocky pulls out the seat across from me. "Who could forget *you*?"

I straighten in my seat like the principal sat down with me. My eyes don't come off him. He's got two white Styrofoam cups in his hands. "You'd be surprised at how many times it's happened already."

"Then surprise me." He sets the cups down on the table, then drops into his chair.

I look at the cups, then him, then the cups again. "You realize I can't drink that?" I lift my hands a little. The chain on the cuffs clicks against the loop keeping them to the table.

"Might've helped if you didn't jump out the window last time," Rocky says.

"So, why'd you bring two?"

His smile falters. He dips his head to the side and takes on the look of a disappointed father. Something clicks. I glance at the door. Someone's coming in? Instead, he's pulling a small key from the hook at his waist. The key goes into the cuffs. My hands are released. Rocky scoops up the empty cuffs and slides them into his pocket saying, "Don't make me regret this."

I draw my hands back. My wrists are redder than I was expecting. There are scrapes from how deep the cuts went. I rub one of the sharp lines gently with my thumb. I can't get the cut Jag had out of my head. How much of what happens to me affects him too? How connected does this heart thing go, really? Is it everything or just really bad things?

I reach for the coffee but pause just as my fingers touch the Styrofoam. "You got any sugar?"

Rocky plucks a couple packets out of his jacket along with a few tabs of CoffeeMate creamer.

"Thanks."

"You're welcome."

I pick up a few of the packets. Tops ripped off; I dump the contents into my cup. By the time I'm reaching for the creamer, Rocky's dropping a couple stirring sticks onto the table too. I dump enough creamer into my cup that the coffee's closer to the color of milk than coffee. Probably too much. Jag laughs at me for it, but Rocky says nothing. He's sitting back, watching me work, his hand around his own cup, though he hasn't taken a drink yet. He waits for me to take mine like I'm going to drink it, then takes a sip of his own. I follow.

It tastes a lot like the stuff Donny started getting and the heat's getting under my skin, making the interrogation room temperature more tolerable.

I take another sip of the warm coffee. With the cup in both hands, I lower it to my lap. Rocky's pretending not to watch me while he lays his phone on the table in front of him. Instinctively, I reach for mine. Of course, I don't have it. There's no reason it would be in my pocket. I still curse under my breath. Rocky's fingers flick over the screen of his phone, opening emails just to shut them again before he even has a chance to pretend to read them. I lean back in the chair and watch him do this a couple of times without pause while he sips his coffee. I know what a stall tactic looks like, hoping someone will crack and say the first word. I've done it a couple of times. Jag's done it to me. I take another sip of coffee. Something moves in the mirror. I turn around to check the wall.

There's nothing there. Not even the shadows that I'm sure are in the mirror. Turning back to Rocky, he says, "Something wrong?"

The shadows aren't behind him. The back room is clear again. "No," I say. I'm going crazy.

Rocky's attention sinks back to his phone. "Crazy what happened with the city council today, eh?"

"I wouldn't know… I don't pay attention to that stuff…"

"Honestly, it's probably better that way."

My thumb taps hard against my thigh. "Why are you being so nice to me?"

Rocky looks up from his phone. "What do you mean?"

"Like you said, I'm kind of a fugitive and you let my hands go?" My eyes drop to the little ring on the table that the cuffs were connected to.

Rocky chuckles. "I never called you a fugitive." He leans forward. "But I'm not really concerned either way. You're not getting out of this room and if, somehow, you manage it, you're not getting out of the station."

"Cockiness was the downfall of a lot of great people, you know?"

"Yeah?" His head drops to the side. "What was *your* downfall?"

I snort, fall back. My arms cross. I look down at my lap while flicking my lip ring with my tongue. "I'm not very good with people."

"Sure. I can see that." Rocky's cup is back at his lips; his eyes are back on his phone. He's waiting for me to crack. He thinks it's only a matter of time until he's filling out paperwork for the murders neither Jag or I committed and the dead guys behind it all are still running around Baltimore, doing more damage and getting away with it since the living can't see how it works.

Rocky takes his phone from the table and slides it back into his pocket. His stern glance returns to me. Something about it is too direct that it's startling. "I just think it's easier to get something when you're not hostile," he says.

"But aren't we?"

"You tell me." Rocky crosses his arms. Relaxed, tired, but not closed off. "How do you keep finding bodies? It's a real talent, you know?"

A laugh comes out like a sneeze. I almost spill my coffee. "More like a curse." My head drops. I put my cup on the table so my fingers can paw at my thighs, get rid of some of the pressure I'm feeling before I can barely sit anymore. "But I wish I knew. I'm kinda getting tired of seeing 'em, Rocky."

"I bet." His voice is surprisingly friendly. His expression's turned soft. Pity.

Reminder: He's not here to help me. He's here to get me to talk and say something he can use to build a case against me and Jag. Doesn't matter what I actually did. The fact I'm here means he thinks I'm guilty of something. I can't blame him; I know how it all looks. He's just doing his job to get a conviction and I'm doing mine to keep myself safe.

"I got a question," Rocky says. "It was you who left the tip the other day, wasn't it?"

"What tip?" I take my coffee off the table and turn away. One leg thrown over the other, my arm hangs over the back of the chair. I take a sip.

"About the body."

"What body?"

"Wayland Cross."

"That wasn't me." My throat tightens. I can't breathe. "I know you think it was because you're giving me details that would contaminate your investigation if you thought otherwise—"

"It was your number that came up on my phone."

I purse my lips. "You're memorizing my number now, Rocky?" My feet flatten against the floor as I turn back to him. "You might wanna back off. You're coming off kinda strong and don't you think your wife would mind that you're stalking a twenty-three-year-old?"

"She doesn't know." Rocky leans back.

"Oh." I set my cup on the table and lean forward. "This is kind of a big secret to keep from your partner."

"If you want to call it a secret. I wouldn't call it anything bigger than some of the things I heard you were keeping from your boyfriend."

"This isn't about *me*, Rocky. This is about *you* and *your* spousal problems. Or maybe it's not a secret at all. Maybe the cartel really did get her, or she died in a fire or *she left your drunk ass*. Help me out here, man. What would you call it?"

"Divorce."

"Fuck." I lean back, exhaling hard.

"Oh, you're familiar?" He chuckles.

My foot's tapping again. I can't come up with anything to say and the ticking clock's only making it more obvious.

"Not drinking, by the way," Rocky says. "Marital differences."

"By marital, you don't mean, like, bedroom stuff, right? I don't need specifics. Just curious. Was it you or her?"

"Me." Rocky laughs. "And it wasn't *bedroom* stuff, it was *work* stuff."

"Sorry," I mutter, reaching for my cup again.

"Don't be."

"I didn't mean it like I caused it or something. I mean

it like, I'm sorry. It sucks." It's stupid I can't even mock him over this. I mean, I could, but it doesn't feel right because I know how much this stuff hurts. Like, maybe my parents never really got divorced. I don't know if they were even married, but when my mom left, I felt it, my dad felt it, and I'm still paying for it.

I tip my cup back. Most of it's sugar that didn't melt now sitting at the bottom of the cup. I wipe my lips with the back of my hand. I wish I had water. "Don't read into that."

"I won't." His lips go flat, but somehow, he's still smiling. "The divorce wasn't bad; this job's hard on everybody."

"You got divorced over your job?"

"It's a lot for people to take. The stress, long nights, worry if I'll come home sometimes. Dinner topics are non-existent or depressing. It's a lot," Rocky says.

"What about the money?"

"What about the money?" He sounds like he doesn't know what I mean.

"Was it ever a problem?"

"Maybe early on, but nothing we couldn't handle. Everything recently about cutting budget though? She hasn't been around for that."

"That's good. Money can be a real issue for some people, you know?" I suck in a breath shakier than I mean to. The mirror goes blurry and fades into gray walls. All the light around me washes everything so it looks the same. A wave of dizziness makes me close my eyes. The room's getting further away, the clock goes silent. I don't know where I am. Glass shatters, breaking on something, then, tumbling to the floor in front of me. I feel pieces slide against my leg. My dad's downing another beer. He breaks the bottle, sobbing, then cuts himself on the glass by accident and smacks me when I tried to help him cause he said I did it to him. A noise in the hall brings me back to the interrogation room. Voices, an exchange of information in the hall, laughter. It's not just Rocky and me. It's not like the elevators or outside Wayland's house or the porch at my place. We've got onlookers, people judging every little thing I do or say, marking down every mistake, every fidget, the meaning behind every scream.

"Hey… Question." I wait until I have Rocky's attention. "When you brought us in here, did you strip a necklace off Jag?"

"I'm not sure. I didn't book him," Rocky says.

"Can you double check and make sure that he has it? It's kind of important."

"I'll see what I can do, but there are no promises—"

"He didn't kill anybody. You need to let him go."

Rocky leans back with a sigh. "How'd the blood get in his apartment?"

"It was there because of me." I'm staring at the mirror window again, imagining Wayland in the corner like I did the first time I was in here, seeing his ghost covered in blood from that bastard he left to rot in Leakin. Everything comes back to me and every stupid thing I've ever done without thinking about what comes next or who it affects. I didn't think about how taking Wayland back to Jag's place could backfire in so many ways, just so long as Jag never knew. That's all that was on my mind. But that turned into him stalking Jag and taking his gun and destroying the place and this… Why couldn't I see anything past those couple of moments where I needed something to seem easy and right and like it'd just work out?

Taking him there gave me what I wanted at the time, but there was so much after that and all the choices I've made have been wrong. Shit's gotten worse for everyone almost every single time.

Which is probably the most jarring thing. Jag knows I can't make good decisions. He's watched my choices backfire on both of us, but he's still here and he still took that stupid piece of jewelry from Ralph, fixing him to me and every stupid decision I make. He's accepted the same kind of a life from me that I took from my dad. I promised I'd never do that to anyone and I can't do this to Jag of all people.

The room goes blurry. Moisture runs down my cheeks and I rock, thinking it'll soothe me some. I squint in an attempt to see through the glass; it doesn't work. Obviously, it's not going to work. I stand up. Rocky tries to hide the alarm that shows in his stiffening body. He's pretty good at faking being relaxed, but I've pulled one over him enough times to know what it looks like when his defenses go up. He's been gotten more than enough times to know he should be prepared for it too.

I go around the table to the glass. No matter how close I am, I just see my face.

Disappointed. Dirty. Tired. Broken.

Worthless.

"You want to say more about what you did?" Rocky says.

I turn away from the mirror. "Can you get rid of them?" I point over my shoulder at the one-way mirror. "I'll talk to you then."

Rocky purses his lips. He leans forward, rubbing his brows. His bottom lip's sucked in when he sighs. "Alright, but you're gonna need to put your hands back on the table before I'll open the door."

I return to my seat. My hands are on top the table again. His cuffs go around my wrists. As soon as they're secure, he's out the door. He's not gone for very long and just as soon as he's back, the cuffs come off again.

My heart's pounding wildly in my ears. Somehow, I didn't think he'd say yes, I didn't think this would happen—I didn't think I'd have to explain to someone how much control the dead have in this city.

After a couple quiet moments, Rocky says, "How'd the blood get there?"

I stare past Rocky to the glass, then I look back at him. My face says we're not alone.

"They're gone," Rocky says. "Don't you trust me?"

I shake my head. "Not really, no."

"What can I do to fix that?"

"I don't think you can."

Rocky sighs. Again, it's the father thing. Disappointment. Frustration. The kind my dad had when he found out I wasn't selling sex like he thought to pay for his habits. "How'd the blood get there, Joey?"

The stiffness in his voice sends a chill through me. It's just short of feeling like an accusation. Next thing he'll probably say is that they've got enough evidence to press charges without my help. This is just a courtesy for Jag's sake. My face is hot, jaw tight. My feet press into the floor so hard, my back's going into the chair. The feeling to run is back, but there's nothing I can do to get out of this room, so instead, the voice hissing in the back of my head I s telling me to take my chances and smash Rocky's head into the table and steal the keys and what comes next doesn't really matter because I'm screwed either way. My finger's in my mouth, nail tucked under my teeth and I'm plucking at skin and dirt and nail so hard, the taste of iron is on my tongue.

"You live together, right?"

My attention snaps back to Rocky. He's leaning forward, arm on the table, shoulders tall. The force is coming out, his patience waning. My chance of getting out of this is shrinking every second I don't give him a reason why I didn't do what he thinks I did. He's never going to believe the truth though.

"Sometimes," I say.

Rocky's posture relaxes again. "To your knowledge, is he seeing anybody else?"

I snort. Stop short. Shake my head. "No."

"There was a girl at his apartment the other day when I stopped by—"

I snort again. "Really? We're doing this again?"

"Doing what?"

"That was *me*, Rocky. You remember?"

"That wasn't you."

"Yes, it was. We stood by the elevators. You thought he was beating me. A group of crows is called a murder, a group of ravens is an unkindness, and a group of badges is called—"

"Bullshit," we say at the same time.

Rocky leans back. His brows come together. He's got this look on his face like he's waiting to call me a liar because something about what I've said is already impossible. It's every minute of the last couple of weeks adding up to the final bullshit the living can't believe. I get it. I used to be like them and even after everything I know, I still can't believe half the shit that comes out of my mouth or the things I've seen. I can't believe that I've gone back to Mortem just by climbing through Armistead like I've done so many other times before. But, just these few times, I went deeper and deeper and deeper until I chose the dark.

I guess that was the difference.

Whatever it means.

Everything around me's going black. Sound fades out. I can't breathe. I close my eyes, imagining Jag in a room not unlike this one, if he's lucky or in a cell next to some guy who likes his handsome face and it's all my fault.

"The blood was from Wayland Cross." I grab the cup from the table. There's nothing left in it, but the remains of the coffee that wouldn't come out with a tip. Bit by bit, I tear at the Styrofoam and drop the pieces to the floor. "He killed somebody a couple days ago and tossed the body in the woods. Probably still there if you're calling the guy missing. I don't know who it was though." My throat goes tight. Even knowing what I know, I can't see Wayland dirty like that.

No. These last few weeks? That wasn't Wayland. It was the city that drowned him in hopelessness and regret, took away his future, and possessed his body. Preying on the innocent is all these people know, which is what made him such a perfect target. Everybody around him only saw another bastard who created their misery. They couldn't admit they did it to themselves because then they'd have to accept they're the only ones who could fix things and maybe it was too late for that.

I stare into Rocky's eyes, looking for the smallest amount of insincerity, mockery, sneering, anger, doubt— Anything that would tell me he's playing a game, but it's not there. "Are you serious you don't remember any of the times we ran into each other last week? It's kind of become more than a *habit*, dude."

"I don't know what game you're playing, but I haven't seen you since the last time you were in this room—"

"Barbara?"

"I remember that, but not you."

"That's because it's how this works."

"How what works?" The dark shadows under Rocky's eyes seem to grow. His fingers tap the counter. He reaches for the coffee cup, finds it empty, and sets it back down. The cup I'd been tearing at is now a pile of shredded foam on the floor. I reach across the table and take Rocky's to treat it the same way. Rocky's eyes follow my hands, watching my fingers. The blood from my busted nail taints the foam. He sighs. "Wayland Cross has been dead for at least a month, Joey. We haven't released that information yet, but he couldn't have been at your house."

"But he was—"

"How?" Rocky's leaning forward again. His voice has gained a harder edge. Not daring, but pushing, more like a badge is supposed to do. The subtitle of his expression is *guilty, guilty, guilty.*

Another snort. My voice is annoying to me. I lean back, crossing my arms and kicking my legs out like I'm sixteen again, pulled into the principal's office for doing something stupid like grinding on the fountain or lunch tables even though I never did that. My guilt never actually mattered; the office never wanted to hear it since everything was an excuse to prove how much of a bad student I was to absolve them of the guilt of being shitty teachers.

Jaw tight, my arms squeeze tighter. "You wouldn't believe me if I told you."

"Try it." Just like Jag, it was a dare, not a challenge.

"You can't laugh if I do."

"I won't."

I meet Rocky's gaze. The accusations aren't there anymore, but there's something else. The waiting disbelief he's suppressed just to see how ridiculous I get. He knew I was gonna say something crazy when I asked him to kick his buddies out. I lick my dry lips. They get drier. I purse them. My skin prickles with everything I haven't said yet. I can't fix the insanity of what's actually happening in this city, what's happened to me, what I know is happening now to everyone. Whether Rocky knows it or not, he's interacting with ghosts every day, but to say that would be crazy, right? You can't just make believers like that. There's also no easy way into it aside from dragging someone to Mortem, and yeah, definitely Rocky would let me pull him into the depths of Armistead without suspicion. There's no way to make this easier for a regular person to take, let alone a badge.

"I died," I say.

Rocky's expression doesn't change. He doesn't move, but keeps watching me with interest, waiting for me to change my story or laugh or say I'm joking and that's not what I meant and here's the real deal, you get it? After some time passes, his lips twitch, probably with the urge to call my shit, but he still doesn't say anything.

"Well?" I say.

"What?"

"Seriously nothing?"

"You told me not to laugh."

"I didn't say don't respond at all." I pick my foot up with the urge to kick the table but drop it back down without doing anything. "What are you thinking right now?

Rocky leans back. He sucks in a breath. His thumb strokes his chin while he scans the wall behind me. He drops his head to the side, a hum clutched in his throat. "What do you mean by *died?*"

"I mean some bastard put his hands around my throat and snuffed me out."

"But you're here now?"

"Yes."

"In your head, how does that work?"

"Nice framing—But it's not *in my head*. It's *in nature*."

"What do you mean by that?"

"You know, the more questions you ask, the crazier it's going to sound."

"Isn't that why we're here today?"

"No." My lips purse again. "I didn't come here to

sound crazy." I shake my head. I don't want to say any of it, but without thinking, like I'd been holding in a sickness all this time, the words come out. It's the only way to get through this. "The dead live under Baltimore. It's not a graveyard, it's a place called Mortem. Kinda like limbo. You get there through Armistead, though I don't really know how and then there's this bitch-and-a-half named Sol who poisons you until the reaper comes to take you to judgment, but you don't really have to go. Like, for real, her entire job is roofying you until you forget who you are so you don't put up a fight—but you can jump into the river instead of going to judgment—whatever that means—but when you jump into Styx, you come back here and you're pissed off at everything and can't die for real again. You can only be collected by the reaper and sent wherever he sends escaped souls. And, like, he's led around by a raven that also looks like a person sometimes and he rips people open to eat their hearts because that's just what he does I guess and—"

"You can't die?" Rocky says slowly.

"I can die now. I made a deal—"

"Alright…"

"I know it sounds like I'm BSing the hell out of this, but I promise, a lot of this shit happened—Not important right now." My teeth grind. His apprehension and seriousness from before are gone, replaced instead with a look that tells me he's thinking I'm actually insane. Not that different from the half a dozen looks Donny's given me any time I might've cried over something legitimately stupid because I couldn't help it. The stupid shit wasn't ever really what made me upset, it was just… the right place at the right time, you know? Like the damn commercial for Father's Day when it's some happy, good-looking guy playing a game of catch with his kid and it's saying to treat him nice since it's Father's Day and he's always been there to support you, so give back. But all I wanted was to wish those words were real and then I hated myself for wanting that commercial to relate to my dad. Then Donny would see me after the commercials went on to something like toothpaste staining a couch or the repeat of some sitcom and he didn't know why I was upset. I never told him either, so I'm pretty sure he thought it was just the normal female insanity when he'd say, "At least you're not as bad as Veronica."

"I knew you wouldn't believe me," I say.

"I'm not entirely sure what I'm supposed to be believing right now," Rocky says.

"That Jag didn't kill anyone; I didn't kill anyone; ghosts are real and stuff's not as straightforward as you think it is." I slump into my seat. The pile of Styrofoam on the floor between my feet feels like my life. Torn trash that's on its way out as soon as I get moved into a cell I'm probably never going to see the other side of and I'll probably never see Jag again and then one day, something'll happen to him and I'll be dead again while he's off in Mortem forgetting about me cause maybe he thinks if he's dead, I've moved on too. Instead, I'm just haunting his old apartment, waiting for him to come back when he never will.

"Is this why you were asking about the grim reaper before?" Rocky says.

"You remember that?"

"Yeah."

"Back then, I'd just met him, and I didn't know what to believe either." Something goes off in my head. Charon's number. Shouldn't matter where or how you put it in, as long as you put the numbers down, he's supposed to come. There'd be no way to doubt entirely everything if he shows up because he should just walk into the booth, right? "I can prove this is all real, but you have to trust me."

Rocky hums, staring at me again. His lips twitch into a grimace. "How exactly do you think you can prove any of this to me?"

"I know a guy."

"With a shovel or a knife?" Rocky chuckles.

"With a raven."

Rocky leans back, crossing his arms. "And where is this guy?"

"I'm gonna need you to let me borrow your phone—"

"No."

"Then get me a pen and paper. Double check there isn't a single badge behind that glass."

"Sounds like you're either preparing for a confession or a murder."

"Don't worry—His bird only eats carrion." I wink. "It means he's only interested in the dead—"

"I know what *carrion* means." Rocky Sighs as he reaches into his ass pocket and withdraws a small notebook. A pen comes from the pocket on his shirt. He places them on the table then pushes them toward me.

Slowly, while looking at him, I take the pen. I clear my throat. My hands are sweaty. I set the pen down to wipe my palms on my pants. My foot's tapping more rapidly than before. Rocky's watching me press the pen to the paper. I tap the counter impatiently as I put down the first set of numbers. A chill goes through me, and I can't stop thinking—What if this doesn't work? What comes next? The bad cop game where he tells me to tell the truth and yells until I say something actually untrue because I just want him to shut up? What kind of questions could he come up with when it seems like I know something but I'm making shit up to cover for it? I know everything about this sounds ridiculous. All of it's dumb. In reality, exactly what's wrong with this situation is fucking ridiculous.

I put down the dash, then a one.

Rocky's lips smack. He shifts, clears his throat. I pull the pen back.

I want to get it over with, but putting in the last numbers will either prove everything I've said or make me look worse. Maybe Rocky'll look at Charon and Val the same way Jag did when he first saw them. He'll come up with an excuse for why they're there or pretend he knows them. Worse: He could try to arrest them. Can a badge even touch a grim reaper like that? Would Val attack him if he tried? I've never seen anyone throw hands at a grim reaper before and the bird can't just be for heart hunting, right?

The last two numbers are written. I set the pencil down. My heart's throbbing. I close my eyes, listen for the rattling chains.

"What are we waiting for?" Rocky says.

"Even with a second chance, the dead can't escape the fear of death," I say.

The room lights flicker. Rocky looks up, back at me. "The hell…" The chains are rattling. The unease hits, then fear creeps in. A pair of dark, red eyes appear in the one-way mirror. I stand up. My chair squeals. I'm stepping back until I hit the wall and gasp. Rocky says, "Hey, are you okay?" but he sounds far away. Another pair of eyes opens, and another, and another, crescendo until the wall is lined with eyes and outlines of ravens like there might be trees hidden in the darkness. The figure in white materializes through the glass. Unlike at the park or the apartment, birds don't spill onto the floor or chairs or anything. The only bird to come in the room is the one on Charon's shoulder. His eyes glow red softly, focused on me. The lights overhead buzz, flicker, then grow solid again.

"That was weird," Rocky says.

Charon's glance moves briefly from me to Rocky and back. "Where is the soul?"

"Uh," I chuckle weakly. My head drops. Not shame, but… A cold sweat wets my neck. "I don't have one this time. I just needed you to show someone something." I nod toward Rocky.

"Do you not understand your boundaries? This is not what we agreed upon." Charon approaches me. Slow, even steps without hesitation. "Stop wasting my time or is this truly all you know how to do?" He glances over the small interrogation room. "Lies, laziness, and recklessness. You are lucky *this* medium is so charitable to your kind."

"I'm sorry—I'm working on it, but I'm not—This isn't what you think it is," I say.

"Who are you talking to?" Rocky says.

"Wait, what?" I turn to Charon. "Can't he see you?" My voice is low.

"No," Charon says. "He's living."

"So's Jag, but he sees you."

"Jagger Locke is closer to death than Stone Grant."

"Uh, Joey?" Rocky says. He braces himself on the table. His eyes reflect the insanity he thinks he sees in me.

My jaw's tight. I try to look at myself in the mirror rather than Charon or Rocky. "What the hell are you talking about? Rocky works in homicide! How much closer to death can you get than that?"

"When darkness is allowed in, it corrodes the soul. While being near death may inspire, it is not nearly enough. Darkness is a choice," Charon says.

"What the hell does that mean?" I say.

"Joey?" Rocky's standing. His expression's stiff, movements slow, hesitant, like he's questioning whether he should jump me and tie me back to the table before I do anything to him. I hate that my first thought is to prove I'm innocent of something I haven't even done yet.

Charon passes by Rocky, heading again for the mirror he came from. His eyes glow reflective in the surface as he looks over his shoulder at me. "Do not waste my time. The next time you call, be sure there is a soul, and stop allowing your mistakes to fester."

"I'm working on it. There's not a lot I can do until I get out of here. Kinda the point of giving you a call," I say.

"You should be aware by now that no one can take action in your place. Your decisions shape your options, you choose the path." Charon keeps moving. "Stop wasting time or disaster will follow." Where the glass should've stopped him, he walks into it. The solid object turns to mist that fogs around him, devouring him quickly as he moves into the distance. Little by little the raven eyes in the glass blink out of existence until they're all gone and the only thing reflecting in the glass is Rocky, me, and the interrogation room.

The paper on the table makes a sound as Rocky turns it to face him. He glances over the numbers. His lips purse, head cocking to the side. He looks back at me and then down. "What's this number supposed to mean?"

"Nothing, apparently." I collapse into the chair I'd been sitting in before. My hands are fists against my thighs. My eyes water and I don't know if it's because I'm tired or angry or upset, but I want to go home and stop going over this again and again and again with no hope of getting to the other side or finding someone to believe me. It's all the same shit I've always dealt with, just a little different. You'd think people would believe bruises, but they'll make up reasons for what's wrong with you, so they don't have to take your word about the obvious. Whatever justifies distance and disbelief, that's the play most people make because no one wants to get involved with anyone else, *really*. Even Wayland said it. He saw all the signs that Jag and I were doing something, but because I never said anything, he rejected it. Hope and desperate ignorance look the same, but they're not interchangeable.

I've been here so many times before; repetition doesn't make something true.

My fingers tingle with a rush. The flash of an image hits my mind. Rocky's head slamming into the metal table, busted open. Charon told me to make a soul next time, right?

I breathe through my teeth. I'm rocking. I only notice because Rocky's watching me differently than before. Edgy. I must look insane. I wouldn't trust me either. Gripping the edge of my chair, a chuckle escapes my lips; I stop it with a groan. My head drops onto the table and another laugh comes out. This one I can't stop. My hands press into my face, wipe my eyes. I mutter an apology. "I said you were gonna think I'm crazy. Any of this helping my case?"

"Josephine—"

"Joey." I meet Rocky's eyes.

Rocky sighs. "Are you covering for your boyfriend? It's okay to say you are. A lot of women have been in your position. I won't tell him; anything you say in here is safe."

"In all honesty, depending on what you've asked him, *he's* probably covering for *me*."

"You might be surprised to learn he's said some… *interesting* stuff too."

"Like what?"

"You're talking about death like you genuinely believe people can come back. If you're serious about what you think happened, we might already be stuck." Rocky's expression says he's judging me in a way he hadn't been before. Pity, sure, but this is more than that. "I know you've been through a lot; traumatic experiences can warp the way you see or understand things to make them digestible. It's not uncommon for people who have been through extreme cases of abuse to disassociate from reality in order to protect themselves. This can take the form of make believe, parables, mixing mythology with reality in a way that your imagination seems real—"

"Thank you, Mr. Psychologist. Appreciate the eval." I turn away.

"You've seen a lot of corpses in the past couple of weeks. Not just regular dead, but brutal murders. That kind of thing doesn't leave you. Hell, even here we're supposed to talk to psychs when we see what you've seen to make sure we don't lose it." Rocky takes the seat in front of me. He pulls it closer. His hand lifts like he's going to reach for me, but he stops short and sets it on the table. "If you were around when any of those people died… it's something else." He leans back. "There's an indescribable feeling that comes with watching the life leave someone's body. I know. I've experienced it and it cracks a lot of people. Doing it yourself though? There's no going back once you've experienced that stain. It changes the way you see people and how you look at life in general, but you *can* make things right. We can offer you protection from your boyfriend—"

"Jag didn't do anything!" I stand up too fast, my chair falls over. Rocky pulls back. His hand's at his belt, reaching for something I don't want to see because the voice that was in my ear is screaming grab him and fight him and he's done nothing but trust me so far when he really shouldn't have. I press my palms to my eyes to wipe the visions away with blackness and pressure. My teeth grind. I'm stumbling backward until I hit the wall, jump, gasp. He's waiting for me to make a move. "You need to stop accusing him, okay? We're not talking about him. We're talking about the ghosts who've destroyed this goddamn city. You know it. You've seen it. Even if you don't remember. You're asking how Wayland could've put blood in Jag's apartment when he's been dead—That's because the dead don't stay dead, Rocky! I lived with a dead man for fifteen fucking years and nobody helped me! I finally got rid of him, but I caught another one since this city is so overrun with angry assholes who think they died before their time."

"What do you mean you got rid of him, Joey?" Rocky's hands are up, casual, but defensive, like he's approaching a wild animal. Unpredictable, probably violent, but uncrossed.

"You should just retire because you're never gonna fix anything if you don't believe because they're never gonna go away. It's proof enough you can't stop them that you don't remember every time we ran into each other when I was dead-dead."

"What does *dead-dead* mean?"

"You remember when you were at Cross's burnt up house like, a week ago or something?" I can't stop the tears from falling now. "You ran into someone coming out of the place who booked it the first chance she got?"

"How do you know that?"

"Because it was *me, you* just don't remember because I was dead."

Ralph's words echo in my head. The explanation of why Rocky and Jag's little brother and so many others couldn't remember me when I stepped away. "As stupid as it sounds, you didn't know my soul, so you couldn't recognize it when I was walking around as *just that*. But we've run into each other so many times… The night of the fire, you followed Jag's car back to his place and asked him why he was in Wayland's neighborhood. He said he was picking me up. A couple days later, you were back because someone broke into his house and you told me about the unkindness and asked if he was beating me while we stood by the elevators. The next day, we met outside Wayland's house. I said my name was Barbara; you didn't believe I had any reason to be there and almost nabbed me, but I ran and then you disappeared. Probably forgot you were chasing me because you blinked and my face was gone."

Rocky's head cranes. His brows pull together. He's gonna say something, but stops himself, pursing his lips instead. He surveys the paper I wrote Charon's number on, still sitting on the table closer to his seat than mine now. Pushing his hair back, he sighs while going back to his chair. He picks up the paper again and turns it over, searching the back for any hidden message I might've left, then puts it back down. "What's this number mean?"

I bite my lip to keep my mouth shut.

"It can't be any crazier than anything you've already said." Rocky sets the paper back down, exchanging it for a stroke to his jaw.

"It calls Charon. I'm supposed to use it if I find any souls, so he can come collect them. I don't know how legit he really is, but he looks legit and I've seen him collect."

"Charon's a Greek myth—"

"Apparently, he's more than that."

"Alright…" Rocky leans back. He strokes his jaw again. Another hard sigh.

I guess that's a better response than Jag gave me, but Rocky has the benefit that he doesn't remember me being at the places I just listed, even if he does remember them happening.

"Not saying I believe you, but if you died and became a ghost, then how am I seeing you now?"

I return to the table. He's tense until I sit down again, though I basically fall into the seat. The legs squeal against the floor. Rocky straightens again. "Sorry," I mutter. "I'm not trying to put you on edge… I just…" My hands go for my pockets, looking for a cigarette out of habit.

Rocky reaches into his pocket, producing a lighter and a box of cigarettes. "This what you're looking for?" he says.

"Can I?" I watch him put the two items on the table.

"If you're gonna talk, go ahead." Rocky's got his phone out now. He taps the screen before laying it on the counter. A voice recorder.

"Humans are made up of three parts. Body, soul, heart. I don't care what your religious belief is, that's how it is. When you die, you get separated. Your soul's the thing that goes to Hell and it's the thing that turns into a ghost when you don't have a body." I grab the box and lighter at the same time. Cigarette lit; I pop it into my mouth. A couple of breaths set the nicotine to work. My eyes flutter to half-lids. I just wish Jag was here. He's always been better than me at explaining stuff. He looks more believable too. I think the lip ring does me in sometimes. "At that point, you're supposed to move on. Charon takes your soul downstairs, and you wait around for judgment. You don't *have* to go to judgment, but if you evade it, you come back up here and you're angry as hell. The whole *vengeful ghost* thing, you know? It's what happened to Wayland. He wasn't a bad person when he was alive, he just couldn't control himself. And that's where mediums come in. I don't know how, but they've got this connection to the other side where they can return your heart to you so you're not crazy. That's the necklace Jag has. The necklace he needs to have, because without it, I don't have a body, so I'm probably gonna go crazy again and when that happens, you end up with Baltimore."

"Now there are mediums involved?" Rocky's head sags forward. "What's the name?"

I stare at Rocky. My cigarette hangs from my fingers in front of my mouth. "I'm not a narc."

Rocky's brow raises. "I'm not asking to make an arrest."

"That's what you said last time I was here."

"What reason would I have to bring in some random yahoo who thinks he talks to spirits?"

"You'll find something. Badges are always real' good about making shit up when they need it."

"Maybe I'm just trying to understand what the hell's happening in my city."

"*Your* city?"

"Born and raised." He almost sounds proud, which I kinda get because Baltimore's my home too, but he's had the ability to leave. I know I wouldn't accept it if someone told me to get the hell out. It'd be nice if Baltimore could clean itself up a little bit every once in a while. The same sort of wish I had for my dad. Instead of giving up, I've stuck around, hoping it'd change its mind because it can't be that hopeless, right?

I don't know why I'm so desperate to hold on.

"I joined the BPD to make a difference," Rocky says. "It's been bad for a while, before I was born even, but I couldn't bring myself to leave. It's one of the things my wife and I fought about. She wanted to get out. She wasn't from here. Actually a Virginian. She only came for college, but we got married, she got pregnant, and she wasn't happy. Something had to give and it was… whatever we thought we had." Rocky reaches for the cigarettes on the table. He lights himself one and quickly uses it. "Maybe heartless of me, but… I don't think the relationship was worth leaving Baltimore for. If it wasn't this, she'd have found something else to drive her crazy and it wouldn't have changed even if we moved over to Richmond or Portland or Hartford or Palo Alto, so I stayed and she left." He takes a puff.

I look Rocky over. He's not watching me now but staring at the wall. He sighs while his free hand squeezes the pieces of loose paper and puts it into his pocket. Whatever he's thinking about has taken him a million miles from here. Until recently, I couldn't make the decision to get away from my dad. It was only with the distance that dying gave me that I was able to do anything about him, and even then… I still want him now. I just understand how long he's really been gone. I should've left a while ago. "You ever regret it?"

Rocky's attention returns to me. He leans back. His hand falls to the table with his cigarette. A light laugh rumbles in his chest. "Don't know yet, but I'm glad I haven't given up on this city. I don't want it to become just another item on my resume or a long memory of horror shows that I don't have to deal with personally, but I know are still there for a hellova lot of people. Plus, no one gets how you could care about a city like this if you're not from it." Puff of cigarette. "All they see from the outside is the reputation and crime and attitude." He's staring at the wall again. Slowly, he nods to himself. "I can't solve everything, sure. Not every case hits my desk, but I can sure as hell try to help when someone calls. That's all any of us can ever do, yeah?"

I know I shouldn't trust him; I keep telling myself that. I know how badges work and every word I exchange with him's a risk that my life will get ruined further, but this time, it's not just me I'm taking down. I've seen it play out so many times on so many TV shows and through all the run-ins we've had with one another. The badges always try and talk like they're people, community members and citizens, not armed with a gun, but with concern. He did it even when he didn't remember who I was.

Still, I don't know how else to fix this. Reminders from both Jag and Wayland bounce around in my head, telling me I can't do it alone and I don't have to. I stall at grabbing a cigarette. Nicotine really does nothing for your nerves when you know it's an excuse. "I don't… know what kind of other shit he does. The medium. He runs a bar and does magic and used to be in a band. That's all I know."

"Who?"

Hit of cigarette. I cross an arm over my chest. I'm not looking at Rocky. "Promise you won't arrest him?"

Rocky smiles with a small chuckle. He sounds the way I wished my dad was sometimes. "Okay… How about unless he's doing something *much more egregious* than backroom drugs, I won't do anything."

My shirt's sticking to my back again, but I'm still really cold. I glance toward the door. I'm in the mirror. I can't help the feeling I'm making the next biggest mistake of my life, but there's no other way out of here. "Ralph Reagan."

"Ralph Reagan, huh?" Rocky says.

"You know him?"

"You could say that. Kind of surprised he's still around to be honest."

"Was something supposed to have happened to

him?”

"Not necessarily… Just an unfortunate life, and you know how those tend to end up." Rocky's staring at me.

Crossing my arms, I purse my lips and sink into my cold metal chair. "No. I don't. Enlighten me sometime?"

Rocky looks me down. "Sure." He chuckles.

I guess that's not surprising considering the reputation BAIT had. KC was known for violent mosh pits, riots, and inspiring acts of insanity that followed his concerts to the point the city banned him from scheduling anything after dark for a while when they were touring. Their in between measure was pop-ups in warehouses or abandoned buildings and underground clubs that no official knew about until it was too late. Still happened. While the band was talked about while it was active, there was a period it exploded just after they disbanded. Bodies showing up at places they tried to play like they were cursed. There were rumors that KC was stabbed, or got into a fight and shot four times, performed, then died. Some of the rumors went wild because KC disappeared and the next thing anyone heard, crazy shit happened at their last few concerts before Ralph opened a random bar hidden in a residential neighborhood. His business is more like a fringe rumor and his history's an urban legend no one's really sure of.

"Can you take me to him?" Rocky stands up. His hands go for his cuffs at his belt.

"Just like that you're gonna let me out of here?" I follow Rocky's lead and get up.

"Let's just say I've seen some things and I've got a case that goes back with hauntingly familiar circumstances. What you're saying isn't the first time I've heard it. It's no coincidence the questions I got lead back to that guy."

"You said you weren't going to arrest him."

"I just wanna talk—"

"I'll show you, but you've gotta do something for me in return."

"More favors?"

I hate that phrase. I hate feeling like I owe someone. Worse: I hate actually owing someone, especially a badge. "Tit-for-tat. Your people are good for that, right?"

"What do you want?"

The back of my head's buzzing with a pain and dizziness that wasn't there before. The room spins. I blink a couple of times in an attempt to clear up my vision. I'm certain they've taken my heart away from Jag. "When I show you that all this is legit, you need to call your guys and have them release Jag. Make sure he gets back all the stuff they took from him when they cuffed him."

"House is on speed dial." Rocky's coming at me now. It's just the two of us in the room, though I keep looking at the mirror behind him, sure I'm seeing movement that's not either of us, but no matter how hard I stare, I'm just seeing myself step back in a doomed attempt to evade capture. Rocky looks bigger in here than he ever has outside of this room. Maybe that's because it's his domain and I'm entirely at his mercy, whereas everywhere else we'd run into each other was a neutral ground where Baltimore was the dealer.

My back straightens as I hit the wall. Rocky reaches for me. His hand around my wrist makes me yelp. I press harder into the wall and swing. Rocky catches my fist with ease like he knew it was coming before I knew I was throwing it. I swear at myself, forcing my body to relax as I mutter an apology.

"I need to step out and clear this with my supervisor. For that, you're gonna need to get back on the table,"

Rocky says.

"You didn't have to grab me," I say.

"You didn't have to run." There's no hiding the moving cogs behind Rocky's eyes, gaging just how much he thinks he can trust me, what's the likelihood I'll attack? What's the likelihood I'll run? For once, he doesn't have to worry about any of that because my running would hurt Jag, so that's not an option anymore.

Though, I guess it never really was.

"Sorry. Running's kind of a habit of mine." I return to the table with Rocky. My cigarette's in the ashtray with his. The pile of Styrofoam at my feet's been spread around the room.

Once I'm secured at the table again, Rocky makes for the door. He uses his badge on the security box hanging on the wall. It beeps as he runs it. He stops with his hand on the doorknob. "While I'm getting clearance, I'll see what we can do about your boyfriend's situation. No promises though."

The word sends an anxious chill through me while at the same time. I'm hot, embarrassed, angry at his familiarity. It's not necessarily incorrect unless you want to say we're a little more than that, but I don't want someone like a badge to know how much Jag means to me.

The door opens with a low click. Someone on the other side immediately says, "How's it going in there, Stone?"

"Making progress." Rocky closes the door. His voice keeps going, but the walls are thick enough to turn the conversation into nonsense and it doesn't take long before Rocky's voice disappears. Then, it's just me, the clock, and my reflection. The ticking catches on my pulse and matches the throbbing in my head. Mixed with how wiped I feel, the harsh lights and everything else tonight,

I'm not coming down from the adrenaline. I lay my head on my arms and keep picking it up to knock it into them again. My eyes close. I try to think about what comes next as I wait for Rocky to return.

NINE.

I'm in the backseat of Rocky's cruiser with the cuffs he put on me attached to the passenger seat. He said he trusted me right before slapping them on and giving me a chance to climb in the car myself. When I said it didn't look like he trusted me, he said, "It's gotta be a mutual thing. We'll work on that." He winked; thought he was being charming.

It's dark outside and the streetlights erase most of the stars, turning the sky into a smooth blanket of black and blue. Glimpses of the townhouses mostly look like framed pictures of back lit moments caught in time, silhouettes of people or furniture as snapshots, never coming back. Paint on the ground by a manhole cover reads WRONG WAY. We go by it too fast for me to see where it's pointing. THEY'RE WATCHING is scribbled in black at the top of a stop sign. Rocky mutters to himself about hooligans, sounding the most like an old man that I've ever heard him. The radio he's got hooked up to the station's walkie-talkies is so low, only a bit of the muttering and random clicks from conversations beginning and ending make it back to me. I lean my head against the seat and watch the neighborhood go by as he follows the address I gave him up north.

BAIT's is just north of Leakin Park, so it doesn't take long to get there. We turn into the neighborhood, and something doesn't look right. The car clock says it's after midnight but the parking lot's empty. There's no one hanging outside, not even for a smoke. The lights in the window along the top of the square building are dim, unchanging, and more like low lights left on for safety than for mood. There's no neon glow or candlelight coloring I'd associate with the regular business hours here. The lots also quiet without music bleeding through the walls.

I survey the storefront again as we get closer. "They should be open." I check the trees. Any ravens? They could've shut down because there was some kind of ghost fight like the other night. Maybe something's wrong with Ralph?

Rocky clicks his lips. He grabs his phone, types something in, then puts it back into his pocket. "You know, everything about you is shady as hell. I'd almost wager it looks like an ambush waiting to happen."

I snort. "Do you really think I'm anywhere near that organized?" My lips draw back, nose scrunched in a sneer. I smile in an attempt to push the tension off my face. "Who would I even ambush you with? No one likes me."

"The gang you and Wayland Cross joined?"

"He didn't join anything. Again, he wasn't a bad guy, and you need to stop saying that he was."

"You told me he killed someone."

"It was Baltimore's fault."

"Circumstances don't absolve someone from accountability."

"Except sometimes they do or people would never get off for killing someone else." I lean as far forward as the seatbelt will allow, pressing my forehead to the plastic plate between the front seat and me. My hands tug at the hooked cuffs. The chain clicks against the bar they're attached to. "Do you have my phone?"

"So you can call in the ambush?" Rocky says.

"If you're feeling so threatened, I don't know why you're smiling."

"I just didn't expect you to be *this* obvious."

My lips purse. "And yet you fell for it anyway." That shouldn't have been a growl. He's doing me a favor and I'm doing this for Jag. I need him to believe that ghosts run this city and Ralph's a medium. "Sorry," I mutter. "As you might imagine, I'm stressed." My foot's bouncing again. I'm smelling the cigarettes on myself and it's making me need one. If he can't see Charon, then this is what everything rides on; I don't have any credibility left—if I even had any to begin with. "Look— All I'm gonna do is try calling the bar owner. There's always supposed to be someone here, but maybe something happened. Like I said, the bar he runs is visited by some shady-ass people.

"Now that you say that, I'm forced to recall… Wasn't there a murder here a couple of days ago?" Rocky says.

"More like a bar fight, but yeah. That was caused by a bunch of ghosts." The memory of the night comes back, but mostly the throbbing in my arms and head and chest from where I got stepped on. There's Wayland's voice as they took him down after he tried to protect me. His eyes wide, frightened, hand reaching for mine across the floor because he trusted me, and this is where we were ending. Then the thug crushed my skull in. I let out a heavy breath and lean back to stare at the ceiling like it'll take the guilt away.

"You okay back there?" Rocky says.

"Yeah, yeah. Just… thinking about some stuff." I hate that my voice trembled.

Rocky reaches into his pocket and withdraws my cellphone. He slides it through the slot in the bottom of the plastic screen. He whistles at me, pulling my attention to him. "Don't make me regret this."

I take the phone with a soft, "I can't make promises like that." The closeness of the cuffs makes it hard to do much of anything, but somehow, I manage to scroll to Ralph's messages and hit call. With the phone pressed to my ear, I wait through the ringing until it hits his voicemail. "One sec," I mutter, hang up, and dial again.

Same result.

It's hard to maneuver, but I press the phone against the back of the seat and type a message.

JOEY	I need you.
	Can you pick up the call?
RALPH	Busy.
JOEY	Im sry
	This is really important
	Plz
RALPH	Ur not the only one whose fucked Joey
	Ralph's not home
JOEY	KC?
RALPH	Where r u?
JOEY	At the bar
RALPH	Fuck

I slide the phone back through the plastic slot for Rocky to take. It slips from my hands, bounces off my lap, and lands on the floor.

"Everything alright?" Rocky's peering at me through the plastic.

"I'm not sure. I want to knock on the door."

Rocky sucks in a breath, exasperation, disbelief, a bit of laughter as he pushes his hair back. He licks his lip. "I had a feeling you'd say that. You're real predictable, you know?"

"It's not a trick."

"You say that while doing everything I tell the rookies not to fall for, especially when dealing with a cute, young girl."

"Are you hitting on me right now, Rocky?"

He stares at me for a long while, a face of pursed-lip disappointment on his features. "You'd be surprised by how many of them will break protocol for a chance at a date."

"Well, they say trust is for fools."

"Who says that?"

"I dunno… But I thought I heard it somewhere."

Rocky pushes his door open and comes around my side of the vehicle. Door popped open, he leans in, unhooking one of the cuffs proficiently in the way like he's done it a million times. He slides the loose end from my wrist to one of his.

"What's this?" I look at our wrists, then his face.

"If anything happens to me, it happens to you too."

"Oh, great. Another one?"

"What?"

"Nothing."

Rocky smiles. I climb out of the car. The front light over BAITs' entrance is on, but weak. That's nothing special; it was never strong. It was all the other lights that helped make the bar more inviting. Though considering their side gig, I don't think Ralph and KC were really going for *inviting the regulars.* That's how you end up dead in the corner once a bunch of spooks lose their shit. I survey the parking lot for any cars I might've somehow missed from the back of Rocky's cruiser.

Nothing.

If there's anyone here, they might be parked out back, but that seems unlikely since that's where Ralph and KC park their car. Across the street, the side of the house reads WHAT'S YOUR NAME? in bold, black lettering. Down the road, someone's radio's blasting distorted techno beats or something. The laundromat at the end of the block's washing the sidewalk over with bright light that doesn't feel like it belongs.

"Lead the way." Rocky gestures toward the door.

I give him a nod, take a breath, and approach the bar. I pray to whatever it is that's out there that Ralph will be on the other side. He'll answer quickly, apologize, saying KC was messing with me because he's kind of an asshole and he was distracted or blasted or passed out and that's why he didn't answer the phone and also why business wasn't open like usual. Then I'll say something like *I didn't know you were narcoleptic,* and it won't make any sense, but he'll say *yeah, too much alcohol will do that to you* and laugh.

After the first knock, no one comes to the door. Rocky clears his throat. I chuckle, my throat's tight. "Ralph's kind of different. Give him a chance."

"I'm familiar, Joey," Rocky says. "If I wasn't giving you a chance, we wouldn't be here right now."

I knock again. The sound echoes off the empty lot, met by the coo of a raven somewhere in the trees that clicks like it's knocking back against the door. The noises those things can make are always alarming. I don't go looking for how many birds there are. I don't want to see if there are seven of them, all watching Rocky cause he's tied to me now. I knock a little harder, getting progressively louder and louder each time. Rocky's breath is visible in the night air as he sighs. Disappointed dad is back. But that's what this whole night has been. If Ralph doesn't answer, we're going back to the station to sit in a cell or interrogation until I crack, or they determine they have enough evidence to charge Jag and I with murder while saying I was obstructing. Then for some reason they still think Jag's behind it despite how I'm obviously the crazy one here.

I feel the pull on my wrist as he steps back. "Wait—"

"There's no one here, Joey," Rocky says.

"It just kinda looks that way—But it's not what you think." I lunge for the door with another fist, banging. "Ralph! Open up! I need you! It'll be quick! I swear!" The pounding gets harder. I should be worried about my voice carrying into the dark and drawing in whoever's hiding. I know the neighborhood. The person in the laundromat's standing in the windows, watching this way. The back light's turned them into a silhouette with reflective eyes. Another person comes up behind them. It's not just watching, but there's something aggressive feeling about them.

They're dead. They have to be dead.

I need to get us out of here before we get a repeat of what happened with Wayland. "Ralph! Please—" Throbbing music comes first, then I'm pulled from the door by Rocky stepping away. The gravel driveway crackles under the movement of a car coming in. I turn to see what Rocky's looking at. A black Riviera with tinted windows pulls in, parks without a care for the lines, and KC climbs out. He comes toward me with long, angry steps. He glances briefly at Rocky before coming back to me. His hair's disheveled, face red, body tense. I've never seen him looking so worked up, but his face, his eyes, he looks like he wants to kill me.

"Why the fuck did you bring that piece of shit here?" KC hisses. The heat of his disposition catches me off guard.

"I need to talk to Ralph," I say.

KC looks over at Rocky again and back. His muscles tighten and his expression is holding back what he really wants to say. "How about fuck you, we're busy."

"I just need him to prove something for me. The badge is harmless," I say.

"Oh, is he now?" Crossing his arms, KC snorts.

"Kailee Charleston." Rocky says.

"Kailee *Chuck*." The light from the street catches on KC's face differently. There's a bruise under his eye. The sleeveless black shirt he's wearing reveals a couple more bruises like handprints. His lip's busted and scabbed over. Though his tongue absentmindedly licks the wound.

"Hadn't seen you in a while. Thought you were dead," Rocky says.

"What'd I tell ya before Big Dick?" KC says. "Can't kill *a fuckin' legend*."

"Legend, huh?" Rocky says. "Is that what the kids are calling killing your dad and lighting the house on fire to hide the fraud?"

"Haha. That's a funny way to greet someone," KC says. "You ever find evidence for that?"

"How 'bout your dad goes missing, body shows up a couple years later at the dumping ground, missing a couple bones, all the while his social security checks kept going to your house..." Rocky meets KC's stare.

"Oh, wow. Nothing. So surprising. Fuck you." He slips his hand through his hair, tying it back in his usual tight ponytail. He turns his attention back on me. "Reagan's not here. Can't help you. Come back later."

KC swings his keys around his hand as he turns on his toes, heading back to his car quickly.

"What do you mean he's not here? I need him right now," I say.

"And everythin's not about you. Sorry if this is your first time hearin' it, princess." He pulls his car door open and climbs in.

My heart's pounding. This is my only chance. If KC goes, Ralph goes, and Jag and I are going to be in jail for murder. I know it sounds selfish and I've spent all of my time trying to not be selfish but still end up too worried about what's going on with me. It destroyed Wayland, it's destroying Jag. And if I wasn't stuck to Rocky right now, I might not have noticed just how messed up KC looked. He wasn't just beat; he wasn't just angry; he was panicking. "Did something happen to him?"

KC stops. He's staring at the graffiti across the street that reads WHAT IS YOUR NAME? "There's a damn good reason he never leaves the bar." His fingers curl around his keys. His foot's tapping and it's infectious.

"Let me help. Whatever it is. It's the least I can do," I say.

KC looks straight ahead. His fingers tap the steering wheel. One foot still hanging out of the car, he climbs out and slams the door behind him as he swears under his breath. His lips pull back into a sneer as his tongue flicks his lip. Then, he goes to the bar door and unlocks it. Shoving the door back, he enters, leaving it open is the only invite he gives.

I check with Rocky to see if he's willing, then the two of us enter the bar. KC quickly shuts the door, locking it behind us. The bar's recovered from the fight that happened a couple days ago. No broken chairs or tables or glass forgotten against the wall. All that's left from the brawl are a few chipped spots in the floor.

KC walks past Rocky and me, returning to the bar where he pulls himself over the top of the counter and reaches for a specific kind of whiskey on the shelf.

"Those the same as your old footwear?" Rocky says.

KC looks down. "Why change a work of art?" I can't see them now, but he's always worn the same set of black, scaled leather boots with metal plating on the tip. It didn't matter that he normally wore torn jeans and band tees. Somehow, it all worked together.

"What do you do for work nowadays?" Rocky says

"Starting this already, are we?" KC eyes me. He uncaps the whiskey in his hand. "Can't you tell? I'm a businessman now. Those perception skills of yours are getting rusty."

"Didn't see you here last week when I swung by," Rocky says.

"I'm a busy guy." He presses the bottle to his lips.

"I don't think that's up to code," Rocky says.

"You gonna do something about it, *Big Dick*?" KC growls.

The bar helped cool some of the tension I felt standing on the porch. Something to do with the charm's Ralph's got all around this place, but it feels different without him here. Weaker, restless, less welcoming. I don't know. There's no one in the bar but KC, Rocky, and I, but there's so much anger pulsing through my legs and into me, it's a storm of emotion so strong I want to embrace it and unleash on everything.

I touch my ass pocket looking for the cigarettes I still don't have. KC sets his bottle down on the edge of the counter while looking at me, seeming to catch me saying something I didn't put into words. He grabs an icy glass from under the counter and says, "You do cider, yeah?"

"If you've got it," I say.

"We're here for work, Josephine," Rocky says.

"It's *Joey*." I move toward the bar.

Rocky doesn't relent. His size compared to mine keeps me from going anywhere. A fight would only result in the cuffs cutting further into my already beat wrists. I turn to face him. "We're gathering intel, Rocky. Isn't this part of your job?"

"Cider isn't intel," Rocky says.

"Address it to the dead thing. I feel like I'm gonna lose my shit if I don't find some way to cool off," I say.

"Welcome to the club," KC says with his lips against the bottle. He takes another swig while leaning against the bar. My glass of cider is sitting in front of him now.

"Ralph's really not here?" I say.

"You can feel it, can't you? A *Terra Santas* without its *savant*," KC says.

"Why the hell is someone always missing in this dumb city?"

"Curse of Bodymore." KC chuckles bitterly. "You take the good with the bad."

"I hope it's not because everybody here's already dead." I try for the bar again. The pull's too hard and Rocky doesn't move. I hiss as the cuffs dig into my skin. I turn to him, try stepping backward this time while I look him in the face. He wouldn't legitimately fight me, right? Stepping back doesn't help convince him to move. I sigh, turn back to the bar, and eye the glass waiting for me on the counter.

"So, what happened?"

KC takes a shot of whiskey. "I don't know." The bottom of the bottle slams into the bar. A bit of cider from the overfilled glass splashes down its side. "I was out on errands. When I got back, he was gone. I went out looking for him, but all I found was trouble. I got a feeling I know who it is, but no one'll say a damn thing. Baltimore's always had it out for him, you know?" His eyes flicker to Rocky. "Different kinda fuckers lookin' for different kinds of gigs. There's a bastard out there been tryin' to get him for ten years now. Can't come in the bar, though. If it's him, my guess is he used some asshole to drag Reagan out or tricked him with somethin' else. Reagan's got no way to fight back when force is used against him."

"What do you mean?" I say. "Whose been coming after him for ten years?"

"*You don't summon the devil by chance.*" Bottle to his lips, KC's eyeing Rocky. His finger taps on the counter. KC glares at me over the top of his bottle, then Rocky, then me again. "That's what he told me when this shit started. He doesn't got a choice in *what* seeks him out. That's all I'm gonna say." There's a slight rock to his shoulders, exposing his restlessness as he shifts from side to side. He reaches for something in his pocket, but stops halfway and his hand comes back to the counter empty. "Now, you need to answer me something before I kick your ass back to the curb." He nods to Rocky, though his stare remains on me. "What's the deal with your new charm bracelet?"

My skin prickles. Heat rushes to my face. I close my eyes and all the helplessness of the last few weeks weighs on me. All I can think of is every bad decision I've made and how it's hurt everyone I gave even the smallest damn about and the pain I caused without ever noticing what I was doing. I rub my arms, hoping to heat the chilled skin. My jaw's hard to work. "The badges took Jag in for murder."

"Really?" KC taps the counter beside his bottle. "He didn't seem like the type." His eyes are locked on me. He's not like Ralph. The irises aren't glowing, he can't see through me or invade my thoughts, but rather than penetrating my mind, it feels like he's squeezing the information out of me because of how much I need his help.

"Jag's not. He didn't do anything but… a ghost did and left some stuff at his place."

"How'd a ghost get into your boyfriend's place?" There's a smartass grin in KC's voice.

My jaw clenches. I don't know how, but it feels like he knows everything about Jag's apartment already. Maybe Ralph told him. Maybe he picked it out of Ralph's brain because they share a connection. It doesn't really matter. Even he knows how stupid I was. Why couldn't I see it back then?

"I brought him there," the words hurt coming out.

"Ah." KC taps the bottom of his bottle on the counter. "Your other buddy?"

"Yeah." I try not to look at Rocky. The more I see his face, the changing expression, the judgment and disbelief and calculation, the more I want to fight him because I know this isn't working. "So, Jag's in trouble and it's kind of my fault because I did some really stupid shit a week ago—"

KC hums with amusement. "Been there."

"What kind of stuff'd you do?" Rocky says.

KC shakes his head, ticking his tongue. "Ah, ah, Big Dick." KC hisses into the bottle. "I'm not the same guy I was the last time ya saw me. Might help ya to keep that in mind." His posture's sagging, but his arms are tight. His tongue slides against the cut in his lip again. He teases that with the tip of the bottle before helping himself to another sip of cope.

Ralph's done the same thing, though he's never hostile when he's blasted. The bottles all over his office and the pot and the way he slurs aren't about pain, but like he's carrying a deep sorrow that I don't think I can understand. He saw into me, but still smiled and felt warm without the pity or anger or desire to pull away that's common when people find out how busted up you really are. Despite how often people say they care, you really find out how much of it's a lie when you show someone the wounds you carry. They think they understand because they were disappointed once, but I've learned that those who brag about charity are usually the least charitable.

"I run a business now," KC says. "Everything's above the board, so your questions can find somewhere else to be."

"Good to hear," Rocky says. "But you really don't need to be so defensive. I'm just a friendly inquisitor."

"I've heard that line before. Next thing ya know you're chained to a table with your asshole stickin' out and a spear going inside while some guy yells at you in Latin to recite John 3:16." KC pushes off the counter with a groan. His legs overcompensate for steadiness. They go stiff and he grabs onto the alcohol shelf on the back side of the bar to keep him up. He puts the whiskey he was drinking under the counter and comes around to the front of the bar. "Joey, I got a lotta shit to do and not a lot of patience. Can you get to the point of why you brought this piece of shit to my bar?"

"I've been trying to explain the ghost thing to him, but he doesn't remember anything and he couldn't see Charon when I called him. I was hoping Ralph could've proved to him I wasn't full of shit," I say.

"Yeah? Well, too bad. Even if Reagan was here, what the hell do you think he could say to convince your buddy? Answer: Not a damn thing," He sneers at Rocky again. His head turned down, his fingers flick, hungry for something he resists reaching for again by putting his hands in his pockets. "So, good luck in prison."

"You guys have some kind of history or something?"

I say.

"We got somethin' alright," KC mutters.

"Ralph could be considered a missing person at this point, right?" Rocky says. "Maybe I can help you with that."

KC's lip draws back. His head drops to the side as an irritated chuckle drops out. "Don't you have something better to do than snoop around *a burnout's* trashy bar?"

"I've never heard of someone who didn't want help when it was offered—"

"You've never understood how much of a liability it is talking to someone like you in any capacity," KC says.

"How do you know someone took him?" Rocky says say.

"Because he's not fuckin' here," KC says.

"Who would take him?" This time when I walk, Rocky follows behind me. We stop a couple feet in front of KC.

KC brushes some loose hair behind his ear. His fingers bare chipped paint, reddish, almost black, not unlike what Ralph had on the last time I saw him. KC gives Rocky a hard, dismissive glance before coming back to me. "Where do I start? It feels like everyone in this goddamn city wants a piece of him. You've seen it too, haven't ya, Big Dick? The bar is pretty much the only place in town where the powers out there can't touch him."

"Why's that?"

KC sits down, leaning against the bar. His legs splay. He brings his thumb to his lip to chew on the nail while staring at the end of the bar leading somewhere else.

Not the bar.

His foot starts tapping. His nose crinkles at the bridge. "Ralph decked this place out for a lot of things. He never leaves the bar because the shit he's runnin' against the wall ain't just for decorations. Everythin' surroundin' this place's either meant to put the dead at ease or keep them the hell offa him. He's got a lotta shit they want, ya know? Get him outside of these walls and he's still just a person. Straddled with extra abilities sure, but human. The dead, Cogs, and whatever else can do with him what they please and they have. He… He gave up everything to help me. Then, he started helping others. He's just that kinda guy. People sense it; the dead know it, the supernatural *pursue* it. They take advantage of him. Always have." A certain kind of sadness shades his eyes as they meet mine. The harsh, overhead light makes his face look inflamed around the bruise in his eye.

KC shifts to reach his back pocket. This time, he doesn't stop himself. His hand comes back holding a small, square tin with a playing card on the front: a man holding a sunflower and a bag stands on a cliff with the sun overhead. The phrase THE FOOL is embossed at the bottom. KC flips the tin open. Inside are a couple of hand-rolled joints and cigarettes. KC reaches for a cigarette. "Ya mind, Big Dick?" He eyes Rocky.

Rocky shrugs. "It's your bar."

KC reaches into his hip pocket. Fishing out a lighter, he pinches the cigarette between his lips and lights up. A deep breath, an exhale, his shoulders sink a bit. His eyes half shut; he goes for another hit. The stress he's holding isn't going anywhere. At least, whatever stress I'm feeling. Maybe it's not his.

"Point bein' there are creatures out there that don't give a shit about his wellbeing. He's just a tool to get whatever the fuck they're after. If I don't find him…" KC glances momentarily at Rocky. "They'll break him and take him. No one wants to see what the fuck happens if that goes down, but I been runnin' around for hours and ain't getting' any closer to findin' him."

"Can't you just, like, feel him or something? Jag found me the other day by a feeling," I say.

"Yeah, no." KC takes a hit from his joint. "All the fancy jewelry he wears ain't just for show. Some of it dampens the empathetic side effect of sharing his body. Most of it came out of a lotta real uncomfortable trial and error. Shit I felt he really didn't need to be feelin'." He snorts. "He can't stop everything though."

"What all can he actually do?" I say.

"Hell if I know." KC exhales. "We might be connected, but I still don't get to see the shit he sees on the other side. I don't know where he goes or who he talks to or anything about what a séance actually entails. All I know is there's shit out there that goes way beyond the Cogs and Servies. It's something I'll never see because I'm not good enough. None of us are." KC pinches his cigarette between his lips.

With his hands free, he looks down at them hanging loosely in his lap. Under the scabs and bruises from street fights are a couple of straight-lined scars, deliberately made to bleed. The discoloration under his nails makes me think of the grime of Baltimore and the sins that clung to Wayland. He closes his hands into tight fists. "I've told him so many goddamn times. They'll take advantage of you as long as ya let them." KC licks his lips. "But Reagan… He's so fuckin' desperate, always has been… He sees value in garbage, thinkin' he can rehabilitate anyone if he just listens to what they need. Tryin' to make shit up for what he never had, thinkin' findin' them a home will bring him one some day. *From filth to filth*—he doesn't get it. That shit only works if ya value somethin' outside of yourself. Most don't and this city rewards it." KC's eyes are trained on Rocky with the focus of a predator anticipating tearing out the throat of its prey. "It's hard on him for a lotta reasons, ya know? Baltimore craves grief. Feels like it's deliberately creatin' it sometimes *just to feed*. Reagan's been tryin' to stop the bleedin' for a while, but he's outnumbered by just how many relish in the destruction."

"I'll help you find him," Rocky says.

KC brings his cigarette to his lips. "*You?*"

"Don't you work in homicide?" I say.

"All things considered, this could end up landing on my desk in a few weeks anyway—pending on how long it takes," Rocky says.

"Don't even joke about that." Smoke carries on KC's words. He stands up so fast, his chair squeaks.

Rocky lifts his hand to say he didn't mean to offend. "Not trying to be pessimistic. I've just been working this beat long enough, I know the general timeline of things." He grabs the keys from his hip and puts them into the cuff on my wrist. His cuff goes next. I rub the raw skin now stinging in the cool bar air. My fingers feel like ice against the heat of the fresh burn.

"You're letting me go?" I say.

"If we're going to work together on this, there's gotta be a little trust, right?" Rocky looks sidelong at me. He hooks his cuffs back on his belt.

"So, you trust me?" I say.

"I don't know if I'd go that far." Rocky briefly looks at KC. "But I got some questions I don't think can be answered any other way. Don't make me regret this."

Rocky is the strangest thing I've ever seen in a badge. Every word that's ever come out of his mouth has been too sincere. His face has always been too friendly. The way he talks is more like he's a normal person than someone trying to control you with the authority given to him by some rando in human resources. He has every reason to call me crazy, drag me back to jail, and build a case against me with whatever evidence he's scraped together. The confidence he has in me is unearned. For every time he's trusted me, I've run away. There's never been pity in his eyes like *you poor bastard.* The dark circles are sleepless nights, maybe from the mysteries of Baltimore that he could never solve since there is no logical explanation to them.

"If at the end of this, there are no ghosts or mediums or walking dead, we're gonna have to have you evaluated for competency," Rocky says.

"I don't know what that means, but if it's a test, I'll probably fail." I wink.

"I figured." Rocky turns his attention to KC. "You want help finding Ralph or not?"

KC's putting his cigarette out in the ashtray on the counter. He slides his tin from his pocket and puts the remainder of it inside. Standing, he sucks in a breath through his teeth. Again, he glances toward the door at the back of the bar then me. He returns to the bar for the whiskey he left under the counter and throws back a shot. Maybe it stung or maybe he's trying to smile, but it comes off as a sneer either way. "If you think you find anything incriminating, forget about it."

"Got it," Rocky says.

KC pauses halfway to Rocky, halfway to the back of the room. He takes a slow step back, points to me and the cider on the counter, then lifts his hand. With a casual wave, he says, "Follow me," and leads us toward the door to the right of the counter.

TEN.

Ralph and KC live in a unit attached to the back of the bar. Stepping through the entrance doesn't feel right. It doesn't look how I expected it to look, but I also couldn't tell you what I expected. Black, shag carpet, dark purple walls, feathers and bones hang all over the place. The lights are kept low, the windows covered with thick curtains and boards that don't let any light in. Candles, matches, and bottles sit on every visible surface, some on the floor. Paper and books wrapped in leather are on the bookshelf mixed with music books, the coffee table, the couch, the kitchen counter. At least three more raven skulls are spread around the room. A dream catcher hangs in the corner, and symbols written in what looks like black paint are drawn on the walls. My heart's throbbing in my ears the moment we go through the home's threshold. There's a heaviness in my body that wasn't there before, making it hard to get my feet off the ground. A single bed's behind a wall that separates it from the living space. There's no door or door frame. It's messy, blankets and sheets askew, half hanging off the mattress in a puddle on the floor while pillows are haphazardly folded or sitting where a person used to be. There's a drum kit and a couple of guitars in one corner behind the couch.

The place smells of pot, cinnamon, alcohol, microwaved meals, and sulfur.

"You really leaned into that whole *occult thing*, huh?" Rocky slows his pace as he steps into the living area. He glances around the room. A half wall without a door divides the sleeping area from the living room, but the apartment is a one-room studio otherwise with the kitchen separated from the rest only by carpet versus tile.

"If you'd seen what I've seen, you might too." KC slips into the kitchen, setting the bottle he's carrying on the counter. Immediately, he's at the fridge taking something out of the freezer. "Reagan's kinda fanatical though. Get him started on something, and he goes in hard."

Rocky reaches into his pocket, drawing out his notebook and pen as he steps forward. A hanging bird skull taps him on the shoulder. He backs away, putting some space between it and him. "You got any human remains laying around here?"

"Discover one to find out." KC leans against the kitchen counter, a new bottle in his hand.

Rocky writes something down. He steps further into the room, crossing into the side where the bed is. There are two doors against the back wall on that side. One leads to what looks like a walk-in closet and the other to a bathroom. Rocky returns to the living room. "This is where he went missing?"

"I think they took him out back." KC points to a

long, black door with a black rose hanging upside down on it near the center where a peephole might've been. An unopened cardboard box sits by the door. There's a dent in the side like someone kicked it. Ralph's name is on the label.

Rocky nods in acknowledgment but doesn't make a move for the door. He turns back to the wall he's standing near and scans the symbols drawn on it. They appear as a mixture of runic symbols not unlike what was written around the Orianda House on the other side of the River Styx where Charon said judgment was handed out. In between those shapes are swirls and dots, slashes and stars not dissimilar to the shapes going up and down Ralph's arms. "What do all these symbols mean?"

"Are you here to pick up decorating tips or look for a missing person?" KC says.

"Alright…" Rocky turns back toward the room. I grab the front door handle. The knob jiggles, locked. There's also a chain on the upper part of the wall, something made of smooth materials, maybe leather, a cross, a couple of beads.

"You really go all out when you decorate, huh?" I say.

"Clearly not enough," KC says.

"Everything in here's got some kind of magic to it?" I say.

"If it looks weird, probably," KC says.

I pick up one of the notebooks from the coffee table. Obscure, handwritten markings decorate the front. Inside, the lettering's the same as Ralph's tattoos and the symbols on the wall and random graffiti phrases you can find around town. Mixed into the chaos on one page are some English phrases written sloppily with a question mark.

Nash. Durand. 10. Chapel Valley.

"Who's *Benjamin Church*?"

"I dunno." KC shrugs. "He goes into trances sometimes and before he *comes back to himself*, he'll just obsessively write shit. All his books over there are like that." KC gestures to a shelf overflowing with different sized notebooks stacked on top of each other. Among the shelves are a couple music or cult books, but mostly it's notebooks. "Looks like a purge."

"Does it ever mean anything?" I flip through the rest of the notebook. None of it makes any more sense than the first page. If anything, it looks more like the spray of a scattered brain that's spilled out.

KC pops the cap off the whiskey he's holding, though he doesn't drink it yet. "At first, he really didn't say much about anything he goes through, but finally, he said the language in there'll drive a mortal crazy to be read verbatim. Something about it messes you up if you're not one of *them*."

"What do you mean *them*? What are *they*?" I say.

"Hell if I know. I think they're too fucked to be *angelic* for what they've put Reagan through. He had no idea what he was signing up for, but they were happy to take advantage of his ignorant desperation when offering him *the gift*." KC goes for a drink, but stops. His eyes are distant.

"What is he?"

KC's fingers curl harder around the bottle. "Didn't the reaper tell you? He's a *Medium*." His sharp eyes turn onto me. He sips the whiskey. "Fuck if I know what that means but the toll's not kind, ya know? He locks himself away and can get stuck in this shit for days. Shit tears him apart. He can't fight, can't leave the bar. Inside and outside of this goddamn city, there are things waiting to cop a feel of whatever he's become. For what ends? I don't fuckin' know. He can't get out of it though. He made the deal; he *belongs* to them, so when *they* call, he answers, and he makes shit for people when he feels it."

"They… being the Cogs?"

"Or whatever's above them. I get the feeling the Cogs are just the beginning. What else is there? I don't know."

"How do you know he's not with *whatever* right now?"

"Because *the door's* unlocked." KC shrugs more irritated than passive. "You think I wouldn't check that first?" He takes another sip of whiskey. His nose scrunches like the taste got to him. He caps the bottle and puts it back in the counter, trading it for a bottle of water from the fridge. He snaps the cap off as he returns to the counter. Half of it's gone, fast. "Everything over there sounds like bullshit because it is. They'll say we don't get it, can't see *the whole picture*, but then refuse to elaborate on why the picture's even so damn important."

Something sounds like a growl. KC slaps the bottle down on the counter with a crunch and says, "Don't fuckin' touch that!" He runs across the room to where Rocky's standing in front of a large, flat door. Dark paper that looks like water wraps around its edges.

Next to the door is a short end table, with a couple of drawers, more of Ralph's notebooks, and a single, short white candlestick in a glassy silver tray. Weirder than the candle itself is the flame. It's white, almost blue—the same color as Ralph and Charon's eyes. There's no wax melting down the sides, and carved into it are symbols that match the ones on the walls and probably Ralph's arms. The flame flickers in a way that says it's not fake fire.

KC steps in front of Rocky. Without resistance, Rocky takes a step back. "This where you keep the bodies?"

"Oh yeah, of course." KC elbows Rocky. "It's for séances, dumbass, and you don't belong in there."

"Sounds delicate," Rocky says.

"It is." KC remains still, in front of the door. He's not touching it and his back curls away from the wall, but he keeps himself between Rocky and the door, even taking steps forward now that he's between them, urging Rocky to step back. Rocky doesn't move until KC's so close; he's stepping on Rocky's shoes and though he relents, he keeps his eyes on the séance room. It's not the same way I was drawn and stuck, but with the curiosity of a skeptical badge.

"You two have become quite the pair over the years," Rocky says.

"Yeah? Five seconds in my door and you've got a whole read on our situation?" The area under KC's eyes is getting redder. "Go ahead, Big Dick. Enlighten me. Tell me what you think you know." His hands are fists.

"Probably better to back off on this one, Rocky," I say.

"I'm not here to make any arrests," Rocky says.

"That's what every pig says to get in the door," KC says.

"I'm not making accusations either," Rocky says.

KC shakes his head. "There's too much on the line. Ya need to focus on what ya said you came here to do or get out. You're not a guest."

Rocky turns away from the door. His next focus is the sleeping area. The tables beside the bed are cluttered like everything else in the room. A half empty bottle of Jack sits on the floor in front of the nightstand with a bit of a stain showing in the matted, but dried carpet. Underneath the black lamp with a tattered shade are two orange pill bottles. Rocky picks up one bottle, examining the label and the small, white tablets inside. "Phenothiazine? Your guy on anti-psychotics, Kailee?" Rocky goes for the second bottle, looking over the label of that one too. "I hate to see this is what's happened to him."

"Shut the fuck up." KC meets Rocky in the bedroom to snatch the bottles away from Rocky. "Touch something like this again and we'll find out how far up your ass my foot can go." KC takes the bottles to the bathroom just off to the side of the bedroom.

"Knock it off, Rocky," I hiss. "I actually don't need my relationship with these guys messed up, especially not cause I dared to trust *you*."

Rocky's writing something on his notepad. "I'm not trying to say I don't believe you, but I know these guys and shit's not looking great around here, Joey. If Kailee didn't lose it and chuck the body somewhere, a gang probably targeted him. That kid's always been messed up, in and out of the hospital for thirty years."

"I *know* what it looks like, but that's the problem. You think it's a normal situation. It's not. There's so much the living refuse to see because no one wants to admit they aren't in control." My voice breaks into a laugh. I shake my head to knock it off. "No one wants to believe it, but we live in Hell." My shirt's sticking to my skin again. "Just ignore your intuition for a bit and keep looking. It'll make sense or it won't, I guess, but you have to keep looking."

Rocky's staring me in the face again. Lips pursed. He writes without shifting. "For the record, you *are* coming off as insane."

"I figured." I turn away. "But I'm hoping that means we're one step closer to you figuring this out, yeah?" I pluck my shirt away from my skin.

Going back to the living room, I head for the front door. I open it. The cool fall air instantly freezes against my wet skin. I step outside. Just as I'm closing the door, Rocky comes through it, stepping carefully onto the gravel path. There's a little bit of light from an overhead lamp beside the door. What used to be windows on the outside are boarded up from the inside. The glass is jagged and busted out. KC comes to the door without stepping outside.

Rocky watches the ground carefully as he moves. First, he approaches the window to the left of the door. Glass isn't just in the gravel, but tucked inside the busted windowsill. The wooden planks are thick with more symbols written across them. Scratch marks like hands dig into them, dragging across the wood texture. There's discoloration from blood, maybe knuckles hitting too hard too many times. There are cracks in the wood where it was punched, but didn't break even though it should've.

"Looks like the neighborhood's gotten rougher." Rocky gestures to the window he's standing by. "Or they always been like this?"

KC shakes his head. "The boards've been up for a while for obvious reasons. We like to keep the house dark and secure, you know? Windows make it easier for nightmares to slip in." KC leans forward a little bit. His head passes through the door's threshold. The gravel crunches under his step as he comes up alongside Rocky. "The glass didn't used to be broken, though. But it was when I got back yesterday, and Reagan was gone."

"You notice any other property damage?" Rocky takes his flashlight out to examine the window. He points the beam into the window frame and passes around the edges slowly. I'm at a different window, phone in hand, light pointed at the frame. A couple smears of red and brown fingerprints crowd the broken glass and leave trails against the shattered pieces. The wood plank on my side reads HE WILL HAVE U and CANT HIDE FOREVER and DEVIL.

A sound in the distance is like a bird choking, then a

caw, broken into breathy segments that sound like crying. Grass or leaves crunch with movement somewhere in the same direction.

"There are some tire tracks over there too. They slashed shit up on the Riviera. Tried to bust the windows in, dented the door instead." KC points across the gravel driveway. The back of BAIT's is surrounded by a small, wooded area that separates it from the rest of the neighborhood of tightly placed townhouses, strip malls, pawnshops, and discount grocery stores. The trees almost give a feeling like the place is hidden and without light beyond the front step, it also makes the black Riviera blend into the trees. "There's some wood on the ground over there. Not sure if it was a snapped branch or a bat. There were some prints by the car before too, but they're gone now."

Rocky walks across the parking area. The light from the house porch doesn't light the gravel more than two feet away from the door. Rocky's Mag-Lite does most of the work and overpowers what little illumination my phone had been offering.

"All those markings inside, they don't really… come out here even a little bit?" I say.

KC shakes his head. Arms crossed, his fingers tighten around his bicep. "From what he told me, *Terra Santas* works for a specific place with a specific boundary line. Think of a holy location. I mean, you can try to put a blessing on something limitless, but the bigger the pond, the thinner the spread until it doesn't work at all anymore. Shit like this costs life. Doing up the house right takes a lot without him trying to bless the whole damn neighborhood." KC sighs. "It sounds oddly specific, but that's because everything with the dead's an *anally retentive definition*. Specifics are required and if you fall out of that in any small way? Fuck you. Rituals are like that. One of the reasons they don't like to communicate with humans is because we don't play by the same rules. They don't understand it; we don't understand them. It's best to just stay away from each other as much as we can."

"How does that work with Ralph? He's human too." I go back to where KC's standing.

"Technically, yeah, he is, but he's got two minds now. I don't totally know how it all works though. Like I said, he doesn't tell me much, so all I can do is notice." KC looks at the sky. The clouds are too thick and the light from the street's too overpowering to see anything overhead, no matter how dark this back area is. The moon's hiding behind a couple of clouds, making the area darker than it needs to be. Another caw echoes from the leaves, broken, distorted, turning into a sob. The leaves crunch on the other side of the car. KC's head turns sharply. His muscles tense. My legs burn with a building need to run. I stumble back, catch a glimpse of Rocky's shoulder on the other side of the Riviera, and push my heel deeper into the soft ground.

Every car, radio, crackling step Rocky takes is amplified. It feels like I'm hearing his breath even. Twigs snap like bones breaking mercilessly. The smell of sulfur slips into my nose with the light smell of rain something too familiar and morose. Someone's hiding in the dark.

"Two minds… Is that what he meant when he said he translates shit?" I nip at my nails.

"Yeah, sometimes."

"What's it all for?"

"I dunno." KC grunts. His foot kicks at the gravel and his lip draws back. "From the shit I've seen, I wonder if anyone's worth the grace Reagan's dollin' out. Most of us'll plow through others in our chase for impossibilities. Buryin' a body ain't shit in the grand scheme of things, right *Big Dick*?" KC raises his voice just a little.

Rocky turns back to us from where he's standing at the Riviera. "A lotta people would agree with you, yeah. Most of the murder I see on my desk is over something stupid. Cold fries, bumped into someone, honked at a traffic light. Often they don't do anything, but wrong place, wrong time and suddenly they got the guilt of every bad thing that's happened to someone. That's when it's not gang-related, anyway."

"That's really it?" I say. "Because for the last couple of weeks I've been tailed by the dead. Wayland aside, all I can think about is this big guy I saw in Hell the first time I was down there. He jumped in the river while we were crossing and then he found me again top side and killed me for no reason."

KC chuckles. "Sounds about right. You're being haunted." He reaches for his tin of hand-rolled cigarettes and lights up. "Last night, there was some guy here talkin' about how fresh thirteen-year-old pussy is. Came back to kill her and her dad after her dad shot him. Two nights ago it was a sixteen-year-old who sold ice cream to this banger and it melted on his fingers. She's dead; he was laughin' about it." KC takes a puff. "There are some people who don't deserve kindness. Too far gone, they don't give a shit. Reagan ain't given it up yet that most people ain't worth his sacrifice. He can keep tryin' but there are people who ain't turning back. You can't help anyone that don't want it and believe me, there are people who don't want to come back to humanity. Fuck, there are even people who trade it in for something more—"

"Speaking," Rocky's voice comes across the driveway, loud, strong, and commanding. Not like he's talking to us or a criminal, but a subordinate. A raven chuckles. The leaves rattle with someone making a run for it. Definitely a person, but at least they're retreating. "Shit. Any casualties? Alright. I'm on my way." Rocky's coming back toward us, slipping his cellphone into his pocket. "Sorry, but we're gonna have to cut this short." Rocky unclips his cuffs from his belt. Jaw tight, hands tighter, without giving me time to react, he slaps one cuff around my wrist. The pull he gives is not enough to do anything but push the metal deeper into the bruise I've already got.

"We can't just abandon this, Rocky—" I say.

"We're not abandoning this. Rain check it." Rocky gives KC a nod, something that says, *I'm not taking you, don't worry.* "If you need someone to look into this sooner, call the department as soon as I leave. Get the forms filed. They'll assign it to someone as soon as they can."

KC rolls his eyes, hissing.

"Can I go through here to get to the front?" Rocky gestures toward the apartment door KC's blocking.

KC steps aside with a growl. Rocky's dragging me forward with the cuffs and even a little bit of resistance hurts more than I'm expecting. A burn, a sting, sometimes a jolt of pain that goes up to my elbow. KC slams the door once we're inside. The lock clatters. "Well, ain't that a kick in the dick? Thanks for stoppin' by. Guess we'll get together again in another ten years, yeah?" KC swipes something off the nearby shelf. Glass shatters on the floor. He curses under his breath.

"Look, I'm sorry something happened to Ralph," Rocky says. "Happens a lot in this town and to be honest, I'm surprised it took this long for him to disappear—"

"Unbelievable—"

"But something's happening at the station and it's not

anything I can ignore."

"*Justice?*" KC says.

"Some might call it that," Rocky says. "Someone came in, trashed the place, and…" He looks at me. "Ran off with Jagger Locke."

"What the fuck, Rocky!" I lunge at Rocky with my hands out. Turning around, he catches them steadily. My attempt to shove is nothing against the strength he has or the pull of the cuffs or the way he grabs my freehand and uses it to swing me against the door and pull both my arms behind my back. Still, tears gather in my eyes. I grunt, pressing into the wall to try and escape him. He shoves me harder to hold me steady. "You were supposed to keep him safe!"

"I have just as much reason to be suspicious of you," Rocky says. "Everything you've told me since your arrest has been nothing short of a delusional break and now it's crossed gang lines? You're getting your info from a doped-up orphan and hoping his murder suspect buddy will tell you how to fix death."

"Oh my god, Big Dick! It's been ten years! If you've got nothin', ya need to let it go," KC says.

Rocky pulls. This time, I fight to stay as the cuffs cut into my skin. He could pull me over if he tried, but he doesn't. Instead, he puts his hands on my shoulders and tightens his grip. "Understandably most people who go through this have some kind of psychotic break." Rocky looks me in the eyes. "You're taking it as well as anyone in your position could expect, but you're trusting the wrong people and you're not seeing clearly. We need to get you the right kind of help so you can process what's actually happening around you."

KC's laughter is hysterical and angry. "Goddamn fuckin amazing, eh?!" He grabs the plastic bottle off the counter and chucks it. The crinkle of plastic is light. The glass bottle of whiskey he brought from the bar is next in the air. It shatters against the wall by the door. KC's buzz is getting into me and feels more powerful than whatever he was wired with when I first came in. The voice in my head's back, louder than the soft murder of before, telling me to crack Rocky's skull in. I close my eyes, but the image of his corpse in my hands haunts me no matter where I look and it satiates my building anger with a tease of ecstasy. I'm panting, alternating eyes closed and open and all I can think of is how I want to make his heart match mine by ripping it out of his chest and chucking it at the ravens waiting in the trees outside.

"You just don't goddamn get it!" KC throws something else, metal this time. It bounces off the wall and rattles on the floor. "You think everything is so simple 'n straightforward, you can just see it all!"

Rocky quickly clips my handcuff around the door handle leading back to the bar. Then, reaching for his hip, he turns to KC and slowly approaches, putting some space between him and I. "Were you behind the attack on the station?" he says.

KC's nose twitches. Disgust. He holds back the laughter this time. The tension makes his head shake. "No, you dense motherfucker. But if the dead broke into your place and took her boyfriend, then she's being haunted. They won't stop until they get her and everywhere she's been is gonna be a target. You understand that?" KC keeps planted firmly where he is, though his heel bounces.

"The dead?" Rocky repeats. "Is that a new gang? I've never heard of them. What kind of trouble is she in that they'd be *hunting* someone like her?"

"Check your hearing, pig," KC says. "I said *haunted*, as in, by ghosts."

"Are you kidding?" I say. "Does this come back to

the first decision I made to go looking for Wayland? And now Jag and Ralph are in this because he got involved even when he saw the warnings signs?" My eyes water. I can't breathe.

"Don't think yourself so special," KC says. "This city's been huntin' Reagan since the day he was born. You just gave it another opportunity to strike."

I wipe my face with my free hand. My back falls into the door and it becomes the only thing keeping me on my feet. "I don't understand—Why does he do this, then?"

"Sometimes people are worth more than the trouble they bring," KC says. "I haven't ever been easy on Reagan either." He looks across the room, his eyes tracing the symbols and skeletons and charms hanging from the ceiling. Everything in this place is either an ode to the lifetime of their friendship or something put in place to protect them. There's a hole in the wall closer to the bed. One of the guitars on the wall has a cracked neck and a dent in the body. "I put him through so much shit, it's hard to understand why he even bothered with me… Ya know the kind of situation he had to be in that somehow lookin' at me gave him hope?" KC chuckles bitterly. His eyes fall to the shattered glass on the floor from the bottle he threw. "People ain't the same when they love ya. He sacrificed his freedom to bring me back and carries my burdens. He saw everythin' about me and the shit I thought about him and still…" KC sneers, shaking his head, he wipes hard at his cheek and forces out a bitter laugh. "Most people won't do this. Won't even do the bare minimum for someone else. But Reagan? He gave me everything I didn't know I needed. I'd do anything for him. It's the least he should get after everythin'." KC glances past Rocky to me. His stare's reading me, but not in the same way Ralph's could. He blinks a couple of times. The stress drops a bit from his posture. He turns back to Rocky. "Lemme come to the station with ya."

"Excuse me?" Rocky says.

"Why would you want to go?" I say

"If it's a ghost, I got a decade under my belt dealin' with this shit," KC says.

"What makes you think I'd trust you anywhere near a crime scene?" Rocky says.

"You said you felt bad for how Reagan ended up. You think I killed him. I'll prove I'm not full of shit if you do the same." KC crosses the apartment until he's standing just before Rocky, meeting his gaze. "Trust me, sugar tits. I'm an absolute golden boy." KC pats Rocky on the arm.

Rocky takes a breath. Sighs. "Alright. But give me a reason to arrest, and I will."

"Party." KC grabs his leather jacket off the back of a barstool at the kitchen counter. Slipping past me, he pulls the door open that I'm stuck to. He steps out of the house, going backwards into the bar.

Rocky watches KC exit the apartment then looks at me. I don't have anything to say, so whatever questions he's got in his eyes, I can't answer. It's okay. Doesn't seem like Rocky knows what to ask either. He approaches me and uses the keys to take the cuffs off the door. He slaps the loose end around his wrist, probably not trusting me more because he doesn't trust KC, which, okay, I get it. I'm not sure I trust what KC's doing anymore either and if he asked, I don't know if I could lie convincingly enough.

KC's waiting for us at the door, his arms looped with his hands in his pockets. "After you," Rocky says with a gesture. KC complies. He pulls the door open and steps out ahead of us. Once Rocky and I are out, he locks the door.

Rocky leads me to the car and puts me in the back just as he had before. "You're riding with her," he says to KC over his shoulder.

"Fine by me." KC goes around the backside of the cruiser. "I'm the one that asked to tag along. Be rude if I didn't play by the rules, yeah?" He waits for Rocky while I'm being pushed into the back seat. For the first time, he feels rough, forcing me into the car and snapping the open end of the cuffs into place inside. Rocky shuts the door and goes to the driver's side. KC steps back, giving Rocky room to open the door before climbing in without hesitation. Rocky climbs into the front seat quickly. The car's started before he's got his seatbelt on.

"Stone, you there?" The car radio clicks when the transmission ends. Rocky turns the volume down on the device and brings it to his ear. Whispering nonsense is all we get now; even his response is a mutter. After a couple of exchanges, he sets the radio down on the stand. Maybe a bit harder than he meant because it bounces and he looks at it, sighing again. His eyes are in the rearview mirror. They meet mine immediately. He looks like he's going to say something, but instead, he just peels out of BAIT's.

ELEVEN.

Going south toward the Font Hill station, a townhouse reads DON'T CLOSE YOUR EYES on the board covering an upper floor window of someone's home. Rocky's left the radio off so there's no sound but whatever Baltimore makes on the other side of the glass mixed with the random clicks of Rocky's walkie-talkie saying nothing. The headlights flash over a wall saying NO HOPE and LOL and a huge dark spot on the ground that doesn't look like paint so much as someone left behind. A bit of metal catches on the light. It might've been a knife, but it went by too fast for me to tell.

THEY ARE LOOKING, JO reads the side of another brick wall.

I lean back, trying to catch another glimpse of what I just saw—because there's no way it should be my name on the wall, right? At least not spelled out like that. There's only one person who ever really called me Jo—

At least, up until recently when Jag dropped it too.

"KC?" I mutter.

He turns to me from the window.

"Did you see that graffiti just now?"

"No. What'd it say?"

"You're gonna think I'm crazy." I purse my lips.

"Really?" He chuckles.

Telling him exactly what it said might mean nothing to him unless he makes me explain everything I thought when I saw it. I pull my hand back to reach for my phone. The cuffs dig in. I drop my head back. "Probably a stupid question, but is there a way that the dead can communicate with this side once they move on or whatever?"

"Why are you asking?" KC says.

"Because I keep… I keep seeing these things. Messages. They look like they're from…" I glance through the plastic barrier separating Rocky from KC and me. His attention's on the road, but it doesn't mean he's not listening. I lower my voice to say, "Wayland. The last few days, it feels like he's been talking to me." My skin prickles with a chill. "Graffiti keeps saying my name. The other day, I felt like it led me to his body. Now, I think he's watching and knows what's going on with the Big Guy."

"What'd you see?" KC says.

"'*They're looking Jo,*' That was the way he always talked to me, but he's supposed to be processed and moved on. Like, I dropped him off at the bar and he was drinking. He was supposed to go to the other side."

KC stares at me for a long while, looking annoyed that I'd ask anything, like I'm stopping him from finding Ralph or going where he wants to go rather than filling time while we're in the back of a car. "Sorry. I'm new to this shit.

KC sighs irritably. "The souls of the dead never really leave." He adjusts so he's leaning into the crack between the seat and the door. His legs spread so one foot's planted on the seat, knee in the air and the other hangs in a long stretch coming to my side of the car. "Influence and memories. Handprints left behind by people who came before ya or are lookin' out for ya. The city speaks to people in different ways. The shit Reagan sees when he looks around is only kinda like this shit I see—but that's because he's been in my head. If you're seein' stuff from your friend, he's probably okay."

My nose burns from the building tears. I pull at my hands to wipe my face. The cuffs stop me again. I lean forward and do my best to reach. "He's not in Hell or something?"

"Did the reaper take him back?" KC says.

I shake my head.

"Then no, he isn't damned and he's probably fine."

A tear rolls down my cheek. My nose stuffs instantly. I don't know if I'm in pain or if I'm happy, but if he's not suffering or trapped in the same hellish disaster that my dad got dragged into when Charon ripped him apart, then it's gonna be okay. I want to cover my face, but I can't, so I turn my head to bite my arm to stop the sob from coming out. My eyes close; I use the moment to breathe. "Thank God."

KC chuckles. "Why ya think Reagan does what he does? A corrupted soul dragged back has rejected mercy. That's what Poena is; that's where Charon's special deliveries go."

"Ralph works *against* Charon?" I say into my arm.

"Not exactly. Charon's a function, Reagan's a loophole. They're not against each other, the just don't work the same beat."

I mutter a thanks.

We pass by the building my body was dumped behind. The lights in the parking lot outside the station are normal. Badge cars reflect blue and red and white, all on. Broken glass litters the asphalt around the cars, some of them even busted up and dented and broken. Windows around the station are busted up too. Stone walls and hoods of cruisers read FUCKERS and PIGS and UR FKN DEAD BITCH.

"Looks like someone left your callin' card," KC says.

"Party," I say.

Rocky laughs uncomfortably. I laugh too, then swallow hard. The phrases aren't anything special. Probably've seen them a dozen and a half time before with so many intended targets. The only difference now is they're a little more personal. Messages for me to find in broken glass that create a setting I'm used to with broken bottles, anger, and resentment for shit I don't even know about. There's never an answer or an end to the anger. It always just is, and I wonder if in Baltimore, it's something that just will always be.

"What happened here?" I say.

"Station had visitors while we were gone," Rocky says. He parks the cruiser behind the line of desk badges standing between the parked cars. There aren't many of them. The anemia of the nightshift isn't immediately obvious, though they are fewer in number than I had expected.

"Looks like more than one," I say.

"Looks like rage." KC tries the door, but the handle does nothing to unlatch, locked from the outside. He leans back, pressing his head to the seat while he stretches his back and sucks in a slow breath like he'd just been slapped. His face twists in pain as he hisses. It turns into a soft chuckle on exhale.

"You okay, KC?" I say.

"Oh yeah… Fuckin' riot over here." Emotion seeps into his voice. He says I don't understand anything, but the way the anger carries is like the way regret eats you from the inside until the pain consumes you and you can't think anymore. He softly chuckles. "I got places to be, let's fuckin' go." His foot bounces slightly and he drops his head back, stretching his neck.

"What's the hurry?" Rocky says.

KC softly chuckles. "What the fuck do you think?" He sucks in a breath.

"Is it Ralph?" I say.

"Yeah, yeah, yeah, yeah." KC's repetition carries pain.

"I'll be right back." Rocky's got the cruiser door open already. He doesn't wait for a response before it snaps shut behind him.

KC presses his palm to his eyes. He chuckles again. This one feels more caustic than pained. "If I end up in prison because of this, doesn't matter what Reagan says, you're banned from the bar for life." He turns his head to me. His fingers split, allowing his brown eyes to peer between them. "Ya got it?"

"Yeah." My shoulders slouch, the cuffs dig into my wrists again and I force myself upright. "Sorry about the trouble. For you and Ralph."

KC drops his hands. His elbows are on his knees and he's leaning forward so his head touches the seat in front of him. "Reagan ain't doin' anythin' he didn't sign up for, but when the time comes, stay out of my fuckin way and we won't have a problem yeah? Just—Fuck." KC punches the seat in front of him. A jolt goes through me. Violence and drive unlike anything I've felt before. It makes me pull at the cuffs, even against the cuts forming from the sharp, metal edges. "Just a warnin' and I'm only sayin' it cause I know you're feelin' it: They're diggin' into Reagan. The harder they push him, the more I feel, the more you're gonna get it from me." KC groans, leans back, and rubs his face again. "This ain't a fuckin' game so try to keep your head on, yeah?" He lowers his hand. His hair's messy again. With his jaw tight, his lips press into a flat line. There's a cold distance in his eyes, even as he looks directly at me. There's something about them that's making it look like he's not there in the way someone checks out before they do something really messed up. His feet press into the floor and he thrusts himself against the back seat. "There it is... Fuck," KC says through his teeth.

The silence in the car's noticeable when Rocky pulls the back door open beside me and it feels unbelievably loud. KC's body shifts sharply. He's on one knee, hand braced on the back of the driver's chair and the backseat we're on like he's going to lunge.

"You're clear to go inside." Rocky's getting the keys from his belt loop. The cuffs fall into his hand. He looks at me straight-on. "Whoever broke in left a couple of messages and I think you might understand them." Rocky glances past me to KC and back. "Assuming what you've said about ghosts is true, I think whoever left the messages were after you." Rocky pauses, staring at my wrists, noticing how much redder they are then before. To be honest, I didn't notice how bad they'd gotten. "What happened here?" He points.

"Impulses," I say.

Rocky licks his bottom lip. His weight adjusts from one side to the other. "I'm going to need you to fight it. Don't run."

"I'll try."

"And don't worry," Rocky says, looking past me to KC. "No cuffs. You're not being detained." He steps back to give me room to climb out of the cruiser.

KC's already coming across the backseat after me. He

jumps out. The soft soles of his leather shoes make a hard splat when he lands. "Didn't ask, Big Dick." KC doesn't wait for permission before making his way toward the station building. His movement through the cars puts the badges on defense.

A couple of them are yelling for him to stop, but Rocky's quick to say, "They're witnesses. Gonna ID some stuff for me," so nothing escalates. They don't try to hide their confusion. One of 'ems got a hand near his belt, another two are ready to bolt and grab him.

Still, they don't seem like they trust Rocky's in his right mind. If he's letting us into whatever's going on, he's probably not. If anything, KC and I look like we shouldn't be here because he and I dress like we've come looking for trouble. Hell, they know I've been in interrogation at least twice in the last few weeks. But KC's got a busted lip, black eye, ripped jeans, a culty band shirt with Latin saying something I don't know, and a criminal record. The steel plating on the edge catches in the parking lot light. The way he walks is like he's got all the power and he's waiting for the first person to challenge him for it to show no one can take it from him. His movements are sharp, more daring than fearful as he goes past badge after badge without slowing down, flinching, or peering in their direction.

The parking lot lighting illuminates his red knuckles, exposing them as being darker than I realized in the car. I press my fingers to my wrist. The skin's more sensitive than I was expecting it to be, but I don't look down. If KC looks like that out here, I don't want to see what I actually did to myself—what I ended up doing to Jag.

As another random badge approaches, Rocky waves them off, but there's one standing at the top of the stairs by the busted open glass doors. His uniform still has folded wrinkles in it. His badge doesn't say rookie and he doesn't look that young either. His hair's short and black, but what stands out the most is the discoloration in his face. Red around the eyes, torn skin along the knuckles, and the mild scent of sulfur as we draw near. Slight, dark tendrils look like they're coming out of his eyes to wrap around his neck, but they're not there after I blink. Maybe the smell isn't him, but the inside of the station. I know that's an excuse even as I think it because he's got the look like the dead guys ready to go at Ralph's place, but somehow, I still want to hope this city isn't made up mostly of the dead and the badges aren't so corrupt they let them get away with everything.

Instead of waving us off like the others, Rocky approaches him with a smile. His disposition with Rocky says he's been on the beat for a couple of years and they know each other pretty well. He says, "You work fast, Stone. Find the perps already? Record time." The edge of the badge's lip twitches. He glances at me, then KC, then me again. He smiles. I don't like how he's looking at me. I'd say it's just the normal suspicion of a badge to a brat, but he's not giving KC the same look. The left side of his face twitches a little.

My hands curl into fists.

I want a cigarette.

I'm being paranoid, right? He's dead, but every dead man in Baltimore doesn't work for the Big Guy.

I shove my hands into my pockets to keep me from making a mistake.

"Consultants," Rocky says. "Joey, KC, this is Officer Henney. He's going to bring us up to speed on what went down."

"You really gonna call a couple of *punks* consultants?" Henney says. "For all you know, these two could be connected."

"What would make you say that?"

"They've got that look about 'em," Henney says.

"Yeah, I got you, but they've been with me the past hour," Rocky says.

Henney chuckles. "That doesn't mean anything, but if you're sure… Who am I to question *Detective Stone Grant?*"

"Ah." Rocky rubs the back of his neck. "Just catch us up on what happened."

"Yeah. Right." Henney leads the way inside. The glass window at the entrance is thoroughly shattered, lying in pieces on the ground. Rocky says, "Be careful it doesn't go through your shoes." The cement steps outside are covered in HA HA HAs of different shapes that disappear and reappear across the hall, doors, receptionist desk, and chairs in the lobby.

"Someone got real busy while they were here, huh?" I say.

"Kinda surprising, really." Henney stops once we're center in the receptionist's lobby. The last time I was here—or the only time I can really remember being here not led by a badge—was when I dropped my pants off after getting sucked into the ground at Leakin. The lobby walls read OINK and LOL and EVIL EVIL EVIL WOOOOOO with some dumb cartoon version of Satan speedily drawn beside it. Faces in different colors are tags down the hall where the glass isn't totally busted out.

"Looks like someone really hates your guts." KC gestures to a crude paint job behind the receptionist's desk: A couple of stick figures wearing blue hats hang from the ceiling with large red holes in their heads and a messy GOTTEM beside it like it's a game of hangman.

"Might surprise you how easy it is to piss people off in this line of work," Rocky says.

"Not really." KC clicks his tongue with a grin. He reaches for the door behind the receptionist's desk. It doesn't move. He steps back, crossing his arms as he turns to the badge. "If the door's locked, how'd a bunch of *hooligans* get inside?"

"We're still trying to figure that one out." Henney runs his badge on the magnetic box on the wall behind the office desk. The box beeps, the door opens with a pull. "Either they used a different entrance, or they got a badge somehow."

"Right…" KC mutters.

Henney leads us down the hall. "So, the perps came in and made a beeline for what they wanted like they knew where to find it. There was a handful of them. They made some noise, threw hands, but overall, it was chaos, and no one really knew what the hell was going on. They forced their way into the back. They had firearms. We were more or less forced out of the office. Crossfire, ya know? We couldn't do anything in close quarters. Then, once we got everyone cleared out, we noticed they tried to get into evidence. Caught one of 'em briefly, but the guy was strong. Threw a computer off a desk and things picked up from there." Henney points to the nearby office space where a thick computer monitor that looks older than I am is sitting on the floor, screen cracked. The tower, still attached, lays flat with most of the cords pulled toward the screen. The phone from the desk is unhooked and busted. Papers, a pencil holder and its content, and the trash can are toppled over. "They got away, left a mess, and no one can give a description. That's what's weird. We're trained for this kind of thing, but none of the officers on duty could come up with anything on what they looked like. Hair color, skin color, height, weight, clothing *style*. Everyone was sure they weren't wearing masks at first, then it's maybe, then it turned into a ring of 'don't know' and guessing. I've never seen anything like it."

"*You* can't remember what they looked like?" KC says.

"Yeah. I'm in the same boat," Henney says.

"You're a fuckin' liar." KC advances toward Henney, reaching with tight fists.

"Watch it," Rocky says.

"Right…" KC turns away. Something catches his eye in the office and slowly approaches. Dragging fingerprints, brown and red and gray, move against the tan-painted walls. Fresh. The smell of sulfur's stronger at this end of the hall. A large wet spot darkens the carpet, going under the door. "Hate to break it to you, but you're gonna need to buy into this *occult shit* real quick if you want to solve anything," KC says. "Criminals and corpses run this city. You figure that out yet?"

"Give it a bit and I might understand," Rocky says.

I've only been here a couple times now, but I'm pretty sure I recognize the walls outside the interrogation room I'd been put in. A large office space is to the right, while the doors continue on the left, but the gray on gray on gray is now disrupted with FEAR FEAR FEAR FEAR in different sizes and colors and styles not unlike the catacombs of Fort Armistead. Another line reads DON'T LISTEN TO THE THEM on top of fear. Then, on the door that I'm sure is the interrogation room I was in, it says

LOOK 4 UR BOY
    WON'T FIND HIM
LOLOLLOLOLOL
    GET FKN FUKED BITCH.

I stop in front of the door. Read it again. Curse under my breath. This asshole thinks he's really gonna get the best of me because he took the only thing that matters anymore. He's wrong. If anything, he's not the only vengeful dead that's not gonna stop until he is taken care of.

I turn around. Rocky's closer than I'm expecting him to be. I take a couple steps back.

"You feeling alright?" he says. "You look sick."

"Yeah. I'm gonna be… I'm just dealing with the incompetency of the BPD again." I growl. My fingers are combing through my hair in rapid succession, attempting in vain to sooth the anger that's getting to be more and more. I eye the messed-up office and think what would it really matter if I threw shit around a little? I'm seeing red and black and gray walls that are begging me to fight with Rocky so I can slam him into them. The reality of his size over me isn't coming into the equation because in my head, I can do whatever the hell I want and after I get the first hit in on him, I know I'd be feeling good. The pain and ache of the loss and failure and betrayal get less and less every time I get closer to pushing Rocky over the edge.

An elbow thrusts into my back. I jump, hands are fists, I swing. KC takes it. "Chill," he says.

"I don't know where it's coming from," I mutter through my teeth.

KC nods at Henney. "Bastard's playin' a game."

I shove my hands into my pockets. "But why?"

"Revenge feels good. Your enemies want you to suffer. That's it."

"That can't really be it," I say.

"People are generally trash, Joey," KC says. "Get used to it." He knocks me again with his elbow while passing.

My hands smack into my thighs and I'm chewing on my lip, pulling at the ring, doing anything to keep myself busy while I go further down the hall, so I don't slip up. Every breath feels like I'm cursing while the voice in my ears is getting louder. A shadow at the end of the hall moves. It looks like bars coming from a blocked window so I can't escape, but there aren't any windows like that. The shadow on the floor feels repulsive to get near, as it's urging me to return to Rocky, shrink the space, get more tempted to do something.

Three doors down from where I am, an interrogation room's got a busted door with hinges broken off. Gray, disrupted by messy, black paint it says TAKE CAUTION with dripping edges. The air in here smells a lot more like sulfur than it did in the hall. Next to the words is a poorly written broken heart.

The necklace!

"Rocky!" I come back out of the interrogation room. He's so close, I bump into him. I take a step back, fighting the urge to swing as I turn away on my toes, hands back in my pockets. "I need you to go to wherever it is you keep peoples' stuff when you lock 'em in a cage. See if his necklace is in there."

Rocky purses his lips. "I can't just leave you here."

"We've got your buddy to watch us. We'll be fine. Please—I need to know if they took that," I say.

Rocky checks his watch. He looks at me, then KC, then Henney. The stare makes him hum. "You got this, Henney?"

Henney laughs. It catches in his throat. He won't stop eyeing me and pretending he's not. "Yeah. I got 'em. What's the worst a couple of delinquents can do in the station anyway? One sound and every guy in the parking lot's ready to go."

"You're right about that." Rocky gives me a look, then goes once more to KC before he turns around and exits the office lobby. At the end of the hall is a door, no markings, but with the same small, gray box next to it. He runs his card against it and disappears inside.

I run my fingers through my hair. My eyes are burning and I'm pacing down the hall nonstop.

Everything that I can remember about the Big Guy's playing through my head, but most of what I remember about him is just a fuzzy feeling from the time at the bar or the fear of when he was choking me out or what it was like to have his rage bearing into me when my feet were off the ground. I don't know where he would be and there are too many gangs in this town to just start showing up in territories asking to be taken to their leader. Guy might not even belong to a gang.

"KC, what the hell is wrong with ghosts?" I say.

"What's wrong with fuckin' people?" KC says. "Shit don't go away when you die. It gets worse. *Freed* from the *shackles* of *mortality*, what the hell you think's gonna happen?" KC rolls his head to the side. He reaches for his ass pocket and withdraws his cigarette tin. He keeps his eyes on the walls like he's reading hieroglyphics. The area in front of me reads GODDAMN BITCH four times.

"People get this idea of who they wanna be and take it, whatever the cost. Your life, my life, nobody fuckin' matters." KC pulls out a cigarette and sticks it behind his ear. His tin goes back into his pocket. "You came to Reagan for a reason. Humanity lost leaves a person without composure. If you can get that shit under control, you can be fuckin' unstoppable." KC's eyes flicker to Henney. The guy's watching us, arms crossed, fingers curled, body jerks and he stiffens again.

Henney looks at him, but makes no move forward. KC nods me over. "Your big guy don't know what the fuck's wrong with him, just that he's driven and unstoppable, even to himself. He might think if he takes you out, he'll get that control cause he definitely didn't feel powerful next to Charon. Doesn't matter what your relationship was before. He's got a whole different life going on in his head that he's made up and thinks is real.

At this point, he ain't gettin' ya out of his head until one of you are dead again." Moving into the office, KC turns a corner too sharp. The metal edge of his shoe catches on the wall with a thud.

"Don't mess around in there." Henney comes to the doorway of the administration room.

"It's called *investigating*, Lil Dick," KC says. "Maybe wait for your buddy to get back before you try 'n show off, yeah?"

"Show some goddamn respect," Henney says.

KC snorts. He lifts his middle finger. "You might fool the livin' in that outfit, but you ain't foolin' me. There's nothin' dirtier than a badge that won't stay dead."

Henney reaches for the gun on his hip. "You wanna run that by me again?"

A slight cringe twitches at KC's expression. His eyes catch on the red ring he's wearing. He puts his arms up as if surrendering, though his fists are tight. "No. Sorry about that, officer. Didn't mean the disrespect," KC says through a stiff jaw.

Henney lifts his hand slowly from the pistol. KC turns away in retreat. His eyes are darker than before. Black lines leak from the sockets. He blinks and they're gone, but that doesn't stop the feeling I'm getting.

I follow him away until we're at the other side of the office. KC's eyes train on the graffiti, less like he's reading it, more like a distraction as he taps his foot. He flicks a cigarette into his mouth to chew on the filter. His hands dive into his pockets. No matter how closely he's watching the wall, he keeps glancing toward Henney.

"That guy's dead," I say.

"No shit," KC says.

"It looks like Rocky can't tell. Why? Jay saw it when something was wrong with me."

"A living soul can rot. The lines blur between the

living and the dead if it's bad enough. You can see it, your boy can see it, Rocky can't cause somehow he ain't seen enough rot to taint him." KC sucks in a soft, but hissing breath. He leans against the wall. "If his soul ain't rottin', the only way to prove this shit is exposure." He breathes out harder, like a sigh coping with pain. He pulls the cuff of his jacket up. Against his pale forearm is a long, fresh cut. Red seeps from it. Pulling the jacket sleeve down, he closes his eyes again.

"What does that look like?" I say.

"Nothin' good." KC exhales hard, a soft groan that turns into laughter. From the way KC's anxiety's getting into me, I think he's fighting back his impulses more than the pain. He laughs and my heart flutters, trying to get out of the violence whispering in my ear. KC pushes off the wall and quickly crosses the room. He looks at the graffiti and damage like that's the reason for his movement, but he goes right for a loose piece of trash he kicks across the floor.

"You wanna go back to a cage?" Henney snaps.

"Said I'm fuckin' sorry, pig. What do ya want?" KC growls.

Henney's hand's back on the gun. Rocky re-enters, holding a clear plastic bag and Henney relaxes. The top of the bag is labeled LOCKE, JAGGER, A. with a number in small print on the upper right corner. Wallet, keys, lighter, cigarettes, belt, and the necklace. I guess I'm lucky badges don't like to do favors and Rocky didn't follow through putting that back in Jag's hands. "Do you see what you're looking for?" Rocky holds the bag out to me.

I cross to meet him in the hall. I'm reaching for the bag. As soon as I'm close enough, he pulls it away from me.

"Tell me what you need," he says.

Henney glances over the bag. Something catches his eye. He twists his head to the side a bit. His lips quirk. "You really think that's a good idea, Stone?" Henney slowly approaches us. "Those are confiscated goods for someone I'm pretty sure is not this chick."

"We're finding a line right now, Henney," Rocky says. "Sometimes you gotta break a couple of rules to find the truth. Just make sure the office doesn't find out."

"You're not as straight-laced as I thought you were, Rocky," I say.

"What did you need?" Rocky holds the plastic bag up again.

I point to the heart-shaped necklace at the bottom. Henney's eyes follow my finger. It's not like he hadn't seen the necklace when the bag came out, but now, he can't stop looking at it. Arms uncrossing, he steps forward, leans in, and cocks his head to the side.

"You steal that?" Henney asks.

"I *made* that," I growl.

"Did you now?" Henney grins, his stare lifts from the rock to me only briefly.

Rocky purses his lips, pushing a sigh, posing the question of what he should do, how much he should say. The same questions I've been asking myself are now hitting Rocky as he works on what he can tell his coworker without sounding like he's come to the same level of insanity as me. What do you even say when you're not sure what you believe yet? He examines the necklace at the bottom of the bag. Light catches on the darker parts near the blackened edge. "You should let me take care of that, Stone," Henney says. "You seem like you might be getting too close to this investigation."

"I don't think so." Rocky steps back.

Henney shoves his hand in my face and pushes me back. Then, he's lunging for the bag. His gun's in his hand, pointed at Rocky.

Rocky releases the evidence bag to Henney. "What do you think you're doing, officer?"

Henney backs away. He rips the top of the bag open. He nears a desk and pours the contents out. "Getting what I came here for and then some." After dumping the bag out, he scoops up the necklace.

"Don't touch that!" I run into the office.

"I knew the bastard was lying," Henney says, gun trained on me. "Now, come to me. We got somewhere to be—"

KC charges past me, slamming his elbow into Henney's back. The necklace flies out of Henney's hand. I run to it, fishing it out of the plastic bag. I shove the necklace into my pocket. Henney's reaching for me. KC holds Henney to the ground. In the struggle, he reaches for a desk while thrusting his hand into KC's face, trying to grab both a weapon and the upper hand. KC's fist slams into Henney's face. "Welcome to the club, buddy. Nice of you to show, eh?" His laugh echoes off the walls. He slams a fist into the guy's face again. Teeth chatter. Henney finds his gun in the mess of papers beside him. With it in hand, he smacks the butt of the pistol into KC's head hard enough he rolls off.

Henney stands. His sights reset on me. The darkness is coming, deepening the blackness of his irises and infecting every area around his face as the tendrils grow out of him, wrap around his neck, and disappear into his shirt collar. "Gimme the necklace, bitch." He walks toward me, gun pointed. Still, with his empty hand, he reaches for whatever he can that's nearest and tosses it my way. This time it's a mug and a grunt. The tendrils from his eyes wrap around his wrists, pulling his grip tighter. His body trembles as his head bounces in a way that's too familiar. My fingers are shaking too. "Give me the necklace," he says again. He pulls the trigger. A bullet blows past me.

"Put the gun down, Henney!" Rocky says.

Henney turns the gun on Rocky. Papers fly underneath KC's foot as he runs at Henney. The gun turns on him next. KC rams Henney. A shot fires. The metal ricochets off the ceiling or a desk or something, but it doesn't seem to impact KC as he takes the badge to the ground again. KC's fist is back, then slamming into Henney's face. A knee to his chest, KC pins one of Henney's hands with his while the other now clenches the guy's neck. "Where's Ralph Reagan?"

Henney claws at KC's arm with his free hand. "I don't know who you're talking about!"

KC's lips are crooked, grinning, showing just the tip of his slightly jagged teeth. "Wrong answer." His hand leaves Henney's throat to curl into his hair. With just as much ease as he'd had getting into position, KC draws Henney's head into the air and slams it into the ground. "Where the fuck is Ralph Reagan?"

Henney spits in KC's face.

KC releases a mixture of a growl and a chuckle. "Wrong fuckin' answer, buddy." In that moment, a glimpse of his old self comes back. The lead singer of Bad Ass Idiot Train, rumored for starting fights and giving people signatures in ways that give them scars instead of ink marks that'll wash off after a couple of days. The guy that started riots with just his stage presence, where he raided bars and laughed about it because no matter how much trouble he got caught up in, he somehow got away. He influenced people without saying anything and started his shows with fist fights. Everywhere he went, people whispered about how he might be a cult leader or killing people and keeping trophies no one could find or a treasure chest of his bloody history hidden somewhere in Leakin that no one comes back from if they go looking for. The rumors really picked up once the band disappeared, but out of all the urban legends, the one about his voice is the one that traveled the farthest across the Maryland and back. Everything he was, he did, he made… He could bring people to their knees, down to blood, to tears, to giving up their life all just by singing.

One rumor even went so far as to say a concert eleven years ago resulted in the suicide of thirty attendees the next day, all killed themselves the same way.

His influence was so bad, some started calling him a siren. It wasn't even his presence that did it. Days before he'd show up for a concert, locals would board up in preparation for the crazy coming to town.

"Stop!" Rocky yells.

Henney shoves his hands into KC's face again, trying to hit his nose. He doesn't make it this time. The following kick is a cheap distraction that KC doesn't fall for. KC knee's Henney in the chin; his head flies back. The opportunity comes and KC uses the break to pick up the gun sitting on the spilled trash within arm's reach. He presses the gun's muzzle against Henney's head and without hesitation, *boom, boom, boom, boom, boom*. Each sound is an exclamation of hatred not showing in KC's otherwise blank eyes. Cartridge empty, he's still pulling the trigger, the clicking doesn't seem to register. The body underneath him goes limp. KC stands up, giving Henney a shove as he gets off the floor. Blood colors KC's bleached denim. Brain matter spills all over the office paperwork, desk chair, and loose electronic cords that had the bad luck to be nearby.

My head's buzzing and I can't think of anything but turning on Rocky next and getting the same feast from him.

A wall in front of me reads STAY CALM, JO where I don't think it said it before.

"What the hell are you doin'?!" Rocky snaps.

"Somethin' *not good*," KC exhales hard. Again, pain, delirium, anger. His eyes are tainted black from the tendrils seeping out of his face. His stare is fixated on Henney as Rocky trains his gun on him.

"Put the weapon down," Rocky says.

KC's head twists slowly. Blond hair drops over his shoulder while brown eyes tinted in red refocus like he's seeing nothing but Rocky. His palm opens. Carefully, he reaches toward the desk.

"Don't move." Rocky reaches for his cuffs."

KC's arms are shaking. "I'm putting the piece down, Big Dick. Just gimme a second, yeah?" Carefully, he sets the gun on the edge of the nearest desk. He closes his eyes, inhales deeply, and mutters something to himself.

"It's not what you think, Rocky," I say.

"I don't want to hear it." Rocky quickly approaches KC.

"Badge or not, that guy was already dead," I say.

"Knock off the bullshit, Josephine."

"Would you listen, Rocky?"

"This has gone on long enough—

"That guy's a fucking ghost!" My voice should echo off the room walls, but instead, the sound proofing around the office eats it. My skin's on fire. I'm breathing hard, worse off than KC who looks just short of losing it if pushed. My necklace feels like it's burning against my thigh and my heart's beating so fast. The bloody mess grows on the floor around Henney's head. The splatter around his face hides everything until his eyes shoot open again. Henney wipes the blood from his face while his free hand pushes violently to get off the ground as fast as he can, his focus is KC.

"What the hell—" Rocky's saying. His gun retrains on Henney. "How—"

"Welcome back, bud." KC swiftly turns toward Henney.

Henney's on his hands and knees, charging the short distance between him and KC. He uses KC's body to stand upright, shaking, disoriented, and clawing his way up KC's pant leg. KC grabs the guy by the shirt, other hand reaching for Henney's head again. In a practiced movement, KC's fingers twist into Henney's hair and he snaps his head into the nearby desk. The crack of the front of his skull is hard, loud, and blunt. A bloody imprint's left behind. KC slams the guy's head down again and again and again as arms flail in a quest for freedom and success at landing on KC. Bits of face and bone and nose break off sporadically between blows. Even as the body goes limp, KC keeps going until the front of the skull collapses entirely. Henney's weight sags before KC releases the hair and shirt. Henney slides off the desk.

There's too much gore for the body on the floor. I know—I know it should make sense. I watch what happened, I saw the pieces fly and Henney come back like he was unaffected, but still it doesn't feel real. Was I really only out for a couple of minutes before? It had to have been longer. Back when some banger smashed my head in at BAIT's, the badges were already locked and loaded in by the time I woke up. They tend to take their time with crime scenes. It couldn't have been as quick as that guy had come back, right?

"How exactly does this whole 'not dead' dead thing work?" I say to KC.

"Depends," KC says. "But consciousness and recovery aren't the same thing."

"Can the living see him?" I say.

"Only when he animates again—Or if they saw him get knocked out."

"What the hell am I seeing right now?" Rocky says.

"Thought it was pretty obvious." Turning to Rocky, KC nods at Henney's corpse. "Whatever you think you know about this guy or this world, give it up." KC blows a stray hair out of his face. "He ain't mortal anymore, *Big Dick*. He's going to keep coming back because he ain't got a *body*. You get it yet?"

"No." Rocky stares at KC.

"Rethink everything you think you know about me or Reagan," KC says. "Badges don't run this city. The dead do."

I duck into the office room, shifting beyond Rocky with a quiet, "S'cuse me." I pull a pen out of a mug that says *Baltimore's Best*. I grab the nearest piece of paper next and put down Charon's number. I've barely got the last one in when the air in the room shifts. The feeling, the vibe, it's like the air was sucked out of this place. I don't know how else to describe it. KC takes a step back. He blinks rapidly, pulling his hair out of his ponytail and putting it back in as his glance moves from the body to the door to me. Instead of fierceness, his expression is one of incomprehension as he stares at me.

The air rattles and vibrates in a way that gets under my skin, overpowering my sense of self, telling me to run away as fast as I can cause the reaper is coming. Office doors fly open, smacking against the walls with a loud crash. A raven flies in, landing on one of the empty desks. Another follows suit, taking up space on a different computer desk. Several more fly in, landing across the room and watching the biggest of them enter, followed by the slow fade of Charon. The office lights wash out his pale face, making him look more like a corpse. His usual platinum hair goes white too. Carefully, he steps around the papers, fallen trash, and busted computer without looking down.

Despite his shoes being white, Charon pays no mind to the puddles of blood or spilled gore as he approaches the dead man's spirit. The rattling chains grow louder as he nears. Even as he walks past me, they're going and going and going until they're causing an ache inside of my head and the heat under my skin's burning to the top. My mind's screaming to run away even though I know nothing's going to happen to me.

"And you are…?" Rocky says.

"You called the fuckin' reaper?" KC growls.

"What the hell was I supposed to do?" I say.

"That guy was our lead, Joey!" KC takes a step back just as Charon approaches him. His hip bumps into the desk. His lips perk at the edge in a momentary grin. "Hey, Char. Long time no see, but you mind leaving this sordid loser alone for a little while? We were kinda in the middle of things."

Charon stops to look at KC. "Kailee." His eyes glow brighter for a moment. "Where is *the medium*?"

"Busy," KC says.

"You've lost him, haven't you?" Charon says.

"Nah, don't worry about it."

"I know you're lying, Kailee." Charon's closeness makes KC wince. "You have a responsibility to keep *that thing* safe?"

"Yeah, yeah, yeah, yeah. I got it. Don't act like I don't know fuckin' better. I been at this a while. I know what he fuckin' needs," KC says.

Charon leans over the corpse. His eyes glow brighter in the silent moments that pass as he surveys Henney. "Patterson Tower."

"Patterson Tower, huh?" KC says. "That's where Reagan is?"

"I do not know, but it is where he was going to take Josephine after procuring her," Charon says.

"Huh. At least we've got a lead," KC says.

I'm still putting space between us until I run into another desk. Charon steps over Henney. He squats near the head while reaching into his pocket. The white chain of his clear crystal whatever is wrapped around his hand. He holds it over the body. Thin, slim chains extend from Charon's pea coat. The metal bindings wrap around the lifeless form while Charon holds the crystal over Henney. His delicate fingers squeeze the chain. Quickly, they restrict. The chains squeeze the ghost body tighter and tighter as bits of light break off to be absorbed by the crystal hanging from Charon's hand until the body is gone. Charon slips the now glowing crystal back into the inner pocket of his blazer. The chains that once held Henney recede into his jacket, disappearing without a trace.

Though my heart's racing, this isn't the same feeling I had back at Leakin or the apartments when Charon had gone after conscious ghosts who had enough wits about them to run. It's the same thing that happened with my dad. While he was passed out, there wasn't any of the excess struggle or fear or pain that hurt like those other situations.

It's weird to think about someone's death. One day they're with you, screaming at you to come back or don't talk like that or go to the corner store for cigarettes and the cheapest whiskey on the shelf. You can feel them against you and you're living a nightmare you can't escape, then, the next day they're not there and you're left thinking you're crazy, feeling how things were different yesterday. Someone else was there and real and you could *feel* him and now he's nothing.

Then you realize when he left, he took a part of you

with him. Your life, your history, your family, your future. That person's gone and now you can't blame them anymore for holding you back from anything when your life still doesn't change.

There's no miracle to his demise, just the promise that you'll always be lacking something and you missed your chance with him, with your friends, with everything that's happened up to this point that could've been different.

Everything's too messed up now and there's no going back.

Charon raises his glance to me. His eyes glow brighter, reflecting a soft blue against his cheeks that can't be washed out by the dull fluorescents overhead. "You would do well to find the source of ire directed at you, Josephine." Charon turns to me.

"I'm working on it," I say.

Charon turns away, making his escape for the office door.

A shadow stretches over Charon's form from behind. Thick, the beast's edges run jagged, the shadow carries on too long for a human and spreads over me. I step back, bump into a desk again, trapped. A couple of red lights reflect from the darkness. The creature in black moves closer. Though the room looks like it's getting darker, the shadow grows smaller until it turns into Val. He wipes his nose with the back of his hand. Something catches his attention. He lifts his head to give the air a sniff. Scanning the room, his dark eyes lock on me. He steps around Charon, hands in pockets, head cocked to the side. His tongue keeps going over his lips. He inhales rapidly, sniffing the air more and more as he comes nearer. My hands are shaking and for every step he takes toward me, I'm stepping back and back and back until I hit the wall, jump, gasp. He's closer than he was before and moving faster.

"Heart's out, huh?" Val says. His body straightens the closer he gets to me. A trash bin falls over as he bumps into it. He coos without looking down, laughter echoes like the birds in the woods that sounded like they were mocking me.

"Don't look at me like that," I say.

"Like what? How am I looking?" Val says.

"What the hell is going on?" Rocky says. "Who the hell are you?"

"Back off, bird. I won't go easy on ya even if ya got a pea brain," KC says.

"He can't help it," Charon says. "He runs on instinct, and a small, bare heart? The ravens cannot resist. I do not think you understand how dangerous this is. If he consumes your heart, there is no getting it back."

Val doesn't take notice to KC and lunges at me.

I duck under Val's arm and run back to the office. My sneaker catches on some loose leaf. I trip forward and fall onto a desk. I grab at a keyboard and yank it free, hoping the cord pops. Just as I turn around, Val's on top of me. His hand clamps around the desk beside me as the other presses into my chest, hard. I don't know why I hadn't thought he'd be strong. The smallest touch has unbelievable strength that shoves me onto the desk. There's no fighting against it, he's immoveable. I swing the keyboard at him. He jumps back, laughing and the ravens spread around the room laugh with him, sounding more like robotic men mimicking laughter than anything.

"What the hell's wrong with you, Val?" I'm off the desk. He lunges again. His claws curl into my hoodie, nails so sharp, they tear the fabric instantly and pull at my skin. He's breathing so hard, he's panting as his eyes survey my body hungrily. I swing the keyboard at his head. It bounces off him without so much as a pained noise. His freehand slides down my chest to my hip, talons desperately reaching for my pocket. I pull back. His hand in my clothing, hooking fingers into skin.

KC's fist slams into Val's face. Val staggers back, hand loosened. His eyes are darker than normal, nose flaring. He screeches. The sound's high-pitched, intense, and terrifying. My ears ache and the sound amplifies the longer it goes on. Fear and dread and despair fill me to the point my body wants to give out. I hold onto the nearest desk to keep standing. Then suddenly, Val isn't himself anymore. Not a man, not a bird, but this thing made of shadowy limbs and tentacles as his form grows larger. In the darkness, a large beak takes shape. Eyes open on the top side of it. Eight of them, and once all of them are open, his mouth gnashes. Two wings turn into four then six and full of uneven, wispy black and purple feathers. Huge, sharp claws form against the tile, stop, reach for KC. In a move too quick to track, KC's thrown across the room. He smacks into the wall and falls to the floor, gasping for air.

"Fuckin' bird!" KC snaps breathlessly.

"Val, come back to me," Charon says.

The screeching doesn't stop immediately, but the shadows rescind. Val's size returns to what can be contained in his human body. He twists his neck, snapping as it pops back in place. His eyes are still pitch black, his nails longer than normal, and his teeth just as sharp. His head pulls into his shoulders and his face twitches. With every blink, the color pulls back into his irises. By the time he reaches Charon, he looks normal, if not slightly agitated. He drapes his arms around Charon's shoulders and falls onto him like a bird landing on the arm of his master. He's panting softly, tongue hanging out as his nose presses into the back of Charon's ear. He won't stop looking at me. "Char, I need to eat it…"

"You've had enough," Charon says. His attention flickers to me. "You should know better than to carry that around."

"Yeah, I'm trying to correct that," I say.

"I cannot stop every raven from hunting you. Return your heart to your body or you will be consumed," Charon says.

Val's still watching me from where he stands behind Charon. His tongue keeps sliding along his lips. He moves closer to Charon, less like he's trying to be near and more like Charon's the only thing stopping him from coming at me again. He groans in a way that sounds like a messed-up caw.

"Stop creeping on me!" I say.

Charon snaps his fingers in Val's face. One of the other birds somewhere down the hall makes a sound like it's choking. Val blinks a couple of times; his expression changes from his hungry focus to nothing to confusion. "What did you say?" Thin, serious eyes are wide, watchful, attentive and curious. His stare breaks and he looks down at Charon. He straightens his posture, though his arms remain wrapped around Charon's shoulders. He finds me again. Instead of insatiable hunger, he stares at me with apprehension. "You don't gotta look so scared." He laughs.

"I'm not scared," I say.

"Okay." Val laughs again. His arms slip away from Charon and into his pockets. He turns first towards KC, but doesn't linger there long before looking at the door he and Charon entered through. A trail of red leaks out from his eye. Heavy, the drop runs quickly down his face. It makes me think of the birds in the parking lot before, when their feathers appeared wet or matted and their eyes were red in the moonlight. It always proceeded finding someone dead. My heart's racing. Sulfurs stuck in my nose and I'm not sure if it's really there or just me, but I put my hand to my nose to dull the smell. It doesn't work. "Val," I say.

"Yeah?" His dark eyes turn back on me.

"What's that?" I point to my eye where the blood drop would be on him.

"Shit," KC says."

The thick, dark line moves down the side of Val's nose. His expression drops into confusion. Gently, he presses his fingers to his face and wipes at the drop. The blood smears on his cheek where he touches it. A bit of it sticks to his fingers. He stares at the color for a moment, his head twisting to the side. His lips part into a smile.

"Tragedy," Charon says.

Val slowly brings the moist finger to his lips and licks it clean. He touches his face again, looking for more.

"What does it mean?" I say.

"The medium is suffering, Kailee." Charon stares at KC.

"I'm fuckin' workin' on it." KC growls.

Charon turns around. His peacoat flicks up in wind that's not there. He goes back out the door he came through and as he builds distance, he's devoured by the mist. Val follows as a shadow to the man in white.

The color comes back to the room. Rocky's staring between where Henney's body was, where Charon went, me, KC, the bloody spot on the floor again. "What... the hell was that?"

"Collections," KC says.

"You saw it?" I say.

"Not good enough," Rocky says. "What the hell?"

"I told ya." KC slowly meanders toward Rocky. Rocky's postures stiffens; he reaches for his gun again. KC lifts his hands like he's harmless. He smiles briefly.

"*Nothin' good* breaks the blinder." He pats Rocky on the shoulder.

"That was the grim reaper, Rocky," I say. "The one I told you about? Charon."

Apprehension flickers across Rocky's face. "I need you to tell me why I'm remembering you dying ten years ago, Kailee." Rocky's looking at KC.

KC smirks. "Welcome to the other side of *seeing*, Big Dick. It's an absolute *blast*."

A soft ringing fills the office. I startle. Rocky says, "This is Stone. Font Hill. Yeah. It's been a…" He looks at KC, then me. "A night. What you got?" His demeanor changes. The air in the room shifts. His shoulders go rigid, something else on his face changes. Not fear, not anger. "You're kidding…" he mutters. He looks at KC then me. "Yeah, I'll be over there soon. No. There's nothing here. I dunno, Rodgers, but I'll be there soon. Copy." He hangs up while sliding his phone back into his pocket. He reaches for his cuffs. "We need to go."

"What's it this time?" KC says.

Rocky eyes KC. He sighs hard. "Crime scene. Real grisly."

"What kind of grisly?" KC says.

There's another pause. Rocky maybe weighing whether he should tell either of us details. I look unstable, he and KC have a history that doesn't do either of them any favors, and his brain's probably running laps trying to make sense of what just happened with Charon and the bird. Rocky could just throw KC and I into a cell until we confess to something we didn't do, or he could get on with believing in ghosts because as sketchy as KC or Ralph or I look, there's no way around what Rocky just saw.

"Overly brutal. Patterson Tower. Victims aren't gang related. Looks like a couple of visitors ran into someone having a real bad day," Rocky says. "Not unlike what we found in your boy's car." Rocky gestures to me.

I'm reminded of when I opened Wayland's trunk a couple of weeks back. The body, the headless, handless corpse of a thing lying in its own blood, mutilated and destroyed beyond recognition. I still can't imagine Wayland having done that to anyone. Even when regret made its way through me to the point of losing control, I still can't see *his* hands, always so gentle and wanting to help ripping someone apart like that, destroying their face, and wanting to break and torture and hide who they were. But then, I'm back in Leakin, finding him in the trees with five bags of some other dead guy he didn't seem to have trouble dismembering. He only worried what I'd think. And then I remember him in his bedroom when his house was on fire, and he was slamming that knife into the guy's head again and again and again. He didn't hear me when I said his name, and when he finally broke out of what was wrong with him, he didn't look like himself, even when his voice sounded normal.

KC walks by Rocky. "Charon said it as a tragedy. Innocence be damned." He pats Rocky on the shoulder, friendly, but it's still gets Rocky to put his defenses up. KC laughs. He turns around as he walks so he's stepping backward. "Now that ya seen Baltimore's secret, ya better get used to this. Shit goes deeper than any of us know." KC turns back around. His step has a bit of a swagger to it as he sways.

"You can't think you're coming to another crime scene after what you just did," Rocky says.

KC stops, turns back around, stares. His lips pull into a sideways grin. "The blood on my shoes a little too much for ya?"

Rocky sighs. "Among other things. I should have you

detained."

"You really gonna tell me you need more convincin' after a visit from the reaper?" KC says.

Rocky looks at me, rubs his face, and sighs again. "You think you're gonna walk outta here looking like that and not catch the attention of every officer in the parking lot?"

"I'll pit stop in the boy's room if it'll make ya feel better," KC says.

"I don't need you messing up crime scenes," Rocky says.

"Take what I'm doin' as the gift it is, Big Dick. I'm trying to keep ya from gettin' yourself killed at the hands of *the nothin' left to lose*," KC says.

Rocky works his jaw. He looks at me more like he's checking to see if I've got anything as obviously wrong with me as the blood splatter on the steel plates of KC's shoes or the stains spotting his bleached jeans that you could maybe call mud in the lights at Leakin Park, but in the office fluorescents, it's obvious he's wearing a crime scene. The badges outside were already skeptical of letting the two of us in here. It's only a matter of time until they come in, see the gore the dead badge left behind, but no body, and formulate theories about what happened. None of them right, but all of them implicating KC and me in something else we have no way to explain ourselves out of if you don't believe in the supernatural.

Rocky seems to realize this because he's staring at the puddle his buddy left behind, sighs, and says, "Make it fast." The puddle's gonna implicate him in something too. Neglect, aiding in the disposal of a body or something. Maybe we can explain it another way his buddies outside will understand. If we get out of here soon enough, it'll buy us some time to come up with a cover story. KC doesn't need to be shown where the bathroom is, but then again, it's just down the hall and we passed it coming in. When he comes back, his shoes are clean, his pants are wet like he washed them in the sink and dried them with paper towels. Most of the discoloration is out and what's left is hidden a bit by the moisture in the pants. "Be-tee-dubs, your bathroom's wrecked too."

"I figured," Rocky says.

"Hope you didn't have a favorite urinal," KC says.

We're out the front door. Rocky gives some kind of report to the guy waiting outside, saying to hold off going inside until the chief from another station shows up. I wasn't really paying attention and kept going for the car. Fair enough when every badge in the parking lot got quieter the moment they saw me. Ravens sit sporadically on the light poles, all watching as I pass, cawing, laughing. One of them flies down at me. I run toward Rocky's car.

"You're gonna wanna watch out for that," KC says. "Don't take Charon's warning lightly."

"I don't plan to," I say.

The raven that dove at me is only a few feet away. Unlike a couple of weeks ago, it's not just a bird now. I saw what Val could become. Was that what he really was inside of that body? Were all of the ravens like that or just him? I'm not messing around with this shit anymore.

If a raven gets too close, I'm kicking the shit out of it.

Rocky doesn't take long filling his buddies in with what was probably the first story he came up with. Brief, but accurate to prepare them for what they might see inside. There might be victims they haven't heard of or something. He climbs in the car and waits until we're driving to say, "They told me Henney wasn't here. Hasn't shown up for work in three days."

"Yeah," KC says with his head leaning against the window. His eyes shut, he yawns. Each bounce should bother him, but he acts like he doesn't notice when his forehead hits the glass at each crack in the road.

"How is that possible?" Rocky says.

"That's how the dead work," KC says. "The logic? I dunno. Some kinda magical bullshit beyond what our little human pea brains can understand. Reagan could barely translate it for me, and I still don't fully get how it works. Something like: When I died, if I moved on, my body woulda looked like my body. When I came back as a spirit, my body was my body, but no one could recognize *me* unless they *knew* me in a way. Like my soul. Like Reagan. Then, when I got a heart, my body became a John Doe, my death was gone, and I got to keep living with some stipulations. I'm a normal person so long as someone living has agreed to hold my heart. If I move on for real, my body and death are mine again. Reality arranges itself in everyone's head to make sense of this shit. Erasing faces and memories, twisting nature— humans aren't the only creatures that manipulate shit to make it believable." KC leans back. His head now bounces against the seat. The way he cranes his neck doesn't look comfortable, but he folds his hands in his lap and almost looks peaceful.

"That explains the Barbara thing at Cross's house," Rocky says.

"Yeah," I say. "You just don't remember because you didn't know me and you can't see the dead."

"How do you fix that?" Rocky says.

"You can either *die* or get pretty damn close to it," KC says. "But don't worry about it. What you saw back there with your buddy should help you out some. Let the dark sink in a little more, and you'll start living like the dead in no time."

Baltimore passes through the window with a brick wall reading DON'T BE DUMB and TOO LATE.

Another wall says DUMB BITCH. I'm getting really sick of the dead bangers stalking me.

Mirroring KC, I lean back and close my eyes, hoping for at least a moment of silence. I don't need the city criticizing me for everything I already know. Though, I always knew better, didn't I? I've just pretended that I don't, so I never had to stop and think about what I'm doing, what I didn't want, how I'd hurt people, how something would hurt me. I never wanted to be like my dad, who couldn't think past whatever he felt in a single moment. He only pursued what he wanted or what he thought would alleviate what he felt. I don't want to be that, but… Every time I close my eyes, I see every choice I made out of the same impulse of need. I've walked right into my dad's path and the only thing that can follow me is destruction.

At this point, I've kinda gotta a record of it, you know? Ralph said your path wasn't set in stone, you could change it and you weren't doomed to the prediction of who the universe thought you would be, but I don't know if he's actually right or just wishful because from where I am, I don't see a way to escape this if I keep on living.

TWELVE.

KC won't stop fidgeting and it's getting to me. He's saying "keep it together" while his foot bounces and he's looking out the window and slapping his fingers on his thighs to something that sounds like an old BAIT's song. I'm not sure if he's talking to himself or me. I tell him, "You're getting to me," and he just goes, "Yeah, yeah, yeah, yeah," obviously not listening every time I talk. I know the rocking and tapping and shifting's putting Rocky on edge and I can't blame him. KC just filled a badge full of lead even if he was already dead and Rocky's trying to process everything he's seen—which is way worse than anything Jag saw the last couple of days while coping with the truth. Then, if what KC said about souls getting nabbed is true, then Rocky might be remembering the news of whatever happened to Henney when he first died and maybe he's getting back the interactions with me where he found my body, but it was a Jane Doe instead of being me.

My hands aren't cuffed, so I can see Rocky banging the steering wheel to music that's not playing. Either he's picking up on my erratic energy or this is how he processes how everything he thought he knew is wrong.

Again, I don't blame him. It's a lot to take in.

Graffiti on the side of East Baltimore Street townhouses read THEY'RE WATCHING and DON'T LET UP and THAT PIECE IS A LIAR and GONNA GETCHA LOL. Ravens line the street, peppered on rooftops. One of them sits on the bright yellow sign for *BUTT'S AND BETTY'S*. The closer we get to the park, the more the buildings are washed in red, blue, and white light. Police cars pack the entries to the street all around Patterson's. Crowds from the neighborhood gather on the sidewalk, standing on their toes and whispering to maybe catch a glimpse of someone else's tragedy so they can talk about it tomorrow with neighbors while saying *I'm glad that's not me*. Rocky pulls onto Pratt to park. We're not even stopped yet when KC's grabbing for the door, grunting when the lock stops him from getting out.

"This is an active crime scene," Rocky says. "I have to clear you with the crew before you can do anything." Rocky pushes his door open. He's hanging out his side of the car, looking at his watch, the tower, giving a sigh, and then the door closes and he's off. It's well after three in the morning. It's a weird feeling to be this wired and drained at the same time. I didn't get much sleep last night because of the nightmares left behind by Wayland's body. Picking up the car at Leakin Park with Jag feels like it didn't happen just a couple hours ago.

I really don't notice I'm biting so hard until I taste blood, check my face in the glass window, and see it's busted. There's a firetruck and two ambulances. Someone at the base of Patterson Tower's coming toward the edge of the park with his focus set on Rocky. The two of them meet. There's what looks like laughter from here, tired, but still something friendly before it looks like the first bit of description makes it to Rocky and he rubs his face. He points toward the car, turns back, and the two of them go into the park in the direction of the tower.

"You think he's actually gonna take us in the tower?" I say.

"Dunno." KC leans back. His legs splay again, taking up as much room as he can easily do in the backseat. "Didn't make much sense to leave us at the busted up station though. Regardless of whatever he believes, he knows he saw something, he knows that place ain't safe, and he knows we know somethin' he don't. Whether he intended to let us in on his new trouble ain't got anythin' to do with why we're here. Remember that." KC closes his eyes. His arms fold behind his head. *"You're a useful tool until you're not."* Looking at him a little longer, red blurs his eyes. Busted vessels. The scab from his lip looks like it busted open and his cheek's got some color that wasn't there before.

"You doing okay?" I say.

"I'm no stranger to brawlin'." KC smiles, but cringes at the pain pulling at his lip.

"That thing… Val—"

"Yeah, whatever you do, avoid touching the bird. He's not really about that and he'll tear your soul a new one if he gets his claws on ya."

"But you socked him," I say.

"Yeah, so? If I wasn't charged with takin' care of Reagan, Charon woulda let that thing tear me apart."

"He's *that* important?"

KC opens his eyes to peer toward me. "Yeah, he is, and ya don't wanna be on the other side of that bird when he pops off." KC's head drops forward. He runs his fingers through his hair, tugging out his ponytail that he's quick to put back in. "I assumed you never got into it with him before. You don't seem to catch it that he's not a person. He doesn't think like a person, doesn't act like a person. He looks kind of stupid because he is, but that doesn't mean he's not dangerous. If you fought him over your heart, your boy woulda died."

"What about Ralph? Is he okay—after what happened with Val?" I say.

"Like I said, the only reason I'm not torn up is because of him." KC's leg's bouncing. "Shit's a lot bigger than your missing boyfriend, Joey." He drops his head back and rolls his neck to the side. I'm not sure if he's feeling the same rabid energy I'm getting from the park or if he's anxious or if it's all coming from me. "Reagan's my responsibility. I know you got your own shit to do and it's nothing to do with mine. Stay out of my way and I'll stay out of yours, yeah?"

"Yeah." I look down at my hands.

KC inhales hard. He looks out the front window briefly. Rocky's not visible. He glances out the window at the sidewalk of people on the other side of the police tape. His fingers dig into his thighs.

"What makes Ralph so special?" I say.

KC looks over at me. "More than any of us can begin to understand. He's wasted zero time in offering his life for whoever the hell shows up in his. All the years with him, and I barely understand how many fucks on the other side want to use him. I don't think I'll ever fully get it either. To *them*—whatever they are—most of us are meaningless wretches waiting to get abused and corralled across the water to whatever the words *final destination* implies." KC stares down at his hands. His fingers slowly curl. "But Reagan's different. They chose him for somethin' bigger because he looks at everyone and sees the best someone can be. Even after he's gotten the worst of your secrets. I ain't leavin' him to deal with whatever the beings on the other side throw at him. What's happenin' to him right now would be much worse if he had to do it alone and believe me, he would be alone. Always has been."

"Ralph means a lot to you."

"Yeah, he does." KC turns to me. His eyes soften. For a moment, the pounding of his foot slows, though it doesn't stop. "The only reason I'm here now is because for some reason he didn't hate me for what I did to him. He saw what I'd done and still wanted to call me family. That's just how he is. He only sees people for who they could be. Fuckin' stupid. I don't even remember the last time he earnestly used the phrase *I want* in context of something for himself. He's always helping someone else, meeting their needs, facing *their* demons." KC meets my stare. "He's never had anybody to do the same; I at least owe him that after everything he's gone through."

My fingers curl into my thighs. There's nothing I can say to that because I know what it feels like too. Wayland gave up his life for me and when Jag accepted my heart, he did the same. I can't understand why they'd care so much about a piece of trash dumpster fire like me, but I'm not so dumb I don't understand how much they gave up for me. Out the window, the crowd's gotten a little bigger. One of the brick buildings we're parked next to says CLOSE YOUR EYES; THEY WILL TAKE YOU; DON'T TRUST WHAT YOU SEE.

A slight pop. The sweat squeals under KC's shifting ass. He stretches his arms out to pop his joints. "Look alive, kiddo. Big Dick's comin' back."

"You don't need to call me that." I sit up.

KC smiles. "Sure, I do." He winks.

Through the front window, Rocky's visible again, coming toward the car quickly. He's already stepping off the sidewalk from the park. He rubs his eyes. I know it's an illusion, but they look so much darker than they did before. At the car, he pulls my door open first. "Don't run."

"I won't," I say. "Don't you know? I'm *invested* now."

"And…" Rocky steps back, giving me room to climb out of the car. "Prepare yourself. It's… pretty grizzly."

"Party," KC says.

"I got it, Rocky. This isn't my first rodeo," I say. The asphalt under my feet reads YOU CHOSE THE DARK in white chalk. I mutter back, "Liar," like whatever put that there will hear me. My ears fill with an impatient whisper that doesn't make sense. It's coming from the nearby crowd, but they aren't the only ones talking. A figure, thick, too dark to see anything but an outline, steps away through the crowd. It moves like a splotch against the people until it gets to the back of the crowd and runs. Light from the streetlamps catches on its face for a second, illuminating dark eyes and tendrils going down the neck. "Hey, hey, Rocky… Did your guys, like, see anyone coming out of the park?" I'm reaching for him without looking. It's not going to bring the figure back, but maybe there's another one out there.

"The officers I spoke with didn't say anything like that. Why?" Rocky says.

"Cause I'm thinking they might've forgotten a couple of things…"

KC climbs out of the cruiser. His sudden weight hitting the ground makes me snap around, heart racing with the fear that he's going to be one of the souls hiding in the onlookers. If that guy was connected to the Big Guy, then he'd know me. Would he attack me like the others? I shake my head. I'm going crazy. Not every ghost in Baltimore goes back to the Big Guy. They've been around before I pissed him off and they'll be around when that guy's gone too.

KC's staring at a fat raven quickly coming toward us down the sidewalk. He puts an arm around my shoulder and turns me toward the park. We're walking, by his force at first, hand holding my arm hard, but I move with him. I grope my pocket, looking for my necklace. It's still there. I take it out and put it around my neck before tucking the gem into my hoodie where it won't be seen. The heat gently burns against my chest where it touches my shirt. At least I'll be more sure it's there. Once we hit the sidewalk, KC releases my shoulder and says, "Stay away from the ravens." He turns to Rocky. "How many dead?"

"Just one," Rocky catches up. He and KC keep pace beside each other as they beeline for the tower. "Mangled. Maybe random, maybe gang related. Either way, got in the middle of someone's bad day."

KC takes the lead toward the park. His movements are fast and precise. He's not a badge, but he's an overpowering front man again who can go wherever he wants and isn't afraid to walk through a badge line because if they stop him, he's ready to start a brawl with the support of whoever's near lusting for the sound of the trigger. KC takes the cigarette from his ear and puts it back in the tin as we near the police line. Rocky walks alongside him with ease where I have to jog to keep pace. Their legs are too long, their speed a minimum problem for them. Rocky nods to the badge at the edge of the park. He grunts something as we pass. The guy's face twists with confusion, but he stands down. The only protest he shows is turning to his buddy and saying, "What the hell?" as we move on.

"If it's just grizzly though, we might be lucky enough

that it's just a ghost trying to get back into Hell," KC says.

"What's that have to do with Patterson Tower?" I say.

"Because it's not just a historical monument. Like Armistead, it's a tunnel to the other side if you know how to use it."

I stagger.

KC snorts, says, "Don't let that stop you," and keeps going without pause. I have to speed up to catch up. A weight that wasn't on the street comes when I step into the grass. It's not the same as going to Leakin where yeah, it's dark and smelly and you know there are bodies before you get there, but at least they're hidden in the trees and brush and stuff. Patterson Park's curated by the city. Here, there aren't any trees or garbage piles to hide the dead in. Patterson's is a tourist spot in a way that's different from Fort Armistead. Still an old military base in a way, Patterson's was used during the Civil War. Like I said before, anything worth seeing in Baltimore's watered by the blood of history and then we dared to build neighborhoods out of the burial grounds of decades past.

I think that's the only type of history this city knows. I mean, we've got a 7-11 where the Ouija board first popped up and there's a gravestone to the guy somewhere in the city.

This place is supernatural; anger on top of anger with people trying to correct for things that happened to them when they were alive by punishing those who had nothing to do with it. Then their actions create more anger, more violence, more victims, more uselessly spilled blood and broken families that will continue the legacy of every unhappy Baltimoron who couldn't get over himself.

From the street, a badge car whistles. Someone yells,

"Stop!"

I turn around to face the crowd. More faces blur into the anonymity of the dead who have given up. They can't all be dead, right? I rub my eyes. They're still faceless, distant neighbors I can't recognize. The stiff grass crackles under my foot, too loud and hard. The snapping feels like bones breaking. It makes my bones pulse where my dad broke my arm when I was ten. He never thought about it when he lost his shit. It was just like one moment he'd be crying and sipping on a bottle or shoving cold mac into his face. He'd mutter with the TV, mimicking what people said like he'd get the chance to live their lives instead of his own, then the next, I'm running down the hall or trying to lock the door or hide where I think he won't find me. He'd hit so hard and fast, then he'd cry. The next day, he'd act like he didn't know what happened. I never knew if he was pretending, so most of the time, I couldn't stay mad.

The time he broke my arm, he saw me coming in from school. I hadn't figured out I needed to sneak in yet because usually, after I left, he'd forget I wasn't in my room until I came up the steps again as long as he didn't see me go out. But I snapped the door shut too hard. He dropped his mac on the floor and spilled Barton's on himself. He grabbed me by the arm and tossed me into the card table I sometimes ate at when I was desperate to be near him. Then, he broke the arm I used to open the house door, like it'd stop me from being able to open it tomorrow or ever again.

Some of the park trees are anemic. Their long, thin branches create frames for the sky, illuminated by a bright, nearly full moon. The branches don't light though. Somehow, they're too dark and absorb the light coming from the sky or the streets, they're tinted the wrong color, looking more like trees out of Mortem than the trees from my hometown.

Patterson Tower stands in the distance. Its sharp, straight edges are lit yellow in a way that almost looks like the building's on fire. The golden outer walls only make the large windows on each story appear darker on the inside, like stepping into a void. The light couldn't be off though. I've been to this park enough before. There's always been something otherworldly about the tower. If that's where the murders happened, then there should be lights on inside.

Bright red eyes glow on a branch outside the tower. Scattered ravens. Way more than seven. They're everywhere, following me.

No.

They're here for the body.

One of them jumps from the branch and flies toward me. I put my hands up in defense. My jaw tenses. A scream never did anything but make him more angry, so I learned not to do it when I got scared. The moment passes. KC glances over his shoulder at me. His step slows down so it's easier for me to catch up.

As we get to the tower, Rocky nods at the badges standing outside, showing them his own merits as we approach the door. "They're with me," he says without stopping.

"The hell you doing bringing a couple of punks to a crime scene, Grant? Your turn to watch the kids or something?" one of the badges says. His voice is sharp. He tries to hide it with a laugh, but it comes off too cocky.

"Something like that," Rocky says.

The doors to the tower are open. The smell of sulfur's thick, even outside. Inside, a body lays in the center of the floor, a man, not much older than Jag. Black shirt, jeans. I'd worry it could've been Jag if he didn't look so different in every other way. His hands are smashed, his chest is ripped open, clothing torn, and skin peeled back like fingers had dug in relentlessly. His head's hanging off the spine, jaw open, and his face is destroyed, similar to how Wayland had left that guy in his trunk.

Bile burns the back of my throat. I cover my mouth and nose with my arm, trying to use my hoodie as a way to filter out the smell and the sight I don't need anymore. I close my eyes, but the image of them just gets worse. I open my eyes again and their chests don't look like carcasses raided by Val anymore. Now, they look like a more typical crime scene, but worse.

"I don't think we're dealing with a ritual," KC says.

"What do you mean?"

"This is the sign of a mad ghost, not *someone* hunting for ingredients."

"What kind of ingredients are you gonna find in a body?"

KC nose scrunches, his jaw tightens in response to the body. "To break the natural order, it cost life." KC meets my eyes. "Different creatures in this city want different things. Whoever took your boy might have nothing to do with Reagan. The dead lust for power and revenge, the supernatural either want him dead or enslaved. Depending on who's got him, he's either gonna be bled dry or they're gonna try and break him. The collection of bones makes me hopeful we're on the right track though."

"What do you mean break him?" I say.

"You ever have your soul violated?" KC's words are so stiff with a knowing that I don't understand. A pain laced in his voice and pity in his eyes for something he's seen that's beyond me. I shake my head.

"I hope you never do." KC turns back to the corpse. "Either way, he doesn't have much time."

The soft tap of footsteps accompanies Rocky's presence coming up behind us. "Whispering because you solved the murder?"

"Humans are brutal, but they ain't got anything on the destruction of the dead," KC says, walking over to the woman, watching her with his full approach. "You want to see the real shit people can do? Kill 'em and nature takes over."

I turn my head away. The body isn't real. None of this can be real—It's just a couple more props in a mad town made for Hollywood horror flicks.

I have to repeat the phrase to myself until I believe it, even if it's impossible.

KC makes his way up the stairs.

"Where are you going?" Rocky says. "The body's down here."

"Observation deck. I'm just lookin' around. Don't worry about it." KC doesn't slow as he climbs, even as badges are yelling at him, "What the hell?" and "You shouldn't be in here." Rocky's quick to say, "He's with me."

It's weird. Because KC's presence has disappeared. The tower's not that big. His movements should still be audible since this place is built to betray your every little movement, but there's nothing coming from KC. I follow up the stairs to find him and even the badges that had been talking before aren't making noise. The whispers should carry, but it's like we're in a void.

KC's standing just at the top of the stairs on the fourth floor. His thumbs are hooked in his pockets. Beyond his shoulders, it's not Baltimore that's outside, but Mortem. The doors on the upper floor are open, exposing the outside. Wispy, black branches like bones reach for the violet sky. A sweep of black light moves through the mist that draws further back until the Old

Town Mall appears in the distance at the other end of the trees. My breath catches in my throat. "We where I think we are, KC?" I say.

"Yup," he says. "Welcome back to Hell."

I slowly approach the set of open doors and the small balcony that runs around Patterson Tower. The air's empty, feeling too light and the familiar numbness of Mortem seeps into me. The whispers of aggression from the walkie-talkies and shuffling badges are gone, replaced with a mind instantly wiped blank and feelings that have a hard time manifesting. I reach for my pocket. Find a box of cigarettes. I didn't have those before. "How is this possible?"

"Death on an altar creates the connection. Patterson Tower is a tunnel to Mortem, a lot like Fort Armistead." KC comes up behind me. "There are a lot of 'em in Baltimore. You just gotta know where to look."

"So, the first time I got to Mortem was because someone *died* there?" I say.

"Probably." KC looks at me over his shoulder. "Think back. Maybe you saw 'em."

"Is this an old monument thing or is there something else?"

"Fuck if I know." KC shakes his head like he's got a bug flying around his ear. His expression is neutral and distant while his muscles seem more relaxed than they had been before we entered the tower. He approaches the edge of the balcony with crossed arms. Scanning the view exposes a small world contained by purple mist at its edges. The old Town Mall is a brightly lit patch of buildings in the middle of a bundle of black trees and dark leaves clinging to their branches with no winter on its way. Across from where I am now is the tall, sandy building of arches with no windows jutting into the sky until its eaten the mist. The last time I was here, Charon called it Poena, but it looks a little different this time than it had before. Looking at the building makes me feel dread and lost and dizzy, and scared. I want to look at it, to see what it really is, but my eyes won't stay open. My heart pounds so hard, my fingers shake. I grab onto the railing and let my eyes close.

"You ever been this close to Hell before?" KC reaches for his ass pocket, withdrawing a box of cigarettes and the tin he had before.

"Yeah." I exhale hard. "Like two days ago." The scars on my arms burn. Not the new ones, all the old ones from the history I try to forget when my sleeves are down.

"We should talk to the locals." KC says. "Charon said the badge was meeting someone here. Instead we got an opened altar. So someone's hangin' around for a reason or they're trying to escape." He tosses the box of cigarettes to the ground and pops his tin of rolled joints open. As he lights it, I reach into my pocket for cigarettes too. The label's Jag's regular, but they're still not mine. They took everything from me when we were at the police station. I don't even have my phone. KC holds his tin out to me. "The ones on the right are cigs." After I take one, he offers me a lighter.

The nicotine helps keep my thoughts in my head.

KC smacks the railing. "Let's go." He goes back into the tower.

"We're going through the forest?" I say.

"Duh. How else we gonna get to the Mall?"

"What about the Liquor? Won't it bring us back here?"

KC lifts his left arm and pulls his sleeve back A silver chain bracelet around his wrist. "Don't worry about it; Reagan's given me a couple of his tricks."

"The dead really like jewelry."

"Ancient civilizations didn't offer precious metals to the other side for nothing." KC lowers his arm.

"Should I assume all of Ralph's rings do something then?"

"Yeah." KC's at the stairs. "Compact, easy way to create a portable talisman. Not everything fits in rings, necklaces, or bracelets, but a lot of basic shit like protection, sixth sense, a little extra power when you punch." This time, he lifts his right hand, showing off a black band on his ring finger.

KC moves quickly down the first flight of stairs. At the ground floor, no one's there. None of the badges that yelled or tried to stop us as we climbed to the top. The body is gone and Rocky isn't anywhere either. "Where'd everybody go?" I say.

"Still in Baltimore." KC puts his cigarette back into his mouth.

"Why didn't they get sent here with us? We were all in the tower, yeah?"

KC shrugs, plucks his cigarette out, and exhales. "Call it a dead thing. I don't fuckin' know, Joey. You keep askin' questions like there're logical answers to magic."

We hit the second-floor landing. KC leads the way down through the lobby. The doors at the front of Patterson Tower hang open. A stone path made of the same sparkling, sandy color as Poena lead through the mud and grime with one path leading toward the trees, disappearing into the mud that buries it and the other leading toward a small bridge that runs over the river and toward the golden front door.

"What if there's nothing at the mall?" I say. "I have to find Jag—"

"Then go find him." KC stops walking. He turns around to face me. His eyes hold something in them they didn't have before. Fire, anger, the darkness of the dead that have haunted me since Wayland's death. "I'm gonna be honest, Joey. I don't give a fuck about your boyfriend, okay? The only reason we're together right now is because your ghost problem's hooked around my medium. If you wanna chase after dead leads and graffiti, then by all means, fuck off. I haven't ever needed you and I still don't." KC closes the space between us. His presence is overwhelming. The nearer he gets, the more I want to step back, look down. He grabs the front of my shirt. The surprise forces me to meet his gaze again "If I don't prioritize Reagan, no one else will. So, you can go after your boy, but I'm not giving up mine for you." KC dips down the path toward.

I look back at Patterson tower briefly before chasing after KC toward Caedis Silvis.

We're down the path outside of Patterson without stopping. The pressure to slow down hits me the closer we get to Caedis Silvis. KC slows too, turns around, and keeps stepping back. "You're gonna wanna stay near. The bracelet's not as good as what Charon's got."

"Right." My skin's suddenly hot and I'm sweaty, but the Liquor takes that away, leaving me feeling empty and content again in a matter of seconds.

I speed up to catch up with KC. My feet sink into the mud. The Liquor smells sweet, but burns my nose a little bit too. My skin tingles with the feeling of being dunked into *nothing*. It's tempting to think I can go back in time and experience things again to see things I missed and make different decisions so no one will get hurt.

That's the worst thing about all of this.

You only get one chance to do anything and once it's gone, it's over. Your mistakes live forever in hearts made of stone that others will carry around with them. I don't want to do this anymore. I take a puff of cigarette to ignore the branches that don't feel right under my feet.

It's only made weirder by the aggressive greed of the mud that sucks my shoe in every time I take a step. I focus on breathing. Any time the anxiety spikes, Mortem takes it away after only a taste of the air. Another puff of cigarette. I'm almost wondering if this cigarette is real or a prop for Mortem. It feels too good. I glance up toward KC. The only sounds around us are his breaths, cigarette breaks, the crunching branches under our feet. "Sorry." My tongue flicks across my ring. "I didn't mean to make it sound like Ralph didn't matter."

KC's jaw is tight with the next puff. "That's how it always has been and probably how it always will be. People don't understand sacrifices that are made for them until it's too late."

"Yeah, I know." I rub my eyes, and let myself follow KC just by his shoes so I don't have to look at his hands or his back or his face and see the disappointment or anger or anxiety that I feel coming into me from him.

I say nothing else and focus only on getting through the path and returning to Caeve Mortem.

THIRTEEN.

It's a relief to hit the pavement of Cavae Mortem. The mud can't grab at us anymore, and after however long we'd been walking, I'm more than certain it wasn't just a game my mind was playing on me. Every step was hard, every stick hooked my foot. We didn't hear any sounds that weren't our own. We didn't see anyone in the trees. We can only hope whoever made the altar is here somewhere.

KC doesn't slow as he makes his way toward the courtyard. We pass by the shops that back home look abandoned, but here they're distractions to keep the dead busy so they don't see their end coming. I don't remember the words on Andy's or the pawnshop looking like gibberish before, but now, the signs are nonsense, the glow in the windows feels empty, and whatever the place is made of looks cheap like movie theater props. The music from Postmortem crawls into the streets the closer we get. Caedis Silvis isn't *that* far, but the Liquor in the air insulates the same way that it catches the light to scare you from wandering too far, I suppose. The closer we get, the more the sound of the courtyard is able to bounce off the buildings and trees and streets, but it feels hollow and dull. I step onto the courtyard's brick path. A pulse from the bar's soft rock goes through me. The numbing effect of Mortem amplifies. I hold my breath, not ready for it to hit. My ass pocket's heavy again with something that wasn't in it two seconds ago.

I reach for it.

A box of cigarettes comes out.

I toss the box to the ground. It melts into the cement. A moment later, it's back in my pocket, making my lips feel lonely and tempting me to put the poison into my mouth, even if only for a little while. I bite my lip ring and toss the new box onto the ground again. By the time we're at the bar, there's another box in my pocket. KC's through the door, going past the tables of rowdy souls playing cards for made up currency or the guy who looks like he spent the last few years of his life at a hospital exchanging stories of how he died. He laughs about it the same way someone might tell the story of how they got their pet dog or lost their first tooth or lied about homework and got away with it. The laughter from the one corner quiets just long enough to hear the guy in the scrubs say, "Then, I died!" and laugh.

KC climbs onto the bar step and leans over the counter saying, "Hey, Sol." He cringes, looks down, looks back a Sol with a flair in his nose. Everything about him says lunging, but he pins his arms under the body like it's what'll stop him from reaching too soon. "Long time, no see."

Sol turns from the shelf of nonsensically labeled alcohol to KC. It's so strange to see her like that. Looking like my mom, but he seeing something else.

Every time I see her, I want to find what memories I have of her and check if they're as bad as the feelings I have when I think about her. The way Sol looks makes me want to talk to her, thinking maybe when I was a kid, I just got the wrong impression because I couldn't understand, because I was a kid and if I talked to her a little more, I wouldn't hate her so much.

But then I remember Sol's not my mom; what she says isn't the truth and she doesn't know anything about my mom, only what I remember of her and how I want to feel.

With KC's approach Sol tries to hide her surprise, but her usual forced smile falters for a second. "Kailee." Her smile strengthens again. "Welcome back. How are you doing?"

"You don't gotta make up small talk. You and I are both busy people," KC says.

"Okay," Sol says.

"I've got a couple questions for ya though. First, you see a suspicious soul hidin' somethin' come in here?"

"Kailee, I can't—"

"Your only job around here is to keep the peace, right? Wonder what the gearheads in the *end* would do to you if a total mutiny took place and every ghost under Baltimore went looking for a way out. Feels like today might be the day to test that—"

"I can't do revenge, Kailee—"

"Don't call me that, and take *his* face off. You're a fuckin' disgrace." His eyes lock with Sol who isn't moving now. It's strange, like time's frozen. Even the noise in the bar turns softer, the lights look like they've dimmed and are flickering, struggling to keep constant at least.

The smile fully leaves Sol's face. Her expression becomes distant and inhuman; the mask she's always worn gone. She still looks like my mom. If she dropped the look for KC, what did she become? Does she still have a face at all for him to see or is it blank like some of the other people in the bar who are missing their eyes or their smiles or what might've been left of their souls? Is there something about her face that couldn't register in the same way the dead don't up top? She looks the same to me, but something's not right with the music anymore. It's going off-key. The ease I felt before from Mortem and the Liquor are dampening to make me feel a building anxiety stating that doom is coming. The hair on my arms is standing now and my face is hot. My foot bounces, not to the beat of the music, or anything. I'm just getting that crazy feeling back.

"I don't understand what you're asking me," Sol says. "You should sit down and have a drink. Tell me more about what you're thinking. I want to help you." Sol grabs a chilled glass from under the counter. "What's bothering you today? If you tell me, I'm sure I can do something." She's got the glass under the tap and in front of KC before she's done talking. She leans her elbows against the counter. A small smile comes to her lips as her hand slowly moves across the countertop until her fingers find KC's. Pain pulls at my chest, remembering her doing this same thing to Wayland, probably wearing my face and how much she'd like to do it to me wearing my mom's.

Irritation digs into KC's expression. "Okay. Cool. We're doing this then?" He jumps off the bar. Turning back to the room, he locates the nearest table, nearest person, easiest one to turn around with a tap on the shoulder. His target responds to the probe. Blank eyes, a distant look. This guy's already checked out, living in a dream state until his turn comes to boat across the river. KC meets his friendliness with a punch to the jaw and a growl that echoes off the interior of Post Mortem. Everyone at that guy's table stands up.

The energy of the room shifts. The conversation and laughter from before is gone as the dead sitting at every table around the bar sits back slowly, attention gripped by the anger in the air. Tapping, clapping, kicking, cussing, a glass goes flying off a table. The voice in my head's getting louder as heat buzzes under my skin telling me to grab shit too. Now's my chance to pick a target and make them bleed. There's a cup in my hand and before I have time to question where it came from, I'm throwing it in whatever direction I'm facing. A table flips in the corner. A snarl, a chorus of curses. A dead guy in the other corner punches someone and that collapses another table. Someone else calls that guy a bastard while the one on the ground's saying, "That all you got?" He latches onto the other guy's leg and bites down on his ankle.

"Wait—!" Sol runs around the bar.

KC's got another guy in his grasp, hand full of shirt, fist back with red knuckles from already hitting the guy three times. The chaos around us whirls to a pause of panting and broken glass and the feeling of Lethe seeps back into the air. "What was that?" KC says with a hard exhale.

"I'll answer what I can," the words sound insecure coming out of Sol's mouth. "I don't know a lot, but I'll answer what I can."

"Glad you came around." KC drops the guy he's holding. The air again shifts right with KC's mood. It's so not like what I remember at BAIT's, but then, I was knocked out when things quieted down. I don't know how a frenzy stops once it starts, but it has to be different on the topside when you're not surrounded by all the Lethe that wants to drown out the misery and keep the peace. For a second, it feels like the air is overdosing me on the stuff and there's a fight between the part of my head ingesting the mist and the voice whispering in the back of my ear.

And just like that, the bar returns to silence; the building rage and thirst are gone with the fight as spirits help their tablemates off the ground. Tables and chairs correct themselves, broken glass, spilled food and cards and games melt into the floor and reappear where they should be. The laughter and conversation and drinking continue like nothing happened.

"What the hell was that?" I say.

"Don't be like that. You've seen a frenzy before," KC says, patting me on the shoulder.

"Not like that," I say.

"Don't get a big head. This isn't how it works topside. You start shit, it'll lead to absolute destruction. To get something going down here takes a lot more energy because of the powers that be that make this place function," KC says.

From the shift of silence to the jovial conversation, it all feels so much more hollow than it had before. Like I know this place is called *Hollow Death*, but it had done a pretty good job putting up a facade of something else before. Even when the food and drinks came out of nowhere, it still felt like there was some worth in the objects here. Now? Everything's so… dumb. It's *so* dumb. The cigarettes in my pockets are fake. This room is fake. The people are fake. Everything here is fucking fake, meant to make you feel good and it works for most people and it's so good at what it does that I know this and I want it to work on me too.

"Back room," Sol says. "Now." She keeps looking at the entrance to Post Mortem like she's expecting someone to come in. She's waving KC and I behind the bar. She glances at the door then around the bar, checking the tables. KC gives Sol a half smile that disappears just as quickly as it came. He doesn't bother looking at me as he makes his way toward the room. I follow KC into the back room I don't remember even being there before. Maybe it wasn't there before and Mortem popped it up and it's another trap and it'll eat us for being annoying souls that caused trouble.

Instead of another illusion, the door contains a small, simple, and nearly empty room. A round table, four chairs, nothing else. There are no windows or decorations but a couple of picture frames with blank canvases inside. The patterns on the wall match the floor and ceiling in a dark wood that looks like it's the same outside in the main bar, but it's darker here somehow. I wonder if there are supposed to be snapshots of things Sol thinks people want to see in the empty picture frames, but because it's just us and we've been causing problems, she's not putting anything together.

Or maybe she puts good memories in the frames and those have been lacking for a while now.

I don't want to sound ungrateful. It's not like there weren't good times with Wayland and Donny and Jag, but it's like… none of those moments actually feel like they belonged to me. They don't feel like they belong in my life or that I was actually experiencing them at the time because while I was smiling or felt kind of okay, I felt bad since I was away from my dad and why should I feel okay when I know he's at home drinking himself into another stupor so he can forget he's there alone?

When I was out, if I thought about it too much, I'd start to think my mom was right to walk away because it was so much easier to have nothing to do with him. The more I'd think about it, the closer I got to worrying I might be like her one day.

KC sits down on the far side of the table where his back's to the wall and he's facing the door. I sit to his left, the chair across from me's empty. Sol comes into the room last. She shuts the door gently and turns around without moving away from the entrance.

"I thought I told you to take his face off." KC's nose scrunches with a sneer. "It's an insult ya think you're anywhere good enough to even pretend to be him. Take it off, yeah?" He grunts. "I don't wanna have to beat it off."

"You can do that?" I say.

"I'll damn well try." His eyes lock on her. A residual of his energy flows into me. My foot's tapping again. I put my hand on my knee to make it stop.

Nothing about Sol changes from what I can see, but KC relaxes, and he leans back. He runs a hand through his hair, combing it with his fingers as he closes his eyes and let's his head drop forward. A heavy sigh comes out. "Back to business. You see anyone shady running around here lately?"

"I don't know what you're saying," Sol says.

"Oh? You wanna go for round two?" KC pushes his chair back.

"No," Sol says. "I mean, I do not understand your question, be more specific."

"Okay…" KC exhales hard. He glances around the walls, more like he's looking for the way to phrase what he's thinking. Was Sol genuinely confused? All those times before when I was asking her questions, did she really not get what I meant or was she just good at pretending she didn't understand. KC clears his throat. "Anyone new come to you asking for Lethe or feathers or other shit we use for rituals?"

"No. No one's asked me for anything," Sol says.

KC glances at me. "You see anyone duckin' around

the courtyard? Guys that don't look lost, but look like they're lookin' for somethin'?"

"I haven't seen anyone like that either," Sol says. "Up until you got here, things had been fairly uneventful."

"Fantastic." KC sighs. "Either no one's been here *yet*, ya don't notice intruders, or you're lyin' again."

"I'm not lying," Sol says.

"You aren't exactly programmed to help—" KC sucks in a breath, gripping the edge of the table hard. His eyes go wide, his jaw clenches, and with his next breath comes a soft groan and a muttered, "Fuck." His body starting to rock where he's sitting as his fingers grip harder and harder at the table.

Instead of it bouncing off the walls like it should, the room devours his cursing and it doesn't allow his voice to escape.

He presses his hands to his ears and his body curls inward. His breathing becomes more labored. Another groan. Redness spikes underneath his jacket, dripping down his wrist. Bruises form too, black and blue splotches on what little skin he's got exposed. He wipes at his head, eyes closed. His face is on the table, then he's sitting up, back arched. He exhales hard, unable to be still. "Hold on, Reagan," he breathes out. "Keep it together."

"What's going on?" I say to Sol.

She responds in something that isn't a human language.

"What?" I say.

She shakes her head. Her face changes in a subtle way, saying that she was missing something in her eyes a second ago that's there now as they rest on KC. "There's nothing we can do," she says. "It's *his* vitas."

"His what?" I say.

"His *body*. On the other side. Something is happening

to *the medium—*"

"Is this from a ritual?"

"I don't know."

The weight of my heart in my pocket is so much more than it was ten seconds ago. KC's continuing pain only makes it worse. Ralph went through this for me. Suddenly KC's anger on the other side of Caedis Silvis makes sense. Does KC go through it every time too? When I did it to Ralph, all I could think about was my pain, Wayland's passing, and getting home to Jag so I could forget everything for a while. I've been using everyone around me, just like my dad used me to numb his pain. So many people keep sacrificing their well-being for me and putting themselves through so much pain when I don't deserve the kindness. Why would anyone go through this for me?

"Mediums are a special creature, Joey. They don't come around often and their abilities are beyond my understanding," Sol says. "However, I do know you can't bend reality to your will and pay no *respect.*"

"How in the hell is self-destruction *respect?*" I reach for something to throw. There's nothing to grab, so my fist lands on the table instead. The voice in my head's getting louder, overpowering the volume of KC's hissing. I need to be moving. I need to do something with this energy or I'm going to drive myself mad. I lean against the wall and then I'm bouncing on it with my hands pressed to my ears while I hum in an attempt to forget I'm in Cavae Mortem.

For the first time, Sol's expression breaks. The distance returns to her eyes. She still looks like my mom, but there's a coldness to them that makes her inhuman in the same way that Val looks like a person, but feels like a bird or the way that Charon looks like a snot-nosed brat from LA, but he doesn't feel like it at the same time.

There's a presence that he's bigger than anything I've ever seen… And he's just a servant to the Cogs or whatever's up there. Sol is the same. Brown eyes go solid. She's not the passive, sweet-talking barkeep who tries her best to drug you while telling you what you want to hear. She's some kind of monster from the afterlife like Val eating hearts, trying to eat me at the station or the fish in the Lethe or the echoes hiding in the Liquor, all wearing things that look familiar so they can draw you close, grab you, and bury you forever. Their faces are illusions hanging over the monsters they're hiding or maybe they're masks dressing up ideas my mind can't comprehend.

I don't blame KC for screaming at her to take Ralph's face off. Just the idea of what my mom's memory might be hiding from me… or that my face was used on someone else I love to trick them. Offensive isn't a strong enough word.

"You're all so arrogant to think you can command anything in the universe to bend to your will," Sol says. "Dead or alive, you humans come down here and for some reason, you think you are still in charge. All you've gotta do is say so and the universe will bend to your desires. Sometimes, you plead or bargain, but mostly your kind makes demands. You scream, thinking that if you don't bend, if you reject what's in front of you, everything else will too and suddenly the world is changed. Maybe it's how the world of the living works. When you're alive, do you simply make demands and everything falls into place as you please?"

"No," I say.

"Then why do you all come to Mortem, which has not been given over to mortals, and believe that it would be run that way? Your kind are sentimental; your kind are angry; your kind are irrational and entitled and destructive and selfish and because of that, you believe you should be in charge, you'll go so far to summon—"

"I never said I should be in charge, Sol. I just don't know where you creatures get off thinking you're holier than humanity when every goddamn thing you do is lying, deceit, and causing pain—"

"Don't blame us. Your suffering is the fault of man."

"How is this my fault?"

"Humans make demands," Sol says. "When not met, you take what you want anyway. You destroy trust and kingdoms for selfishness and power. Why does a medium suffer to provide? Because that is what those afflicted by humanity can't escape."

"If humans are that bad, then why would any of us go through that kind of pain for anyone? Let alone strangers?" I say. "Ralph doesn't know me but as anything but a customer who comes in on the regular to forget her shitty-ass life. I'm sure I'm not the only one with a sob story drowning in a bath of 120 proof on the weekly."

"I don't know, *Josephine*." Her voice sends a chill through me. The way she says my name isn't something I can protest against this time. She actually feels dangerous. "Humans aren't rational. Why would a stranger harm themselves for the benefit of others? Why take on the pain of those around you at your expense? I don't know. I see no purpose in giving those who have already died another chance. If you had cared about life, perhaps you would've been more careful, and you can't expect something to change once it has died. But I've seen all types have such disregard for the living that I have never understood suffering to reward them with a second chance." Her eyes fall upon KC.

My legs are shaking, fighting me to remain still and get no closer. My hands curl, skin stinging, heat's getting to my head, and I can't think, can't think, can't—I knock my head into the wall again. I shake it. Hand to my eyes, I press my head harder into the wall.

It's only then that I realize KC isn't hissing anymore. I'm not sure when it stopped. I survey him, sitting back at the table, panting, rubbing his face, cheeks flushed and everything's sweaty. Discoloration on his skin shows bruising, but everything else is too covered to see further damage.

"Hey… You okay?" I say.

"Yeah," he hisses, arm still covering his face. He takes a couple of long, deep breaths, forcing himself to go from panting to a sigh.

I drop to the floor, using the wall to ease me down. The building pressure I'd felt in my head's gone. Shakily, KC pushes himself up to sit. His head drops into his hands. He closes his eyes muttering. "Fuck."

"What the hell was that, KC?"

"*The priest.*" He takes a deep, shaky breath.

"What?"

"Clock's fuckin' tickin'. Either we break Reagan out or that guy breaks him." KC's head moves a little as he stretches his neck gently.

"What the hell are you talking about? Who the hell is the priest?"

"It doesn't really fuckin' matter, does it, Joey?" KC stands up. "I told you this shit's bigger than you know. Reagan doesn't leave the bar for a reason and this is one of 'em." KC's fingers shakily run through his hair. He undoes the ponytail. His long, blond hair falls loose around his shoulders.

"What's going on? What do *they* want from Ralph?" I say.

"He talks to things, real big things, gets into souls that are harboring God knows what. They call on him, tell him to do things. He can access places and information no one else can. He says some of it could destroy me; that means it could destroy him too, but he doesn't ever consider himself when he gets to work." KC's eyes lock with mine. He's always had a serious look about him, but nothing more threatening than he's got now, when it comes to Ralph. "There's more shit out there than I understand and pretty much the whole bar's set up to protect *him* from it. Them. All of it that'll use him up and spit him back out."

"This happens every time he does a séance?" I say.

"To different degrees, but Reagan does more than séances," KC says. "Where it ends? I'm not sure, but that's what the rest of *those things* want him for. And he got into all this shit because he decided to give out a second chance to someone who didn't deserve it." Standing, KC's legs wobble. He uses the wall for stability as he makes his way toward the door. "We need to do something… so we can find *him*." He stops, leaning against the wall as he eyes Sol. "If you really haven't seen anythin', then sittin' back here's a waste of time."

"What are we going to do then?" I say.

"Hell if I know," KC says. "Guy could be anywhere."

"Think he has anything to do with the big guy or Jag?" I say.

"Maybe. I dunno. I really don't know much about this guy beyond the way he stalks Reagan," KC says. "You don't know anything about *him*, do you Sol?"

"I can't answer that," Sol says.

"I figured you'd say that," KC grunts.

Sol's eyes are on me. I hate the way she looks at me and the way she tries to look so normal and accusatory at the same time. It doesn't help that she's wearing my mom's face. I can't stop wondering if that's the same sort of accusation she showed me the last time she saw me.

Did she even pause for a second to consider if I should go with her or did she know there was something wrong with me too? Did she think about what would happen to me at all?

"Thanks… I guess." KC says. "We'll look around." He puts his hand out to push Sol, but doesn't touch her. She moves without the prompt. He grabs the door handle. "Maybe Big Dick'll saw something at the park we're missing. That's what his entire job description is, right?"

"Shit," I say.

KC glances over his shoulder, finding me still at the table, though he's standing now. "What?"

"Rocky—I forgot about Rocky. Shit." I pace across the room. "He's gonna think I ditched him on purpose."

"So, explain to him ya fell into Hell when we get back." KC shrugs. "Whoops." He opens the door with a grunt.

"I don't think he's gonna buy that. It's kinda why I came looking for Ralph in the first place," I say.

"We better find him then, huh?" KC steps out of the room, stops.

His head cocks to the side. "Excuse me?"

I peer around KC to see what he's staring at. There's a man in the bar, staring at us, meeting KC's gaze, frozen like he hadn't meant to be seen. He's lanky with a little bit of muscle, a little too tall, and the black tendrils moving along his arms are thicker than what I've seen before. They wrap around his exposed neck showing from his open jacket, across his jaw, and dig into his mouth, ears, and dark, inhuman eyes. He looks like the guy from the forest.

Everyone else in the room is at their tables, talking like they notice nothing. The guy's eyes turn on me, and refocus on KC when he takes a step forward. The guy says something that looks like, "You." For a second, everything's in slow motion.

KC steps forward saying, "See somethin' ya like, buddy?" KC's dashing across the bar just as quickly as the lanky guy's running out the front of Post Mortem.

"Bastard!" KC yells as he runs.

"What the hell?" someone at a table says then slinks back into whatever he had been doing before KC bumped him.

I go running too. I can't let KC get too far ahead of me. On the way out the door, I run into someone. They offer a typical Baltimoron greeting of "Dumb bitch," without getting up. The lanky guy and KC aren't immediately visible in the courtyard. I go down the brick path a little, looking both directions. No way they could disappear so quickly. If they stepped into the street or headed toward Lodgings, the mist might be hiding them. Further down the courtyard to the right, I catch the backside of KC running into the building that should've been the Old Kaufman's, but instead it said THE BIN. The door closes quickly behind him with a snap.

My heart's throbbing. I'm light-headed. The heart hanging around my neck is heavier than it was twenty minutes ago. KC's chasing after someone because the person who gave me that second chance is missing and hurt and the guy holding my second chance might be with him.

It all sucks and I don't know how to make it stop. The Liquor tugs the anxiety out of my body. Mortem reminds me there are cigarettes in my pocket. For a second, it all feels so tempting because if I just sucked on that cigarette and sat at that bar, I could forget who I've hurt and how I've hurt them and that I don't know what the hell I'm doing or if I'll be able to help Jag.

He shouldn't have even been in jail, I shouldn't be

trying to prove I'm not crazy to a badge that has no reason to believe me or KC or Ralph or anyone, but every choice I make just seems to ripple into hurting someone else. Ralph might be in shit because of me. Maybe he's not, but Jag actually is and I can't check out while he's in jail or waiting to die because he gave me more chances than he should've. I have to help KC find Ralph so he can prove to Rocky that Jag's innocent, and then I'll figure out what to do from there, if I'm even worth the trouble I'm putting Jag through.

I can't think too hard about it because every time I do, the cigarettes get a little more tempting.

So instead, I run down the courtyard, making for Kaufman's to find KC and hopefully get a lead.

FOURTEEN.

Kaufman's in Baltimore is a huge building that should have nine steel gates over the store front. The upper windows should be blocked with glass so dirty, you're not sure if they're black from darkness on the inside or covered in something. It used to be a department store that sent out catalogues to families who could go make a day out of shopping for just about anything on any of their floors. Furniture, electronics, repairs, clothing for the whole family, toys, stuff you didn't even think you needed, but the second you saw it, you were struck with this sense of, "How did I even get by until now? I'm sure they played cheerful Christmas music around the holidays and featured loving homes between the pages with Santa putting gifts under a tree and if you came at the right time, you could even meet him in the lobby. They did their best to paint a picture you'd want to see yourself in, that maybe you could build if the right stuff was offered to you. Then, maybe you'd come by and spend a couple hundred dollars trying to take the future you saw for yourself on the pages of their catalogue.

Kaufman's in Mortem isn't the corpse of a building from decades ago, rotting away between other businesses brought back from the dead. It has a bright paint job of black, purple, and pink. The carvings are silver-plated, intricate, and look like bone or web. The windows feature warm home settings or mannequins that look too much like people I know. One of the mannequins looks too much like me, but her skinnies are sky blue, she's wearing a blouse and silver bracelets and little hoop earrings while she smiles alongside someone too fit to be my dad, but he still looks like him in the face.

I guess he's my dad if he had a better life.

The glass doors part when I step in front of them. Inside, there's nothing but a white canvas of mist and nothingness hanging above the pale, peach marble floor. I step through the door. The place materializes instantly and my brain's having a hard time reconciling it with what I had been looking at two seconds ago. I'm going crazy, been going crazy, this is all just bringing it out more.

Rows and rows of clothing aisles form with the hoods of cars showing in the back and escalators leading to the second floor. The walls are decorated in an old-timey way. I'm not sure how else to describe it—like the original Kaufman's, there are wall carvings along the trim, gold and brown wallpaper, pictures of what the place used to look like, and how things have changed. Soft chuckles and giggles and talking echo like people are actually here give the place life, but I don't see anyone. Soft, but playful piano music plays through speakers, telling me to come in and take a look at what they've got in the back.

This place… I wonder if it's really a mirror of Baltimore or it's just putting something on the face of something familiar—Like everything else I've run into down here so far.

"Hey, kiddo Can I help you find something?" The

voice is too familiar, even if it's distorted with friendliness that's so unlike him and the fakeness that Sol carries around whenever she speaks. I turn to the source. My brain can't connect what I'm seeing with what I know. The man standing in front of me's some weird version of my dad. I say that because never in the twenty-three years that I've known him has he combed his hair to the side like that or kept his face shaved or looked at me with wide, alert eyes and a warm smile. His shirt isn't stained or ill-fitting, but a pastel polo with jeans that aren't baggy or too small, stuck under his gut. A thick, golden watch hangs on his wrist. Black hair speckled with gray is combed back and he's got slightly darker hair growing on his upper lip. The start of a mustache in the rest of his stubble.

"What the hell are you doing here, Sol?" I say. "Take that face off."

"Sol?" the thing says. "That's not me."

"Well, you're not my dad—"

"Look, I know thing's've been a little difficult between us for a while, *Josephine*, but I want to make it up to you. However I can—I know it won't be easy and I don't deserve your forgiveness, but I really want to make things work. I wasted so much time in that chair, making you clean up my messes and apologize when I hurt you. Josephine—I want you to know that it wasn't me. Not the real me, anyway and I love you—"

"Shut the fuck up!" My hands are going into his chest, shoving him back then they're on my ears to block him from saying anything else that might convince me to give him a chance. "I'm not here to get empty words from a dead whatever you are who thinks he's doing me a favor by saying all the shit my dad never did! You're not him! You can't be him! Take his face off and get out of my way!" I run deeper into the store. My eyes are burning with tears moistening my cheeks. The Liquor acts quickly, working its magic to take the pain out of me. I can get why some people would fall for this facade. Everything about this place makes you want to get comfortable so you can play along with the feelings of relief or satisfaction you've gotten that maybe you never felt at all in life. It's so much easier to let go of everything, sit down, and let yourself get numbed by Mortem's spell than to fight against it.

I'm moving without direction and I don't care enough to stop. I don't want to look back in case that thing pretending it's my dad is right behind me. I just hope he can't teleport to try that stupid trick again. I've wanted that shit so bad for so long, it's so dumb. An impossible, sentimental desire that Mortem seems too eager to feed because it works. If he keeps at it, I don't know if I'll be able to resist again. I can already feel myself wanting to sit down and listen to him apologize and say he was proud of me and ask him if he wants to go to the bar for a drink and catch up or something, but I can't let this place make me forget about Jag.

I pass aisle after aisle filled with products that look soft around the edges like they're made of dreams painted in water color. Like the bar, people stand around the store with soft murmurs and music playing through invisible speakers. The words don't make sense, but they make me feel more comfortable.

My sneakers are silent as my feet hit the ground. No one behind me makes a sound either. Not because they're not there, but the Bin's manipulating perception, making it harder to know if I'm being followed.

I know, it's stupid to think about because why the hell would some supernatural creature need to chase me when it seems like they've got all the power in existence while I'm in their den? If that's what you can call this. If

I see that thing again, I'm going to punch it in the head. Maybe that'll knock the face it has no right to off. If nothing else, both that thing and Sol deserve a good cross for the kind of shit they pull down here.

Whatever's in control, it's getting smarter. That thing saw my mom's face wasn't working at the bar, so it went for my dad instead, probably getting into my brain and memories and feelings the same way Ralph does and figuring out what I want the most. How stupidly bad I'd hoped my dad would change in the end before he moved on or I moved on or both of us died. None of that happened, which only makes me wonder if people can even change or if you're one bad day away from living through the rest of forever as the worst version of yourself. It can't be the latter, right?

My legs ache. I stop in front of a wall of televisions playing some scene from some part of Baltimore filled with graffiti. A shadow slowly moves between the buildings while candlelight illuminates the edges of the sidewalk in white paper bags. The screen goes black. A voice says, "WHERE THE FUCK ARE YOU, JOSEPHINE?" sounding too much like my old man. A sob breaks into anger. "What'd I do to you? What did I *do* to you? What the hell did I *do* to you?" He keeps saying over and over again. The sobs are getting worse until he's choking himself. The screen illuminates. The picture's not clear, but even with the blur filtering over it, I still know it's my house, lights out, Dad in his chair from behind the television screen, illuminating him from the front. His arm hangs over the edge of his chair, his pistol loosely gripped in his hand, the muzzle of it touching the floor. His head lulls to the side. Red bleeds through the back of the chair like it had been shot and was dying too.

"Dad?" I step closer to the TV. Doesn't matter how

many times I tell myself this isn't real, it's a trap, don't look at it, don't look at it, don't look at it—My body's moving on its own and some other voice in my head sounds just like me saying, *Don't miss your last chance to talk to him. He died because of you. Make up with him.* My chest hurts. My fingers reach for the screen. Touching it, a soft current of electricity goes through me. A head. Goosebumps. A wave of relief.

"It's going to be alright," my dad says from behind me.

A hand's on my shoulder. I pull away from the TV, turn around, and step away from the figure.

The thing that looks like my dad is standing next to me, hand floating where I had once been.

I press my palms to my ears before he can sound like Dad again. "I told you to take that face off, Sol!" My voice cracks. The screaming is caught in the walls of the department store, being silenced. Even though I'm loud, it doesn't travel and it's between the two of us like I'm whispering.

"I swear to you, I'm not Sol, Josephine—"

"Like hell you're not—I delivered the piece of shit face you're wearing to Charon and he told me dad's not here anymore. You really think I'm going to believe you're him, wandering around like the good dead who don't jump in the river when I know what you creatures are like? You don't care. You just put on a face to manipulate people and I'm sick of it!" I'm still stepping back.

The thing that looks like my dad's coming toward me, saying, "You only make it harder on yourself by rejecting the comforts Mortem has to offer. Aren't you tired of suffering?"

"No, guess not. I've got enough to live for right now and I'm not looking for comfort, so go help someone else." I draw my fist back. The punch is strong, leading, it pulls my body forward. I've never been a good fighter, mostly just scrappy; that was only good enough to get a shot in and move before getting knocked on my ass. My fist hits his face. His grunt sounds just like my dad the last time I landed something on him. I flinch, pull back, wait for him to grab me by the arm to continue our usual dance.

Instead, he grabs his cheek. His eyes are big and watery. He looks like he's going to cry.

"Is this what we need to do in order to fix things?" he says. "You can hit me again if you need to, Josephine. It's the least I can—"

"Just leave me alone, alright? I don't need your help and I don't want anything to do with you!" I put my hands up as I step back too fast. My shoulders run into someone standing close behind me. I pull away, throat tightening to hold the yelp in as I swing another fist.

Backing toward the thing pretending to be my dad, I almost hit a shelf. A burst of nerves comes from inside of me and goes out again with a breath of Liquor.

"Holy shit." Wiping the sweat from my forehead, I rub my eyes.

The rows of aisles blur together. I check over my shoulder. The TVs that had once showed my house and my dad in his chair are now bright, empty light and the thing that looked like my dad is gone. The shop doesn't feel real anymore. The bright lights are clouds that are pulling me away. A soft buzzing builds in my ears. The white screens are getting brighter, attempting to overpower the image of the floor and aisles to make me feel like I don't exist anymore. I close my eyes and press hard on them. "Where the hell is KC?" I run my fingers through my hair, pushing my bangs back. "I didn't realize Mortem was like this," I mutter. My hair slips out from behind my ears as soon as I start walking again.

I put my hands in the air. Not a shrug. They're just above me and my head dips to the side. "Ugh…" I rub my face again. My arms drop to my sides.

There's a squeak. Rubber on linoleum. It's weird because there's been none of that the whole time we've been here, now, suddenly my shoes are giving me away. Around the corner, I'm not alone anymore. A guy with long brown hair, kind of shaggy, wearing jeans a little too tight for a man his age and a sleeveless shirt is standing with both hands and pants covered in grease. He looks up at me. His gray eyes meet mine. Too familiar. Everything about his face is too familiar even though I've never seen this guy before in my life. I'm sure of it.

"Joey." He puts something back on the shelf. By the time it leaves his hand, I don't remember what he was holding anymore and I can't stop looking at his face. Slowly, he comes toward me. "That's your name, right?"

"Who's asking?" I swallow.

"I've been waiting to meet you, ya know?" He laughs gently. The laugh gives it away. He sounds just like *him*.

"Who are you?"

"Sorry—Roy Locke. Jag's dad?" Roy says.

Chills go down my spine. The Liquor's not working as well as it should. I shouldn't've asked because all it's going to do is make me want to stand here and ask him a million questions just to see if he really is who he says he is so he can tell me all the things I've never learn about Jag on my own. "How? Haven't you been dead for a while now?"

"Yeah." Roy rubs the back of his neck. "I've been waiting for Jag to catch up. I've got an apology to make. I'm hoping he doesn't come too soon, but the waiting is killing me, ya know?" He laughs again and it's the same kind of relaxed laugh that Jag always has when he's got the TV on low and he's not paying attention to it. He's watching me or he's tired or he's texting someone, but he's in a good mood after finishing a beer and we're chilling without jack shit to do and that's how we like it.

"You'll be waiting for a while," I say. "Jag doesn't have plans to die any time soon."

"I figured. Think you'd mind waiting with me?" He slides his hands into his pockets. They stand the same way. Their postures the same, their mannerisms are the same, everything is the same, even after the years apart. What's it been? When Jag started working at Bodymore five years ago, his dad had been dead since he was eighteen.

Almost ten years ago, and Jag still hasn't forgotten all the time they spent together. It stayed in his body and his voice and just the way he is. I guess that's not so weird. I lived with a ghost for fifteen years and I could never forget my dad. I wonder how much of me is just like him. Is it my temper? The alcoholism? Am I so clingy that it makes Jag uncomfortable, but he's not sure he can say anything cause it might set me off? Did I get any of my dad's good qualities? Did my dad even have any?

"He really misses you, ya know?" I say. "He thinks about you all the time."

"Yeah…" Roy sighs. "I did some stupid shit. Too bad you don't really think about that until you're on the underside, eh?"

I'm breathing slowly. My visions going in and out and I'm staring at Jag's dad's face trying to memorize how he looks but also just trying to see him. This isn't real. This *can't* be real. This can't even be what he looks like because I don't know what he looks like. It's just Mortem making him look the way I'd think he would look, right? Using memories of Jag's face and morphing them into someone older who doesn't have any of Jag's mom's features. Jag's real dad died long enough ago that he'd have moved on or jumped in the river by now. He wouldn't have all this information and he definitely wouldn't still be waiting around the courtyard of Mortem. Plus, I've only been here a couple minutes and every time I slow down, Mortem's trying to suck everything it can out of my head to send me back to the bar and get on with the program.

I know this, but looking at Jag's dad shows me a part of him that I never got the chance to see. I want to pretend I don't know better because this is someone Jag cared about, so even without having met him before, I care about him too.

My heart's throbbing in my ears. My fingers are pulsing. I close my hands into tight fists. I can't stand the feeling. "Are you—"

A soft grunt echoes from somewhere above. A slap, a pound. "Open your goddamn mouth!" KC's voice cuts through the air, sharp and explosive. It doesn't echo so much as strike and disappear.

Jag's dad looks at me with concern in his face. "Maybe we should get out of here?" He chuckles awkwardly. "We can talk at the bar?"

"Ya get one more shot—Fuckin' tell me!" Another crash.

Jag's dad puts his hand out to wave me toward him. The voice is already in my head, urging me to return to the bar, lining up the questions for me to ask him that would fill my head with things I made up about Jag, but sound more convincing because they're said through this creature that's reaching into my head and taking my guesses on what I think Jag's dad would be like.

Someone further down in the Kaufman's showroom slams their fist into someone else. Jag's dad suddenly walks past me saying, "Oh no, oh no, oh no," and I know for certain that's not some hellish version of him, but a kind of customer servant of the dead. As soon as he passes me, this shadow of a person splits his body in three or four or five different ways. Like a ghost coming out of his form, they don't take on physical appearances of their own, but act likes shadows leaving his body and disappear into an invisible mist as soft voices attempt to consolation through whispered affection.

I'm standing by the stairs that go to the next floor reading HOME AND PEACE. The pounding from before's more consistent. Fist on flesh, body to the floor. It's coming from upstairs. I run.

I'm at the top of the stairs and running through what feels like endless space of furniture and floor and clothing racks and show rooms. Anything you can pack into a shop is here. The fact none of it's necessary or it's just as fake as the box of cigarettes that keeps spawning in my pocket makes it all the more ridiculous just how many tricks there are here. Everything about Mortem's a pacifier to ease the wandering soul with distractions until Charon delivers you. Superficial, like the alcohol at the bar, the faces you'll meet in passing, the home they'll make for you at Lodgings. The only things there that are real are the stories you'll hear and forget once you're had enough Lethe.

"Open up, Cherry Pie!" KC says. Another crash. Sounds like someone slamming into the floor. Skin on skin, a slap, a punch, a growl, KC saying, "Motherfucker!" with a laugh and another punch. He's on the floor next to a shelf of wires, cords, phones, and a back wall of TV screens showing a raging concert at its height. The lights here aren't the sterile, bright fluorescents of the first floor, but something dimmer in submission to the atmosphere on the screens. Red lights flicker over the audience. The view's on screen's from the stage. The singer's playing the guitar, watching the people in the audience as they make eye contact with him and bounce harder. Their lips move clumsily with his. Beer spills from cups held in the air and I'm smelling it and cigarettes and sweat. The music's getting louder, familiar songs played by an indie band, though it's not coming from speakers. It sounds like I'm at the concert, just off to the side of the stage.

The music goes off-key. The voice isn't singing with the band anymore, but it becomes clear.

It's KC.

The crowd throbs and swells, getting more and more excited until a cup is dropped. A fit of glory turns to one of rage and smacks someone's jaw just off of downstage right. KC flicks the mic cord as he takes to the front of the stage. I look down at him on the ground in front of me. The guy underneath him's got a swollen eye, blood coming down the side of his face, and a split lip where he bit himself. KC's got his hand around the guy's neck and the other is pulled back in a fist, waiting to strike again.

"KC, what are you doing?" I say.

"BPD call it *interrogation*." KC repositions himself so his knee presses into the guy's stomach. Both hands go around the guy's neck. It shouldn't matter. The guy's not moving. "Give it a sec." The tip of KC's shoe presses into the floor, leveraging his weight to press harder.

My body's swaying a little. My foot's tapping again, following the speed of KC's music and the energy from the crowd around us. Something crashes downstairs. I'm not sure how there's no one else on this floor with us or where the creature that was following me went or why every bit of furniture that was here is gone and every direction is wall to wall televisions playing the same party mix, same perspective, same concert losing its shit and turning into a mosh pit of fists, fury, and bruising.

The screens flicker. Separately, they turn black and get bars through them, turning the picture fuzzy and doubling it like TVs about to go out. The sound's ahead of the picture with Ralph's voice coming through the speakers. "You okay, Kace?"

"Yeah, yeah, yeah." He's pacing hard and sharp across some dark room, arm swinging as he keeps his head down. "What makes ya ask?

"Something's felt kind of off tonight."

"Yeah? Weird, cause I been feelin' like fuckin' fire." His voice is sharp, almost a hiss. KC picks up a half-empty bottle of water from the makeup counter. He looks it over with pursed lips before deciding to down it. "What makes ya think somethin's wrong? Is it just *one of those feelin's* again?"

"I dunno. It's just… You haven't looked like yourself tonight. I wondered if you noticed anything." Ralph pauses. Gray eyes are staring at KC with concern in the mirror. "The last couple of nights you've been worse. With the fights. Have you noticed? Rose's been worried you're gonna kill someone."

"Rose is a fuckin' lame ass." He hisses, tossing the empty plastic bottle into the nearby garbage. "I'm fine." He licks his lower lip. "And there's nothin' goin' on." The point-of-view on the TV's like seeing Ralph through KC's eyes. They're in a makeshift dressing room of some kind. There's flaky-looking lights, folding tables, and a temporary line of mirrors behind Ralph. The place is still pretty dark.

"Are you on something, Kace?"

"What? Who the fuck do you think I am?"

"I know. I just… I'm really worried, KC. Look at your hands."

He does. His knuckles are red, swollen, and torn. Cuts and bruises crawl up his exposed arms. Even in the mirror he's got a scabbed over busted lip and a black eye glowing in the room's soft illumination. KC meets Ralph's eyes in the mirror. "What's wrong with the way I look? Too trash for you?"

"That's not what I mean—"

"I know my kind of *filth* isn't your bag. Doesn't matter if you *were* born in a dumpster. You've always been better than me, yeah?"

"That's not… That's never been how I feel," Ralph says. "What happened pre-show?"

"Nothin'." KC comes closer to Ralph. "You been fuckin' Rose behind my back?" His arm goes around Ralph's shoulder and he pulls him in, giving Ralph a tight squeeze. "You scared of me, Reagan?"

"I care about you, KC." Ralph meets KC's eyes, chuckles weakly. "I know you've been having nightmares. You pant and groan in your sleep. Every time we go out, it's like you're looking at something that's not there. You're chasing down fights, avoiding me."

"I said don't fuckin' worry about it, Reagan." KC squeezes Ralph's shoulder so hard, Ralph winces. "I'm fine, I'm not havin' nightmares and I'm not avoidin' you. Why the fuck would I do that? Think *I'm* scared of *you*? Who the fuck could be *scared* of you, *Ralph Reagan*?" KC steps away from Ralph, going back to the makeup counter. A mini fridge sits underneath. "I'm the same I've always been. Maybe you're just finally seein' it." He grabs a water bottle, muttering, "Ya never shoulda moved in with me."

Twist the cap, a click, he looks at himself in the mirror, Ralph's reflection behind him. He hasn't moved, but a light glows softly in Ralph's eyes while darkness builds behind him. Tendrils against the wall like tentacles slide across the floor. A couple of red dots flicker against the back wall. A soft pounding races in my chest, echoing the panic on the screen. KC turns around. The darkness is gone. The eyes are gone. There's laughter coming through the other side of the door, inhuman, sounds more like a bird.

Ralph's eyes seek out KC's. When they find them, his expression softens. He doesn't so much look like the calm, collected drummer who'd been best friends with a wild man for over a decade. He looks tired, worn, fearful, and concerned. The gentleness and warmth in his features feel unjustified.

"Fuck, I hate your face sometimes." KC snorts into the plastic bottle he's holding.

"KC—" Ralph takes a step forward, but stops himself from getting closer. "I don't know why, but I've had this feeling like something bad's about to happen all night, and I don't want anything to happen to you."

"Ah. Ya know how goddamn pathetic you sound?" KC chuckles.

"Yeah, but I—"

"And if ya don't stop, people are really gonna think you're suckin' my dick. You want that?"

There's a soft glow seeping into Ralph's eyes. His face distorts so he doesn't look so much like himself, but a face with a dragged mouth and blurry eyes, smeared around like a charcoal drawing. KC steps back. "You need to go," KC says. A sense of repulsion and fear and desire goes through me, matching KC's motion on screen. His fingers slide along the countertop, looking for something and seeming irritated at only finding a makeup brush.

KC rubs his eyes hard. Ralph's face doesn't clear, but instead, black tendrils expand against the walls behind him. A soft voice whispers through the sound of the post-concert saying *he hates you, do him the favor* nonstop.

The wall behind Ralph says ALL THIS FUCKIN TIME and FAKE in small scribble. The room blurs with pulses of tension. The sounds of the party on the other side of the door fade out, getting dimmer and dimmer. There's a caw that screeches over it all with a laugh. KC looks up.

Seven sets of red eyes turn into seven ravens sitting above him, watching him, laughing sporadically.

"Get out!" KC says.

"What's wrong?" Ralph reaches for him.

"Don't fuckin' touch me." KC swings. His fist slams Ralph square in the jaw, knocking him into the door. KC closes the space between them. Another punch, then another punctuates his voice. "Don't talk to me! Don't look at me! Don't fuckin'—Don't!" His voice is so loud and so raw, it cracks. KC's hand wraps around Ralph's throat. Ralph's eyes are wide; the gray glow's gently. Inside his expression is a vulnerability and softness so foreign, I feel disgusted looking at it. Maybe that's just KC's feelings getting me again. I don't wanna look at the screen anymore.

Ralph chokes, saying KC's name through gasps as he reaches desperately toward him. His fingers gently tug at KC's shirt. KC blinks. Whatever was distorting Ralph's face is gone. All that's left is this guy with a busted, bloody lip, runny liner, and eyes watering with fear not for his own wellbeing.

A distorted sound disrupts KC's focus. Scratching at the door and on the walls mixes with the music filling the night's air, interspersed with frantic cawing.

KC Freezes. "Fuck." He growls. The spots on Ralph's face are already gaining color. He draws his hand back, and a print's darkening around his throat too. "Shit," he hisses under his breath as he steps back, turns away, paces to give the energy in him somewhere to go. "Sorry, Reagan. I—I didn't mean to—I—"

"What's wrong, KC?" Ralph's gray eyes search KC's face, speedily moving in a desperate need for answers.

"I don't know." KC shakes his head, almost like he's trying to pull himself out of something. He presses his hand to his face, covering his eyes. My skin heats. My chest hurts. Guilt goes through me and brings with it this feeling of shame so bad, I want to disappear. "I just—" He wipes his jaw. "Some shit's been goin' on with my head. It's been worse. I just… I wanna… fuckin' everything. I swear to God." He looks at his bruised hands. Blood's tucked under his nails. There are jabs up his arm, not self-imposed, but something tore through him out of anger or aggression. The knife cuts. He looks back at Ralph. The redness of his cheek shines bright, even in the dark dressing room lights. A flash of disgust hits me again. KC's hands turn to fists. "I need air, maybe a cigarette." He chuckles. "I got somethin' goin' on. Forgive me, yeah?"

He stares at Ralph for a long while, waiting for an answer.

"Yeah, of course, KC." Ralph says softly. KC shoves Ralph away from the door and slams it behind him. Again, the screens around the room flicker, not all at once. Some pictures are slower to change; some stay black while others come back with KC going down the hall. Graffiti on the venue walls read SHOT UP, BURNT, LOOK OUT, CHOSE THE—FAILURE.

The screens are still out of sync, everything doubles. A shadow moves in the hall. KC falls against the wall, gasping. He groans to himself. A fat raven stands at the end of the hall in front of him, staring with big, obsidian eyes and a smugness that birds shouldn't have. "Get the fuck away from me!" KC runs down the hall, kicking at the bird as he goes. It flies into the rafters where it keeps watch on KC's retreat.

Moving through the venue halls, doors have two frames, people have two shadows, and everything's blending together. KC shoves the bathroom door open with his shoulder. Three stalls line the far side of the room, no doors on any of them. The blue wall around the toilet separating it from the sink reads IDIOT on repeat and then MURDERER and DIS APPOINTMENT and HAHAHA and YOU THOUGHT YOU COULD RUN? Under those is a phone number and under that is KILL KILL KILL KILL in red.

KC turns on one of the sinks. His hands are under the water while he looks himself in the mirror. His face is flushed. His blond hair, pulled into a ponytail is loose and messy and sticking to his face. Dark bags hang under his eyes, turning them mostly black and mixing with the bit of smeared eyeliner he's wearing. He stares down at his hands. The water turns a light shade of red. He draws his hands back and wipes them on his pants. He turns the faucet off then back on. The water's clear again. He wipes his eyes. "What the hell's wrong with you, Kailee? Why did you just... do that to him? Jesus Christ—He's all you've got." His foots bouncing. "Get it together, yeah?" His hands curl around the edges of the sink, giving him balance to steady. "He's never done shit to anyone... so why do I hate him so goddamn much?" KC slams his fist into the mirror. Shards fall into the sink below. Blood trickles down his knuckles as he hisses. "Fuck." He grabs a couple paper towels from the bin, sticks them under the sink, and wipes his face down. "Maybe it's time he moved on, yeah? I'm really gonna fuck him up if he doesn't, huh?" KC sneers through a pant.

The bathroom door flies open; it bounces against the wall with a rattle. Someone grabs hold of KC by the shirt and slams him into the toilet stall. KC swings to hit whoever's near as he pushes off the wall saying, "What the hell, man?"

"What the hell, you," says some guy in a leather jacket, ripped jeans, his shirt's from another band, but the image is too blurry to see what it is.

"Stall's open if you wanted to use it," KC says. "I'll try not to laugh when you sit to take a piss."

"Think you're a funny bastard, eh?" The guy's snarling; his anger's abnormal. Too much like my dad's when he really lost his shit. It's too much like the Big Guy when he grabbed me at the bar. The guy holding onto KC has black eyes and tendrils coming from them, going around his neck, up his arm, around his fingers.

"Not at all. I ain't a funny *funny* bastard, but am a *fuckin'* bastard though." KC on the screen says just as he pulls his fist back. The punch is intercepted by the guy in the leather jacket before it lands. He uses the hold on KC's fist to pull him in. The screen flashes. A groan of pain comes. The perspective pans down. A knife's sticks out of KC's ribs. He growls a curse that never turns audible.

The guy in leather pulls the knife out and thrusts it in a second time, then a third. KC's legs go weak. "Gonna… lose your load… shootin' it that fast…" KC grunts, falling to the floor. Something's holding him up. The toilet stall. All over the tiles, the floor says GOOD and GOTTEM again and again and again. It carries onto the walls where it hadn't been before along with HAD YOUR SHOT and AIN'T THIS YOUR WISH? and LEAST IT'S NOT AN *OVERDOSE*.

The guy in leather's muttering to his buddies. It's too quiet to hear under KC's breathing until the muttering turns into, "You shouldn't be in here." The guy smacks KC down. He hits the floor hard with the door no longer holding him up. The guy kicks KC in the side. KC grabs at his clothing. He curls into himself, knees attempting to block the holes in his chest. A kick to the spine is next. The TVs fill with a couple of feet, brown suede shoes covered in mud. "Doomed to disappoint, eh? Shoulda figured. Look at your fuckin' family. Rest in piss, Charleston." The guy leaves the bathroom. The door slams. YOU CHOSE THE DARK is written in red on it.

The monitors flicker a couple of times before going dark across the room with the image of the dirty bathroom and KC's pleading, pained breath calling for Ralph. Blood drips from his lips to the floor; I taste it in my mouth too. Everything's black, though the sound of the raging music still plays through the walls, muted. Muffled speech of angry people fighting and panicking and talking about wrecking something in the venue hall. Then, the bathroom door opens again, and Ralph is saying, "KC! KC—Hold on, okay? I've got you!"

The monitors obscure. KC and Ralph aren't in a dingy bathroom anymore, but instead, something with cleaner, more commercial stalls even if it's trashed. Stall doors hang off the hinges, toilet paper and plaster lay everywhere from broken sinks and urinals and pieces of the ceiling tiles that got busted up with something else. The screen goes to the bathroom door and Ralph's standing on the other side, the parking lot windows behind him. His eyes widen the moment he sees KC. They gloss over as he mutter's KC's name.

KC chuckles. "Surprised?

"You're supposed to be dead." Ralph says. "What are you doing here?

"What's it look like? I'm having a fiesta." KC meets Ralph's eyes again. So much fear, so much concern, so much compassion lace his expression.

Then, there's a thud, a gasp. The screen turns black

and the image of bloody hands dropping a body in the darkness of Leakin Park. Flicker. It becomes Ralph in a lit room, staring into KC's eyes. "What else did you see?"

"Everything."

KC chuckles bitterly. Shame fills my chest. "And you still wanna help me?"

"Of course, I do, KC," Ralph says softly, tears streaming down his cheeks. "I love you." His thumb strokes KC's face.

"You shouldn't." KC snorts, part bitter, part disbelieving. "You always were hopelessly desperate, you know that?"

"Yeah."

The screen goes black.

The real KC in Kaufman's pulls the guy from under his knee off the floor and slams him back down. "Turn it the fuck off!" His voice carries across the empty walls like mine refused to do before. It bounces down with anger, urgency, and a fire that sets the walls alight. The monitors shut off at the same time. The sound disappears. The room's empty of anything, but us now and walls of black screens with nothing else to say.

"What the hell's going on?" I say. "What was that?" I point to the screen.

KC pushes his loose hair back with his free hand. The guy he'd been beating lays motionless on the floor, pinned under KC's knee. He takes a breath. "Never been to the Bin before?"

"No."

KC snorts. "You thought Sol was bad, she ain't got shit on this place. This place is a snare for the dead, to trap you and make you forget who you are, where you came from, and what makes you human. It'll use every torture method it can come up with to push you out of your skin." KC chuckles bitterly. He slams a fist in to the dead guy beneath him, reflecting the heat and anger that's been building in me since the monitors around us started playing. KC's panting through his clenched teeth. Sharp canines catch in his smile as his eyes go wide.

The dead guy underneath KC comes alive again. A hand reaches up, trying to claw at KC's leg to find freedom. KC drops back down on top of the guy, one hand to his neck, the other to his face. The dead guy attempts to gouge KC's eyes or grab him by the hair, but finds no success.

"You wanna bite me? Do it, bitch." KC shoves his palm into the guy's mouth. "Wanna stop suffering? I want a location. Old man. Sunglasses. Red glove. Looks like a priest." KC slams the guy's head down. "I know you fuckin' seen him!"

The guy bites KC's fingers. KC draws his hand back and bashes his fist into the man's teeth. Both hands grab at the guy's head to slam him harder into the ground while his voice echoes, "Woo!" and "I could do this all night, sweet cheeks!" finishing by spitting on the man's face.

KC slams the guy's head down again. He grips the side of the guy's head as best he can before smashing it into the floor rapidly. Pieces of bloody bone snap out of the guy's head, scattering on the clean linoleum underneath. His knee presses harder into the man's stomach, holding him to the floor. Blood's coming out the man's nose, bubbling, and he coughs as he chokes on his own blood until he stops breathing. His eyes close, his body goes limp, and the screaming torment of the man's anger and pain dissolve. With the submission, KC keeps going.

A tapping comes next. The bells. A soft whistle. The rattling chains and sense of unease. I step back from it, touching my chest to make sure my heart's still there.

The raven's red eyes give it away, glowing, making it seem like it came through the screen. It lands on the ground not far from where KC is. KC pays it no mind. The chains keep going until Charon forms out of the clear department store emptiness. He stands at the head of the bloody, uncooperative man.

"What are you doing, Kailee?" Charon says.

"What's it look like? Getting information. You know the drill." KC's fingers hold the dead man's head down with a palm against his forehead and the other at his neck. "This could be easy, but the fucker won't talk, so we've been a little creative."

The dead guy's eyes peel open. At first, they're slim, his teeth are bared and chipped and he's sneering, but then his eyes move from KC to Charon standing over him. The sneer turns into fear as he presses himself away from KC and into the floor like it offers him any chance to get away. "N-no!" He growls. His head swings, arms flailing toward KC in an attempt to be set free. It doesn't work. "L-let me go!"

KC's attention turns back to the dead guy. "Oh, that what does it for you?" His fingers lace in the guy's hair. Using the hold, KC lifts the guy's head. "Where is *he*?"

The guy's eyes go from Charon to me. A look of recognition flashes over his face. "You—He's waiting for you at Kaufman's—"

"Where's. My. Medium?!" KC lifts the guys head and slams it into the floor with each word.

"Kaufman's! Take the bitch to Kaufman's!"

"If you're lyin' to me, you better hope Char's put you away for good." KC draws his hand back and lands one more hard punch in the man's face.

"In desperation, humanity will do whatever it takes to give them some feeling of control," Charon says.

"It's not desperation if it works." He looks up at

Charon without loosening his grip.

"I was talking about your friend," Charon says.

"Oh." KC chuckles. His fingers close harder as the guy starts to struggle for freedom. Charon and KC exchange eye contact in a way they hadn't before, referencing something that couldn't be seen. *"Do as thou wilt,"* KC says as he stands.

"The medium is suffering; *recover him* before he *breaks,"* Charon says.

"Working on it." Once he passes, KC flicks his head to the side. A soft crack. He rolls his shoulders. His knuckles pop. Charon's chains are rattling, and the bloody faced ghost is racing to his feet just as Charon's bondage races to grab him. KC's quicker, but still not with the same urgency I feel to get away. Val's looking at me, licking his lips, keeps going to my chest where the necklace hangs. He approaches me, head cocked to the side. My heart's warm against my skin and the heat goes through my clothes to my fingers as I feel it. I step back slowly, turn on my toes, and run for the stairs.

I hit the landing at the bottom. The department store is mostly gone. Another empty show room, walls black and blank with glowing TV screens all the same as upstairs. Instead of playing a dirty bathroom in a dive or a makeshift greenroom or a stage, it's an empty warehouse littered with garbage, piles of clothing, a smell of sweat and dust and abandon, cigarettes, alcohol, piss. Broken glass scatters everywhere as the camera pans to a body laying in a puddle of its own blood. Black t-shirt, his jacket, his trim hair, broken aviators he shouldn't've even had because it's dark outside. "You did this," snarls the same voice that called me a bitch when it pinned me against the wall and choked me out. "If you just died like you shoulda—"

"Get out of my head!" I scream. My skin's so hot

now, my clothes are clinging to me. I close my eyes as I run across the empty space, telling myself it's not real, it's not real, it's not real and Jag's not dead. Nothing around me matches like it should. His laughter's met with my childish sobs as I hid in the closet as a kid, reminding me too much of how Jag found me a couple days ago.

I've always been like this. I sought refuge in the dark, hoping to turn back time so my dad would come back and it worked. He sat in that chair for fifteen more years, keeping me from being alone. Or at least, that's what I'd thought, but time hadn't gone back and his being there was the isolation I couldn't escape and kept making worse. Yet, with Wayland gone, I tried the same thing. The sobbing on the TV's too much and it's getting to me. My chest hurt, my legs are weak and I can't breathe cause that hurts too. It feels like a dagger's piercing my lungs and since I'm already holding my breath, there's nothing I can do to make it stop. I press my hands to my ears.

My skin prickles as I run, and my voice is coming through the speakers, desperate and pleading for my dad and Jag and saying I love him and my lips are following along with the screaming of my childish desperation to not be alone. I'm getting dizzy from the wave of emotions hitting me. The floor's moving sideways. The Liquor's no longer of comfort or maybe it's not even trying. It's everything KC said; I want to forget and a drink with Sol sounds so good right now. Especially if the picture on the wall is right and Jag's dead now. He might be waiting for me at the bar. If he's dead, he'll never forgive me for what I did to him and I can't forgive myself. The best option would be to forget.

"It's not real, it's not real, it's not real," I say to myself in an unending loop as the screens try to convince me that everything they're showing me is true and I should just give up. I have to keep talking or I'll repeat what they say and if I repeat what they say too much, I might actually start believing it.

My eyes water; the floor blurs together. I don't know where I'm going or how long I've been running or why I'm even here. My dad's standing near the door — or at least, the thing that looks like my dad. Instead of wearing a smile and the *sorry* of before, he's got blood running down his shoulders from where it came out the hole he put in himself. He's got a gun in his hand too. I turn my head the other way while saying, "You're a real bastard, you know that?" as I go out the wide Bin doors waiting for me with nothing visible on the other side until I'm through them.

The Old Town Courtyard comes back into focus, turning from purple outlines into a full color picture. The music from Post Mortem's soft, but it brings a levity that wasn't there before. My cheeks are still moist, but I'm not crying anymore as the Liquor floods back into me with each breath, doing its job and silencing what the screens inside were trying to rip out of me. I wipe the tears from my face with the back of my hand.

"You good?" KC says.

"Yeah." I wipe my eyes again. Black eyeliner smudges off with the moisture.

I don't see him at first, but he's standing a little way down the courtyard. Hard to miss if I hadn't been distracted by everything else. The other dead moving from place to place come back into view. They don't take notice of me either. No gossip, no glances. I don't even seem to exist to them. KC stands by a dark globe built into the brick, it's covered with stuff that looks like moss but is red in color. He's got a joint pinched between his fingers and is blowing out smoke.

I go to him. "That's one hellova trick they've got in

there," I say.

"They don't like failure down here," KC says. "Theirs, anyway. Ours don't matter that much."

"Sucks for them that humans like to mess with shit, huh?" I say.

"Not without cost. They take what they can. Consider it punishment." KC puffs of his joint. Exhale. "Like, yeah, Reagan can break a lot of rules, but it doesn't come without cost. The dead seek him out wherever he is, either yearning for whatever he can give them or to destroy him. The universe's desire to tear him apart is unreal, but he gives home to the wicked in hope that they'll find peace and move on. Mostly, it doesn't work." KC turns around and makes his way down the courtyard, toward the street.

I quickly catch up to walk beside him. His long legs move him with effortless speed. "Where are you going?"

"Baltimore," KC says.

"Charon was inside the Bin. Don't we need him to get out of here?"

"Unless you want to tear up your boyfriend, we're not using Styx," KC says.

"Then how the hell are we going to get back?"

"Through the séance room." Without stopping, KC continues toward the street. In the distance, a bright, red sign reads LODGINGS, and the hotel canopy comes into view.

FIFTEEN.

The billboard outside Lodgings says TAKE A REST next to a person lying on a mattress that looks too much like a mix of a coffin and one of those beds at normal hotels that all have the same sheets and no comforter so you're cold all night, no matter where you stay. I don't think that's what it said before. The sign changes, showing a pair of scuffed up, soiled shoes. They look like mine. Skaters. Blood and mud caked to the sides, destroying the white trim. The words YOU'VE BEEN BUSY slide onto the screen.

"Shut up," I mutter.

CAN'T WASH IT OFF. DRINK INSTEAD, the sign reads.

I drop my head to watch the ground. Hopefully, it doesn't throw Mortem's opinions at me next.

The weird thing about Lodgings is it doesn't feel like it exists until you step out of the courtyard. It's in the mist that hides Mortem from the Old Town Mall until you get further away from the light. Otherwise, all you see is the big red LODGINGS glowing in the sky. Get closer, and the sign says whatever it wants, what it thinks you want to hear, what'll drive you crazy. I don't know anymore. I guess now it feels like Mortem's lashing out at me. Doesn't seem so crazy after what KC's said about it.

Lodgings is a hotel made out of the old rubber factory that actually stands in its place in Baltimore. It has an overhanging canopy reading SLEEP and an empty standee where it looks like someone should be waiting to greet us. After what happened at the Bin, I'm sure there's supposed to be someone around here to draw me into a room, but now that's twice no one's been waiting. Is it something wrong with me or does Mortem think it's best bet to get me into a room is to leave me alone?

KC stops with his hand on the glass door. Again, it's foggy, you can't see anything on the other side but the light's on, gold finish, and the vague shape of the front desk. "Whatever you think you see," KC says, "Don't pause. Don't look. Don't listen." He glances back at me.

"I don't think you need to worry about that. There wasn't anyone here last time," I say.

"You'd be surprised at how things can change."

"You say that like it's alive."

"Somethin' like that." KC pulls the door open and goes through, making a beeline for the elevator. He keeps his head down and presses the elevator button quickly. He turns his back to the front desk and puts his arm against the wall, leaning his forehead against it to use his bicep to block his vision as he continues to press the button rapidly.

I mirror his posture, keeping my head down, using my bangs as a wall to stop me from looking around the lobby in search of the next familiar thing Mortem wants to throw at me. My heart's throbbing loudly, the unease is seeping into me, gradually. First, the fear, then the anxiety of something sneaking up on me, but the silence comes fast and it turns into a flutter of excitement. I don't know why that's there. Everything here's fake and there was nothing in this stupid hotel before. I remember ripping open the desk drawers and busting out the windows in my room to test just how far this place would go to keep up the facade. It didn't try beyond a photograph of my bedroom, complete with sounds like my dad was on the other side of the door, in his chair, with the TV up keeping him company.

A couple of taps against the floor. Soft steps. Someone enter the lobby, not through the door. Maybe they'd been sitting in one of the chairs on the other side of the room and I'd missed it because I wasn't looking. KC's feet are still on the floor. Even if KC's tapping his toe, it's not in time with the steps that are coming from behind me.

"Don't look," KC says like he's reading my mind.

"I'm not gonna look," I say.

"*Jo?*"

My breath catches in my throat. I'm not ready for his voice.

"Wayland?" I exhale his name.

"*Joey,*" KC says harder.

My head lifts. Wayland's standing in front of the customer service desk with a small key in his hand. It's got his name on it and the number nineteen hangs from the tag.

"Hey," he says. His voice is so soft, he's practically whispering. His hand goes to his pants. He slips his key into his pocket and wipes his palms off. "I didn't think I'd see you again."

"No, that was me," my voice is slow. "I mean, I didn't think you'd remember me."

"How could I forget?" Wayland rubs the back of his neck. His lips pull to one side with the kind of bashful smile he has always had for me. It's so warm, so him. My eyes water. Clean, hair combed, not a speck of mud or blood or gook from the woods on him. He looks just like himself before Baltimore destroyed him; he looks like he *should*. I brush my eyes like I'm tired.

"*Joey*," KC snaps.

"I was just about to head up," Wayland says. "At the bar, they told me to come over here to 'hang out and I might see something familiar.' I didn't know what to expect. I didn't know they meant *you*." His exhale is filled with relief. His eyes won't stay on me, but he keeps looking this way. "Did you want to hang out or something? I got some studying to do, I think. Maybe? We could turn on some music or whatever instead. The tests not really that important." He slowly closes the space between us. His hand touches my arm.

Goosebumps form all over my skin. His eyes are so bright and big and the suffering and fear and sadness that were in them the last time I saw him are gone. Finally, the Liquor's done something right. Wayland never should've felt guilty for what Baltimore did to him.

He smiles more warmly, relaxed. "It's good to see you, you know? Feels like it's been forever." He laughs softly.

I nod because I can't speak. His hand tickles mine. Our fingers intertwine loosely. I still remember what it felt like when he grabbed my arm on the stoop at my house as he backed me toward the door. The pressure and desperation and pain in his lips against mine and the guilt that filled me for never noticing the way he looked at me or for making him listen to me talk about my problems with Jag. For never telling him what Jag was to me or making him figure it out on his own or hoping that since I didn't call Jag and I a *thing*, we didn't really exist as a *we*.

I believed the same thing. I thought if I didn't give our relationship a label, then it didn't count and I wasn't at risk of losing anything I cared about, but Jag has been more than a friend for a while now. I was only taking advantage of him by not saying it and I hurt Wayland by not being clear.

I pull my hand away from Wayland's. Knowing what I know now, I can't do this. All these little actions that didn't use to mean anything say so much more now. "I thought you moved on, Way." I wipe my eyes while looking away at all the intricate details on the lobby wallpaper instead. Look too long and you notice how the curls aren't the right width. The shapes get messy and lack uniformity, and the color shifts like splotchy shadows or spill stains hidden under everything.

"What do you mean?" he says.

"Like… You were on the other side of judgment." The words taste bitter coming out of my mouth. He shouldn't be here. He shouldn't be dead; he shouldn't be forgotten; he shouldn't be listless. "I thought Sol helped you along. KC said you were on the other side because you were leaving me notes—"

"Oh." Wayland laughs that awkward way he always has. Tight throat. Heat on his cheeks. He turns away from me, slipping his hands into his pocket. He pulls the key back out to give his finger something to do by toying with the tag. "No. KC's wrong. I never sent you any messages. I've been waiting here for you because I was hoping that maybe you'd come and visit and we could go on together. Once I'm on the other side, I can't talk to you anymore, you know?"

"Yeah…" A chill goes down my spine. "You sure about that? I mean, KC and Ralph are kind of pros at this. They've been doing it for a while. They'd know, right?"

"Maybe, but… You wanna believe that and miss what could be or you wanna try to go back to how things were?"

I meet Wayland's eyes again. He's watching me carefully. But his eyes aren't right. They're too dark and glossy and more like a mirror. They look empty. The soft smile on his face isn't right either. It's not the same as the people at the bar who aren't fully there. It's inhuman in a way that doesn't reach his eyes because he doesn't have a soul; he's not a soul; he can't be that deep. This thing is closer to Sol or my dad or Jag's dad in the Bin. It's so weird. Even though he looks vacant, his eyes are still swollen with sadness like he's been crying and he's got that busted lip from when Jag punched him the other day.

"Wayland, we *can't* go back," I say.

"Don't you at least want to try?" he says.

I know it's not him, but a voice in my head keeps telling me I'm wrong and I'll mess it up again if I don't give him a chance. Stop asking questions, you're crazy, you've always been crazy and self-sabotaging and you know it; how is this any different?

Something dings behind me.

"We're going, Joey," KC grabs the back of my hoodie. Another hand gets hold of my arm and I'm stumbling back while Wayland says, "Jo! Don't go!" and lunges for me.

KC pushes me into the elevator; my muscles fight against him in desperation to meet Wayland. I'm not in control. I'm shoved into the wall in the elevator by the buttons. Pinned there, KC pushes the close door button again and again and again until the metal mirror doors shut. At the same time, he's pushing a floor number.

The wall panel where the controls are shows a full set of ten by five buttons, but only one has a number on it.

Sixty-nine.

Once the elevator starts going up, he releases me and

I pull away from the wall, swinging my arms like I'm trying to get the gross feeling out of my skin because of what that thing was doing to me. The nerves and nervousness and guilt and everything pull my muscles to chase after him like it'll give me one more chance to go back to the way things were. My skin burns with embarrassment. I keep my face down as I pace from the corner because I can't stand still. The voice is still there telling me to go back to the lobby, *he's waiting for you. Talk to him. You know how long he's been waiting? Look at you, abandoning him again.*

"I told you to keep your head down," KC says.

"I tried." I smack my open hand into the wall. I'm not angry, but the energy of everything is going through me and there's too much of it. A button appears on the wall panel with a zero and it's flashing, telling me to hit it. If KC wasn't standing between it and me, I'd have already pressed it. The impulses are strong; Mortem's stronger than I gave it credit for.

Turning away, I grunt under my breath. Everything in me is fighting to turn back to the button panel. "There wasn't anyone down there last time. I was caught off-guard is all—"

"It couldn't manipulate you like this last time."

"How do you know?"

"*It gets in your head.* That's the power of Mortem." KC rubs wary irritation from his eyes. "You ever wonder how Reagan always knows what to say when he's *serving?* What you need? Everything about you when he made your fetish? He half-lives on some plane, where minds, thoughts, memories and emotions are. He can just touch it and see everything, but then your shit becomes his shit. He lives through what he sees, ya know?"

"Great." I rub my eyes before crossing my arms tightly over my chest. "So, nothing in my head is safe?"

"Word of advice," KC says. "Next time you take a trip down here, don't believe anythin' ya see or hear *ever*. Close yourself off; tell yourself everything here is fake. Coming down here when you're dead, they stick their tentacles in you harder. Doesn't matter that you've got a heart again. They know you're defying the natural order and they want to put a stop to it. There's a reason I don't come down here unless I have to. You might be able to talk to a reaper because his job's delivery, but servies are different."

"*Servies*," I say. "You've said that word a couple of times. Do you mean Sol?"

KC nods. "Reagan calls them *Servus ad Mortem*, slaves to the dead. Their entire existence is the entrapment of souls. Make you forget your life, purpose, reason for being, and anythin' ya care about. They gotta make you malleable so you move on. It's not malicious so much as it's a function, which kind of makes it worse. There's no reasoning with a computer program, ya know? Servies are only slightly different in that they interact more directly with humanity so they can feign what looks like human interaction. Even then, they're limited to the bounds of comforting wandering souls to keep them out of trouble. Funny that no matter how thorough they are, some of us still won't play and end up slippin' through the cracks"

The elevator dings. The doors open. KC steps onto the floor that looks nothing like what I was on when I explored Lodgings before. Where my floor looked expensive with flowers and vines and fresh, new carpet, here, the carpet's tattered, old, and stained in large splotches. Red, brown, black. Mud. Alcohol. *Other things*. The walls are wrapped in spotty wallpaper, varying in shade. Broken ceiling to floor length mirrors hang at even intervals. Cobwebs crowd some of the edges near the roof. The lights on the walls imitate small stage lights pointing down the path. Not sure if it's supposed to be a dive or a dressed up abandoned hotel or some amalgamation of places KC's been to before.

"When Sol says she doesn't know something…" I say slowly.

"Sometimes she's lying, most of the time, she just can't answer," KC says. "Her function doesn't allow her to answer a lot of things. Whatever's programmed her has created an internal imperative so that she can't answer in a way that's helpful to the dead. There's not much of a difference if you're living. It's just the reapers can't take you and though the Liquor can mess with you, it's mostly toothless."

"What about Ralph?" I say.

"What about him?"

"He's still human, right?"

"Mostly, though he shares his existence with whatever's on the other side. Supernatural with the strengths and weaknesses of a human. When he does a séance, he talks to all kinds of shit. I dunno what, bigger things, he won't say, goes beyond the reapers and the servies and the Cogs. They got their own purposes and every last one of us is just a drop in a bucket to be used in whatever their big cosmic game is. Reagan's only said one name to me so far. *Olintia.* It's who he talked to when he became a medium. She made the ring hanging from his neck. He said she was nice. From the way he came out of séance that day, she probably was. Most of what he deals with roughs him up, but that's just the nature of taking a physical form into a spiritual place. We're not made for this and bending the natural order always comes with consequences.

"Servies aren't that complicated. They exist here and don't understand things from any perspective recognizable to humans. They don't get your distress or pain or fear. They never did and they don't care. Everything in Mortem is like that. A function that serves the universe or whatever."

"What about you?"

"What about me?" KC's pace slows. He turns around, but continues to walk backwards. "I'm just a dead asshole who met the right person at the right time and somehow didn't fuck it up. I get the same treatment as you. The only pull I have around here is I'm not afraid to get angry to get what I want and they know I'm in charge of keeping Reagan safe so they can't do shit."

He stops at a door that looks more beat up than the others. The wood's discolored with mildew, water damage, and dents from a knife. The air smells like fungus has been growing for a while. The carpet stinks and squelches under my foot.

KC sticks his key into the lock. Twisting the knob, the hinges squeal softly as the door opens. On the other side is a recreation of Ralph's and KC's place back at the bar. The bed with black sheets is messy still, everything pushed to the foot of the mattress or hanging over the floor since no one can be bothered to make it. Smoke and candles. All things occult hang from the ceiling and line the floor with some of them even looking recently used. Posters and a guitar and a TV in the corner. Even a cup on the counter where KC'd set one when we left while a couple of plates sit in the sink. The bathroom door hangs open as at the far side of the room. The windows are boarded up and covered by plush, black curtains. The only thing off about this place is that it looks more put together than the room back at home where the thugs had broken in and left signs of their fight on the door.

Still, there's an unnatural visibility to the place even

before KC flicks on the lights.

"You ever feel like you're living outside the world?" I say.

"Pretty much every day since I was born," KC says. He's in the kitchen, turning on the sink, washing away the blood that got on his hands back at the Bin. His dark eyes stare into me. "Don't take that as more dramatic than it really is."

"How else am I supposed to take something like that?" I chuckle.

"As a statement like it is." He flicks his wet hands in the air, then wipes his palms on his ass. He crosses the room for the closet at the other side of the apartment. His stained shirts on the bed, he kicks his shoes off. His belt buckle clicks as he pulls his belt loose and slips inside the closet. There are scars on his back. Cigarette burns, old knife wounds, graffiti by choice, ritual, and circumstances too familiar to me. "Everyone's so goddamn ready to put a label of 'special sob story' on every part of what it means to just be alive. You're not special because you don't feel like you fit in, or you got a shit hand. Don't ask me to feel bad for ya, yeah? We all gotta put up with bullshit and work to get what we want. Find some place to be or don't, but if you're thinkin' of askin' me for pity? Nah. What a buncha narcissistic bullshit to ask me to care about your baby problems. Get over yourself." He kicks his pants into the corner of the closet. A new pair on with no stains, he's wearing a copy of the band tank he had on before when he comes out. He picks his shoes up, and sits on the bed to put them back on. "No one owes ya pity." He pulls on his leather jacket as he stands. "You're lucky if anyone thinks ya got value at all." KC glances at me as he crosses the room.

He stops at the door that he didn't let Rocky touch earlier. The whole thing's almost invisible as it blends into the wall. His fingers slide into the hole and he pushes into the door. Something clicks. The door slides open. On the other side of it is a small room, totally black, feeling endless. Burnt candles of different sizes lay on the corners and near the edge of the circle. A small pile of black feathers sits on the center of an old circle, no longer complete. What little light seeps in from the room causes symbols like those on Ralph's arms to reflect in the darkness.

KC steps through the room without pause. My sneakers slip on something. Another feather. The little bit of light spilling from the open door illuminates a couple of spots on the bottom edges of the walls and the floor. They're caked in brown and red residue that looks like it used to be liquid.

"Don't waste too much time here," KC says.

"Something happen if we do?" I say.

"It's just not our space to spend time in, alright?" Anger seethes through KC's teeth. He shuts the door behind us. On the far side of the room, across from where we came in, KC gropes the wall until he finds another small hole. Finger's inside, he pushes the door open just the same as he did the first and slides into the wall. On the other side of the opening is Ralph's and KC's apartment.

"That's it?" I say. "We're back in the real world now?"

"The *Living* world, but yeah," KC says from the closet, light now on. "That's one of the functions of a séance room."

Something on the other side of the door thuds. KC pauses in the séance room's exit, staring. Rocky's standing on the other side of the bed, going through the nightstand drawer. The blanket that was on the mattress is now on the floor.

"What the hell are you doin' here?" KC says.

"You been in the closet this whole time?" Rocky says.

"You got a warrant to be going through my shit?"

"If I come back with a warrant, I'm not stopping until I find the bones." Rocky pushes the nightstand drawer closed.

KC moves out of the séance room and waits for me to follow before snapping the door shut. He walks around the wall separating the sleeping area from the living room. The front door hangs wide open. "Fuckin' riot. You bust my door open too?"

"You ran off with my suspect," Rocky says.

"I didn't run off with shit," KC says. "But you can have your prisoner anytime. I got places to go. People to see."

"Wow, you can't do that to me," I say.

"You're not my problem." KC dips into the closet. The light flickers on.

Rocky looks from the closet to me. He's got that stern distrust in his eyes again. I can't blame him. Another time he trusted me, took his eyes off me, and I look like I booked it. It wasn't even on purpose. His hand's at his belt, finger the cuffs. "I checked that damn closet. There was nothing in there." He slowly approaches as he watches me. I know he's surveying my face, my hands, my posture for any sign that I'm lying so he can push me harder until I tell the truth. He's not gonna get anything more believable and I know it sucks. You can't explain this shit. You can't explain Baltimore, even when you're someone like KC who's been dealing with this shit for God knows how long.

"I told you, Rocky, it's not what you think." I sigh, rub my eyes. My fingers come away black. I know eyeliners all over my face again.

"Then what is it?" Rocky says.

"KC, can we just use the door for like, a second to show Rocky the other side?"

"No." KC snaps a drawer shut hard from the closet.

"Alright…" Rocky's attention trails KC now. "Pretend I believe you're not a murderer. Where do you think you're going now?"

"Kaufman's," I say.

"Shut your goddamn mouth, Joey," KC growls.

"You think your missing person's at Kaufman's?" Rocky says.

KC leans against the frame. His eyes lock with Rocky's. He's quiet for a long while. His nose scrunches and a mad energy is coming off of him. His heels bouncing and it's causing mine to. The fresh red lines down his arm almost look like their glowing. The damage Ralph went through while we were in Mortem feels louder now. "I *know* my *missing person* is at Kaufman's."

"Why would he be there?" Rocky says.

"I don't fuckin' know. Ghosts set up shop in the weirdest goddamn places. Maybe it's because the Old Town Mall's familiar and spooky enough to keep people like you from wanderin' around." KC returns to the closet and comes back out of the with a metal bat and throws it onto the bed. He goes back a second time and when he comes out, he's tucking something into the back of his pants beneath his leather jacket.

"I'm pretty sure you can't legally carry, Chuck," Rocky says.

KC eyes Rocky. "It look like I'm packin', Big Dick?" KC nods toward the bat on the bed.

"Show me what you got behind your back," Rocky says.

"That'd spoil the surprise."

"Nothing about that answer screams *trust me*."

"I get that a lot." KC takes the elastic from his wrist

and slides it into his hair, tying his locks into a tight ponytail.

KC turns his back to Rocky, lifting his jacket and his shirt. His jeans are tight on his body, leaving no room to hide anything as a sheathed dagger sticks out of the back of his pants. "Didn't know I was your type, *officer.* That why you been chasing me for so long?"

Rocky hums, taking a step back. "You're planning to run in there and knock down a bunch of bangers with a bat and a knife?"

"A gun ain't gonna do anythin' but piss 'em off and let 'em know we're there," KC says. "Once we get my heart back, you can call the reaper, assumin' they didn't put up any protections." KC drops his jacket. He flicks his hair out from under the collar of his jacket where it'd been trapped. "How you feel about swinging, Joey?" He nods toward the bat on the bed.

"I'm not so great with a bat. Can I get the knife?" I say.

KC reaches to the back of his pants were the knife's tucked in. He pulls out the plain, mostly black sheath. It's got a couple golden, mystical eyes embossed on the handle. "Don't lose it." KC glances across me at Rocky. "Watch your head. It might get a little rough in the neighborhood." KC grabs the bat from the bed. With it propped on his shoulder, he heads toward the door.

Rocky turns to me. The cuffs are off his belt now. "You can't think you're going with him."

I know it's a mistake to say anything to Rocky. Any trust I might've gotten from him is gone after what happened at Patterson Tower. "Look, I'm sorry for losing you. I didn't try, but believe me when I say something bigger is going on here than gang wars. You saw Charon at the station. Explain that."

Rocky says nothing.

"If Jag's at Kaufman's, I have to go. I can't let anything else happen to him because of me. Throw me in a cell after that if you want, but at least let me go look for him this one last time." I'm looking Rocky in the eyes. He's evaluating me. His focus only breaks when KC hits the lights off in the closet. His steps heavy and fast as he goes for the door, grabbing his keys off the hook by the wall.

"Don't move." Rocky half turns to face KC. "If you're going in, we're callin' for back up."

"Nuh-uh." KC snorts. "I ain't lettin' you put Reagan in that kinda danger." KC slips the keys into his pocket, turns on his heels, and crosses to Rocky. He's close enough, Rocky squares off. "You forget what happened at the station?" KC's neck cranes. His head slowly shakes. "*Bam, bam, bam, bam.* You shoot a ghost? You're fucked. Frenzy 'em up, everyone's dead. Now multiply that by however many fuckers are in that hive. That's not even getting' started with the shit you don't understand. *The priest.* If you're living, he can make you see shit that don't exist. Whatever power ya think ya got is neutered when dealin' with this shit. You wanna go out in a blaze of glory fighting the dead with your squad? Then have at it, but do it some other time when I ain't got shit to lose."

"You're talking about something impossible, Chuck," Rocky says.

Pushing his hair back, KC chuckles. "You wanna know what happened ten fuckin' years ago? Then come along for the ride, Big Dick. Maybe you'll finally see how bad Baltimore really is 'cause this place ain't normal." KC crosses the short distance to Rocky while he talks. I'd expected Rocky to step back, maintain the space between the two of them, keeping the threat lower, but he doesn't, even as KC stops right in front of him and the two are eye-to-eye. "I've spent every day of my life for the last ten years being around the dead of this city. You know what they want more than anything? More bodies, more power, more grief. Most of 'em are angry; they want to be angry and they want to make whatever poor motherfucker they can pay for the pain they feel every day. Don't matter if they laid eyes on you today or yesterday or three years ago. None of us can get away from the Baltimore's ghosts and there'll be a hellova lot worse waitin' if anything happens to Reagan."

A soft tick is the only sound. KC's breath. His tapping foot. My heart's throbbing in my ears. "Shit." KC backs away with a hiss. "I'm out." He crosses to the back door of the apartment. "If ya feel like comin', I'm drivin'. If not, have a good life, don't come again." He pulls the door open and walks out without waiting or looking back. I follow out after him before Rocky can grab my arm and make a different decision for me. The apartment door closes behind me. Rocky's less than subtle footsteps hit the gravel behind me. His hand's on my shoulder. My body tenses and a hiss escapes.

A burning feeling makes my arm go numb before the pain registers. I'm breathing before I feel the wetness and the sting turns into a sharp pain. The heat turns into a growl in my throat. Something's stabbing through my arm. My vision goes spotty. I stumble forward, reaching for anything to help keep me standing as a wave of dizziness threatens to throw me over. KC's too far away to reach, the car's not close enough either, and the trees are all too far off the side of the path. I hit the ground. I push to sit up. "KC," I breathe out.

Rocks, trees, birds watching, six of them? Seven? Eyes, the graffiti reading HAHAHAHA. It's all in my head, right?

Tears pool in my eyes. I grab handfuls of gravel and

fling them, gasping. Baltimore mocks me by sending my voice back as an echo in the sky.

"Breathing, Joey," Rocky says.

"What's happening?" I say through my teeth.

It doesn't matter if KC says anything. I'm hearing ringing and buzzing and then far away and then nothing as everything around me's going in and out and black. The night's eating the streetlights and the gravel's eating the earth until I can't think of anything but the pain burning and dripping down my arm. It's a knife going through my skin, sharp and deep and unaffected by hesitation. I can't keep my eyes open. My cheek stings with the familiar feeling of a slap. My head slams into something. A hiss and the repeating voice going to die, going to die, I can't die—"He's going to die, KC!" Baltimore says back to me, using my voice.

The pain subsides. I'm laying on my back. I don't know when I got here and my face is wet. Someone's hanging over me. A blur or a shadow, the face messed up. All they've got are teeth and a taunting grin with a head back lit by a light pole at the street.

KC's ponytail falls over his shoulder. He touches my face, using his thumb to gently open my eyes. "You there?"

I push his hand back with a weak swat. "Yeah. I… don't know what happened." I exhale. My cheeks are burning now that the moments passed, my emotions have come down, and I'm reliving whatever just happened through the distance of memory.

Rocky's on his knees next to me, wrapping a piece of cloth around my arm, holding it tight in his big hands. A chill goes through me. I'm trembling. My fingers curl gently, reaching for *him*. I'm thinking *I need you* again and again and again. I'm so cold and my eyes are heavy. Is that Jag or me?

I wipe my eyes while KC wraps my arm with bandages. "What the hell just happened, KC?"

"Reagan told ya, yeah?" KC's eyes meet mine. "You're connected through your heart."

"What did they do?" I say.

KC looks over my face, my arm, and my eyes again. "My guess? Anger management. These aren't the signs of a ritual. Coulda been worse, but your boy's probably fine for now."

Rocky offers me a hand to get back to my feet. My vision goes spotty and I stumble back, gripping onto Rocky for balance. My eyes close again. My head drops forward.

Everything's too heavy.

I'm exhausted. I don't want to do anything but go home and lay in Jag's arms and feel safe against him, but that's not an option until I get him back and even then, I don't know if I'll deserve it.

"You sure you're okay to do this?" Rocky says

"I owe it to Ralph and Jag and everyone who's ever given me a chance. The reason anyone's in trouble is my fault because I didn't follow through. That's always been my problem, you know?" I meet Rocky's eyes. "I just… run… from everything and it's only made things worse."

"You've got one thing going in your favor." Rocky crosses his arms. He's looking past me. KC's at his car. At the sight of the dented door, he growls to himself. He pulls the door open and tosses the bat inside. KC's car door shuts. "Between you, him, and Ralph? There are a lot of blanks that I can't seem to fill in with real answers. If it wasn't for that, we wouldn't be talking right now."

A chill goes through me, then heat and my eyes close. Everything Wayland sacrificed for me plays through my head. The times Jag's gone out on a limb to chase after me or he's offered to fight my dad or he looked like he was really gonna go in and lay my dad out because of what he saw on me, even when I didn't ask. He's gone to jail for me now while Wayland lost his life… and Rocky is losing his sanity over trusting me.

The temptation to go back to Mortem is there again. Forget everything, forget what I've done to people, forget the worst of my impositions and how I've hurt everyone around me and move on so they don't have to suffer because of me anymore.

I open my eyes again and Rocky's still there, staring, waiting expectantly. "Thank you for trusting me, Rocky. I know I've given you every reason not to and you're a badge which like, gives you double reason to not trust a liar like me, but I… just… thanks… for seeing me as more than some kind of scum to clean up or ignore. It means a lot that you actually seem to give a shit, you know?"

"I told you," Rocky says, "I try to earn the badge every day. That doesn't come without getting the trust of the people I serve at least *sometimes.*"

I meet Rocky's eyes. "I've always run from everything because I was scared of what might happen if I showed I cared, but… it's only made things worse. I guess playing dumb doesn't do shit to trick the universe."

"Yeah… I'd guess that lying really doesn't work against God," Rocky says.

"Who knew?" I smile weakly.

An engine roars to life. The window on the passenger side of the Riviera rolls down as KC slams on the horn. "You comin' or fuckin' what?"

I look to Rocky. He gives me a nod. "Yeah!" I say before turning to the car.

I hold the knife tight at my side. Its weight grows the closer I get to the vehicle, knowing what I'm going to have to do, but part of me doesn't really mind. I helped

Wayland dump a body in Leakin; I shot my dad in the face a couple of times. I should be able to use a knife on someone, right? Especially on a couple of ghost bastards. The bodies of the dead I've seen over the last few weeks plague my mind. They should sicken me and it's weird they don't while the voice in the back of my ear's saying *nothing lost, don't worry about it.*

KC's got the engine on by the time I get to the car. Since Rocky wants the back seat, I have to push the seat forward and wait for him to climb in.

The radio's blasting. I tap my foot from the passenger seat, waiting for us to get to the Old Town Mall.

I don't know what's getting me so hyped. I've never been one for violence—At least not until I died. If you can believe it, I fucking hate it. I don't even like watching romcoms where people think it's funny to slap someone else. I always hated seeing that kind of shit on TV; I've hated seeing it follow me the last few weeks; I've hated feeling like everyone in this city really wants me dead and I've hated feeling like I wanted to contribute to the deaths of others. Like, not caring, like tossing those weighted bags of someone's missing person into the bushes the same as a cup from KWIK TRIP or a used condom or whatever that's got no use anymore. I hate thinking of how I was a few weeks ago with Wayland and I don't even feel like that was me. But the memories are there and my body hasn't forgotten what anything I've done has felt like. It's just… something I have to live with.

I'm glad Wayland's not around anymore to hold onto worse. He doesn't deserve the guilt that Bodymore put on his shoulders. This city's obsessed with violence, though I don't know if it's the city's fault or the people who built it. Maybe humans and the city are just easy scapegoats for something bigger.

I can't help thinking it. I need some way to get out of what I am, you know? I never wanted to be like my dad. I was never actually scrappy. I just liked the excuse and pretended I was a lot more trouble than I honestly ever got into. It kept people from getting invested if they thought I looked like a delinquent. They saw a lowlife, a dropout, someone who wasn't going far. Maybe I'd become a prostitute who'd hit a dumpster in a couple of years or a burnout who'd be found under an overpass with track marks to show the progression of my bad life getting worse until I finally reached escape.

Most people stay away from early signs of failure. They write you off as fast as they can so they can say *not my problem* when trouble hits and *not surprised* when your body shows up. Rocky's said pretty much that when talking about KC and Ralph.

Nobody wants to get involved in something they think's doomed from the start, you know? Waste of time. Waste of space. The sooner you run off, the sooner you can dissolve into nothing as the city eats you, your neighbors forget you, and you become nothing but more fuel for the rage you don't have to stick around to see play out.

Rocky's in the backseat with me. Probably didn't trust me behind him and it gives him a better vantage point on KC, but still, he looks crunched with the seat so far back, his knees are at his chest. His head's hitting the ceiling. He doesn't say anything about the discomfort though.

"Rocky." I put the knife on the floor, so he doesn't have to edge so much from me sheathing and unsheathing it out of the nervous energy buzzing inside of me. "Do you think Baltimore's doomed?"

"In what way?" he says.

"The violence, misery, selfishness... and whatever else you see on your papers in the station." A bitter chuckle rolls around my mouth. "It doesn't seem like it'll ever stop. You really think there's anything we can do about it? Everyone's always at each other's throats. From the second you're born, it's like your dad wants to cut you."

"I've been offered jobs in other cities with fewer problems, more support, and bigger budgets. Where the cases aren't as consistent, the brutality isn't so banal, and the pressure's not as high. I might still be married if I'd gone to an easier town."

"Why didn't you?"

Rocky sighs. Awkwardly, he rubs the back of his neck. "Baltimore's hurting. I'm not sure what it is that's made it like it is, but her pain's not a good enough reason to abandon her. She's my home, my history, part of who I am. I can't leave her to self-destruct just because things look bad. If everybody did that, there'd be no one helping anyone when they hit a hard time. You know, people are more than whatever a snapshot at their worst moment captures."

'What if it never stops hurting? It's been like this for a while."

"A cycle's hard to break, yeah, but it's not impossible. Maybe I'll never see the benefit of the work I do in my lifetime, but I want to hope that by the time I retire, the best of my efforts contributed to pulling this place out of Hell and making it better, even if it's just for a couple of people." Rocky looks at KC, the back of his seat. His lips tighten, his heel bounces once against the floor. "I've had times where I've failed. Saw warning signs and injuries and questioned if I coulda done more. I don't want to live with the guilt of who I could've helped if I didn't run."

I don't know if I believe him because I can feel the city thirsting through me. There's so much rage trapped in the graffiti around the town, in the broken buildings, abandoned and ignored by the people who are supposed to take care of them, but lived in by the people who have no other choice or who love them anyway. The voice in my head has been tempting me to do worse and worse since I started hearing it. If that's not Baltimore calling me, then what else is it?

Lights shine on the buildings outside. A sidewalk reads I WANT MORE above the outline of a body. The real mark of a grave? The city's simple, never-ending demand for blood? An argument or protestation against my thoughts?

It doesn't matter. I mutter, "No," because even though I don't know how I'm going to change, I know I don't want to stay as the same thing that's gotten me into the trouble I'm in now.

SIXTEEN.

KC parks the Riviera on Aiquith Street near the entrance of the Old Town Mall. The courtyard's dark with only a few lights spread throughout working, buzzing, and flickering on and off. I don't think it's an accident a couple of them are on. Music's coming from somewhere. The thumping's muted like a car stereo in the distance, bouncing off the streets and the Old Town Mall's bricks. Birds sitting on rooftops pick up the sounds, distort them, and mimic back a mess.

KC's got the bat over his shoulder as we cross the street. He pauses before stepping onto the sidewalk. He puts his arm out to stop me. Rocky steps on the back of my heels. We apologize at the same time even though I didn't do anything.

I step over the sidewalk.

The feeling of the Old Town Mall courtyard washes over me. It's different from Mortem, but it's the feel of abandon. Broken places have a different energy about them, you know? Like the life that used to be there is still hanging around, but you also get the feeling that things shouldn't be like this. It's like going to an empty playground. The feeling of nothing when there should be something, a disassociation from humanity. Not everything in the Old Town Mall's abandoned, but it all looks like it would be. Some of the businesses are in partial working order. Some of them are busted up, but still used. Some of them just look dirty and rundown, but more than functional — like the discount grocery store on the corner.

Though, the Old Town Mall isn't really welcoming, the night somehow makes the place even less inviting. Shadows move soundlessly between buildings, but then when you do hear someone walking or a pebble being tossed, there's no proof. People sleep and live and hide and wait in these places, both boarded up and with open windows. Not all of them are malicious, but you don't know who is in here for what.

Two months ago there was a story at the top of the paper about a couple of guys from out-of-town sneaking into Kaufman's to shoot a video. They were tailed inside and by the time they came back out, a handful of thugs were waiting, beat the shit out of them, and jacked their equipment. Never found out who they were.

Probably ghosts. Those guys were lucky to get out alive.

People look at the abandon here and think it's like any other city, but Baltimore's abandon is just our lives worn down.

You don't think someone should live in that house because it looks like no one's lived in it for thirty years, but somehow, it's got power. Boards over the broken windows are more of a sign that someone cares about the place and is probably living inside than a show of abandon. Dead plants, overgrown grass, kids' toys in the yard.

No matter how beat we look, we keep on going. It's the Baltimoron way. Whatever you gotta do, you make shit work.

The darkness leads people off the streets. Whoever's dumb enough to step out of the light is at risk of disappearing, regardless of what you look like or whether you're strapped. Shadows turn to tendrils that find a way to trip you or go up your pant leg or make you scared so you're not watching where you're going and you smack into a wall while running, giving whatever's following you the advantage it needs to catch up. The only people that like to come around the Old Town Mall at night are adrenaline chasers, junkies, indie film makers, the scabs of Baltimore trying to avoid detection, and randos playing for internet clout by doing something spooky. The ones in the most danger are always those from out of town. They observe the Old Town Mall from a safe window on the other side of a computer screen, but when you step onto the path, it's a completely different feeling. The whole city's got a different vibe to it than the couple of times I'd been to Richmond, but places like the Old Town Mall are even more different, like digging into the chest of a corpse that can wake up and grab you.

This place isn't as abandoned as it looks, and now, I feel like I can see it.

The restaurant on the corner has boards in the windows while the beauty shops facing the street have metal gates tightly protecting their fragile, glass storefronts. The window in front of *Jowlanda's Beauty Salon* is busted out, laying shattered over the brown seats below the window with a plastic bottle of Barton's, a couple empty cans of Natty Boh and Four Loco, cigarette butts, a lighter, a pen with shit on it, and a purple Swisher's wrapper. A piece of dirty white clothing is shoved against the building, looking like someone's stained underwear. The few lights that are working illuminate the interior of the abandoned shop. There's nothing inside but shattered mirrors, garbage, a torn-up beauty chair, and the smell of rot, piss, and alcohol left behind for too long. There's a hint of sulfur in the air that grows stronger the closer I get to the buildings.

A shadow at the back of the shop moves, dipping into a door not visible from the courtyard.

An unkindness sit across the rooftops. The moon's bright, large, and round. The courtyard lamps are flickering, amber and white. For some reason, there's both washing over the brick. The ravens' eyes glow crimson against the dark sky, mixing their hungry speckles in with the stars.

It's the strangest thing to live in a city of the dead and maybe that's why it's always felt so off being with my dad. He hasn't actually been here since the day I started first grade. I lost him a long time ago and every word he said to me over the last fifteen years was an echo of his misery in an attempt to drag me down with him. I don't know if it was because he wished to damn me for what my mom did to him or if he hoped if he pulled hard enough, he could get out of the sorrow he'd gotten himself stuck in, but I'm glad I never fell in.

A whistle echoes off the old buildings. Energy's coming from the ground, going up through my legs, and filling my body. Anticipation, excitement. It tickles under my skin and makes old scars in my arm ache. The air chills me, but does nothing to quench the rising tempest that's getting whipped up by the intimate whispering between the buildings.

Baltimore's constant call for action.

Lights flicker on where they shouldn't. Shadows gather in the windows, busted out, boarded up, blocked off by steel bars in an attempt to keep them protected. But there are so many more people here than I would have guessed and they keep coming to the windows like they are hiding in the back room as an audience waiting to build.

The small supermarket to the left has a bunch of signs talking about a sale because you know everything in there's from dumpster diving. The outlines of lost lives that've sought refuge here peer through the foggy glass, faceless. Everything's blurry, impersonal; the lights flicker on, yellow, revealing a new form each time they shut off and come back on. The jewelry store across the way gets two new shadows in the upstairs window above the shop. Then, the liquor store's got a man and a kid standing behind the glass door.

Most of the shops have jagged metal gates pulled over their entrances because if they didn't, they'd end up like *Jowlanda's*. I look over my shoulder. Now there's the shape of an older woman, a younger woman, and two kids standing in the busted-out window. The gate over *K's Jewelry* says RUN RUN RUN RUN. The gate next to that's on an unmarked building and says DON'T ASK. Next to that's the *Old Town Pharmacy*, half of the windows are exposed, the rest covered with planks of wood that read NARC and again and again and again. *Sister's Fashion* has sloppy flowers painted across it with RIP and COME BACK TO ME BABE while the store next to it has one of the words in the store name covered in black spray paint and letters added to the end of the uncovered words so it reads FINGERED. The gate underneath reads BITCHES LOVE COCK MORE.

The lights are flickering over Cooper's Liquor, but the door's open and the smell of a grape cigar's coming out. I'm sure something's moving inside. A chair scrapes against the floor. A glass bottle falls. My body's stiff, heart racing, skin hurting like I've already been slapped and I remember what it's like to have my back against the wall. My dad's voice rattles in my ears, not begging me to spend time with him like at the Bin, but begging me to forgive him just before he says *fuck you*.

"Stop looking," KC says.

"Who's there?" I say.

"Who do you think?" KC says.

A caw comes from above. The line of ravens across the rooftops have doubled.

Down the courtyard, a guy comes stumbling out of the old Kaufman's. He's got a light step and something in his hands. His laughter takes over the air in the otherwise silent courtyard. Hands in front of him, he squeezes them into fists, swings, laughs harder. The ravens atop the buildings start to click, one after another after another until the clicking turns from a metallic sound to a weird, robotic laughter.

KC stops where he's at. He puts his arm out to stop me. The guy strips. Whatever he's holding falls out of his hand. Light catches on it. A ring. The metal clicks on the ground and it's like that click was a mark saying go. One, then two, then a handful of ravens dive from the rooftops. The first hits his head, the next, his shoulders. The birds take him to the ground. The laughter turns to pleas as the ravens pin him and the biggest of them rips at the ghost's body, tearing at his skin and crunching his bones in its beak as if it were made of soft tissue. Screams of agony fill the courtyard. Fists uselessly fling at the bird. As the heart becomes less, so did the soul pinned to the ground until he was no more and all that was left behind was a barely visible shadow of where he once laid and the birds pecking at the stone for whatever crumbs his soul might've left behind.

His is not the only smear of life left on the pavement.

Their black eyes lift. The light catching on them turns them red. They focus on me. The first of the birds flings itself in our direction.

KC swings the bat as one of the ravens lunges. It

shrieks, retreating to a nearby rooftop. He goes to where the ring fell, picks it up, and examines it. "Guess that makes sense."

"What is it?" I say.

"One of Reagan's rings. If this random fucker's got one, the rest of his jewelry's probably been handed out." KC slips it onto one of his fingers.

"Won't they just come after you next for that?" I say.

Smirking, KC shakes his head. "Two things: I got a heart and it belong to Reagan."

"What's so special about the jewelry?" Rocky says.

"Every fetish is tied to who made it or who the intended wearer is," KC says. "Reagan's essence is in every piece of jewelry he wears, meaning the ravens won't attack whoever's wearing them. Think of it as if they're wearing his scent. The ravens know Reagan's soul, but they can't do anything so long as someone's carrying his shit."

"What about my necklace?" I say. "Val was obsessed with it—"

"Because it's a heart. It doesn't belong to Reagan, it belongs to you and the fuckers live off that shit." KC looks at me. "You don't wanna end up like that guy? Then don't slow down." KC turns on his heels to face me, still, walking backwards. "Nothing personal. They're just animals." He gestures to the ravens lining the rooftops.

I focus on the walk so I don't trip again. Paint's peeling on some place called the FOUNTAIN OF YOUTH TABERNACLE. Grate closed, the graffiti reads YOUNG ASS INSIDE with a poorly drawn ass next to it. One door down is a brown building with busted windows. A yellow sign with white letters reads YOUNG LAND as the store name. There are pieces of old, cheap candy scattered on the pavement outside the window along with another crumpled piece of clothing. Maybe a child's pair of underwear. A steel grate covers four panels of the next wall with the biggest grate reading METH HEAD. The smallest says 4. The other two read U FORGOT UR BIT DIT and STFU LIBRA and TIFF PLZ.

A light flickers in front of the building. Across from it are abandoned-looking shops. A red three-story with black metal bars across the front and boarded up windows on the second and third floor. A brown building with windows melted from fire. HORROR is written on what's left of the yellow sign and NO SHOOT ZONE on the metal grate. Then EVIL EVIL EVIL EVIL is in smeared chalk all over the bricks out front. White dots like the eyes of a monster hide in the shadow cast by the light.

"Stop slowin' down," KC says.

"You seeing the footprints though?" I say.

"The dead've been busy. That's it." KC glances at the birds lining the rooftops then to me. "I'm not warning you again."

The purring caw of a raven echoes down the courtyard. Deep, guttural, daring. The fattest one I've seen so far is on top the building neighboring the liquor store. He's staring at me with interest and hunger. The boarded-up windows underneath him read EAT ME and FUCKED TO FINNA with a figure sprayed in black that's so messy, I can't tell what it's supposed to be. A long, red line goes down the black thing, looking too much like the blood that dripped down Val's face earlier.

TRAGEDY is written across the top of the building, just under where the raven's sitting.

"They're gathering, and it's not the smell of your heart doing it." KC fingers tighten around the bat's handle as it remains slung over his shoulder.

"Careful, Rocky," I say.

Rocky's gaze meets mine. His smile's like something I expect him to wear when he's working late at night and doesn't want to be there. The kind of face he makes when he's thinking of his ex waiting for him at home knowing she doesn't want him around anymore. Wary, fired, anxious, and hesitant.

"Just don't want you to die is all." I nod toward the birds. "Seven or more ravens means they're waiting for someone to go."

"Good to know." Rocky's hand's on his gun, though his attention's between the buildings. There's no movement in the courtyard. It sounds like there are footsteps down the way. Still, looking forward, you can't see anyone.

A light from the liquor store's just enough to reflect off the ground outside the building. The ravens caw. Laughter. I reach for the necklace hanging around my neck. My heart resonates with warmth, like metal that'd been sitting near a source of heat. It makes my fingers tingle to touch and the nervous energy I felt before amplifies. One of the birds above sounds like it's choking. It jumps from the rooftop and lands in front of me. I pick up a can from the ground and chuck it at the bird. It retreats, returning to a nearby rooftop. Landing, it peers down at me still. I breathe out, hard.

Ahead, the old Kaufman's is four stories tall. It has nine metal grates over the front entrances and windows, each numbered in faded black. Eight says BITCH over the pale number. The metal banner over the door's faded, but has embossed words like FURNITURE, THE GREAT HOUSE, ISAAC BENESCH & SONS, and CARPETS AND RUGS. Most of the windows from the second to the fourth floor are blacked out, boarded up, splattered with paint or blood or a mess from God knows what. Some boxes are visible from the ground on the highest level. Whatever paperwork the owner of this place hasn't bothered to get rid of or maybe he's using this building like an old storage unit. I don't think that's the greatest idea, all things considered, but people generally aren't smart when their primary concern is convenience.

"Big Dick," KC says. "I'm only gonna say this once: Don't let your guard down once we're inside and don't go chasing after ghosts. You're probably gonna see some things you don't like. Ignore it or don't go in."

"Making your excuses already?" Rocky says.

"I'm doing you a courtesy, old man. Take it or leave it, but don't get in my way." KC turns back to me. His eyes are sharp, his head's bouncing, he takes another breath. He turns back to Kaufman's and walks down the line of metal doors. Arrows on the cement point further along and say TRASH. The metal grate that would say two is lifted, revealing a pair of red double doors with large, glass windows in them. A couple of bones tied together hang over the door. Bloody handprints mare the entrance. Wood blocks the view of the inside. The ground is stained with blood between the tiles and footprints, leading into the shopping center.

KC's paying little attention to all that though. Instead, he's staring at a mark on the ground in front of the door. A kite-shape encompasses a perfect circle. "Bingo," KC says. His muscles tense. His head flicks to the side, cracking his neck as he rolls his shoulders.

"What is it?" I say.

"The old man's calling card." KC grabs hold of the door handle. "Hopefully, he's still here, so I can put him out of his fuckin' misery." The briefest glance gives him the confirmation he's looking for without words and opens the door.

The air's different after stepping inside. Something's thicker, making it feel easier to breathe. The fear, panic, and anxiety have been cut in half and instead, I've got this feeling that's similar to when Jag's holding me.

"KC, why's it feel like this in here?"

"Because it's a den." KC nods toward the door. "If he's still active in here, don't believe everythin' you see. Might not be real."

"More of that?" I say.

"Yeah, more of tha—" There's a grunt; KC's punched in the stomach. He sucks in a breath, spits out blood. He's swinging the bat fast and hard. Before I see anything, it hits something hollow and meaty. A thud echoes off the entry. A body drops. He draws the bat back and slams the end of it down on the head of some guy who hadn't been there before. A crack comes, the bat pulls back, and KC slams it in harder. The head pops. Not like you see in the movies. It's not like a *bam* and red's splattered on everything. It's more like blood runs out his ears and his nose cracks and blood comes out of that too. There's a fissure in the top of his head and more stuff's coming out his eyes. KC kicks the guy hard enough he rolls over. He steps over him, then, the metal tip of his boot presses into the guy's neck, crushing down without restraint while he takes the top of the guy's skull.

Entry point: his eyes. The bone snapping echoes, multiplying the horror as the end of the bat caves a hole through the front of the guy's face and goes straight to his brain. It hits something halfway through. KC lifts the bat and slams it back down through the skull. It pushes through whatever it got stuck on before and hits the floor. KC pulls it out. The end of the bat comes out red. KC steps over the body.

Rocky steps forward, grabbing KC by the shoulder.

"That—"

"Dead." KC pulls out of Rocky's grasp and turns on his heels to face him. "Been that way for a while." KC lowers on top of the guy, picking up each hand and going over his fingers, sliding off the jewelry he finds, but only keeping some of it. "Lucky day," KC says, slipping on a silver ring with a small pink and white speckled stone on it.

"What's that?" I say.

"Reagan's second favorite ring." KC goes through the guy's pockets next. Patting him down, he comes up empty. "Don't see it here. We'll have to keep looking."

"You're into graverobbing now?" Rocky says.

"I'm just taking back what is *mine, Big Dick*." KC returns to a stand squaring off as Rocky approaches him. "If you were worried about graverobbin', you shoulda checked up on me years ago."

"Is that a confession?" Rocky steps closer.

"Prove it," KC says.

My arms swing out in front of me; I'm stumbling backward, trying to get my bearings back as someone gabs my shirt and turns me. My back's against the wall on the other side of the hall. Quickly, a hand's at my throat. All the air's out of my lungs. I can't breathe in the air that's too thick to be Kaufman's. This place wants me to die—That's all I can think as my feet come off the ground. My fingers curl around the hilt of the knife KC gave me. I gasp for air. Knife drawn, I thrust it toward the attacker. Something bursts, the pressure gives. His hand loosens and he's stumbling back until he falls with a thud. The knife's sticking out of his eye as he's screaming. He grabs at the hilt to pull it out. A gush of blood and brain matter trails behind, painting half the guy's face in red. KC shoves the knife into the guy's throat. He goes as far in as he's able until the tip either hit the floor or the guy's skull. Then, he pulls it out. The guy's other eye opens—The one that I stabbed. It's dark, but there's the look of a black, shiny globe on the inside as blood seeps down the edge of his eyelid like tears. Light reflects off his inhuman iris. He can't pull his eyelid open the whole way.

KC releases the blade's hilt and uses his thumb to force the guy's eye open while his other hand holds against the guy's mouth. KC hisses, jerks back, but doesn't raise his hand. "Fucker—!" He punches the guy's cheek, harder this time and the blood makes a wet splat.

The guy's screams turn into nothing but air and a whistle through the holes in his throat. The memories of Wayland's mangled body just a couple of days ago are still fresh. My eyes burn. I run to where KC's bat is on the floor. I grab the wall for support and use the bat like a cane. I can't get the smell of fresh gore out of my nose and when I close my eyes, I see the pain still on his face. Whatever the hell they did to him, whatever he said last before he collapsed and city thugs ran off with what remained of Wayland's life. A sneer's on my lips and I'm breathing hard, thinking *do it again, KC.*

I shake my head to get the anger out. My vision keeps going red and black and I can't focus on anything but the closest body for me to slam the bat into. The sting's coming back to my arm. I gasp, feeling a fist in my stomach and a slap on my face, but there's no one in front of me. I brace myself and swing.

"Whoa—" Rocky approaches. "You okay?"

"Yeah." I blink my vision back. "I think. I dunno. I got punched in the gut or something." I get an eyeful of the bastard on the floor.

"Hey, hey, hey. Wake up. You in there bud?" KC's slaps the guy's dry cheeks. How ginger he is makes me need to check on the one who's head got busted in. That guy hasn't moved yet. Assuming he's a ghost, how long should it take before he gets back up?

After a moment, KC wipes his bloody fingers on his pants, leaving prints on the fabric from both his hands and the way that guy's hands clawed at him to get up. Just like he did with the last guy, KC picks up the guys hands and plucks off the jewelry. One ring hits the floor while he takes the other. He pats the guy down, digging into the guy's pants pocket. KC withdraws a silver ring with a round, purple stone on it. The ring's small and delicate, hanging from a chain. "There's our favorite." KC mutters to himself as he slips the two rings into an interior pocket of his leather jacket.

KC squats back over the guy, taking hold of his chin and squeezing his cheeks, hard. The veins in KC's arms stand out against his skin, the muscles are tight. KC whistles and mutters. "Ya gonna be dead, ya gonna be dead, so get up while you can, honey." He releases the guy's cheeks to smack him harder across the face. The blood makes a wet splat. "Ya hear me, buttercup?

"You killed another one," Rocky says.

"What's it fuckin' matter?" KC says. "You call me a killer already, don'tcha?"

"Sounds like a confession to me," Rocky says. "When'd it first happen?"

"What's another piece of rot in the pile?" KC says.

"You act like killing doesn't mean anything—"

"At this point, it doesn't." KC pins the guy to the floor by his neck. "You already know what ya think of me and nothin' fuckin' matters, yeah? You don't give a shit about why I do what I do just like ya don't give a shit about a man who beats his wife to death, huh? We're all the same kinda garbage that gets ignored until its convenient." KC smirks and returns his attention to the corpse underneath him. "I don't give a shit anymore. Do whatcha gotta do, Big Dick, and I'll do my thing. But let me warn ya, once you know what matters, ya don't mind crossin' certain boundaries and there ain't no going back. A threat's a threat, no matter what color they're wearing." He pinches the guy's chin again, squeezing harder each time. He uses the grip to pull the guy's head from the floor and ram it down again.

Thud.

Clatter.

Blood splatters across the floor from all the holes in his face and the slit in his neck. The eye that I didn't stab pops open. In the other, the lid hangs heavy, unable to fully open. Blood seeps through the closed lid. The guy's body stiffens. His hands press into the floor and he's pushing up, reaching for KC with one hand. KC grabs his arm as it comes for him and pins it back to the floor. The guy reaches with the other. Fingers slide up the guy's skull to lace in his hair. A handful of shorter dark locks and KC slams the guy into the ground.

The guy snarls, back curls, and he reaches blindly for KC in an attempt to shove him off. KC grabs the hand coming at him and takes it back to the floor. He slaps the guy's face, saying, "Hey, hey, hey, buddy, come back." KC leans in closer. "I don't wanna fight ya. I just want ya to tell me where I can find my people. That too much to ask? Can ya talk? Give it a try, cause I ain't got much patience left, yeah?"

"Get bent!" the guy chokes out through his busted throat.

"Nah… Not feelin' it today." KC thrusts the knife through the guy's remaining eye.

The guy screams, body spasming. His voice tries to carry, but KC shoves his hand in the guy's mouth to stop it from going too far into the building. If that was meant to stop anyone else in this place from knowing we're here, I think it's too late, but seeing him unable to cry out is still more satisfying than I'd like to admit. I glance back toward the glass door opening of Kaufman's.

"This don't gotta be hard, buddy. Believe me, I'm hatin' this as much as you." KC mutters, yet his voice is grounded and deep, a threat that gets my blood hot and makes me feel not like running, but fighting. KC's fingers close around the knife's hilt and he twists it in the guy's skull. The guy screams into KC's hand. His back curls, but KC uses his weight to flatten the guy against the floor. He pulls his hand back saying, "Where the fuck's my medium?"

"Loading dock office—" the dead guy gasps.

"The old man with him?"

"I dunno," the dead man mutters. "He was, but I dunno—"

"Thanks," KC says. "Told ya it'd be easy." A chuckle breaks his words. He grabs the knife back out and slams it into the guy's chest. The guy underneath KC goes limp.

I don't know if he's really gone this time or if he's faking it, hoping KC gets up. Something clatters behind me. I spin around to check out the body of the guy KC knocked out before. I don't know how much time there is between getting knocked out and getting back up. Henney didn't take long to come back at the station, but then my dad also didn't come back when I was still at the house. The guy on the floor's unaroused. He hasn't even moved his arm to flinch since KC knocked his head in with the bat.

"That guy wasn't a ghost, was he KC?" I say.

KC looks from me to Rocky back to me. "I'm not going to answer that. You can read between the lines."

"Okay, fine. Then tell me, why isn't Charon here?"

"Remember the symbol out front?" KC nods toward

the door. The symbol on the ground is still visible through the foggy department store glass, even if the lights in the courtyard aren't all that bright. "That marks this place as a den. I don't entirely know what that means other than this is a kind of alternate reality that bitch ass controls. The old man's got power above the reaper, can't come here, can't pick up the dead until the den is gone and if the den disappears with the body inside, the body goes with it forever."

"How do you get rid of a *den*?" I say.

"How do you get rid of a rat?" KC's watching the guy he'd just stabbed. He puts his foot onto the guy's chest to hold him down while he pulls the knife out of his chest. He draws his foot back and slams it into his side. "Fucker." His palm springs toward me. It takes me a moment to register that KC might be asking for the knife's sheath. I hold it out to him. He takes it and snaps the blade into the sheath.

"Hey—" Rocky's moving toward KC.

"If you want that body as evidence, you're gonna need to drag it outside in the next five minutes." KC slides the knife into the back of his pants.

"That a threat?" Rocky steps in front of KC.

"You're in over your head, Big Dick." KC steps forward. When he doesn't move, KC pushes him back. "If you can't take the reality of what we're dealing with, there's the door. I ain't puttin' on the breaks if you get in my fuckin' way. Things are only gonna get messier from here." He makes a beeline for the loading dock.

"You look insane." Rocky grabs him by the arm.

KC pulls away, chuckling bitterly. "What's new about that?" He takes a step closer. Rocky takes a step back. Seeing the retreat, KC keeps pushing. "You're gotta wanna reframe how you see things. Everyone's always lookin' for answers that set you apart from people like me, sayin' *I'll never be like them*, because it's easier to swallow than reality since insanity's a lot more common than anyone wants to believe." The light catches on the metal tips of his shoes. Somehow, it reflects in the dark color of his eyes as he locks stares. Rocky hits a wall. His hand goes for his pistol. KC doesn't relent. "Real insanity sets in when you only see what you want when you see another person: resources to be mined or obstacles in the way. That's *you* right now."

KC stops about foot from where Rocky is. They're stares are locked. "Don't get the wrong idea about me." He shrugs. A chuckle. A step back. "I try to live an okay life, *but by the books,* but I ain't Reagan. I don't got that kinda mercy. I'm only around now cause I owe someone my life and I don't trust anyone else to take care of him the way I know I will. Everythin' about my being here is selfish." KC stops in front of Rocky. "You wanna know what drives the dead? Put a bullet in your head and see what surfaces when ya hit rock bottom. Otherwise, maybe stop by the bar some time. Talk to Reagan about Baltimore. He's seen worse than you can imagine, but goddamn he's so idealistic, he sees blood in the gutter and thinks someone's signalin' SOS."

"Sounds like he abets criminals," Rocky says.

"He offers a line to the lost and it's more than the BPD ever did for the victims of this city."

"That look like hope to you?" Rocky gestures to the corpse with the caved in skull.

"Looks like gang violence." Lips pursed, KC smiles and turns away. "City negligence. Poor bastard." KC steps over to the body.

"You don't get to blame anyone else for your actions—"

And I don't gotta feel guilty for doing what I had to, to survive." KC cranes his neck, looking it the corpse.

"The only rule in this town is take care of yourself cause no one else will. *From filth to filth*, there ain't much else in Baltimore. You and I both know it." KC pushes the guy's head with the tip of his shoe.

The guy's not gonna be in there.

The only way he can come back now is by jumping into the river if he's got enough anger to remember KC's face through the temptations of forever on the other side. KC spits on the guy's face, picks his foot up, and crushes his nose.

"That's a crime scene—"

"Then take it outside." KC swerves from the direct path to make his way back to the guy he'd stabbed. KC grabs hold of him by the arms and pulls him toward the other corpse. It leans against a wall with a pipe built into the wall and going along the bottom edge. "You wanna borrow me your cuffs?" He puts his hand out toward Rocky.

"No, I don't," Rocky says.

"If ya don't wanna do this for me, do it for Reagan." KC's hand remains out. "We both know he doesn't deserve this shit; he's never hurt anyone."

Rocky approaches KC fast. One hand's going for the cuffs, the other's just above his gun. His eyes lock on KC though, watching his movements, ready to parry. He gets a handful of shirt. KC swings his knife, followed by a right hook. Rocky let's go and backs off just before anything hits him. He lunges for a second time, getting a handful of KC's shirt and catching KC's blade as he tries for another swing. KC growls and chuckles at the same time. His head's shaking. His muscles aren't big, but KC's beating Rocky's strength with a swing of the bat, a hand in the face, and a reckless abandon that Rocky doesn't have.

Rocky releases his hold on KC, putting space between

them for safety.

"Fine." KC sheaths his knife. "Have it your way." He takes a couple steps back. He tucks his knife into the back of his pants and picks up his bat from the floor. When he finds it, he lifts his hands and shrugs. "The dead don't play by mortal rules; I don't either. We'll leave him here and *you* can get stabbed. Ya think you can reason with him when he gets back up? Good fuckin' luck. If it were that easy, we wouldn't be here. People in this city got a knack for turnin' destruction into home and then we wonder why the hell everythin's a mess. Chasin' endless bodies around Baltimore just to forget who did it's kinda your bag, yeah? The BPD is the real horror show." KC turns on his heel and makes his way toward the back of the store and likely the loading dock.

The wall behind Rocky reads SAVE OUR KIDS in white and blue spray paint. I didn't think there'd be any graffiti in Kaufman's. Honestly, I didn't think this place would be so easy to get into either. It's still under private ownership. I guess that never stopped anyone from sneaking in, especially since losers shooting video for online followings made it look safer than it really is. I'd have thought the handful of stories about urban explorers getting mugged would've been enough to result in a private security detail or upgraded locks. But instead, the grate's hanging open and no one seems to care. Though now that I'm thinking about it… Maybe the owner did get security, but when the bangers moved in, they took out old management and now, maybe we'd find a body curled over in a bathroom or supply closet if we went looking.

I know what Wayland said; I know what Rocky said; I know what my dad did, but I still can't believe how seemingly easy it is for normal people to put an end to a life. I mean, I should get it. I didn't think twice about wanting to kill Donny the other day after he pink slipped me. He didn't deserve it, but at the time, I just couldn't think of anything else. And then there was shoving that gun in my dad's face…

I really didn't think that hard about it until it was too late and he was gone and it's like what the hell is wrong with me?

In those moments, I thought if I'd left him, I'd be pulling the trigger on him, so I couldn't leave. I didn't want to be the reason that happened, but in the end, I didn't indirectly shoot him; I picked up his gun and did it myself. If I think about it too much, I can feel myself ready to do it again. The calm, the climax, the release of everything he held over me in that goddamn house.

Then, just as quickly as I pulled the trigger, it was gone.

I remember the vague feelings of anger and staring into my face and Jag's body pressed against me on the sink so I didn't do anything stupid, but the impulses I felt at the time were so powerful I couldn't get them out of my head, even when looking at Jag.

It was never about thinking. At those times, there was just no way and all I wanted to do was end everyone and everything for the little high that it was gonna give me. Like a drug, the climax of power and pleasure, the sparks left me feeling so good.

If I didn't think about it, maybe I never would've stopped. Maybe I would've gotten worse. Maybe I would've become the monster Rocky already thinks of me of as and Jag would be dead.

I approach Rocky fast. Hand out. "Gimme the cuffs."

"What?" he says.

"I don't want you to die. Give me the cuffs." One hand's going for the cuffs, the other's just above his gun. His eyes lock on me, watching my movements and the body on the ground where KC had left it. The corpse groans. Both Rocky and I look at it.

"This isn't about mortality, Rocky. You saw. It'll keep coming back whether you believe it or not," I say. "But give your eyes a chance to convince you of what you've seen so far. I'm not the only one telling you this shit."

The corpse awakens with a snarl of curses. His face is still darkened with blood pouring out the socket I popped. Though it looks like his eyes are back. Both wide and white and staring at me. He pushes up and lunges for it at the same time Rocky races to pick it up. They both get a hold at the same time. Rocky shoves his foot into the guy's face, slamming it hard into the wall as he pulls the gun from his holster. He points it at the thing's head and pulls the trigger twice. Blood splatters against the wall; its body goes limp.

Rocky holsters his pistol. The sound of metal hitting the floor echoes in the show room while Rocky exchanges the weapon for his cuffs which he gives to me.

"I guess you win this one," Rocky says.

"Party." I lock half the pair on the wrist of the dead man then the other half on the pipe running along the floorboards.

Rocky's at the corpse KC bashed in with a bat.

"What are you doing?" I say.

"I'd be an idiot to listen this much, but leave a body alone if Chuck says it's going to disappear." Rocky pulls the body across the floor, leaving a trail of blood in its wake. "I don't want a single life to be lost if I can help it."

"What do you think is gonna happen?"

"I dunno, but ironically, I'd rather live on the safe side." Rocky pulls the body out Kaufman's entrance and leaves it against one of the other grates outside. He gives a look to the shadows lining the foggy, yellow window on the other end of the courtyard, then comes back inside.

"Let's find Chuck," Rocky says, checking over his hands for blood, then wiping them on his already soiled suit. "I want to get the BPD in here as soon as possible."

"You can apologize to him later," I say.

"Don't think I'm *that* convinced yet."

"Give it time." I run ahead, leading to the loading dock.

The department store walls argue with themselves. It might not be the creatures from below hitting in my ears, but someone's talking to me and covering up what everyone else is trying to say. Every time I blink, there are more and more words on the walls and the way the lines cross, it's making my head feel like there are too many frantic voices are talking at each other.

DON'T MISTAKE
    MAKE^
BROKE   BROKEN   BROKER
GONNA STEAL ALL THE DAM MUNNY FAM
HE EATS OUR BABIES
U THE REASON WE LIVE IN IN HELL
DON'T BLAME ME DEBRA
DON'T LISTEN TO THE NOISE
ITS ALL NOISE
ITS ALL NOISE
ITS ALL NOISE
DON'T LISTEN TO THE NOISE.

KC's peering in the loading dock window, foot bouncing, hands resisting reaching for the knife in the back of his pants. At the sound of our steps, he glances sidelong at us. "Damn… I thought for sure the banger woulda got ya," KC mutters before shoving the door open. "Lookin' for your boss, baby cakes!" His voice echoes in the loading dock. "Where's that old motherfucker?!"

"Who the hell are you?" some banger says.

I make a run for the door. Rocky grabs of hold of me and doesn't let me go. "Don't be anything stupid."

After a moment I say, "I'll try."

Rocky doesn't let me go as we edge closer to the door. Everything inside's gearing up. The voice, the anger, it's getting into me. The two act as a reminder of the places I occupy. Control and frenzy; caution and risk; not alive, but not dead yet. Really, I could go either way though.

SEVENTEEN.

"What the hell does he think he's doing?" Rocky says. "He's gonna get himself killed."

"It's too late for that, Rocky," I say.

We're at the loading dock, the double doors are closed, foggy windows at the top of the door give a peek into the back room. Dirty fingerprints smudge the glass with bloody handprints decorating the door's surface. The space under the window says KEEP YOUR HEAD DOWN. I peer through the glass window in the door.

Adrenaline's running. I want to get this over with and go find Jag. But for everything KC and Ralph have done for me, I owe it to help them first. I can't keep being selfish; I can't keep acting on impulse. It's always the wrong move.

Plus, I don't even know if Jag's in this stupid building or what the bangers have to do with Ralph's old man. Charon can't collect anybody, I'm weaker than the Big

Guy and if what KC said is true and Jag is here, then if Jag dies, it could end up that no one finds his body. Rushing in now wouldn't just make me a bigger idiot, but it'd get more people killed.

I look through the window on the door.

On the other side of the glass, the feeling of KC's stage presence is coming back, overwhelming. The legend that made him dangerous feels real. Worse then what I've already seen him do today.

The two guys sitting at a cruddy plastic card table stand up. Playing cards are scattered on a fold out table. One of the loading doors hangs wide open. Another door off to the far side of the rooms also open, looks like an office and there's blood splashed against the concrete coming out.

Symbols mark the floor around the room made of blood and chalk. A couple of feathers and beer bottles filled with different things, not beer. More blood, water, dirt, something else I can't tell from the distance. There are more bones against the wall behind the bangers and graffiti that reads BANG BANG BANG and GOTTEM and BALTIMORE IS MINE.

Ralph isn't anywhere visible in the room though, but I'm praying he's here at least so KC can find him.

The darkness is too much.

Ralph happily gave parts of his life to me so that I could have a second chance.

I don't care about the rules when the universe is fine burning people out. Anyone willing or dumb enough to be taken advantage of becomes fodder for the greedy and that doesn't stop with the living.

KC rolls his neck, his knuckles pop and he rolls his shoulders like he's getting ready for a fight. KC kicks the doors open. "I think you've got something that belongs to me." Hands up, he slowly swagger's forward, hips swinging with each step, bat lowering to a ready position.

"The fuck you talking about?" one of the banger's says.

"Who the hell are you?" Another says, coming from the far wall near the office. "We don't owe you shit."

"I'm not askin' for a debt to be paid," KC says. "I'm here to take back what's mine." KC swings at the nearest body. The dead guy isn't fast enough to dodge and the bat hits him with a loud *thunk* that echoes off the empty loading dock walls.

Three more bangers come from the far side of the loading dock. "Motherfucker." One of the bangers draws his knife and charges.

"Sweet talk's not gonna get you a date, buttercup." KC swings the bat at the guy with the knife. Misses. The knife lunges toward KC. He staggers back, swings again, hits the guy in the back of the head. He drops. KC keeps swinging like he's hit a frenzy.

Mash, splatter, squelch, crack.

The sounds of the body breaking.

The guy furthest back pulls a gun. He glances toward the office. The briefest of looks, takes aim at KC, and shoots.

The bullet lands. KC's leg stiffens. He looks down at the fresh hole, blood seeping through his bleached jeans. Another bullet. KC drops to his knees with a sound halfway between a chuckle and a sneer. He falls forward, but weakly rolls himself onto his back before giving up.

Graffiti on the ceiling says BOOM BITCH.

There's no second hole in KC. This time, the guy with the gun drops it. Another bullet. Rocky's taken aim. A third round goes off and the guy who'd had the gun drops.

Another bastard's coming up on KC with a knife. I dash from the loading dock entrance.

"Joey!" Rocky's saying from behind me.

I don't let it slow me down. Across the room, I'm grabbing the bat off the floor and swing at a banger just as he lunges at KC with his knife.

KC rolls over. The knife hits the concrete. My bat hits the guy's back, and KC's got his knife unsheathed, grabs the guy by his neck, and shoves the blade into the guy's face. The banger drops; KC pushes him off. KC climbs to his knees and searches the guy quickly. His fingers, his pockets, KC takes all the jewelry he finds.

"Shit, shit, shit," KC mutters. He glances down at the hole in his thigh, checks over the ground for something, then looks back at me. Realization hits as he sees the bat.

KC takes a breath, blowing the hair out of his face. His nose scrunches, lips curl back He draws a sharp breath. Two bangers on KC. One draws a gun, the other a broken bottle.

KC grabs the wrist of the guy with the gun, yanking on the wrist to pull the gun free from his grasp. He whips the guy in the back of the head, making him drop to his knees. KC points it at the banger's chest and shoots, one, two, three, four, five.

The banger drops.

A blade catches on my hoodie, putting a hole in the fabric, but missing my body. I swing the bat. A loud thud echoes in the empty room as it collides with his head. He reaches for me; hand full of my shirt, dragging me closer. I swing the bat again and again, working through the searing pain in my arm as I scream. The guy drops to the ground with blood splattered across his face from his broken nose and whatever exploded to come out his ears. A guy with a knife swings at Rocky, who meets him with a bullet to the chest and a shove to the side of the head to push him away. The blade catches on Rocky as the guy stumbles back.

Rocky curses under his breath.

The angry banger lunges at me, taking me to the ground. Hand back, my fists in his face; his hits the floor by my head. He flies off with Rocky's foot wedged into his side.

My bat lands on the guy with a knife, only hard enough to get his attention to turn. I swing again. He catches the bat this time as he faces me.

I book it for the other end of the loading dock, doing the best I can to keep space between them and me as I hear Rocky swinging behind me. The bat's in his possession now.

Something hits my head; I hit the ground. Roll onto my back. The guy's on top of me. I thrust my feet into his stomach. He growls, lands a punch, I bite my lip and taste blood.

Another couple of shots ring off, hitting the banger in the chest. He goes down. Footsteps come up behind me. I turn swinging the bat. Rocky says, "It's me."

"Get the fuckin' rings then call the reaper!" KC's voice echoes off the walls with command.

KC's eyes are wide and black, darkened with the seeds that Baltimore buries inside of its residents, sending tendrils running down the side of his face, along his neck, and out of his hands as the darkness consumes him. He pulls the guy down and flips him over. Knife out and back in. He trades it for the gun the banger's got and thrusts that into his mouth, emptying what's left of the load as his voice echoes off the loading dock in a "WOO!"

The loading dock goes quiet. Action turns to the sound of fleeing footsteps out the open door and down the alley until all that's left is panting breath.

I go to each body, doing the pat down I saw KC doing and grabbing whatever I find on their hands and in their pockets without discernment. I know Ralph wears a bunch of rings, but I don't know what any of them look like or what matters and if these are the things keeping the ravens away, it was better to get all of them.

As I move to the next body and repeat, I'm waiting to get up or for someone to come up behind me. The bat's off the ground and I hear footsteps behind me. I gasp, turn around, ready to scream, but it's just Rocky.

KC's limping his way to the office on the other side of the loading dock. He reaches the door with a growl, a hiss, a fuck, and Ralph's name as a sigh. KC darts into the room.

I glance side long at Rocky. He and I are stepping over bodies, backing away from the bangers without taking our eyes off them as we quickly follow KC.

The office is empty, one of the lights is on, and some light weakly snaking in through the broken, tinted glass. There's an old desk pressed against the wall, a half-burnt candle that doesn't look like it should be there, a dustless spot on the desk where it was disturbed recently, and a pile of clothing in the corner. All black. All easily recognizable.

Ralph's pale body lays on the floor, blood pooled on the concrete beneath him and smeared all over his skin. Hand prints, drag marks. There'd been a struggle before he couldn't fight anymore. Not all of it could be his. There's too much; he's not cut enough, though his arms are bleeding with strikes down the center.

Gently, KC rolls Ralph onto his back. He's naked, parts of his body only blocked to me because of how KC's craning over him.

The tattoos are more pervasive than I'd realized.

Foreign symbols, sigils, and runes wrap around his neck, wrists, elbows, and shoulders, connected by flicks of black ribbons that pool around his chest. They run down his hips, draw around his thighs, and grow dimmer as they make way down his legs.

The way the ink pools on his chest looks like an eye or a malformed heart, the source of everything wrapping around him. The black symbols aren't the only ones on his skin. Alongside them are streams of red, purposefully cut to look more like letters that aren't in harmony with what's already on Ralph.

The scars he carries are more extensive and visible too. Not just purposeful cuts going down his arms, but things that look too much like the glass marks my dad left on me with his empty bottles. Ralph's pale skin is only made paler by the bruises running along his body. They're worse on his lips as if he'd been held down, kicked in his side, the shape of hands around his neck.

He's not moving. I can't tell if he's even breathing. From his expression and the color of his skin, he looks like a corpse.

KC's got a finger pressed to Ralph's throat. "He's alive, but I don't know if he's awake. Mind turning around for a sec? He don't like his shit looked at."

"Right." I do as KC says.

He gets up and retrieves the clothing from the corner. He lays Ralph's pants over his lower half while carefully coiling his t-shirt to pull over his head. "You got the rings?" KC holds his hand out.

"Yeah." The word stumbles out of my mouth. I dig into my pockets, until I've got everything I grabbed. KC drops the handful of metal onto the floor and picks through them, skipping over some rings with memorized familiarity. Compared to the madman of a moment ago, the gentleness in KC's touch as he picks up a ring, identifies it, and slides it onto the correct hand, correct finger, makes him look like a different person entirely.

"What the hell are you two into?" Rocky says. He's

standing over Ralph, though not close enough to be in arm's reach of KC. Eyes trail down Ralph's body, maybe trying to make sense of everything he'd been exposed to in the last couple of hours.

"Honestly, Big Dick?" KC says. "I dunno. At this point, we're just along for the ride."

Ralph's breathing labors. His fingers curl weakly before his head drops to the side and his eyelashes flutter. His eyes open with a soft blue glow illuminating the usual gray. "Kace?" he breathes out. "Is it really you?"

"Yeah, *Reagan*. Don't worry, it's me. I got you."

Ralph weakly reaches for KC.

KC takes Ralph's hand. "I think *he's* gone. I'm gonna get us home, yeah?"

"Thank you," Ralph breathes out.

"You don't need to thank me. Just hold on, okay?"

Ralph closes his eyes.

"What the hell's going on here?" Rocky says.

"All things considered, I'm sure you've got a guess," KC says, suddenly sharp again, but even then, he's softer than he was with Rocky before.

I've never heard KC's voice so soft or seen his handling of something so gently, like dealing with something precious and delicate. I knew they were close, but I don't think I understood how close and I still don't think I do.

Ralph carries KC's heart, so that means something. I would do anything for Jag, but this is so much more than that. The intimacy, the care, the look in his eyes makes me think too much of the look I see in myself when I think of all the shit I've done to Wayland and Jag.

Guilt.

The memory and feelings from the Bin flash through my mind. The feelings of pain and anger and sorrow from those moments. What the hell did KC do to Ralph?

"You call the reaper?" KC says.

Voices, a groan, a string of cussing comes from the other side of the office door.

"Doing that right now," I say, pulling my phone out of my pocket. Charon's number is in the caller and I hit send.

The lights outside in the alleyway flicker.

"You got Reagan's necklace?" KC says.

I'm shaking my head. "I didn't find it on any of them."

Hanging metal lamps rattle as if a small earthquake is tilting the room.

"The big one," Ralph mutters.

KC looks down at Ralph. "What's that?"

"Your heart…" Ralph's hand is trembling. He squeezes KC's hold. "I had to protect it. Tacitus would've…"

"It's okay, Reagan," KC says. "Just tell me where it is."

"Big guy… upstairs. Told him… protect it for power," Ralph says.

"You got that?" KC says.

"Yeah," I say.

"I'm gonna need you to go get it. Preferably before the raven you just called finds it, yeah? Then we'll call it even."

"Got it," I say.

The sense of unease is back and the need to run ignites with the gentle rattling of chains in my ear. With Ralph's eyes barely open, red liquid builds around the bottom like tears, building to overflow down his cheeks.

Tragedy.

KC combs Ralph's hair gently.

Rocky's stepping back until he's at the office entrance, eyebrows tight with apprehension and confusion. He opens the door to peer out.

The cursing gets louder. Someone spots him.

"In or out, Big Dick," KC says.

"I'm going out," I say.

"I'm coming with you," Rocky says.

We duck out of the room, closing the door behind us. Immediately, the bangers' attention is on us, but it doesn't last long.

The windows fill with black feathers on black feathers; cawing and croaking and the laughing of ravens imitate life they don't understand as little red balls glow against the glass. The closed loading dock doors fling up on the tracks, opening. Fog makes the path that the ravens follow before they land on every surface they can. The bangers back up, looking for a means to escape. It's useless with the birds anticipating where they will go next and landing before them with gnashing beaks, bitter cawing, and control.

The warehouse doors the bangers are trying to move won't open. The windows won't smash, and the ravens guarding the other side snap through the cracks to make sure the souls of the damned don't escape. I'm stepping back as the chains get louder.

Charon's not the first to come through the loading dock door. Instead, it's a long, dark shadow, a body that stretches over me with appendages like tentacles and feathers growing in all directions to envelop the room. What started as the body of a man distorts into more limbs as a caw mixes with a growl and a laugh. The form's no longer a man, but a beast. I turn to the open loading dock doors that lead back into the department store.

With no other choice, the bangers charge Charon and Val, weapons drawn.

Val's head's crooked on his neck. His eyes reflect

crimson in the shadow of his body that isn't all visible outside of a blur on his actual form. A loud sound of excitement, hunger, poisonous thirst, bird-like and human, echo off the walls. Val licks his lips. His fingers tighten, nails grow. I back up until I'm against the wall hoping he doesn't notice me. The bastard with the gun takes his shots. The sound's eaten by the warehouse walls.

Val lunges forward, no longer human, but some kind of shadow of a raven, a monster with wings upon wings, eyes along his beak, and a carnal hunger. The tendrils of shadow hold the man with the gun on the ground as the creature that was Val takes him.

The snarling is beastly, terrifying, and supernatural. It hurts under my skin, to my core. The heart hanging against my chest burns with a fear and pain too vast to explain.

A voice in my head is screaming. I don't know what I'm seeing anymore but Val's shadows tickle my legs. Rocky's loud steps echoing behind me give me a kind of twisted comfort that maybe if the shadows tried to tug me, he'd catch me just to hear me say thanks to a badge one more time.

I'm going to die next. I need to get out of here.

I go running for the loading dock door. Charon's white suit acts as a lantern against the shadow of Val's new form, saunters into the room. The beast has moved on. Screams of pure terror and damnation and demented suffering echo off the department store walls.

Charon makes a sound. Feels like judgment. A chuckle. A snotty little brat telling me I'm not getting away from his pet.

Before Val has a chance to turn his hunger on me, I have to get Jag free.

EIGHTEEN.

I'm back in the main showroom and the sounds of Val consuming the souls of the damned somehow aren't making it this far. There are only a couple of ravens spread across the room. They look more confused and left behind than rabid and under the command of a monster who only pretended to be one of them. Old elevators with cages over the doors sit near the center of the room. Beside them are the stairs. The wall inside the elevators reads COME IN, but all I can think of is the elevator in Mortem and the creature that looked like Wayland trying to get me to stay. There was something in his eyes that was so bizarre, so inhuman-like it was uncomfortable, but even as I knew that and felt the crawling under my skin and the burn in my body from the way everything about my soul told me to stay the hell away from him, there was still something so convincing that I couldn't resist talking to him.

All the evidence has been in front of me the whole time in how I should've behaved or acted or when to call it quits, but I never wanted to believe it. Even now, with everything I've seen, I still don't want to believe in the power of these creatures that pretend they're like us through the shallowest imitation, but they don't have what humans have. Charon collects souls, but he doesn't have one. Val might look human some of the time, but he'll never be one and he doesn't understand what it is that he does to us. I don't know what the purpose of any of this is or what machine these creatures are working under to keep functional. Whatever's going on isn't keeping Baltimore under control.

"Where we going?" Rocky asks, less like he's curious, more like he wants his thumb on the beat.

"I dunno, upstairs?" I turn to him and while I'm doing that, I'm stepping back. "But I don't want you to get hurt, not because of me."

Rocky chuckles, smiling in a way that's too pure and nice and kind in a way I still don't deserve—especially not from him. "Then we'll split up, so when you get yourself into trouble, I can come in and save you. It's the BPD way."

"No, Rocky, it's not." I shouldn't be able to chuckle, but I do. I don't expect him to keep his word on splitting up. It's such a shit idea, but coming here was a shit idea and following me was a shit idea and everything I do's a shit idea, but he still went with it, so I'm climbing the stairs on my own, running I don't know where, hoping that the Big Guy's still up here and that he's got Ralph's heart but he's also got Jag cause I don't want to worry about the old guy KC mentioned tormenting Jag in the same way he went at Ralph because I'm selfish like that.

I don't want to keep looking.

I want to know Jag is safe and my mistakes aren't still

biting me in the ass.

The stairwell door on the second floor is locked, so I go to the third, and it's locked too. The fourth isn't though. I'm not dumb enough to overlook that this could be a trap, another setup made by the Big Guy to lead me into an ambush. Bigger than me, he's going to have the upper hand and if I don't stay ahead of him. All I can do is move, stay low if there's anything to hide behind, and hope I find Jag before the Big Guy finds me.

I peek out the stairwell door. It looks like an old office room with a single desk left behind, a door on the far side, rusted file cabinets, and a random, stained mattress in one corner next to cigarettes and bottles and garbage from fast food places. Something touches the back of my neck. My fingers tighten around the bat and I turn, swinging.

There's nothing there. I hold my breath. Look around. Watch the shadows for movement or the walls for someone on the other side with a new warning to give. I'd even take mockery at this point, but there's nothing.

No warnings, no echoes of the screaming I thought I'd catch from below from the devoured souls or hunger and failed attempt at escape that only left them in more pain. As bad as noise can be sometimes, at least it lets you know you exist.

Maybe that's why my dad always had the TV blasting.

I move through the room. Keeping low isn't going to do much there's no furniture, but I pretend like bent knees will let the shadows wash over my body like a blanket and keep me hidden a little longer. I close the door carefully behind me. It's heavy, made of metal, and letting it go could've made it slam.

Just then, that sound echoes across the floor. A door not near, but not far, threatens to send someone my way.

I dip into the corner behind an old filing cabinet and wait. Dust flits through the air. The lights from the courtyard flicker brilliance across the furniture left behind, turning skeletons into empty sales shelves and chairs and couches with broken legs, and a body in the corner.

I listen for anything, but there are no footsteps, no voices, no one going down the stairs or breaking something or slamming another door. I move through the office doorway to another room. Immediately there is a large window and a sign that looks like it's pointing to a back hall. Storage? Security? I'm not entirely sure. I glance behind me toward the show room and meet a wall. Maybe this is the storage area. A rusted set of filing cabinets sit against the wall, cigarette butts litter the floor, a dirty pair of socks lay crumpled next to a single muddy boot looking wet.

The floor smells like sulfur and blood and my body doesn't want to move. The cold fall air seeps in the buildings cracks and nips at my skin through my clothing.

There's movement down the hall. A grunt. Pacing. It echoes off the empty floor.

This place is so different from how Kaufman's was in Mortem, but it somehow feels the same. Broken shelves that've been forgotten since they've got nothing else to offer visitors, shattered glass and busted mirrors because no one wants to see how far they've fallen when they're covered in scars and so much blood, they're not sure whose it is. Trash litters the floor from cigarettes and cigars and McDonald's. In the corner's a broken camera and a KWIK STOP cup filled with piss, acting as a makeshift toilet to avoid getting stabbed in the alley out back. The walls are blank windows filled with the dark sky. A raven's framed on the roof across the courtyard, looking this way. If I stare long enough, I get dizzy and feel the pulse of pain that tried to grab me as I ran out of the loading dock. Instinctively, I reach for the necklace around my neck to make sure my heart's still there.

It is, but it doesn't stop the pulsing under my skin, the echo of KC's bloodthirsty screams and the bam, bam, bam of every bone cracking on the cement. I feel it in my body. His anger, the bangers, everything they've done to me and what they did to Ralph that makes me want to burn Baltimore down until I find the Big Guy like taking him down will count as getting revenge on this city. It's not reasonable. It won't do shit but leave me homeless and if there's one thing I always wanted to avoid, it was being seen by my neighbors.

"Dumb bitch," the Big Guy's voice is a snarl ricocheting down the hall. "You finally came." I turn around. At the far end, the Big Guy's there, pointing a gun at me. He doesn't aim it, but charges.

I run away from the Big Guy, holding onto the bat and ignoring the spikes of heated pain going through my arm. I pass by maintenance and janitorial and electrical and more storage to a door that's slightly ajar at the end of the hall. The sign on it says SECURITY. A gun goes off behind me. I dip into the room. The bullet bounces off the metal door. The Big Guy stampedes down the hall after me, his weight shaking the floor. Windowpanes slap like they're shaking in fear or cheering him on to rip me apart again. I shove the metal door closed and hit the deadbolt. The hinges look weak. Another bullet goes off, piercing the door. The Big Guy slams his fist into the other side. "You come all this way to run?" he hisses.

"I dunno!" I back away from the door. "You go through all this trouble to one-pump it?"

There's a wall of old TVs flashing white and fuzzy but not showing any picture. They're marked with tape and sharpie, but instead of saying what the rooms are, it's more like FRONT, RACK, DECK, PECKER, BACK END. Red and brown boot prints mark the floor. A soiled mattress sits in the corner surrounded by garbage, more blood, cigarettes, and a burnt corner of fabric. Then, there's Jag, bound, lying on top of it with arms tied behind his back, his ankles tied together, and something in his mouth. His skin's pale. He's not wearing a jacket and red marks go down his arm in the same place they were made on mine not that long ago. He doesn't have the benefit of the bandages though. Blood stains his jeans and runs down his fingers. He's got a busted lip and a black eye. The squealing door draws his attention to me, where it goes from warily defiant to surprised.

"You're really here." I pull the gag from Jag's mouth.

"Yeah, I am."

"I'm sorry J. I'm sorry about all of this—"

"Don't worry about it. We need to get out of here." He cringes, sucks in a breath.

"Yeah." I look over his lap. His arms are black and blue. Blood dried to his lip is also oon his pants along with a new seeping hole.

The bullet the Big Guy just shot off. The same hole is mirrored in my leg, though the blood's harder to see in my black skinnies. I breathe in a sharp breath. Ignore the pain. "I'm so, so sorry, J. This was never supposed to—"

The door rattles against the frame. Metal screams in surrender, alerting us that it's not going to last much longer.

"We can talk about it later," Jag says.

I don't have the knife anymore to cut the knots holding Jag to the chair. One of the bottles by the mattress will work. I grab one and smash it on the floor beside the bed. The glass cuts through the ties. The door rattles again, metal threatening to give in with the next fight. "Can you stand?" I say.

"Yeah." Jag pushes himself up from the chair. His step's a stagger, but he moves like he's already got a plan. He hand's out and he says, "Gimme the bat." I do. He points for me to stand where his chair is, then he goes to the security door entrance. It rattles on the hinges as the Big Guy throws himself against it. During the lull between body slams, Jag pulls the deadbolt. The next ram knocks the security door open. The hinges pop and the door slams into Jag standing behind it.

The Big Guy's eyes lock on me. He's not human, not with that look. It's not like my dad's. It's not just regret, it's something worse and deeper and more caustic. The darkness inside has consumed all of him and turned his eyes into empty pools. My face reflects in them, distorted by his fantasy of agony and fervor for suffering. Hanging around his neck is KC's heart.

"You're not gettin' away this time, bitch." He's faster than I'd expect from someone of his size. Jag smashes the bat into the Big Guy's head. He turns around, swinging his arm with a snarl. Jag jumps back. Grunts to cover the groan. My muscles go weak as I trip, my left leg paralyzed.

"Gotta get moves better than a drunk, old man if you wanna beat me," Jag says. He swings the bat again, aiming for the Big Guy's nose. The Big Guy catches the bat before it hits. He yanks Jag forward by the bat Jag refuses to let go of. I grab a bottle from the floor by the mattress and smash it into the back of the Big Guy's head. He releases the bat and swings around again. His eyes focus on me. The dark tendrils move through his face, down his neck, his arms, moving under his skin and forcing him to move quickly.

My visions going black too and all I can think about is the feeling of making him bleed and scream and fighting me for mercy like my dad did back in the trailer.

Another thunk. The bat hits the Big Guy in the head. Red comes out his nose. He turns around and Jag buts him in the face immediately. The Big Guy staggers. Jag reaches for me. I grab hold of his hand and we're running out of the room. He pulls the door shut behind him.

Maybe running's not the right word. Jag uses the bat like a cane or splint on his left to help strengthen the muscles when he steps. The limp's still pronounced and each bounce hurls a new wave of nausea and dizziness through me. My pants stick to my leg as more blood comes out the hole. I don't want to look down, to see just how bad it is because just like everything else I've dealt with in my life, so long as I don't look, I can pretend it's not a problem no matter how bad it hurts.

I'm not sure when I started to slow down. Maybe it was just Jag's steps have always been longer than mine, but he's leading now. We're going down the stairs. The Big Guy's heavy, shuffling steps echo all around us and it's hard to tell where the hell he is.

"We need to get the necklace he's wearing, J," I say. "It belongs to Ralph."

"You kidding me?" Jag says.

"No."

Jag groans softly. "Alright. We'll figure something out."

We pass the elevator and make it to the stairs. The door slams shut behind us. Jag let's go of my hand so he can use the railing to help go down the steps. They're hard to take and each one sends a powerful shock through my body that threatens to make my legs give out beneath me. Jag's grunting every other step he goes down and keeps saying, "You okay?" and I say, "Yeah."

I don't think it's that he doesn't believe me, but it

gives a distraction that I know I appreciate. Everything sweaty and hot and my clothing's sticking to my skin and my hair is gross and I'm panting so hard. The sound of the Big Guy echoes from the room above. Something metal hits the wall, followed by a growl. Furniture being tossed around. A glass window shattering. A scream.

Above us, the door at the top of the stairwell smacks against the wall. Anger bounces off each stair. At the speed we're going, we're not going to make it back to the lobby. Jag peels off at the third-floor landing and I follow. He pushes the stairwell door open. I go through and as I move, I'm reaching behind me, looking for him, needing to make sure I see or feel him so I know he's not lost and I'm not alone and he hasn't disappeared on me again. His long strides get him to my side fast. This floor's mostly desks and boxes and trash. The windows lining the front that look out into the courtyard are mostly covered with wood. Some of it rotted. One panel says HIDE another says GOTTEM.

I slow down until I stop. My hand finds Jag's shirt before he runs into me. I look back; he's looking at me with confusion. All I can think is he's real, he's here, and I need him so much, it's unreasonable. I pull him around a wall. The sound of my breath bounces off of everything around us, threatening to give away our position as the stairs creak beneath the Big Guy's weight and the stairwell door slams open.

I wrap my arms around Jag tightly. Yeah, it's dumb—It's stupid in that moment, but I just fucking need him. Maybe he needs it too or maybe he just feels it and is giving me what I want like he always has.

His arms are tight as he holds me against his chest. He's strong the same way he always has been, in the way that made me feel safe when I got away from my dad or when he helped me out of the cage my dad made for me that I couldn't escape on my own. Every time I've needed him, he's been there for me, ready to fight battles I didn't want to burden him with. Ready to follow me into mistakes so I wouldn't get into trouble alone. Ready to care about me when I was busted and chipped and angry because of everything that had been done to me. None of it was his fault, but he took me in anyway and helped me survive.

I wouldn't be alive without him.

God.

When did I get so pathetic that just a couple of hours apart made it feel like I'd never see him again? My hands curl into his shirt. The heat of my heart presses against him and calms the darkness whispering destruction into my head. I don't know when it got so intense, but it's unmistakable when the silence is gone. My eyes burn and blur. Time's so slow and I'm thinking we shouldn't be doing this, the Big Guy's right here somewhere, catching up, but I don't want to let go.

I pull back to take the fetish from around my neck. I'm putting it on Jag saying, "Can you hold this for me."

He nods, letting me put it on him. "Sorry I lost it for a little while.

"Not your fault."

"You trusted me."

"You trusted me too." My voice cracks.

"We're even."

I shake my head. "Not at all, but I'll try to make it up to you."

"You don't owe me anything for this, Jo."

I can't keep it together. Everything from the last two weeks hits me all at once and I'm just thinking of where we are, how hurt he is, yet somehow, his voice can still be so gentle.

A chair smashes into glass, bounces off the wall.

Metal file cabinets scream from the assault they're put under as the big guy moves. Jag pushes off the wall. He grabs my hand with his and presses the butt of the bat to the floor to give his leg more stability. He glances back toward the room. A couple of doors run the other way that might lead us back to the stairwell and give us an escape from the Big Guy. Jag's tugging me forward saying, "Just a little further," while his confidence gives me the strength to push through the weight that makes my body want to give up. We round the corner at the end of the hall, hitting another office space filled with boxes. On the other side of the room is a door to the back end of the stairwell.

Everything shakes around us as the Big Guy approaches, running down the hall. He's in the empty doorway. Eyes focused on me. I can't call Charon until I get the heart back. He's running across the room. Jag swings; it doesn't work. The Big Guy catches the bat, pulls it out of Jag's hand, and punches him in the face. Jag hits the floor. My face throbs from our established bond. Then, the Big Guy catches up and grabs me by the shirt. He's stepping us back and slams me against the cold wall in some twisted déjà vu of the first time he saw me in the bar up here. His hand's around my neck. I can't breathe. My feet aren't touching the ground and I'm kicking, desperate to try and get away before I lose any ability to fight back. I land a couple of hits, but he's not grunting. His eyes are pits of darkness with nothing but hatred and destruction and vile desire.

I claw at his arms, raking my fingers across his skin, but through the laughter and the rage and the growling, he doesn't notice.

Both hands are around my throat now. His nasty breath's in my face, heating my cold cheeks and filling my nose. It's a bitter taste in the back of my throat, force-feeding me his rot. My vision's going black and black and black again. The boards behind the Big Guy say FUCKIN LOL and FAILURE and KNEW IT like there are more dead who've been following me around just to see when I'd fail if that's really all they do. I don't need spectators of Baltimore making bets on how long other losers will survive. Jag's on the ground, gasping and choking and I'm not sure if I'm hearing him. I feel his name getting caught in my throat as the hands tighten, catching the sound before it can leave my mouth. My voice cracks. My throat hurts and the sound of desperate life echoing around me sounds too much like me.

"Dirty bitch," the Big Guy snarls. "You thought you could get away with it, what you did to me. Always entitled. Always fucking…"

My head feels like it's going to explode. My feet press to his chest, too weak to do anything. My head lulls against the wall; I can't grab him anymore. As my arms fall at my sides, all I can think is *Jag's going to die, Jag's going to die, Jag's going to fucking die and it's all my fault.*

A bullet strikes. Blood splatters in my face. I don't know how the bullet doesn't hit me too. Another through the chest and I'm thinking that one must've gotten me. Three more shots echo and my ears are ringing. The hand around my neck loosens. The Big Guy turns around, looking for the offense with what little time he has left. Rocky's standing behind an empty shelf, using it for cover. The Big Guy makes a run across the room. Halfway, his legs give out and he drops to the ground. He lands with a thud, a squish, a gasping pant, and a splatter as he hits the floor. Another bullet goes through his head.

"Got him," Rocky says.

"Rocky?" I say.

"Didn't I say I'd save you if we split up?" He

chuckles.

"You might not be as bad as I thought," I choke, trying to breathe.

"I earn the badge yet?" Rocky says.

"You might be too good for it." I climb to my feet. My legs shake a little. I go to where the Big Guy's laying facedown. "I gotta get the necklace he's wearing." I pull at the chain, trying to get the heart out from underneath his weight, but he's too much. Without hearing him, Rocky's beside me, lifting the Big Guy's shoulders just enough to let me pull the necklace out from underneath him and work it over his head.

I shove the necklace into my pocket. Rocky drops the body and we both retreat quickly, knowing what's to come if we don't work fast enough to stop his revival.

I pull my phone out of my pocket. The screen's more busted than it was before, with cracks destroying the picture of Wayland and I that I had as my wallpaper. I curse at myself as I tap the screen, hoping that it works. The dialer pops open. I put Charon's number in and hit send.

My phone's in my pocket. The first bird flies into the windowsill. He's on his way.

I can't take my eyes off the Big Guy. For what he did to Jag; For what he did to Ralph and KC; for what he did to me. He represents everything wrong with Baltimore. The rage some use to justify hurting others, the blame that gets flung around at any innocent bystander lucky enough to be in eyeshot. Wayland never wronged the banger that killed him; the city took him away. I never did anything to this bastard, but just like my dad, he blamed me for everything he hated about his life. He demanded I give him everything in repentance for shit I never did. He'd take my life and that still wouldn't have been enough because for some reason, Baltimore's bloodlust is never ending.

I approach the Big Guy again, my eyes locked on his unmoving body. "You tried to take everything from me." I slam my foot into his side. "We don't need another bastard in this city." I kick him again. "Baltimore's done with you." Jag pulls me back. My body doesn't want to go. My vision's going dark and all I can see is the Big Guy, on the ground, at my mercy, waiting for me to deliver more of what he deserves.

Ravens fly in and shield the windows, turning into a wall of black feathers and bloody eyes. They're wrong though. This bastard's passing isn't a tragedy; everything he did since getting a second chance is. He left so much carnage in the wake of his regret that everyone else had to pay for it. I'm trembling as the birds build. The lights in Kaufman's are flickering on and off even when they shouldn't and the Big Guy's trying desperately to gets up. He's running, trying to get to the exit before the monster gets in the room.

The doors fly open, and the birds gather in here too. Jag's arms go around me and he's stepping back. My body doesn't want to move, but I go with him anyway. The Big Guy charges toward Charon. Val's shadow extends from the elevators that shouldn't work. He shouldn't be backlit, but his features are nothing but the bird-monster-man as the tendrils of hungry shadow reach across the Kaufman showroom and wrap around the Big Guy's body.

Charon moves slowly from the elevator while Val's monstrous form mounts the Big Guy and pins him to the floor, mercilessly ripping his body open with a sharp beak and talons seeking any heart that may be left on his person. Small balls of dark particles float in the air. Charon draws out his crystal jar. The chain hangs from his hand and consumes the floating orbs, all of them coming to him.

I'm pressing into Jag and that's making him step back more, but I can't take my eyes off the destruction Val's laying into the Big Guy until he's nothing but a dark stain on the ground that's not even vaguely shaped like a person. He's a stain like so many of the weird shapes I've seen all over Baltimore that only look like shadows cast at every hour of the day without reason. He's a man lost to his instincts, anger, and his past, never coming back.

Charon's glowing blue eyes are watching me. "Looks like you've finally assumed your responsibility." He makes a sound like a purr or dismissive hum. "But be warned, if you do not temper yourself, you can be caught up in disaster at any time. The dark is waiting."

Val's dark, red eyes sharply turn to me.

I'm pulling Jag toward the stairs and he doesn't resist. We pass by Rocky who is unable to pull his eyes off the Big Guy's final resting place.

"We need to go, Rocky," I say.

"Yeah." His voice is low, and still looking at Charon as he takes a couple of steps back. Even without the sight of a collection it's hard to understand. I don't blame him for the apprehension, but at least he's not asking questions right now. It gives me time to figure out how to answer them later.

The three of us are moving down the stairs as fast as we can, which isn't very fast because Jag's leg hurts and though I'm running on adrenaline, it's rapidly weakening. I trip when we hit the bottom floor. Jag catches me, groans from the pain that grabs him, and we run into the wall at the nearest landing. His arms go around me. He pulls me to him. I can't help but put my arms around him in return. My heart slows, the pain fades away, and it's easier to breathe. Jag's power, what he's always done for me. In that moment, his muscles relax too an maybe for once, I can give him some of the comfort he's given me all this time.

"Thank you, Jag… for never giving up on me," I say into him.

His hand's stroking my back. It's so nice that even in this abandoned, dirty death trap of a building, I don't want it to end, I don't want to move, and I could almost be tempted to lay on the floor with him for a while until the two of us feel better.

But the weight of KC's heart in my pocket reminds me this isn't over yet and sacrifices were made beyond the three of us. "We need to go to the loading dock," I say to Jag. "KC and Ralph are in there."

With a little space between Charon, Val, and I, it's easier to slow down. We get to Kaufman's lobby without hurting ourselves more. Jag survey's the room.

There's also the trail of bloody footprints going back there from KC's and my shoes, leftover from the guys in the lobby.

In the loading dock, there are no bodies from the bangers that had been here before, but spots in the ground that were darker than others. It wasn't blood, but another burnout ground to ash and mixed into a building, leaving his benign ghost behind and all the graffiti is gone.

KC and Ralph aren't in the office anymore. KC's squatting on the ground beside Ralph where he lays on the floor, dressed. His eyes are closed. The red marks he got while here now look more like shallow cuts and burns. Blood and grime are dried along his exposed skin, while the tears from earlier smear against his cheek in what looks like an attempt to clean him off. He doesn't stir, even as the loading dock door shuts behind Jag and me.

KC stands up when we enter, crosses to me quickly,

and puts his hand out.

I take his heart out of my pocket and give it to him. KC examines it briefly. When he's satisfied with what he sees, he sighs, pushes his messy hair back, and says "Thanks."

KC returns to where Ralph's laying. He mutters, gentle, but too quiet to hear what he's saying. He slips the necklace around Ralph's head. His soft eyes peek open, reflecting a pale blue glow against his cheeks. He looks at me for a moment before he closes his eyes again. KC pulls Ralph's arm over his shoulder. With proper footing, KC positions Ralph's body over his shoulder.

Coming toward us, but doesn't stop as he walks past saying, "Leaving," without stopping.

"He okay?" Rocky says.

"Not really," KC says. "And I'm not interested in standin' here to play twenty questions with a badge."

"Where are you going?" Rocky says.

"What did I just say?" KC growls.

"I'm not going to stop you, but if I'm gonna let you go, I'm gonna need a location so I can ask a couple of questions once I get this place sorted out." Rocky circles his finger as a way to point to the room.

KC sighs. "What's there to sort out?"

"What was happening in that room." Rocky gestures to the office, "and the body out front."

"Oh," KC says. "You got the corpse outside in time?"

"Here's to hoping," Rocky says.

KC turns on his heels. He doesn't stop as he steps backward toward the open loading dock gate. "He needs to be somewhere safe so we're going back to the bar. If we're not there, we'll be at Baltimore General, but I don't think he needs *that* kind of attention right now." KC says. "You startin' to get it yet, Big Dick?"

Rocky's eyes go to Ralph. He's a ragdoll over KC's

shoulder. His lack of movement makes me worried, but not as much as the urgency in KC's step.

"I think so." Rocky lets out a sigh. "I'll come find you in a bit." Rocky reaches for his wallet. He's pulling out a card, moving to catch up with KC. "I lost track of you guys ten years ago. If anything happens, I want you to call me—" He's holding the card out.

KC doesn't take it, lifting his middle finger instead. "You know where to find us now. I'm not callin' a badge." KC goes out the loading dock door and enters the alleyway on the backside of the Old Town Mall.

The air's returned to what it should be, still and quiet, just like you'd expect for an abandoned department store in the middle of the night. "I've got paperwork to file, but I don't think I've got the forms for this kind of report." Rocky looks me over, then Jag, then to where KC and Ralph had been. There's a sigh. His shoulders drop. "You wanna give me your number?" He holds the phone out to Jag. I stare at it for a second. My heart's throbbing in my ears.

Jag stares at it. "What do you need my number for?"

"Well," Rocky says. "I have hers, but if I can't reach it, you seem like a safe bet and if I can't reach either of you, I'll just assume you skipped town. Sound good?"

"We're not skipping town." Jag takes the phone. I'm staring at myself in the glass window going out to the loading bay. My face is a blur of what it should be. I barely recognize myself. Not because I'm drunk or delusional or really even tired. It's just that everything about this moment feels surreal. Jag's never been bad with the badges. He's always told me to calm down, that my getting worked up would only look worse, but he didn't understand how badges worked in the same way I did. But Rocky's not like the badges I always guarded myself against. He's someone who's actually tried to follow through and believed the crazy shit I said, even when he had every reason not to.

I was suspicious of him screwing me over this whole time, when it was only me locking people out that made shit bad in the first place. I never told Wayland the truth and it hurt him to the end; I kept so much from Jag and he got hurt so much until finally he was dragged into an abandoned department store and done over by a dead guy who couldn't move on because of a stupid beef he had with me.

Jag hands the phone back saying, "We don't have any plans to go anywhere, right Joey?"

My name's a surprise and I'm not entirely sure what Jag just said, but I nod and say, "Yeah," anyway.

"Good. Then I'll talk to you tomorrow." Rocky gives a half nod. "Take care of yourselves, yeah?"

"Thanks," Jag says.

Rocky's muttering to himself as he leaves. His phone's pressed to his ear. His voice brightens to "Rodgers, I'm gonna need a team at the Old Town Mall as fast as you can put it together. There's a body. Yeah... I'm sure it's not an overdose. Guy had his head caved in with a bat. Outside the old Kaufman's. We'll need to check the rest of the building. Alright. See you in fifteen." Rocky stops in the doorway of the loading dock. His hand's on the door. He turns around. "If you aren't interested in a trip to the station tonight, I'd recommend getting the hell out of here. We have a body to take care of because despite what *some* think in this town, it's not a matter of *people who don't count* when they die, *it's about finding the body*. Everyone matters."

"No, Rocky," I say. "That guy out front definitely didn't matter."

"Careful," Rocky says slowly. "That's a dark path to go down. You need to remember that no matter who you are, there's someone out there who cares."

"If anyone cared about him, he wouldn't've been here."

"You gotta work on that cynicism of yours." Rocky chuckles.

"Yeah, yeah, yeah," I say, stepping back toward the loading dock doors KC exited through. "If we're done here, we gotta go. Our ride's bouncing and I already know it's too much to ask him for a ride."

"Talk to you tomorrow, Joey," Rocky says. With a nod and a tired smile, Rocky exits the loading dock to wait for his friends in the Kaufman's lobby.

Jag and I enter the alley, walking fast to catch up with KC. Him and Ralph are a silhouette against the moon and streetlights bleeding int the alley from the streets. The air smells like pot and mildew and alcohol more than anything. Ralph looks like a rag doll than a person, his legs unmoving and his body a puppet to KC's will. I don't even know if he's still conscious. Ravens still sit on the tops of the buildings, watching as KC passes between them. At least thirteen of them and all of them are focused on KC and Ralph.

"Don't tell me," KC says. "You wanna ask another favor."

"I hate that word," I say.

"Yeah? Me too." KC won't look at me. "It's all anyone ever wants when they lay eyes on Reagan."

"I just want a ride back to the shop." I hate even saying it because the paleness of Ralph's skin isn't even lost in the darkness. If anything, the moon makes him appear as a corpse. His soft breath and trembling give away that he's not dead, no matter how he looks. "With Baltimore being like it is and people like they are, why the hell does Ralph even bother?"

"Because that's just the kind of guy he is," KC snaps.

"He cared too damn much about the inconsequential life of a dirtbag like me and made a stupid deal some years ago. Unfortunately, his loss was everyone else's gain and"

"*Regret is only the beginning; horror is the transformation; tragedy is the offspring.*" Ralph's voice startles me, though it's hard to hear. I slow down enough to fall behind KC. Ralphs eyelids are open, but just barely. It's given away more by the soft glow of blue, almost white, on his cheeks. His expression is distant, his body lacking any control and bounces as KC walks.

"You don't gotta say anything to them, Reagan" KC says.

"The dark is always waiting. It will make you feel as though you are alone and it is the only option. Don't believe it," Ralph says through panting breaths. "Once you've fallen far enough, it will whisper in your ear. Sometimes, you can feel it touching your skin, guiding your hand, reaching with you as if it's the only assistance you can find when you can't see. It will gently walk you across a line you can't take back, pulling you deeper into disaster until you see no difference between creation and destruction, hope and hopelessness." His gentle eyes lock with mine. My skin heats and a feeling of being exposed takes me over. I try to take a step back, but my body won't move. "Joey, you became your father's tragedy that he couldn't take back. You don't have to be anybody else's. Your fear isn't unfounded; you can let your past destroy you and seek refuge in the darkness where good and evil are invisible, or you can choose to see beyond your afflictions. A soul caught in itself can only spiral out of control as the fountain of perspective poisons every aspect of life until there is nothing, but misery left. Once you've reached that point, no one can convince you otherwise and doing to others what has been done to you is justified.

"Don't allow yourself to believe you are alone. That's the greatest lie of them all. You listen to the murmurs in the dark as they tell you everything you've always feared. As they put their hand in yours and lead you away. Look around. Darkness will try to fool you into receiving its companionship; don't welcome it. Tragedy is not an end, but a judgment for how your soul has been corroded in response to the world."

"How the hell do you think like that after everything you've seen?" I say.

"Because for as much as the darkness pervades, there are many who choose to live through it."

"How?"

Ralph smiles weakly. It reads closer to himself, but he's not all there. The brightness fades from his eyes as they return to their normal pale, steel color. Streaks of blood mark his cheeks as if they were tears of his own. If what Charon said earlier is true, he felt the tragedy of Baltimore inside of him. "There's a beauty in the soul that can't be taken, only given away. Darkness never stops its pursuit. The closer it is, the louder it gets, the harder it is to see anything else." Ralph's eyes close again. "It has no limits on what it will do to try and gain your consent. It will tell you what you want to hear, whisper wishes in your ear, calm the destruction or alienation you feel. It will take advantage of your desperation and make you fear that you can never turn back... but immeasurable pain doesn't mean one can't heal; mistakes aren't damnation; history doesn't prescribe doom. Maybe it is an exercise in terminal grace, but no one deserves to end in tragedy. I believe in the good to grow if you plant the seeds for others to harvest."

"Don't fuckin' push it, Reagan," KC says.

"If they need help, help them," Ralph says.

KC groans. "If you waste my time, I'm leaving you

behind."

"Thanks," Jag says.

We get to the street and climb into the back of KC's Riviera while KC sets Ralph into the front passenger seat. Blue and red lights reflect off the buildings in front of us. The store at the front end of the Old Town Mall says DON'T LOOK BACK and WHAT IS YOUR NAME?

Something catches KC's eye across the street as he stands on the driver's side, door open. Down the street's the form of an old man standing under the streetlight. His body is obscured, boxy, made to look longer than is natural by the priestly robes he's wearing, distorted by the night. A shadow covers his face; he's wearing sunglasses. Under his right arm is a small, leatherbound book, tightly tucked against his body. As his left hand comes out of his pocket, light catches on his skin, turning his fingers crimson. A glove. Brighter than should be possible.

KC raises his middle finger to the guy.

"Know him?" I say.

"Doesn't matter right now." KC breaks his attention and climbs into the driver's seat. He doesn't bother with a seatbelt before turning the car on and peeling out of the neighborhood. KC keeps glancing at the review mirror. I turn around to peer out the back. The old man's still standing under the streetlamps, his long jacket blowing in a mild wind until the darkness devours him like a mist eating him until he's gone.

I want to ask KC who or what that was again, but something tells me he wouldn't answer and to be fair, I didn't really need to know.

Don't ask questions; that's the policy.

Don't get involved with someone else's demons.

The radio's on low, enough to cover the soft sound of

Ralph's breathing. KC's muttering so softly, his voice is only an intimate breathy murmur that's so much softer than how I've heard him all night. Ralph's eyes are closed and soon, the front seat's entirely quiet.

I smell so bad and everything's sticky and my hands are still shaking if I dare to look down at them, so I lean back and close my eyes in an attempt to follow after Ralph. The weight of everything's getting to me and I don't want to be in this car. At least I don't think I'm bleeding anymore.

Jag's hand finds mine on the center seat. Our fingers lace, my heart rate slows. "It's gonna be fine," he says.

"You're always so sure," I mutter."

"Because I've seen some shit." He smiles at me and it's so warm and pure and sweet that I can't believe anyone could look at me the way he looks at me. The way I never thought I deserved. "We'll either get to the other side or we won't and I don't see either of us giving up. We're gonna be fine, Joey."

My skin goes hot. I lean into him. "Thank you… for never giving up on me, J."

"We're a team." He squeezes my hand. "As long as you trust me, you'll always have me."

"No… *You'll* always have *me*." I chuckle as my fingers find my heart against his chest. "You sure about this though? I'm kind of a fucking mess, you know?

"Yeah… but I kinda like that." Jag leans back. He's looking down at me, meeting my eyes while his head leans against the headrest. His face is so soft and gentle and warm and honest. I don't know how else to describe it, but the look in his eyes and the smile that makes me feel like he cares and nothing else in the world matters. I want to believe everything he says. I don't trust anyone else with my life.

I lean into him and let my eyes close. His smell, his

warmth, and the firmness of his muscles takes me out of this city, this moment, and away from every shitty thought I've ever had. It's hard to fight the impulse that every bad thing that's ever happened around me is because I did something to other people and I deserve the punishments I get. I want to reframe everything constantly. What happened to Jag was because of me; what happened to Wayland was because of me; what happened to Ralph was because of me; because all I can see in myself are the faults and failures that reach out to drag everyone down with me in the same way my dad dragged me. It's dark and I never considered that maybe Jag or Wayland weren't letting me do things *to* them, but trying to pull me out of something I couldn't pull myself from.

Maybe if I'd been able to see it sooner, things could've been different.

Pessimism is the bankruptcy of the soul and a bankrupt soul seeks disaster everywhere it goes, so that's all I saw. There's no turning back time to fix the opportunities that I missed or the people I hurt. I can get stuck in all of what could have been or should have been or would have been with all the things I know now. It doesn't matter now. If I let the worst parts of my life paint everything I see, hopelessness will be inevitable.

I open my eyes and the brownstone we pass in succession reads:

SHE AINT HOME and
    WHAT'S STOPPIN HER? and
THE DEEPER THE RED,
    THE DEEPER THE CUT
THAT AINT GONNA LOOK PRETTY
    WHEN IT HEALS
BUT THAT DONT MEAN

IT WON'T GET BETTER

I let my eyes close again. My body falls into Jag's. The noise of Baltimore falls away and so does every final word it wants to have with me. At least for tonight.

NINETEEN.

KC's driving us to Bodymore Bodyshop. He's quiet. I don't know if Ralph's awake. He's not moving, but he's got a soft, jagged breath, laced with pain or terror it sounds like he's trying to control. His hands are trembling and KC keeps looking over at him, sighing, and then inhaling his cigarette angrily. I have so many questions about what just happened, about Val and those guys, and that old guy or Ralph's existence. Like, what *is* he? He's not *just* human with extra abilities. There's more to that because what the hell else does it mean that Baltimore's been hunting him?.

The time's not right. I shouldn't ask—It's not like Ralph or KC would answer anyway, right? They don't owe me anything.

Maybe it's the nerves. My foot's still tapping. The energy's all mine, I think. Jag's hand on my leg is trying to help, but it's just… I don't want to be the cause of another bad thing.

"Is he gonna be okay?" I say.

The car's quiet but for the radio playing low and Ralph's soft, labored breathing. Ralph's hand shifts, marked by the sound of his rings hitting something in the front seat.

KC glances side long at him. His jaw tightens. "As good as he can be under the circumstances."

"You know why the big guy had his heart?" I say. My foot's bouncing. Jag's thumb strokes the back of my hand. I'm exhausted, but his comfort isn't doing anything to pull me back. All I keep seeing is Val tearing those souls apart—knowing that he could do that to me if the timing was right. He almost did it to me a couple of times already. "It doesn't really make sense for a ghost to carry. I mean, I've been doing it all day and I wouldn't trust the Big Guy with something like that."

"I needed to keep it away from Tacitus," Ralph mutters.

"Who?" I say.

"The old man," KC growls.

"If he got KC's heart, he would have destroyed it, so I told that man, it gave him power, but he had to keep it away from the ravens," Ralph says *"Ravens are drawn to power*, they'll take it from you. He got greedy, and Tacitus gave it up. He got what he wanted."

It takes a moment for me to realize he was actually speaking, though his eyes remained slightly open. "What did they want with you?"

"*Power*," Ralph says.

"I told you," KC says. "This city's been trying to get Reagan for a while. That freak showed up the day after Reagan became a medium and has been stalking his ass ever since trying to get whatever it is the other side gave to him. Problem the older bastard has is he can't step foot in the bar."

"How'd he get you then?" I say.

Ralph opened his eyes again. The soft blue glow peeked out, illuminating his cheeks and exposing the bit of red still left behind from the streaks he couldn't fully clean off. He looked so distant. His trembling increases. He closes his hands, curling his arms into his body. "Tacitus made a deal with your friend, bring me to him and he'd deliver you. The officer appeared at my door and brought a few of the living with him. Those alive aren't held back by the safeguards of the *Terra Santas*. They were going to take you out of the holding cell, but you never made it there, so they took Jagger instead. The drop off place was Patterson Tower. Your friend did what the dead normally do when upset and had an outburst before sending the officer to wait for you to return." Ralph trails off.

"Then why did he want my heart?" I say.

"He must've heard me tell your friend the heart gave power. Perhaps he saw yours and decided he wanted to give it a try." The glow fades from his eyes. Breathing hard, the next words that come out make little sense. I don't know if it's the language or the muttering, but the glow in his eyes gets brighter until he closes them again. He mutters a little louder. Something incomprehensible. Pain tears into his voice. His hands curl gently into his leg, then loosen as Ralph loses consciousness.

"Shit." KC's jaw tightens as he glances sidelong then in the rearview mirror at me. "No more questions."

I nod and look out the window.

If there's anything else I need to know about myself, about what I've got, or about what Ralph is, I'll have to wait for another time. I've asked enough from both of them and I'll be lucky if KC doesn't ban me from the bar after all this is over.

We reach the body shop; Jag's limp is worse than

mind and with every step, he's exhaling something that's almost cussing, but he's giving up part way. His car is inside the garage. Donny must've moved it before he went home. Like Jag normally does for me, KC and Ralph sit in the parking lot until we're inside and the door's shut again. I wonder if they'll open the bar again tomorrow. Maybe give it a week?

Will there even be that many regulars at the bar tomorrow night? I don't want to know how many of them at the warehouse he knew intimately. I don't want to know how many creatures stuck around watching that place just for the chance to drag him out and force him to use his abilities for whatever messed up shit they conceived of.

I don't think I'll ever understand the light Ralph sees in the world. Maybe I've just been in the dark for too long. I couldn't see whatever it was Jag or Wayland or Donny saw in me either. Maybe Ralph's just idealistically suicidal. Is that a thing? Seeing hope beyond reason in a way he's got no right to. I don't know how you get there, but KC got there, right? Or at least, he's trying.

Maybe Jag's right that he can show me how to get away from the dread and hopelessness and anger and see what he sees. Maybe that's what KC gets out of being around Ralph too and if that's true, I get why he doesn't want to give that up. I don't want to get away from Jag; I want to see what he sees. I want to know how he sees Baltimore and what's so hopeful that he only saw a future when he looked at me.

Jag slips into Donny's office, the door unlocked. The light flicks on and it takes a few minutes for Jag to come back out, but when he does, there's a bandage under his jeans where the blood's on his thigh. He comes up beside me, medical kit in hand. The air's thick with tension from the question he's burning to ask, but I don't think he wants to since he doesn't know what kind of answer he'll get.

"Sit down. Let me take a look at you," he says.

"I'm fine, Jag—"

He shakes his head. "You gotta stop saying that when it's not true."

Quietly, I do what he says and take a after pulling down my skinnies so he can see the spot in my leg. He wraps it tightly. I don't know if the blood on the pad's from the hole or our hands. Jag watches it for a moment before telling me that I can pull my pants back up. He sets the medical supplies under the chair saying, "I'll put it away later. If Donny asks, blame me."

We wash off in the sink, trying to get as much blood off our arms and legs and hair. I turn the water off, but we're still standing there for a while. Quiet, staring a head, hands clutched around the thick sink lip.

Jag pulls his box of cigarettes from his pocket and offers me one before he takes his own. He hands me the lighter. I've taken a couple of puffs before he gets it out: Whose blood are you wearing, Joey? That's not all the big guy, is it?"

I look down at myself. The black fabric of my skinnies are darker from the water and blood I couldn't get out. The smell of iron and sulfur and rancid human mortality burns my nose and I wish Jag hadn't called attention to it because now it's all I can smell. "Baltimore's."

"You need to be honest with me," he says. "Did you kill anybody, Joey?"

My fingers curl with the cigarette. A chill goes through me. My foot's tapping and Jag's starting to tap his leg with the same kind of nervous energy. The connection's back. The flash of the body in the entry way and KC putting the knife through its head. That guy and the guy at the badge station and the brutality the big guy had when he chased me down the hall. It was inhuman. It makes me think of how Wayland looked almost every time I saw him over these last few weeks. So much blood, first sullying the sweater of a good kid who never even got so much as a parking ticket. Then, it was my dad's clothes. Then, it was Jag's. Everything the Big Guy touched got dirtied by unresisted impulses to destroy.

I could've been covered in Jag or Rocky or Donny or some random dolt in the wrong place at the wrong time, making me think they did something to ruin my life instead of recognizing it was all me. Somehow, I never did that… I wasn't like the Big Guy. I never actually wanted to hurt anyone. I never blamed them for what happened to me.

I made my own decisions; I created my own misery.

I just didn't see the people who saved me from wallowing in it.

Tears pool in my eyes and blur the loading dock. I rub them like I'm tired, then wipe my fingers off on my pants. "No…. No one. I didn't."

I don't know if it's believable. He saw me at my worst; he saw me want to hurt him. I'm a disaster, you know? A dirty mess that was no one's job to clean up and a burnout too painful to watch that people kept getting involved to stop me.

I can't stop the tears, even by wiping at them and pressing into my eyes. They just keep coming. "I don't know why you care about me so much, Jag… I'm not *easy*." The chuckle hurts, but it's the only way I can think of to try and stop from crying. But that doesn't work.

Jag's brown eyes are waiting for me with the warmth and kindness I never felt I deserved. "Easy never had anything to do with it. Every bad day is worth seeing to the other side when you care about someone else."

"I don't think I deserve you, Jag," I say.

"Yeah? If you don't go running off, I'll help you see what I see when I look at you." Jag's fingers brush my hair out of my face.

He pulls me into him. I let him and he holds me for a while in the soft silence of Bodymore Bodyshop. Nothing exists outside of us then. At least in that moment and it's fine. I don't want to move, but we can't stay there.

We return to Jag's car. He gets a couple of towels out of the trunk and puts them over the seats. He checks for garbage for signs of intruders. He goes through the trunk and backseat of his car. With nothing out of order, he pulls the car into the parking lot, locks the shop back up, and then we're heading home.

The board over the door of a red brick townhouse reads DO NOT ENTER. The boarded-up windows on the same place reads EAT SHIT AND DIE. The side of the meat shop on the corner across the street has graffiti of a dark catacomb pretending it's not the inside of Fort Armistead filled with glowing water and illegible letters that look more like the shapes printed on Ralph's arms than letters.

My skin prickles. I lower my head to hide the tears hazing the city around me. My fingers curl in my lap.

Jag reaches past the stick and takes my hand. I tell off the voice in my head saying I don't deserve this. Jag doesn't agree and in this case, I'll trust his opinion more than mine. I've never been able to see myself right. Jag's always had a good eye for reality. Too good, too real, in fact, he couldn't see it when I fell into the grave.

That's the only reason I'm alive now.

Back at Jags' apartment, he's out of the car first. He uses the door to catch his balance and hold himself up as he hisses. Too much pressure on his leg. He forgot and the shockwave of pain shoots up my leg too. "Sorry," he says.

"You don't need to be, J." I meet his gaze as he leans over, peeking into the car. There's a darkness gathered under his eyes. He smiles, forces a laugh, and rubs the back of his neck, ruffling the hair the way he does when he's tired and barely keeping himself awake. The bruises and redness limping remind me of everything I've put him through not just in the last couple of days, but the months and years he's been by my side. Jag rubs his eyes next in a useless attempt to wipe the wariness from his face. When that doesn't work, he slides his aviators back on.

"You doing okay, Joey?" he says.

"Yeah."

"Need help getting out?"

"Probably no more than you."

Jag chuckles. "We can help each other then. That's kind of part of the deal yeah?"

I push my door open. It's heavier than usual. My arms don't want to work, my legs shake as I get on them. So many times I've opened this door and walked this path, not always in the greatest shape, but I think everything's finally catching up to me.

It's gonna take some getting used to, I think.

Jag closes the driver's side door just before I close mine. His arm's hanging at his side. I reach for his hand. My fingers lightly lace with his; he takes mine back. His walk becomes a stroll and I keep wanting to lean into him more and more. It's so dumb, but for the first time in my life, it feels like the lifetime of survival and the fear of getting buried and no one noticing is gone. I could've been a drop in the bucket, not lost—forgotten as a memory no one ever made, living a life that never mattered.

It was all supposed to be easy.

But when Jag told me to *run*, did he know it I'd take it as an invitation? I wonder if he regrets saying anything. Did he expect me to need him as much as I do?

I think I hated him a little that day because for a second, he showed me hope. He was the first person who made me think I might have an ending different from my dad. For a while I didn't believe him and every time he gave me hope, it felt like a cruel prank and I was waiting for the day he took it away, calling me stupid because I actually believed him.

Maybe that's over-dramatic. Maybe it's stupid to think I couldn't have figured things out on my own… but I can think of so many times where it's only been because of him that I was still standing? He was the support I needed when I needed it and he never backed away. I still can't believe he waited for me to see it.

My eyes water: heat burns my face. I rub my eyes with the back of my hand and when I inhale, my nose is stuffy enough to make Jag go, "You still okay?" and I say, "Yeah."

We reach his floor; he's leading the way to his apartment, gently pulling me out of the elevator and down the hall. Everything about his complex is the same as it's always been. The smell of burnt popcorn. Someone's TV going a little too loud down the east hall. Someone else is coming out of their apartment three doors down from Jag's with garbage in their hands, redness under their eyes.

Another ghost hopelessly and sentimentally clinging onto the life they wasted? Maybe.

Humanity really is too stubborn for its own good.

The signs of Wayland's visit are gone with walls so clean, it's like he never existed. In my head, I feel like if I check my phone, I'll have a message from him, but in my heart, I know he's gone and I can't keep calling on a ghost of my former life. If I want to move forward, I can't get stuck on the past and what I don't have anymore. Every time I do, the sorrow comes back and the murmurs return with solutions I know won't work, but get more convincing the longer they stay in my ear.

Jag's apartment is on the right. The number of times I've come down this hall, thinking *I need him* and every time he was on the other side of the door, ready to take me in. His arms, his couch, his bed. He never asked questions because he knew I didn't like them, even when I ignored the signs of everything he didn't like that I kept making him see. Beating heart, black eyes, bruises crossing my body where hands treaded in the wake of my dad's anguish.

I never asked Jag how it made him feel. I didn't slow down to think about what he said or didn't say. I didn't tell him thank you enough for everything he did for me.

But he stuck around.

Jag let's go of my hand to unlock the door. On the way to the bedroom, he takes his cigarettes and lighter from his pocket, setting them on the counter with his keys. I close the door behind me. Lock it. Don't go any further into the house. The room still smells like fresh paint from when the landlord came a couple days ago.

My chest tightens. My heart's pulsing through every inch of my skin and my eyes burn with gathering tears. Things will never go back to the way they were. I can't convince myself that's a good thing yet, and every time I let myself stop, all I can think is *I can't do this, I can't do this, I can't do this*.

Jag comes out of the bedroom.

I wipe the tears from my eyes.

He pauses once he reaches the kitchen and turns to me, a smile on his lips. "What are you doing, Joey?"

"I dunno."

"Why don't you take your shoes off?" He dips further into the kitchen. At the fridge, he leans into it. "Or are you gonna run again?" He chuckles. Shutting the fridge, he places a couple bottles of beer onto the counter. The bottle opener is next.

I shake my head. "No." I use my feet to push my shoes off and kick them beside the door. "I think I'm done running for a while. It's sorta messed a lot of shit up, ya know?"

Jag smiles softly. The bottle opener pops the cap off one of the beers, then goes onto the counter. He opens a counter drawer. He takes something out I can't see. "Hey, Joey?" One of his knuckles knocks against the counter. When I'm looking at him, he says, "Heads up," and tosses something at me.

The thing's a blur of a small box. Velvet in my fingers when I catch it. My heart's racing in my ears. My skin's hot and cold at the same time. My throat's dry. "What is it?" I manage.

"Open it." He takes a sip of beer.

The box is so heavy. God, my face is hot. Everything's on fire and my fingers shake as they move along the lip of the box to push it open. It's not like I don't recognize what it is. Wayland hid the same thing from me. Inside is a black band with a couple of red gem bars framing the top and bottom of a ring.

Jag sets his beer down and clears his throat. His cheeks have a little color on them too. He rubs the back of his neck. "I figured, I'm already carrying your heart, so… I wanted to know if you'd carry mine."

I look up at him. He's waiting for me, like he always has, leaning against the counter with a goofy little smile on his face. "J…" His name's a sigh I can't hold in. "Are you sure you wanna do this?" My voice goes weak, shaking. I laugh to cover it. That doesn't work, so I laugh a little more to try and loosen up. "I died before I hit my prime a couple weeks ago."

"Think so?" He straightens. "Because I think you're just getting started."

"I don't want to drag you down if something happens to me."

"You're worth the risk." He comes from behind the kitchen island.

I look at the ring again. It glows in the kitchen light, making the ring match the way the light catches on my heart as it hangs against Jag's chest. "You're fucking… unbelievable, Jagger." I'm so lightheaded. I don't feel like I'm really here. *This* isn't really mine.

He isn't *mine*.

With my parents and my life, this was never supposed to be the way my life went. I was never supposed to have anything good. I was never supposed to be happy. I was never supposed to know kindness cause how do you ever get it with a family that didn't have any to pass down?

Every part of my body's numb and I can't think because I'm not in it anymore. The box blurs against my palm, becoming just a little black dot, threatening to erase me. Not in a bad way. It's the same feelings that Jag's given me cover when I asked him to.

"Yeah?" Jag slowly saunters toward me. His hips sway with a swagger he saves for when he's been drinking or he's teasing and he knows he's got the upper hand. He touches my arms. Even with my hoodie on, his fingers are fire against my skin that sends heat through my body. They slide gently down my wrist to my hand, taking the ring from the box. Then, he takes my left hand. He slips the ring on my finger while I hold my breath. Once he's done, he catches my chin and dips my head back. I'm falling into his eyes and he says, "What took you so long to notice?"

I chuckle weakly. "You're so lame."

"Hella lame." He smiles.

The back of my neck burns and everything in my head's still trying to convince me this is a mistake.

I'm going to destroy him if I don't run; it doesn't matter what he says, he doesn't want this mess. Part of me still doesn't think Jag knows what he's signing up for not telling me goodbye, in not knowing when to call it quits, in knowing he's going to see and feel what's wrong with me for the rest of our lives.

He's going to learn everything about me that I've tried so hard to keep hidden my entire life. The more he sees me, the more risk there is. What if he doesn't like it? What if he changes his mind?

Should have died alone when I was sixteen to save everyone else the trouble. That's what everyone but Wayland thought. Get fixed or get fucked, ya know?

No one wants to look at problems.

There's no room in the world for people who can't help themselves. That's what they say. Perfect little people go about their perfect little lives and ignore the blood in the gutter and the callousness in plain sight left behind by other people who *helped* themselves. All you gotta do is know how to act and you'll make it. Being broken? Ha.

No one wants to see the damage they left behind or the filth built up in their homes, people hurt and left behind by selfish disaster, calculated efforts, or a choice to pursue desire in a single moment at the expense of anyone who might've loved them.

"J, I can't make any promises that I'll be perfect—"

"I'm not here because you're perfect, Joey." He laughs.

My hand finds his shirt. I lean onto my toes. My lips

press to his and his arm goes around my waist. My feet whirl against the floor. My back's to the bedroom and Jag's walking fast, leading me. My legs touch the edge of the bed. A hand presses into my chest and I'm on my back. I'm reaching for his belt; Jag's already tugging at my pant legs. My skinnies clear my thighs when he stops. His head cocks to the side. He stares. A goofy grin full of teeth pulls across his lips while his eyebrows press together. "What…" A snorting chuckle interrupts. He covers his mouth. "What are you wearing?"

My face is burning. I stare down at him, then past him to the floor, the wall, a lamp and whatever else I can, so it's not him I'm looking at. "Someone told me that wearing a little lace sometimes wouldn't kill me. So… I figured… I'd give it a shot."

"Smart guy." He surveys my body slowly. "You look great."

I meet his gaze. Jag lowers his hand, showing his stupid grin's still there. His cheeks are redder though as he takes it in. His smile grows.

Fuck.

I love that stupid look on his face, the way I know he only looks at me like that and how he's so good at telling me what I need to hear exactly when I need to hear it. No girl with soft hands, long hair, and smelling like peaches is going to take him from me. "You too."

He takes his shirt off and flings it to the floor somewhere. I take mine off too. The necklace he wears for me bounces against his bare chest. Light catches on it, making the red glow softly, overtaking the black. The hole that's usually obvious in the middle blends in with the rest of the stone.

Jag's on top of me again. My fingers find the back of his head and curl into his hair. His lips press to my neck, leaving hot streaks across my skin. With every kiss, he moves us further onto the bed.

Everything's on fire. My heart's pounding so much stronger than ever before. Jag chuckles softly and says, "You like that, huh?" before his teeth grab at my skin.

My back curls. I suck in a breath and hold onto him as if letting him go would make him disappear.

"I love you, Jag," I mutter.

"I know."

"Shut up." I exhale hard. My fingers tighten in his hair and, with the hold, I urge our lips together. The way his body fits with mine has always made me feel complete in ways it's so cliche, that when you hear other people talk about it, it feels like bullshit romance that doesn't really exist. Like the kind of shit dreams they sell in cheap books written by the millions where everything's so idealized, there's no way another person could feel so good. It's dumb, because even the *first time*, I knew I didn't want to live without him, but that's just a clingy girl thing you can't say, right? Still, it felt like more than *just fucking*. I knew it. Did Jag know it then too?

Did he know that when I was with him, the craziness of the world quieted down and everything felt *alright*? He made me think there was something better out there for me, even when I didn't see it for myself.

I don't have my dad as an excuse to hold me back anymore; I have Jag as a reason to push forward though. I want to make sure he doesn't see me as a mistake. I want to love him and it might take me a bit to get it right, but knowing he'll wait for me makes it worth it to try.

When we finish, Jag's laying beside me, holding my body against his with an arm over me. I trace shapes in his skin. He's still kissing my neck.

After everything we've been through and everything I've done to him, every time I screamed at him or threw something since I died or locked him out of my life or made him look at me busted up while he had to pretend not to notice when he really wanted to say something… I don't understand how he can look at me the way he does. I could go on forever about everything that makes him special and why I've been so desperate not to get attached since everything that makes him special doubles as a list for what makes him too good for me. There's no more lying, no more running, no more hiding. He's asked to see all of me and I want to see all of him too. I want to know about his mom and his brother and his dad. What does he love? What's he hate? What stays with him so much that made him ever give care about me because maybe I can learn to see the world like he does.

Through his eyes, it seems like a pretty okay place to live.

The guilt of it all builds inside of me. "I'm sorry, J. I'm sorry about all the shit I've made you go through."

"You didn't make me do anything."

"I saw how bad my mom messed my dad up. I didn't want to do that to you. I didn't want to do that to anyone. I thought that if I didn't get too attached—If I didn't say certain things or acted a certain way, then nothing would happen, and you would move on to someone when you got annoyed."

"Yeah, that's not how it works, Joey…"

"I noticed."

His thumb strokes my skin gently. "You know… When my dad would relapse, he'd do shit *not* like himself. He couldn't help it, wasn't thinking. Sometimes, he felt like an animal, driven only by the impulse to hit the bottle or whatever stupor it put him in again. I don't know exactly what he went through that made him like that. We all make mistakes. It's easy to want to forget, but at the expense of everything else?" Jag grunts. "Stupid shit would set him off and he got out of hand more times than I can remember, but that didn't negate the times when he was fine and trying. It didn't stop him from being my dad or erase the memories of who he was when he was at his best. Lane doesn't really remember because Dad wasn't around long after he was born. Honestly? He doesn't need to know the worst of it either. Dad's bad days didn't define him and yours don't define you either."

"I loved my dad, Jag." My vision blurs. "Things got bad a lot, but he still found a way to stop himself before he dragged me into Mortem with him. That has to count for something, right?"

"Your dad was a piece of shit, but I don't think he hated you. He was just so focused on trying to outrun his demons alone… and that's not something anyone can do." His hand tickles mine, touching the ring he placed on my finger.

I roll over in bed so I'm facing him, then, I'm on top of him. His hands are secure on my hips. I lean down, kiss him, and the night disappears. The city disappears, but I never forget that I'm *home*, in *our* house, in *my* city.

Baltimore's not a perfect place and it leaves its fingerprints on every resident here, one way or another.

The streets are macabre, going from boarded up to occupied to newly renovated and expensive and hipster. From shops with busted out lights and incomplete signs to places closer to town hall with cut grass, fresh paint, and lawn keepers.

Visitors should be warned; this place feeds on grief.

You can't leave your house without seeing someone else's mistakes. I don't think there's a person here who doesn't have at least one ghost from the city following them, but if I'm any indication, that doesn't have to mean we're doomed, right?

This city's crimson and painted bright with graffiti,

brick, and the blood from the vengeful who couldn't find a home, who get what they wanted, who faced down their demons, or the legacy the city left behind by everyone struggling to get by. The deeper cuts make the resentment worse and sometimes, you feel like you can't move on because every time you look in the mirror, the disfigurement's all you see. Your eyes are drawn to the lines of what people did instead of how you've healed. Then you tear them open again and again to justify the destructive desire you feel toward others to cope with the pain.

As long as you're hurting, you can't be wrong, right?

At least, that's what you tell yourself, but then you become the same kind of creature that left its mark on you, ruining lives you don't think about a second time because it gives you a moment of relief and somehow that feels like it works.

The morning comes with the soft *beep* of Jag's alarm. His arm's still tight around me. He groans as he rubs his face. His voice is an intimate mutter he says, "Good morning, Joey," and I say, "Morning, Jag," back.

Nothing else matters.

"How you feel about going to the garage today?" Jag says. "Think you can get along with Felix?"

"For you, I think I can try."

We get ready like the day is normal. It's easier than it should be. I barely feel the pain in my arm and we're in his Mustang before I realize it. Jag's smoking his after-coffee cigarette and the radio's cranked up. The windows are open and the fall air's coming in. It feels like it's going to snow soon. My hand finds his on the center console. Our fingers lace. I peer at him. His eyes are on the road, though he's smiling through his cigarette. I can't help but smile too. Though, I purse my lips to hide the influence he has on me, then I look out the window instead.

One building says, UR ALRIGHT, KID while the one after that says DON'T BE FOOL'D, WE'RE ALL DOOMED.

On the next street, all the doors and windows are boarded up on a row of four brownstones. They each read NEVER GET BETTER, NEVER GET BETTER, NEVER GET BETTER, NEVER GET BETTER. The city's battle cry like it's proud of the state it's in.

A woman comes out of the next house. Her eyes are red, skin drained of the color it should have, making her seem transparent. A kid sitting on the stoop looks the same. A man comes out of the convenience store with a sneer he's trying to contain as he looks for his wallet, unsatisfied, a plastic bag on his arm, a cigarette, already lit, hanging from his mouth. The couple of homeless we pass on Pennsylvania Avenue look all the same. Red eyes, tendrils under their skin, lifeless color like corpses, even in the morning light. A sense of unease comes as we pass and my foot's bouncing.

I think half of Baltimore's dead, looking for purpose and desire when they have a simple need waiting to be met that they can't understand. They're obsessed with a life they don't get to live anymore. They need to make it right but can't figure out how. The cycle's hard to break, but it's not impossible. At least that's what Rocky said.

Since I died, I don't know if I count as part of the failure statistics, but I'm going to pretend having a second chance means something because I want to see the city get better.

I want to be better.

Maybe that's why Ralph risks as much as he does.

While we're driving, I pull out my phone and text KC:

JOEY	hey
	how's ralph?
KC	Stable
	Sleeping
JOEY	Not too bad?
KC	Bad enough.
	He can't be out of the bar.
JOEY	It's that bad?
KC	Yea
	Idk what it is
	Too much shit out there that wants something from him
JOEY	He deserves better
KC	Baltimore's been trying to get him for a while
	Came at him in a lot of ways
	Dunno why.
	Got worse when he took on this shit job.
	it hasn't got him yet
	And it never will if I've got a say
JOEY	Is it ok if I come by later?
	I need to tell Ralph thanks fr
KC	Yeah.
	Might be out of it tho.
JOEY	u know what he likes?
KC	Bring moon flowers
	He likes those for some reason

I put a note in my phone to look for a flower shop later, then my phone's in my pocket. Bodymore Bodyshop comes into view. The windows at the gas station on the corner read FUCK OFF where it's not broken. The white wall beneath it says SORRY JANET in small, blue lettering. I wonder if Janet's dead or just locked whoever that is out of the house.

We park behind Bodymore, a spot over from Donny's car and the station wagon that probably belongs to Felix. Inside, the air smells like coffee. Not the cheap stuff. Felix is standing at the counter, pouring himself a cup. "Hey," he says to Jag.

"Hey." Jag slides his jacket off and hangs it in his locker. He turns around, looking at me. His arms cross and I know he's waiting for me to say something.

"Hey, Mustache," I say. My heart's racing.

"Hey," he says back. "Joey, right?"

"Yeah." I look at Jag then back at Felix. "Jag tells me you give amazing oral."

"Joey…" Jag sighs. As soon as Felix puts the coffee pot back into place, Jag's pouring himself a cup.

"Funny," Felix says. "Said the same thing about you." He chuckles.

My eyes widen. "Jagger—"

Jag shrugs. "You started it." He's smiling and I can't help but smile back. He's easy, I'm messy, but he makes me feel like I'm at home and somehow, he makes people give me a chance in ways I never could. He makes wherever I am feel like home and maybe that every mess doesn't have to leave stains you can't clean up.

Jag nods toward a second cup he poured on the counter that's waiting for me while he steps off with his own *black* coffee. I approach the counter. Felix doesn't race away like there's something wrong with me. I take a couple packets of sugar, ripping the tops off to dump them all in at once. "Welcome to the team, *Felix*." I put the cream in next until the color's watered down from coffee to milk. Both Jag and Felix chuckle. I look at them, but they're both looking away, sipping at their cups like they weren't just exchanging secrets. "Just know…" I grab a stir stick. "J has complete authority on the radio."

"Oh, I know." Felix laughs.

"You trained him already?" I say.

"Like that's supposed to be hard?" Jag snorts. "It only took me about three months to get to you."

"You were keeping track?" I say.

"I really wanted to talk to you." Jag shrugs.

My face burns. "Yeah, yeah, yeah… You and every badge in Baltimore."

"Funny I got to you first."

I wipe my eyes, more like I'm tired than like there's something in them. "Sure…" My chest's tight. I sip my coffee and move from the counter. My hand brushes Jag's as I walk by. He follows me out of the break room. I look over the shop, the couple of cars already loaded into the hydraulics, the corner that Felix now occupies where Wayland's car had sat not even a month ago. So much can change in such a short amount of time. It's hard to see it as something irreversible until something big happens that reminds you not everything's under your control; you're not still in high school; you can't act like things don't change. Rejecting reality as it moves on just means thing's change without you and leave you behind.

Tears builds in my eyes. It shouldn't, but the smell of the damn coffee makes me think of Wayland more and the discoloration in my arm and the badges being everywhere, asking me if I'd seen him while all I could think of was getting away from them so I could find them while he still had a chance. My heart's racing again like I need to run. Go to the park, look for him in the fort again because he's lost and the badges'll never find him.

I'm at the computer, zoned out on today's schedule and I don't know when I got here.

"Hey, Joey." Jag's standing behind me at the bin of

paperwork for the current jobs for the day. "You okay?" He fingers the clipboard to make it look like he's paying less attention to me.,

I catch a glimpse of the ring on my finger. I wipe my eyes again. Black smudges come off on the tips. I curse myself and wipe my fingers on my pants. "Yeah. Thanks…" I turn around to face him. My foot bounces. I shove my hands into the pocket on my hoodie. "I mean, thanks for caring."

"Yeah. Always." The smile on Jag's face slowly drops, like he knows what's trying to sneak into my head. Light catches on his necklace.

"You don't need to worry so much about me, though." I pick up my coffee from the counter and take a sip. "Things are just… different, you know?" I tip my cup toward him.

"I know." Jag comes toward me. He puts his hand on the counter beside me. His hips are close to pinning mine. "Donny actually liked the new coffee enough to pay extra over Folger's for it."

"Wow."

"And I got him to rinse out the pot yesterday." Jag sets the clipboard down, pinning his other hand on the counter behind me.

"Amazing. Next you're gonna tell me you got him to vacuum the shop."

Jag shakes his head. He leans in o whisper, "Nah… He was saving that one for you."

"Party." I snort.

"Hey!" Donny's voice carries in from the shop. I look over and he's standing in the doorway. "I'm only paying ya to be one kind of busy around here. You saw the schedule. Get to it." He goes back to the shop. Jag pulls away, taking his clipboard with him. I open the answering machine messages to start with the missed callbacks and emails from overnight. I put in the number for the first call. My phone buzzes against my thigh. I race to dig it out. I don't know why I'm thinking it might be Wayland or why I'm so disappointed when it says Rocky on the display. The drop down doesn't show anything when I try to view the message. Open, it reads:

ROCKY	Busy?
JOEY	Why?
ROCKY	I need a statement on record.
	About what happened last night.
JOEY	Talk to KC.
ROCKY	Already did.
	Your turn.
JOEY	At the shop.
ROCKY	Also
	Might want you to look at something for me.
	Got time?
JOEY	Pick me up?
ROCKY	Gimme fifteen.

I step into the shop. Jag's channel is playing, he's got his toolbox open next to him, but hasn't started yet. He looks up when I approach. "What's up?"

"Rocky," I say.

"What's he want?"

"A statement and some help with something. I'm guessing he found some dead banger issues, or he wouldn't be asking me for help. I've got a record, ya know?" My phone buzzes in my hand. I look over the next text.

ROCKY	Want me to come with the lights on?
JOEY	I'm gonna tell D so he doesn't freak ur

                        here.
ROCKY   Lights on. Got it.
JOEY   Bastard.

"Be careful," Jag says.

"Yeah."

"And tell D so he doesn't think you're bailing or going to prison again." Jag bumps my arm with his as he walks by.

"Right." I'm not sure if the sadness I feel in my chest is his or mine or the fear that I could now really not come back, that I could hurt him with one stupid, tiny mistake, that I have to think more before I do anything because if I don't slow down enough, he'll pay for my mistakes too. This job, this thing with Rocky, the promises I've made to Charon and my second chance. When did I get all this responsibility?

Nothing's just about what I want anymore.

Weirdly enough, that's actually the most calming thing about it all.

I slip my phone away, watching Jag make his way back around to the radio in the corner of the shop. He turns it up. The room fills with the normal sounds of the classic rock he plays in the car. His voice is distant, but even when he's muttering the words to himself, off-key, he's still audible to me over the music.

Donny's on the other side of the garage in front of a blue Chevy. I go to him saying, "Donny?"

"Yeah?" He glances up from the engine with pursed lips and hands already blackened by grease.

"We got a badge on the way."

"Shit, again?" He groans. "Where's the body this time?"

"You gonna be disappointed in me if I say there's no body?"

"Thank God." Donny sighs. The relief in his laugh is palpable. "But then, what are they comin' for?"

"A statement mostly. There was a situation last night…" My hands go into the pockets; my posture goes stiff. "And he might want my help with something."

"Shit, kid. You're working for the badges now?" Donny says. "Never woulda guessed you to get clean and friendly with the state."

"It's not like that. I'm not working *for* the badges. I'm *consulting* with *one*," I say. "Means I'm still better than them."

"Next thing ya know, you'll be coming around here, asking about taxes or some shit," Donny says. "Don't turn on me, Joey—And especially don't talk to Veronica and come in here on her behalf, yeah?"

"What kind of job do you think I'm doing?" I say.

"Hell if I know. Badges sorta press the hell outta whatever issue they can though, don't they?"

"It's not that kind of job."

"Just stay out of trouble." Donny pats my shoulder. "I don't want a badge showing up to ask for an ID on your body next, okay?" He gives my arm a squeeze while he locks with my eyes.

I don't know how I never noticed it before. The kind of look he's giving me is the kind I always wish my dad would give me. Not the desperation of *please never leave me*, but a kindness that he cares about me and wants me around, but he's not going to tether me here because of it. Even though he might not know what I'm doing, he's proud of what he sees in me. Not the hopeless sixteen-year-old girl I came to him as with nowhere else to be and no skills to show for the problems she's caused, but someone he pulled out of a hole, gave a chance and some encouragement, and is now seeing the potential I had buried back then.

I look at Jag standing by an open engine at a hydraulic lift next to Felix. Not the car I left him with, but the two of them are looking over a clipboard, laughing, pointing at something, and laughing again. "Not gonna happen." Jag points across the room toward the lobby. His eyes catch mine. He smiles. I smile back. "I've got a lot to lose, you know?" Jag turns back to the clipboard, the car, and Felix. "So, I think I'll be okay."

"Good." Donny pats my shoulder hard, then gives it a squeeze. "That's what I've said all along. It just took ya a little while to get it."

"I know." My vision blurs a little. I shake my head. It clears up. "Thanks. For everything." The tears are coming back. I wipe my eyes and laugh. "Veronica really missed out."

"Don't I know it? Ah well. Shit happens and good riddance." He turns away, getting back to his car and the busy schedule I feel guilty leaving to the three of them.

I go back to the lobby to put in as many calls as I can while I wait for Rocky to show up. My cell's on the counter, face up, watching for anything to come in and any time the screen flashes, I'm still thinking there's a chance it's Wayland.

Change is hard to get used to, and everywhere I look, I see him.

I've still got the silver ring he gave me and I'm wearing it on my right hand as a reminder that he's around, but not in the same way he always has been. He's inside of me in the memories and kindness and hope I wouldn't have without him. He's here because I'm here, because he saved my life, because he loved me. I hope he never leaves.

Maybe that make me desperate, and I accept that's one of the things I got from my dad, but... I love them so much.

Donny and Jag and Wayland. I knew, but I never wanted to say it because of how much it'd hurt when they disappeared. I wasn't wrong, but Wayland has a place in my heart and when I go around the city, I see glimpses of him in memories or graffiti that tells me he's on the other side and things aren't as bad as they could've been. Maybe it hurts to think that I'm having a harder time without him than he's having without me, but I have to fix that. I have to remind myself he's not going to be forgotten. His touch is on every person he interacted with. He left his mark on Baltimore, even if it wasn't in the way he intended. He can't help people the way he always planned to, but maybe I can help him do that with the way he's changed me.

Rocky's car pulls up out front. Like he promised, the lights are on.

I tell Donny and Jag that I'm leaving. Donny's like, "You're sure you're not getting arrested?" as I walk out.

"Yeah," I say. "Rocky just thinks he's funny when no one else does." I step out of the garage.

Rocky's leaning against his car as I come out. I climb into the front seat. He doesn't say anything and gets behind the wheel.

"I told you no lights," I say as I put on my seatbelt.

"I didn't want you to miss where I parked." Rocky's pulling out of the lot without his seatbelt. We're at the stop sign on the corner before he clicks it.

"Bullshit," I say.

"Can't help it," Rocky says. "It's in my nature. Isn't that what you've said?"

I groan. "What did you need me for?"

"Townhouse with screaming all over the walls. A crime scene like someone exploded. Someone was there, saw it, but couldn't recall any details of what the killer looked like."

"Plus side, sounds like your intel didn't come from a ghost since the dead can recognize the dead," I say.

"Good to know."

We don't say much else on the way to the crime scene. I keep playing with my phone and open the message thread to Wayland. I don't know if I'll ever stop sending him messages. He was my best friend through the hardest parts of my life. You can't just forget that. Even if he never gets my messages, I don't want to pretend he's not around anymore.

As I'm going to send him a text, I get a message from Jag.

JAG	Try not to scrap.
	We're going out tonight. ;)
JOEY	K
	U always gonna worry this much?
JAG	prolly
	Every time ur out, it feels like ur getting into trouble
JOEY	bad habit
	Working on it.
	Gimme time?
JAG	Yeah.
	We got a lot of time.

My cheeks heat up. I shove my phone into my pocket before I have the courage to say something really stupid and out of character. I'm tempted to look for Wayland's messages again. Go to the past, send him something, and dream there's a future with him in it again. I can't keep doing this. You know, it's a fine line between being affectionate and needy. Between looking like you care just enough or too much or not at all.

I'm still finding that line. I never had good examples,

so I'm just glad Jag's giving me time to get it right.

We pull up to the sidewalk just outside of the brownstone of Baltimore's newest disaster. Badge tape hangs against the door. Red, blue, and white lights flash over the cement and brick like it can illuminate the crime in broad daylight. Rocky leads the way up the stairs, telling the guy at the door, "She's with me," and even though the badge looks like he doesn't want to let me in, he doesn't fight with Rocky. I don't mind giving him the eye when I walk by. I think I recognize his face from years ago when I was skating on the steps at some church.

I guess this is what it means when you don't just have authority, but people trust you.

I trip on something. A loose floorboard that fell from the upper level. You can see the spot in the ceiling. This house wasn't abandoned. If there's anything good about the Baltimoron spirit, I guess there's at least that. Even when we're trashed or broken or busted up or not worth a damn to anyone across the river or out of state, we can still see the value in the rubble. We're a home for the broken and abandoned and kids of murder and blood and death that never stop.

We're not the only ones like this, but it's part of who we are. It's why Rocky never gave up on the city; it's why Ralph never gave up on KC; it's why Jag and Wayland never gave up on me. It's why I'll never give up either.

I step over the plank carefully. Black marker in neat lettering says GOOD LUCK, JO on the floor. I blink and it's gone.

There's a sound like someone choking. A raven chirps and caws and this big ass black bird's sitting on the ground beside the corpse in the living room. I blink again and it's replaced by a man in all black with slick black hair, a face without a care in the world, and bloody fingers going in and out of his mouth as he licks them clean. Charon stands over the body, ripped open, heart missing, soul glowing in the small crystal hanging from his hand.

His chains don't rattle in my ears anymore. The whistle from Mortem's still in the air though, warning me that the other side's close and overlaid with what I'm seeing. I reach beside me blindly, thinking Rocky's there. He's not. I turn around to see him standing in the doorway. "Hey, Rocky," I wait until he's looking at me.

"I see your friends are here." Rocky gestures to where Charon and Val are.

"Nice of you to remember," I say.

"I get the feeling once you see certain things, you can't go back."

"You're right about that." I continue toward the body.

"Careful you don't disturb the evidence," Rocky says.

Charon's eyes glow softly in the dark room. The overhead light's on, but it's amber and has barely any light to it. The windows of the living room are boarded up, like the neighboring homes connected to this one. The TV against the wall's off, the screen's busted. The remote's laying on the floor somewhere in the corner with blood on it. Reminds me too much of the last time I saw my dad's body. The air smells both stale and wet. Iron. Piss. Alcohol. At least this body doesn't make me sick like every other one I've seen before it. For a moment, I'm worried I might be going backward again or my heart's turning to stone.

The bloody mess of a pulp with its head beaten in and a shirt cut in a way I can't tell if it was a knife or Val's fingers, the fingerprints escaping the disaster are obvious. Maybe I'm not dead again but growing up. Sounds stupid to say that when I'm looking at a bunch of gore, but at least I'm not pretending it's not there anymore.

Tragedy's everywhere. Pretending it's not doesn't doh shit but make it follow you and pile on and get worse.

"Humanity," Charon says. "What a disaster."

"It's complicated," Rocky says.

For the first time, Charon briefly acknowledges Rocky's existence with a glance. He surveys the corpse, the bloody wall, the remains of someone's mess of a life. "That's not to say your kind does not come up with creative solutions or stories to explain what you do not understand. However, your kind is driven by emotion. Desperation. Need. Fear. Love. Hatred. These things drive humanity to take and give, destroy and create, live and die. Unlike animals who live off instinct, emotion flows through you. The worst of all is *love*. Sometimes indiscriminate, often not. It is illogical the extents I have seen humanity go to hold onto something they believe is *worth the sacrifice* of their own soul." Charon's eyes turn to me. "The thing that creates passion for charity can equally destroy when taken to an extreme. The line between life and death or good and evil is finer than your kind tend to accept."

His words make sense, but I don't want to believe him. I don't want to look at this mess and think it could be me and Jag because I never wanted to look at my dad and think that could be me and someone else someday. The line's thin, but how do you stop yourself from becoming the next disaster someone else has to clean up?

I understand the sorrow that made my dad take his life, and then when that wasn't enough, he was ready to sacrifice mine too just so he wasn't alone. That's inside of me now, but I don't have to fall into the same path as my dad.

"You gonna give me time to catch this one before the harassment starts?" I say to Charon.

Val stands up, sauntering coolly away from where he had crouched over the corpse. His arm goes around Charon's shoulders as he perches himself against death. Somehow, his bloody fingers still don't affect the white suit. Charon's blue eyes glow softly, then brighter. "You intend to assume responsibility and fulfill your oath?"

"I'm not running anymore," I say.

"Then I am not concerned." With that, Charon heads for the door. Val's a bird on his shoulder again. The man in white disappears into the city painted crimson, never to be touched by the tragedy he cleans up. I turn back to the body with its guts laying on the floor beside it. I wish there was more to go off. A guide to profiling the dead or some way to give me a direction. "Hey, Rocky… What do you do first when you want to find the perp?"

"Look at the signs. Ask around. See if anyone saw anything."

"And if that doesn't work, then what?"

"We hope the case doesn't go cold." Rocky laughs.

I don't.

"Party."

Rocky comes up beside me, he pats my shoulder. His voice is too friendly for the crime scene. "Don't worry about it. The longer you're in the game, the more you realize there's not a soul that goes unnoticed by everybody. Sometimes, it just takes a bit of time to find the trail they left behind."

A broken picture frame lays on the floor behind the body. Glass cracked, some of it remains attached to the wooden frame, some lays the floor. On the wall under the nail, it says NEVER SATISFIED and TIE THE KNOT and BLEED. DRIP. TO STARVING in erratic writing like a finger drawn through blood. I twist Jag's ring.

No one will go unnoticed.

No one will be forgotten.

No one deserves to end in tragedy.

POSTSCRIPT

When I started writing *Bleed More, Bodymore*, I hadn't actually intended for it to become a three-book project. I'd only imagined it being the first book and worked through the first book, but once I got to the end of that book… I realized that Joey's story wasn't over yet, she had unfinished business, unresolved mysteries, and wasn't done sharing her story either. That lead into book two with the discovery of Ralph and KC, who became more distinct in their personalities through the revision process, and become even more distinct in who they are while writing *Grieve More, Bodymore* that they ended up needing their own book.

That's right. Although Joey's story has found it's ending, the story about Baltimore isn't over yet. Maybe you guessed that from some of the elements introduced here like Tacitus, the mention of the *Grief Eater*, and some of the things mentioned in Ralph and KC's apartment. What's going on in Baltimore is bigger than any of them know.

So, if you're wanting answers to some of the things mentioned in this book, and want to know more about Ralph and KC and what's going on in Baltimore, there are a couple of things. First, there will be Bodymore 0 (currently unnamed), which should come out the year following this novel's release. It will take place ten years before *Bleed More, Bodymore* and specifically be about Ralph and KC and how Ralph became a medium. All will be told from Ralph's perspective.

That's not all there is. Over the last year, I've had the pleasure of meeting a very good friend who I believe will be a friend and writing partner for the rest of my life. From November 2022 to February 2023, we were talking about her writing project and mine and we discovered there's overlay between her story and mine. Over that period and onward, we decided that our series would merge. So, she will publish her first book in her series, with the establishing plot and characters, and the second book in her series will be coming to Baltimore where the characters of that series will meet Ralph and KC. Those characters know so much more about what's going on in Baltimore and about Ralph's condition… It's just that none of them know it yet.

It's truly been a blessing to meet, get to know, and work with M.M. Morris over the last year and I look forward to doing many projects with her in the future which include her *Noumena Series* which will have the cross over with Bodymore and take places a couple months after *Grieve More, Bodymore*. In addition to a western series set in the 1800s and separate series set in modern-day Japan.

We've already started working on both, though her efforts are focused on *Noumena Series* while we're working on the western series. I can't wait to share so much more about these characters with you between everything that is being worked on. The magic in Bodymore is so real, and over the last year, Ralph and KC have quickly become some of my favorite characters for the kind of love they have for one another and what they find by being there for each other.

I hope you'll come through the journey with M.M. Morris and me and keep up-to-date with our works.

Her influence is all over the pages of this novel and the prequel, you'll see them more once you see the Noumena series and go back to find where the hints are. It's thanks to her, this book has the shape that it does in the end as Tacitus, the Grief Eater, and some of the other elements she had and that we worked on together built more meaning into this book.

Thank you for going through this with Joey and me and I hope to see you in future books!

Ian Kirkpatrick

OTHER WORKS

Bleed More, Bodymore
(Bodymore #1)
Genre: Magical Realism/Supernatural Mystery
Paperback ISBN: 978-1-7368870-0-4
ebook ISBN: 978-1-7368870-1-1

A mechanic in Baltimore has her life turned upside down when a normal pickup job turns into the discovery of a corpse in her best friend's car. With the friend missing and accused of murder, she must search for him. But one mystery leads into another as she discovers ghosts live in a town beneath Baltimore.

Boom, Boom, Boom
Genre: Satire
Paperback ISBN: 978-17368870-2-8
ebook ISBN: 978-17368870-3-5

A Ukrainian Youtuber living in a border town beside Russia is approached one day by foreign investors who offer him new material for his channel: Military-grade explosives. While war is on the horizon, the investors return with much bigger plans for the Youtuber than simple running an unknown explosives channel.

Dead End Drive

Genre: Satire/Horror
Paperback ISBN: 978-1-7368870-0-4
Hardcover ISBN: 978-1-7368870-9-7
ebook ISBN: 978-1-7368870-1-1

In this transgressive, satire-laced debut, a fourteen-year-old boy inherits his family home and the hatred of all those around him as they seek to seize the inheritance from his cold, dead hands.